DEAD IN THE WATER

ALSO BY JOHN MARRS

When You Disappeared

The One

The Good Samaritan

Her Last Move

The Passengers

What Lies Between Us

The Minders

The Vacation

Keep It in the Family

The Marriage Act

The Stranger in Her House

The Family Experiment

You Killed Me First

PRAISE FOR JOHN MARRS

'Clever, twisted, and dark as mighty hell.'

—Lisa Jewell

'Marrs is brilliant at twists.'

—Peter James

'A proper twisty thriller.'

—Sarah Pinborough

'Whatever you do, don't read this in the dark . . .'

—Cara Hunter

'John's thrillers never fail to keep me furiously turning the pages.'

—Sarah Pearse

'John Marrs is a master of suspense.'

—Jeneva Rose

'This one will leave you with paper cuts.'

—C. J. Tudor

'Tensely plotted and terrifyingly imagined.'

—Harriet Tyce

'A smart, gripping and scarily believable story.'

—T. M. Logan

'What a twisted sinister book that was. Loved it.'

—Peter Swanson

'One of the most exciting, original thriller writers out there. I never miss one of his books.'

—Simon Kernick

DEAD IN THE WATER

JOHN MARRS

This is a work of fiction. Names, characters, organizations, places, events, and incidents are either products of the author's imagination or used fictitiously. Any resemblance to actual persons, living or dead, or actual events is purely coincidental.

Published by Thomas & Mercer, Seattle

www.apub.com

Amazon, the Amazon logo, and Thomas & Mercer are trademarks of Amazon.com, Inc., or its affiliates.

EU Product Safety contact:
Amazon Publishing, Amazon Media EU S.à r.l.
38, avenue John F. Kennedy, L-1855 Luxembourg
amazonpublishing-gpsr@amazon.com

ISBN-13: 9781662527708
eISBN: 9781662527715

Cover design by Will Speed
Cover image: © Tim Robinson / ArcAngel Images; © Natalja Petuhova
© FTiare © RachenStocker © Mr and Mrs Tkachuk / Shutterstock

Printed in the United States of America

For Rhian, for swimming against the tide.

One day your life will flash before your eyes.
Make sure it's worth watching.

—*Gerard Way*

PROLOGUE

It isn't only the water pouring down his throat and filling his lungs that's killing him. It's her, the person who has him tied in restraints and is forcing his head under the surface.

The ice-cold liquid ignites a burn that spreads inside him. He coughs and splutters as he chokes, his body desperately trying to reject it, to force it back out, but this only draws more water in. He tries to move his arms to push his way back up to the surface, but they are restrained behind him. When he kicks his weakening legs, she climbs on top of him and pushes her knees into the back of his to keep him firmly in place. He twists from side to side, the internal burning intensifying as the pressure in his chest builds, making it feel fit to burst. Nothing he does to try to save himself is making the slightest bit of difference.

She wants him dead.

He fights and fights until he is too exhausted to carry on and the life inside him begins to ebb. He feels his movements slow as he becomes detached from his surroundings.

Surrendering to the inevitable marks the beginning and end for him. Now is when he sees it all. Everything that has gone before this moment. All that has made him who he is, unfolding before him. He's been through this before, so he knows what happens: that all at once, thousands of memories begin playing simultaneously.

And somehow, he is able to focus on them all. The people he has loved, the people he has lost, the moments they have shared, the laughter, the passion, the anger, the joy and the regrets. He remembers everything.

And then he sees him. A final image before the water consumes him and it all comes to an end.

The dead child. The one who started all this.

PART ONE

ABOVE

CHAPTER 1

SIX MONTHS EARLIER

DAMON

'A year of challenges,' I blurt out. 'You and me.' I plant my hands on my hips as if this is the greatest idea of all time.

'Like what?' It's taking Melissa's gaze a little extra time to focus on me, a sure-fire sign the alcohol is taking its toll.

I don't really have an answer, so I wing it. 'Once a month,' I grin, 'we'll take turns to challenge each other to do something completely out of our comfort zones.'

Her top lip curls, suggesting she already hates the idea. She looks to Adrienne, the only other woman in our group of ten or so mutual friends, like she's hoping she will offer her a valid excuse to get out of this. Adrienne gives a playful shrug, as if to tell her she's on her own.

Melissa raises her voice to be heard. 'Damon,' she says firmly, 'aren't we already about to step further away from our comfort zones than we've ever been before?'

I look at her, puzzled. One of her fake lashes is coming unstuck.

'Our baby plans,' she says.

'But that's different,' I reply. 'And it's also why this might be our last opportunity to do something for ourselves. We can organise challenges that won't break the bank. Remember, you were the one who told me we needed to be more spontaneous. Try new things before we hit our thirties and get stuck in ruts.'

The truth is I'm not so much stuck in my rut as firmly cemented inside it.

'I meant signing up for cookery classes or going to more gigs,' Melissa says. 'Not wing-walking on bloody biplanes. Every penny counts for us right now.'

Elsewhere in The Abington, our first pub of the night, Steve has selected Neil Diamond's 'Sweet Caroline' on the jukebox, and now our friends are singing along with the *ba-ba-ba*'s. I put my arm around Melissa's shoulders to offer a persuasive squeeze. 'I promise we won't do anything that's going to cost us an arm and a leg, or that'll find us in mid-air. So what do you say?'

Her hesitation means I'm winning her round. 'Okay, if I really have to,' she concedes.

I clink her glass with mine to seal it. Truth be told, I expected her to put up more of an argument.

'Who's going first?' asks Tommy. 'You or Mel?'

'Anyone got a coin to flip?' I ask the group at large.

None of us has. Apple Pay killed coins.

'I've got a coin-tossing app,' Tommy offers and opens his phone.

'Millennial wanker,' I say.

'Heads,' says Melissa. She lets out a huff when it lands on tails.

'So what's it going to be?' Tommy asks me.

It has to be something that won't so much push her from her comfort zone as hurl her. Something cheap, cheerful, spontaneous – and that she'll hate me for. Because where's the fun in serving her something she'll enjoy?

A smile spreads across my face. I've got it.

Ten minutes later and we are in the back room of an ill-furnished but hospitable karaoke bar in Northampton town centre. It's three days after New Year's Eve, and most people are hibernating at home or launching a dry January to pay for their alcoholic sins. Only a handful of punters are here, listening to a woman perform what has been, until this moment, a passable rendition of Whitney Houston's 'I Will Always Love You'.

'I think the climax has eluded her,' I whisper to Melissa.

'Story of my life,' she deadpans.

Two others are waiting to sing before it's Melissa's turn. I've never seen her down a pint so quickly. Dutch courage.

I've chosen karaoke for two reasons. One, I know how much she hates being the centre of attention, and two, she kind of scream-sings, and it's bloody hilarious. Somehow, she can hit notes Mariah Carey could only dream of, only not necessarily on purpose or in the right order. To rub salt into the wound, I've chosen Queen's 'Bohemian Rhapsody', a song with more key changes than a locksmith.

When she at last receives the call, she nervously makes her way to the stage and turns her back on us all. Even after the first *Mama*, I can hear Freddie Mercury's moustache bristling as he turns in his grave. Excruciating, and delicious. When she finishes caterwauling some six minutes later, we can finally stop cringe-laughing and applaud. She hurries off stage and I high-five her. That's why I love this girl. She has bigger balls than me.

But something's off. She's not glaring at me with as much loathing as I hoped for. After an uneasy beat, the reason for her suspiciously cheerful demeanour strikes me: she has something worse lined up for me.

This woman knows me inside and out: my loves, my longings, my likes and my loathings. And there's a list of the last a mile long.

Perhaps these challenges weren't such a great idea.

'Come on then,' I tell her. 'Put me out of my misery.'

She smiles. 'Aren't you just dying to know?'

CHAPTER 2

MELISSA

If looks could kill, Melissa knows she would already be carried away by the rolling waves lapping at the beach ahead of them.

She knows swimming in large bodies of water makes Damon anxious. In fact, he hates it almost as much as mayonnaise, eating meat from the bone and the crackling of static electricity.

After all the years they've spent together, there is very little she doesn't know about him. Though he can swim, and barely tolerates pools, the mere suggestion of paddling about where his toes can't touch the bottom is enough to bring his skin out in red-and-pinkish blotches.

Which is why Melissa has chosen the sea for his challenge.

Damon has employed an increasingly desperate array of excuses trying to wriggle out of it, but she has no intention of allowing him to do so. A deal is a deal.

She has, however, granted one concession she now sincerely regrets on this slate-grey February day: the only way she could get him this far was to agree to go in with him.

Melissa is the first to reach the shoreline of Brighton Beach. Having dispensed with her dressing gown and trainers a few metres back, she tiptoes across the pebbles in a plain black swimsuit. The first wave licks at her ankles – it's exceptionally cold. *Winter*, she reminds herself. *What'd you expect?* At least, from behind, Damon can't see her tightly pulled face.

She turns to find him still some distance from the waterline – stationary, arms firmly folded, a belligerent toddler protesting at bath time. Clamped to his skinny chest are two off-white towels they borrowed from the bathroom of their bed and breakfast. He's wearing brightly coloured orange-and-white shorts he bought at H&M earlier today, because he 'accidentally' left his at home. This pair are comically large on him; the leg holes flap in the wind.

'I look like a sodding traffic cone!' he says, and she doesn't disagree.

'Come on,' she says, and beckons him towards her. But it's as if his feet are encased in solid concrete.

'The sooner we do this,' she says, 'the sooner we can go back inside.'

'I don't want to!' he yells. 'It looks rough out there.'

'It's only a few waves.'

'It's okay for *you*, Miss Former Olympian. You know what you're doing. I'm built for land, not water.'

She rolls her eyes. 'I swam for the county when I was fourteen,' she clarifies, 'which hardly makes me Rebecca Adlington.' She'd been rake-thin back then, she recalls, with broad shoulders and a permanent smell of chlorine about her that she'd try to mask with Body Shop shower gels and cheap perfumes endorsed by the popstars of the day.

She's yet to win another step from him. He can be so maddening. 'Let's not forget,' she calls to him, 'whose stupid idea these challenges were. *Yours*, remember? What's the worst that could happen?'

'My testicles never descend again?'

'The way you're carrying on, I'm doubting you had any in the first place.' With that, she turns around, holds her breath and begins her descent towards deeper water, where a tall wave promptly catches her unawares with a cold slap across her thighs and chest, raising red pinpricks in her skin. She quietly curses.

As if in answer, Damon appears beside her, letting fly a string of expletives of his own, only he isn't keeping anything under his breath.

And then, like Melissa, he's up to his neck in the water.

'How far are we going?' he asks, and adds a theatrical gasp.

She gazes ahead, towards the circular bright yellow swim buoys arranged loosely in a box formation.

She nods at them. 'There and back again.'

'They're miles away!'

'Bah. A hundred and fifty metres at the most.'

She leads the way, choosing breaststroke over front crawl as she doesn't want to leave him behind and offer him another excuse to complain. She turns to check he hasn't tiptoed back to shore, just as a wave engulfs his head. 'Fuck this!' he yells and spits out a mouthful of the salty water. Her smirk is good-natured, though.

Onward.

Melissa assumed that once she began to swim, her body would warm up or she'd grow acclimatised to the temperature. But neither has happened. The current is challenging but she's strong enough to persist until finally she reaches the string of buoys, each with the words 'swim area' painted in black lettering across the sides. Damon arrives soon after and they both tread water, hanging on to the ropes that link the buoys.

'See, that wasn't so bad, was it?' Delivered while panting, this is less than convincing. Melissa holds her hand up in the air and he reluctantly high-fives her. 'It's invigorating,' she adds. 'Ready to head back?'

'Hell yes,' he replies. 'Does Uber run a jet ski service?'

They begin their return journey as they came, with her taking the lead.

This route, however, proves more challenging. The tide is against them and she's forced to shut her eyes as she swims into the waves. 'Not much further,' she yells over her shoulder. She suspects Damon is silently cursing her, because she hears nothing from him. She can only begin to imagine the fresh hell he is concocting for March's challenge.

'I said it's not much longer,' she repeats, and turns her head.

Only, she can't see him behind her.

'Damon?' she shouts, scanning the sea for him. She expects to spot his head emerging from a wave and for them to continue. But there is no sign of him.

Fear envelops her in the space of a heartbeat.

'Damon?' she shouts at the top of her lungs, then focuses her attention on the beach, in case somehow she became disorientated and he's swum past her. But he's not there either.

There is only one other place he can be.

Under the water.

CHAPTER 3

MELISSA

Fear has Melissa in a chokehold as she swims back to where she thinks she last saw Damon, but it's such a disorientating environment, she can't be certain.

It's then that she feels it, a tug against her ankles. Her stomach knots when she realises what's happening to Damon.

Of the eight months she spent backpacking in Australia after completing her A levels, five were spent at Sydney's Bondi Beach, working as a lifesaver. She recalls being shown a documentary as she trained for her Bronze Medallion. Rip currents are narrow channels of water that don't typically drag people beneath the surface, but can pull them away from their intended path without warning. The narrator of the video explained that a person's reaction is more likely to kill them than the current itself.

Melissa takes one more frantic look around her, and when she can't locate him, she takes a deep breath and dives.

Everything under the water is grey, silty and murky, making it almost impossible to see her own hands in front of her face, let alone hope to locate Damon. When her air runs out, she rises to the surface, surveying her surroundings again and continuing to shout his name as loud as her constricted throat will allow.

Nothing.

She takes in another breath, and this time when she submerges, the strength of the current intensifies. Melissa doesn't know for how long it carries her, but eventually she reaches beyond the zone of breaking waves. Another sharp intake of air and she dives again. The water is less cloudy here, but only moderately so, and she wishes she was wearing her swimming goggles because then she might see further and without having to keep squeezing her eyes shut. She kicks with her legs and moves her arms in front of her, mimicking the technique police divers use in fingertip searches of murky rivers. And all the time, she is acutely aware that the longer she takes to find Damon, the lower his odds of survival are becoming.

When the air runs out and the burn in her lungs threatens to set her chest ablaze, she rises, sucks in more air, and dives again and again and again until she is utterly exhausted. The warmth of her tears as they streak down her face is at odds with the water's sharpness. She is fast reaching the point where she might have to consider defeat when, under the surface, she spots colours close by. Orange and white. The colours of Damon's shorts.

She swims towards him, fumbles around until she can grab hold of his arms, then pulls him up to the surface with her. He's unconscious. She cannot hear if he is breathing over the sound of the waves. She turns him on to his back, resting his head against her chest to keep it above water, and kicks hard to get them both back to shore. She thanks God he has a slight frame because it's taking every ounce of her depleted strength to keep them moving.

At last, through sheer, desperate stubbornness, she eventually feels the shingle under her feet. She clambers out from under him and begins dragging him by his arms up the beach, away from the water.

'Please be alive, please be alive,' she whispers as she settles him on to his back and flips to trained paramedic mode, searching for vital signs. There's no air coming from his mouth or nose, no pulse emitting from his wrists or neck.

His heartbeat is absent.

Damon is dead.

CHAPTER 4

MELISSA

'Ensure airways are open and seal their nose with your fingers,' Melissa begins, reciting aloud her lifesaving training. Then she performs two initial rescue breaths. She tries her hardest to avoid cracking his ribs as she begins compressions. She counts to thirty before giving him two more mouth breaths. It triggers an unexpected memory of the first time they kissed. They were fifteen and in an empty kids' playpark as night fell. They were drunk on the bottles of Smirnoff Ice they'd stolen from under her older brother's bed, and it just kind of happened.

They have shared so many moments over the fifteen years they've known each other: their journey is not supposed to conclude on this beach. Not like this. It cannot be her fault he is dead.

Regrets flow thick and fast, like a swollen river bursting through a dam and swallowing everything in its path. If only she hadn't agreed to these stupid challenges. Damon often comes up with ridiculous suggestions after a few drinks. Matching tattoos, cutting each other's hair blindfolded, ziplining, Interrailing, learning how to play the ukelele, hiking across the Pennines. She's shot so many of them down in flames. But every now and again she humours him because she knows why he wants to pursue them. There are voids in his life. And guilt compels her to help fill them.

'Can I help?' a concerned voice from behind them asks. Melissa turns to find a frowning middle-aged man walking a yappy dog without a lead.

'Call an ambulance,' she shouts, then sets to a second round of compressions. The man removes a phone from a tote bag and makes the call.

Statistics from her paramedic training come rushing back. Of how the human brain can survive for four minutes without oxygen, but after that, the chance of permanent damage rises. Time is against her as she begins a third round of compressions.

Random images from their shared history begin to flash like torchlights. Of their honeymoon in Madrid; of climbing over ten-foot-high fences to enter a music festival without paying; of the star he paid to name after her beloved cat Freddie, who was hit by a car; of him joining her for two months of her Australian travels. And of their wedding day, when she promised until death do us part. She isn't ready to become the sole guardian of these memories.

Suddenly, a fountain of saltwater jets from Damon's mouth.

Her prayers have been answered.

Melissa pushes him on to his side where more follows, dribbling down his cheek as he gasps for breath. She rubs his back and reminds him he is safe, and she is here with him. His body shivers, and his teeth chatter so hard she is scared they might chip.

'Pass me those towels and give me your coat please,' she tells the man with the dog, and together they drape them over Damon. He is as white as a ghost and she holds on to him for dear life, irrationally fearing that if she lets go, he might float back out to sea, never to be seen again.

'What about you, love?' the man asks, and it's only now that Melissa realises how badly she's trembling. A combination of cold and shock. Goosebumps march across her flesh but it's Damon's well-being that matters. This isn't something new; it's been this way for years.

Now a woman appears and covers Melissa with her own thick suede coat. Melissa tries to thank her but can't get the words out. She doesn't know how much time passes before she hears the faint sound of an approaching ambulance siren. It brings about a Pavlovian response in her and she leaps to her feet, scrambling into her clothes. She is about to begin dressing Damon when he speaks for the first time.

'Who was he?' His rasp is barely audible.

'Who?'

'The boy.'

She glances around the beach, but it's only the four of them. 'What boy?'

Damon turns to her, finds her eyes.

'The boy I think I killed?'

PART TWO

BELOW

CHAPTER 5

TWO WEEKS LATER

DAMON

The music is playing so loudly I'm struggling to hear my friends. So I find myself nodding or smiling along even when I don't really understand what they're saying. Mum told me I once fell over as a kid and hit my head on a coffee table, rupturing my right eardrum. The hearing in that ear never completely returned so I struggle with it at the best of times. And I think there might be some water left in my other ear because I've been plagued with a whooshing sound ever since I drowned a fortnight ago. Together, they make me feel like Aquaman, minus the chiselled jawline, six-pack and scales.

Shake it off. Act as if you're having a great time.

I actually argued against going out tonight. Back in October last year, I downloaded a '150 Films To See Before You Die' list, and Melissa and I have been working our way through it ever since. I'd have been happier staying in the flat with her, eating my body weight in caramel popcorn and marking another movie off the list. Or even having our friends come over for a poker night. But they insisted on dragging me out on this bar crawl to celebrate.

'Coming back from the dead means you get to do the dumb stuff you did in your teens all over again,' Tommy explains.

A bleary-eyed AJ agrees. 'If I was you, I'd be out every night trying to sleep with every girl who so much as smiled at me. No offence, Mel and Ade.'

'Non taken, Tragic Mike,' says Adrienne.

'Like so many girls gave you the time of day first time around,' Tommy reminds AJ. 'Can't see things changing much second time around.'

Banter. Friends poking fun at one another in a good-natured way. That's what I usually love about this group – they take me out of myself when I burrow down. But even though I'm trying hard, my heart really isn't in it. All my conversations require effort these days. I don't think any of them have truly grasped how close they were to never seeing me again. Why? Because they haven't asked. Melissa told them what happened and I've exchanged voice notes and Snapchats with them. But they have yet to say, 'Damon, how are you really doing after what happened?' And I've yet to tell them, 'I'm a bit shit, actually.' I have seen things they haven't. Things I can't explain. Things I keep replaying every time I close my eyes. Things they will never understand.

I wish I could drink tonight, as booze might've helped to blur the edges. But I can't mix alcohol with the broad-spectrum antibiotics I've been taking. They were prescribed as a precautionary measure in case the water I swallowed was contaminated and gives me an infection. That's the last thing I need. Well, drowning was *actually* the last thing I needed, but the horse has already bolted and the stable door is flapping in the breeze.

I'm in need of a moment to myself so I make a joke about having the bladder of a toddler and needing the bathroom, but I head outside into the beer garden instead. I lean against the wall, taking the deepest breaths my damaged lungs will allow. I cough, another lingering side effect of swallowing so much salty water. I catch sight of the others through the window. They may be here to celebrate my second chance at life but none of them understands what it's like to have actually died. To have come within a whisker of losing these faces and places, of swapping everything for nothing. I should be grateful I'm still here but I'm struggling to move past what I so very nearly lost forever.

I catch Melissa keeping a watchful eye over me out here, from in there. Without her, this would be my wake. She's giving the appearance of having fun, but I suspect she's also finding it difficult. What happened that day in the sea has changed us both. I wonder if, like me, it has taken more of a toll on her than she's ready to admit.

CHAPTER 6

DAMON

The train journey from Brighton back home to Northampton was a blur of images, past and present. Melissa kept trying to engage me in conversation, but my replies were perfunctory. I was still too overwhelmed from watching my life flash before me. Such a cliché, but I'd never imagined what it might be like in practice. At least for me, it meant thousands, maybe even hundreds of thousands, of images escaping from my subconscious, encompassing all eras of my twenty-eight years. And in the fortnight that's followed, I've been dipping in and out of those memories, dwelling on some and reliving others. But always trying to make sense of one in particular.

The boy I think I might've killed.

A red-headed lad, his crumpled body on a pathway separated from a road by trees and bushes. I am standing over him as he lies there, watching him bleeding from his mouth and left ear. Suddenly his eyes open, he reaches out his hand and I stretch out mine. But that's where my recollection ends. If it is a recollection.

Melissa said he was the first thing I spoke of on the beach as we awaited the ambulance. Then I kept repeating it on the way to hospital, where I spent two nights under observation before being discharged.

'You were imagining him,' she told me during visiting hours. 'You haven't killed anyone.'

'The way I saw him . . . it was like my other memories, absolutely crystal-clear.'

'You wouldn't have forgotten killing someone.'

'But you know some of my memories as a kid are patchy. So it could only have happened then.'

She shook her head. 'Come on, Damon. That's not something you're likely to forget.'

I was, and still am, inclined to believe her because Melissa is almost always right.

I pull myself together – for now, at least – paint on a smile, and return to the others inside the pub.

'Drink up boys and girls,' says Tommy, and cups his hand around his ear. 'Time for the next pub. The Old House at Home is a-calling.'

As the others lead, Melissa hangs back to wait for me and we exit together, arm in arm. Only two people on earth make me feel safe, and she is one of them.

'You okay?' she asks.

'Once this ear infection goes, I'll start feeling more like myself.'

'And aside from the infection?'

'Getting there,' I lie.

'Good,' she replies, seemingly placated.

A young woman in a thick, stained coat sits on top of a sleeping bag with an unlit cigarette butt balanced between her fingers. Inside my wallet I find a ten-pound note and give it to her.

'Have you ever walked past a homeless person and not given them money?' asks Melissa.

'I could have so easily been like her.'

I know how quickly I could've slipped between the cracks. Half of children who end up in care have criminal convictions by early adulthood. A further ten per cent become homeless. If it weren't for Helena . . . my thoughts tail off when a figure suddenly catches my attention across the road. He's sitting midway inside a single-decker bus. A young lad with red hair, his head turned towards me, his face expressionless. Slowly he raises his hand and points a finger at me. For a split second, my breath leaves my body, as he looks so much like the boy I saw when I died. Then a van overtakes the bus and obscures my view, and like in a movie, he vanishes.

'Damon!' Melissa yells and yanks me sharply towards her. A car horn blares and I realise I've stepped on to the road. 'Are you trying to get yourself killed again?' she says with a gravity behind her smile.

'Sorry,' I reply, trying to mask the unease in my tone. I don't want her to pick up on how rattled I am and add to her worries about me. 'You know how much I enjoy a sequel.'

CHAPTER 7

DAMON

I snap awake at the sound of a heavy door slamming, followed by a deep, angry voice echoing along the corridor outside the flat. I'm fully clothed, lying atop the duvet. Light creeps through each side of the blind so it must still be daytime. I raise my head, and wince when I feel someone racing Formula 1 cars around inside it, so allow it to sink back into the pillow.

I recognise who's talking outside. It's the young man who lives in the apartment opposite yelling at his girlfriend again. He's calling her a 'miserable bitch' and she's telling him she is sorry. Now, they're stomping down the metal staircase together, him still showering abuse upon her. This isn't a one-off. I don't really get angry, so much so that Melissa once nicknamed me Lake Placid during a one-sided row about whose turn it was to fill the car up with diesel. And I don't understand why people can't talk it out instead of yelling. I've yet to meet my neighbours in person, but based on past experience, I know that tonight they'll be making up with sex so noisy it would make porn actors blush.

I do a double take when I check the time on my phone. *What the hell?* What started as a Sunday afternoon nap has become an epic twenty-hour sleep coma and it's now mid-morning on Monday. The sharp movement makes me aware I'm about to piss myself so I tiptoe to the bathroom like a ninja in stealth mode, fearing I might accidentally dribble down the front of my Calvins. Then, after swallowing three codeine tablets, I return to bed. God knows why, but I'm still exhausted. My eyes glaze over as I stare at the ceiling. And soon enough, I'm losing myself in the sea, returning to the moment the largest of the waves caught me off guard, jamming my mouth and throat full of freezing water. I didn't have time to brace myself for the next wave, which triggered a coughing fit, and before I knew it I was below the water's surface, dragged by a terrifically potent, invisible force. A rip current, Melissa told me later. Now I understand that by panicking and fighting against it, I did the worst thing possible. Soon after, I lost consciousness.

When I think back to it, I'm certain my brain was preparing me for the inevitable, protecting me, wanting me to exit this life experiencing something aside from terror. Hence, as my body began shutting down, the gush of my life's significant moments flooding over me – the instantaneous, somehow simultaneous manifestation of my entire existence.

There was no chronological order to it; it wasn't like starting a book at the first chapter. One moment I was a teenager; the next, I'd reverted to a child and then an adult. Static images and mini-movies all played together, each with vivid clarity. A black-and-red balance bike I'd loved as a toddler; a football tournament I'd competed in as a teen; towering skyscrapers I'd made out of Lego; a poster of my first crush Margot, from the pop band *Party Hard Posse*, that hung on my bedroom wall; a marble run game I was obsessed with building; being hit in the neck by AJ's rogue blue paintball; and being mugged for my mobile phone by a hooded hyena on a BMX. A party I organised when Tommy returned from travelling around America; a Taylor Swift concert Melissa dragged me to; opening my terrible A-level exam results; and the whitey I pulled that was so intense, I never smoked a joint again.

I suddenly realise the only person conspicuously absent from those life events was my mum. There wasn't even a glimpse of her, the person I miss the most.

The good and the bad, I was able to not only recall but *understand* every one of these people and events.

Well, all but one: the dead red-haired boy.

I've replayed his death hundreds of times since then, searching for clues to his identity and whether what I saw was real – or, as Melissa suggested, whether he was a figment of my imagination. Try as I might, I've yet to recall anything else about him – his name, where we were, why I was there, who hurt him or what happened next.

But if everything else I remembered that day is true, why would my brain fabricate him?

My phone buzzes. A text message from Jason, one of my colleagues, asking for a lift to work. We both have shifts that start this afternoon. He only lives a couple of streets from me so I won't need to go out of my way. Yes, I reply, I'll pick him up in an hour.

I climb out of bed, my head still banging, make my way into the bathroom and turn on the shower. I freeze in place well shy of the spray, my body rigid, a Pavlovian response to running water. I'm back under the waves, clawing to reach the surface, failing every time. I should be grateful to still be here and I really am, thanks to Melissa. But I keep dwelling on the fact that I drowned. That for a time, I was *dead*. And I'm struggling to find a way to deal with the enormity of it. Half the time I'm thanking God for allowing me to live, and for the rest, I'm crying for what might have been.

Come on, Damon, I tell myself, *pull yourself together*. I reach my hand out to feel the water's temperature. Ever since I drowned, I can't seem to find warmth. I've taken to wearing a long-sleeved

T-shirt under my work shirt and two pairs of socks in my boots. Sometimes I wonder if I'm actually still dead and floating under the surface of the sea, and this is all a dream.

Stop it. How long am I going to keep thinking like this? Why can't I focus on what I have and what lies ahead and not what I almost lost?

Because it's easier to recall and dwell.

Finally, when the shower is hot enough, I climb inside and close my eyes as the water cascades over my head and down my back.

My tattoos catch my eye. My first was the words '*Offering Others Direction In Sorrow*' across my collarbone, etched there when I was seventeen. I don't even know what it means. It was a phrase I woke up remembering after a dream in which Mum emerged into my subconscious. I think it might have something to do with the way in which she died. My dreams of her are always vague: she is more of a presence than a participant in any dream event. Her name, Bobbi, runs along my wrist. The rest of my tattoos extend all the way down to my hand. They are all linked together to form a sleeve, made up of drawings and motifs I have doodled or found online. Some remained identical from scraps of paper to skin, while others were finessed by tattooists.

Only when the water temperature begins to cool do I turn off the shower and open the door.

And that's when I see it.

A deep red pool of blood in the centre of my bathroom floor. And a child's footprints leading into my bedroom.

CHAPTER 8

DAMON

A hand clamping down upon my shoulder fires the fear of God through me.

When I wheel around, I find only my co-worker Jason, wildly amused by the high-pitched shriek I've released. A woman carrying a basket full of children's clothes on hangers looks me up and down in the supermarket aisle where I'm stationed. I mouth her an apology.

'Did you hear yourself?' Jason gasps between howls of laughter. 'I so wish I'd filmed that for TikTok.'

'Why are you creeping up on me?' I snap.

'I said your name, like, three times. You were miles away.'

'I was concentrating.'

That couldn't be further from the truth. In body, I am here. I'm living and breathing, but in my mind, I remain trapped under the waves off Brighton's coastline.

'You're thinking about that kid again, aren't you?' he asks. 'The one you saw in your dream?'

'It wasn't a dream.'

'You gone all *Sixth Sense* on me?' Pulling an imaginary blanket up to his chin, he trembles and whispers, 'Are you seeing dead people . . . all the time?'

I put my scanner down on my trolley. 'I don't think I can see dead people. What I saw was one dead person as my life flashed before me.'

'So it was a ghost?'

'I . . . I don't know what it was.'

'Your brain's playing tricks on you then, innit? I bet it does all kinds of weird shit when it thinks it's game over. The last thing my pap told us before the brain tumour screwed him over was that he used to be the king of the Netherlands. Nan said the furthest he'd ever travelled was to Wales, and that was only 'cause he got the wrong train to Newcastle.'

'Yeah, you're probably right.' I pick my scanner up again, eager to abandon this conversational cul-de-sac, and move on to the next aisle wishing I hadn't told Jason about the boy. I need to keep it to myself. But I was still rattled by the puddle of blood and footprints I thought I saw on my bathroom floor. They vanished when I held my lids shut. At least I didn't mention to Jason I'm worried I might be responsible for a boy's death.

I suppose I was hoping for a different reaction from Jason to Melissa's immediate dismissal. I should've considered he is only nineteen and not particularly worldly wise. At least sixty per cent of the workforce here is around his age – either students, teens on gap years, or university graduates biding their time until they find a career. The rest are fifty-plus, either dipping their toes back into the working world after their kids have flown the nest or made redundant from long-term careers and left with little other choice.

And amongst this population, you'll find people like me: those who took a stopgap job here years ago, then never left. I'm fast approaching my thirties and still filling other people's trolleys with click-and-collect orders. This is a job, not a career. I don't know what I expected from life, but this wasn't it. However, I'm determined to do better. With our plans to start a family, I need to explore my options and make a move instead of treading water. Poor choice of analogy, I know.

I check my device. I'm taking longer than I should, so I pull myself together. Thirty minutes later, my digital order sheet is empty and I'm making my way through the doors to the warehouse and lining my trolley up against the others awaiting collection. Then I head to the bathroom to pee, checking my phone on the way. Melissa has texted, asking if I want takeout tonight and offers me four options. I choose old favourite Nando's, and she confirms she'll order it online and pick it up en route from work.

As I close the bathroom door behind me, an icy chill blasts through me.

I am not alone.

This time, it's not only a pool of blood on the floor. As clear as day, the dead boy is also here and he's standing in the centre of it. The hairs on my arms rise as he glares at me, head slightly cocked, eyebrows knitted, mouth open wide. I cannot see his teeth or tongue. Instead, there is only a gaping black hole. I think he is trying to speak but all I hear is a rasping, choking sound. Slowly, his arm unfolds and reaches out to me, as if pleading for my help, like he did when I saw him as I drowned. Blood drips through his fingers, some trickling along his arm like red spider legs.

He feels so, so real, and I'm terrified.

And, before my knees can buckle beneath me, I run like I've never run before.

CHAPTER 9

DAMON

I dread going home to the flat. For the last three days, the dead boy has been returning to me when I'm alone. This morning as I was making breakfast, there he suddenly was, motionless and glaring at me with the familiar hollow, empty gaze. I bolted out of the flat door, still in my pyjama bottoms, down the staircase and into the lobby, trying to catch my breath.

When I eventually crept back into the flat, I had it to myself again. I left for work moments later without showering, my toast untouched.

So now I'm delaying returning home even though my shift finished two hours ago. Instead, I sit with a handful of co-workers I don't really know in the staff canteen. It doesn't matter that we are all at different tables scattered about this characterless room. As long as I am with other people.

What the hell is happening to me? What is it I'm actually seeing? Have I brought this boy back with me from the other side like some fucking hitchhiker from hell? Is he a ghost or am I hallucinating? I'm not spiritual and I don't believe in the supernatural, so that leaves a hallucination as the most probable explanation. I am seeing him because I'm going nuts. I ask my phone's AI to look up the words 'brain injury' and 'hallucinations' and learn the two often go hand in hand. When the brain is damaged, it can misfire, creating distorted perceptions. So that's what the boy is. A perception, not a physical manifestation.

Okay, so now I know what I'm dealing with.

However, the relief I thought this explanation might bring doesn't arrive. Because it doesn't explain how I can stop myself from imagining him. It's only been a little over three weeks since I died, so perhaps I must give myself time to heal. Or maybe I need to find out if he once was real, and, if so, why my brain has brought him back to my conscious mind.

I begin googling other people's accounts of what it's like to watch your life flash before you as you die. Searching for people like me.

'It was like reviewing your whole life in one short film,' reads a Reddit post. 'But with no end goal. None of it was judgemental, only a factual representation of my life.'

'For me it was like watching the longest-ever movie condensed into a few seconds but knowing every bit of it was true,' a woman on a YouTube video recounts. 'Each single memory stored in my brain – many of which I hadn't thought about in years – was included . . . passing me by at the speed of light.'

My experience was similar, but with one key difference: I haven't returned alone. And no matter how hard I search, I've yet to find anyone else reporting a stowaway.

Then I go off on a tangent to try to understand how our brains behave when we're dying. A medical study of one patient's last moments claims doctors measuring his brainwaves noted a high and low frequency fifteen seconds before his heart stopped beating. Such frequencies are patterns associated with meditating, dreaming, concentrating and memory retrieval. So something pretty complex was happening inside that patient's brain they couldn't explain. Was it his life flashing before his eyes, preparing him for death? They couldn't prove it wasn't.

The author of another research paper describes her theories as to what a dying person experiences: 'It's as if they know death is coming and the last thing they can do is to get their house in order. They want to review all they've done in their lifetime, all their actions, reactions, behaviours and thoughts. These life reviews allow them to find the meaning to their existence and know they served a purpose.'

This all makes absolute sense to me. Because I think that's what my brain was doing. But it still doesn't explain the appearance of the boy.

I need to think about something else, so I busy myself by updating my LinkedIn profile and trying to make some connections with recruitment agents. I don't know what there is beyond the supermarket that might be suitable for me, but I have to start somewhere.

Eventually, when I can no longer put off the inevitable, I make my way back to the car, drive home and pause on the landing outside my flat, bracing myself for what, or who, I might find inside.

I unlock the door, quietly turn the handle – and see nothing. The television is still switched on, talking heads chattering, in the corner of the room. The morning's hastily abandoned coffee and toast are where I left them on the kitchen worktop. I flinch at a sudden noise behind me, until I realise it's only the couple in the apartment opposite, arguing again. *Home sweet home.* I keep the front door slightly ajar so I can hear their raised voices on one side of me and the television's mindless chirping on the other, hoping the unholy combination might prevent the dead boy from returning. Even if only for one night.

CHAPTER 10

DAMON

'Everything alright?' asks Adrienne from the seat next to me.

'Sure, why?'

'You look a little out of it.'

'That's my default setting,' I try to joke. 'Perpetually bewildered.'

'That's handy, because that's precisely the quality we are looking for in the father of our baby.' Melissa smiles. 'A perpetually bewildered man.'

'Is there any other type?' Adrienne asks.

I pretend to be amused, but I'm not feeling it. Or much of anything else, beyond preoccupied. Powerfully preoccupied. But I'm trying hard to disguise it. Be the person I was before I drowned. I repeat those words to myself. *Before I drowned.* It almost sounds as normal to me now as saying *before I turned on the TV* or *before I ate lunch.*

The walls of the waiting room in the fertility clinic are decorated with posters of couples and single people smiling and cradling babies or holding their toddlers' hands. I'm seeing nothing mirroring our situation: me, my ex-wife and her girlfriend, who I'm trying to get pregnant. We are a reality show waiting to happen.

I absent-mindedly move to twirl the silver wedding band on my ring finger, forgetting it's in my bedside table. It's been three years since I last wore it, the day the decree absolute was granted in Melissa's and my divorce hearing. Right up until that morning, I'd clung to the hope she might yet change her mind, might wake up to the realisation that she'd made a huge mistake and still wanted to be my wife.

She didn't. Still hasn't. She won't.

I first sensed something was troubling her months before she finally sat me down in our (now merely my) flat. The first red flag I chose to ignore was our dwindling sex life. We hadn't even reached our second anniversary when it virtually dropped off the radar. She'd blamed her lack of libido on the final stretch of her paramedic training, a course I'd tried to discourage her from pursuing. She claimed the stress of revision and on-the-job training left her exhausted. I'd tell myself it was fine, that all couples went through this, that it'd pick up. And then I'd have a sneaky stealth wank in the bathroom so she wouldn't feel I was putting any pressure on her. And on the rare occasions we were intimate, she'd become more aroused using the sex toys I'd bought us to spice things up than by my presence in the bedroom. It didn't matter that we no longer kissed or held hands as often. Romance was for teenagers. We were perfectly fine.

Later, when I lost the charger for my tablet and used her laptop, red flag number two appeared: I discovered what she'd really been looking at on the nights she said she was studying in the spare room. She'd regularly been visiting gay porn sites and chat rooms.

'You've always known I'm bicurious,' she told me by way of an explanation. 'I've never hidden it from you. Looking doesn't mean I plan to do anything about it.'

Up until then, I hadn't felt threatened by what I took to be her passing interest in the same sex, nor had it turned me on thinking of her with another woman like it might some men. She'd always felt comfortable mentioning if she found someone attractive. I'd tease her about her girl crushes on Blake Lively and Margot Robbie, and I joked I'd consider going gay for Timothée Chalamet or Harry Styles. She told me I'd be punching above my weight. It was all in fun. *No,* I told myself, *her fantasies are nothing to worry about.* I was lucky to have an open-minded wife. And I convinced myself with little trouble that her curiosity was a phase – and phases, by and large, passed.

The 'we need to talk' conversation came weeks later. No conversation beginning with those words is ever going to end positively for one of the two people involved. And it finished with her tearfully admitting she wanted 'to explore her sexuality further'.

'Explore what, exactly? Sleeping with other women?'

'I don't know,' she said, soon followed by an admission: 'Yes.'

'Is this because of what happened with the—'

'No,' she replied, quickly shutting down that line of questioning.

We fell silent for a moment.

'And what about us?' I said eventually. 'What am I supposed to do while you're "exploring"? Or is this your way of saying you no longer want me?'

'No, no, not at all.' She'd taken my hand in hers. 'I want to, I guess, press pause on us. Who we were when we met at thirteen isn't who we are at twenty-four.'

'I'll change,' I said, failing to conceal my desperation. 'I'll do better. I'll find a better job, I'll explore your sexuality with you, I'll do whatever you need me to do.'

'You need to let me do this by myself,' she said gently. 'With the best will in the world, I can't do it with you.'

Melissa moved back in with her parents that weekend and we would never spend another night together under our roof, until the days following my drowning. Having her there, close by, felt terrific, even if she was wrapped in a duvet and sleeping on the sofa in the next room. I even allowed myself to fantasise this might be a turning point in our relationship. That almost losing me might make her fall in love with me all over again. But life doesn't offer happy endings like so many of the movies we watch.

Besides, she now has Adrienne. And while it kills me to admit it, I've never seen her more in love.

CHAPTER 11

DAMON

This clinic pulsates with the essence of life and what could be, yet I remain consumed by death and that boy and whatever the hell *has been*. I rub my thumb against a tattoo of a semicolon on my wrist, a habit I've developed when I'm distracted, like when I play with my absent wedding ring.

Three days have passed since the boy last appeared to me, and I'm on tenterhooks, awaiting his return. I still haven't mentioned it to Melissa. She'd only tell me what I already know, that I'm imagining him. But in the moments the lad is here, he feels so very, very real. Like if I stretched out my hand, I could touch him. And as much as I want to believe that, even if he existed and his death is real, it has nothing to do with me – I can't shake how I felt as I was kneeling by his side.

Like I wanted him dead.

Thinking those words sets me thrumming in my chair. I concentrate on trying to take deep, silent breaths that Melissa and Adrienne can't hear. Stay calm and get this morning over with.

Our appointment at the clinic is for a mandatory counselling session to ensure none of us are being coerced and that we all understand the journey we're about to embark upon. It's a formality, because we are all on the same page.

It's been eight months since Melissa and Adrienne first approached me out of the blue over dinner at their house, to ask if I'd consider co-parenting a child with them. Melissa and I had miscarried our baby not long before we split up. I was devastated by losing the opportunity to become a dad – the father I never had – but it was hard to gauge how that loss affected Melissa because she never talked about it. Still hasn't. But I think it frightened her off trying to conceive again. Adrienne, however, had always wanted to experience pregnancy. And since a uterine fibroid condition meant she'd be less likely to conceive without the help of IVF, and neither wanted to pick an anonymous sperm donor from a catalogue, they turned to me.

'You can have as little or as much involvement with the child as you feel comfortable with,' Melissa was quick to establish. 'All we'd ask is that you don't dip in and out of their life. Kids need consistency.'

She knows I'm not that kind of man. I have only mental snapshots of my dad, at best an irregular presence throughout my childhood. Stolen moments here and there, more absent than present. Never a proper explanation of where he was or why he'd gone. I will never understand why, *how*, any parent would play little to no part in their child's life. When they first asked me, I was afire with the chance to make that right in our child's life. They suggested I take some time to consider their offer, but I agreed to it there and then.

Which is why we are here today for the next stage in our journey. The girls have saved hard and chosen to go private rather than wait on an NHS-funded list for the next two years. Once we get the go-ahead, STI and genetic tests will follow, before checks to see if my sperm is fit for purpose.

By the time the clinic's receptionist invites us to follow her up a narrow set of stairs, I'm calm again. But it isn't to last. Because the dead boy has reappeared. And I'm transfixed by him. His face is contorted in pain, his black mouth wide open. I want to point to him, shout what I'm seeing to the receptionist, Melissa and Adrienne, but I hold back because I know this is not real. I don't see dead people, I imagine them. I reanimate them. His pleading eyes bore holes into mine; his arms are outstretched as if he's begging me to help him. And then he moves towards me, so close that I see my reflection in his corneas. Only it's not me here, now, in this room; it's me kneeling over him, watching and waiting for him to die.

'No!' I yell at the top of my voice.

The boy suddenly vanishes and I spit out an apology as I hurry into a nearby bathroom where I'm sick into a basin. Then I take deep breaths and rinse my mouth out with cold tap water.

I *know* the version I saw of him when I was drowning was real. And I *know* the version I've just seen of him is imagined. But for the sake of my own sanity, I need to discover once and for all who he is and what happened to him – alive or dead. Only then might he leave me in peace. And until that happens, I fear he will continue edging me towards the point at which I no longer have any sense of what is real and what isn't.

Madness, I believe that's called.

CHAPTER 12

DAMON

I stare at the building from the opposite side of the road. It's been many years since I've been here, but it still feels familiar. It is an unassuming detached house, nestled in a row of identical homes in a nondescript suburban street on the outskirts of London. Above the door is a datestone announcing its 1922 construction. Windows are surrounded by flaking wooden frames.

I hold the daffodils I've brought with me in one hand, and with the other I remove a vape from my jeans pocket. I take a long drag before exhaling a strawberry-scented cloud. I quit smoking last summer, but that dead boy has me on edge. Even though nicotine is a stimulant, my skewed logic promises it will calm me down. And buying disposable vapes reinforces the message that I only need a temporary nicotine hit. I slip it back into my pocket and approach the front door, pinning my hopes on its occupant giving me some much-needed answers.

The bell is silent when I press it, so I knock instead. There's no answer, so I knock again. A faint voice comes from inside.

'Let yourself in!' she shouts. 'You know where the key is.'

She can't have been aware I was coming, so must be expecting someone else. I crouch to shout through the letterbox. 'Hi Helena, it's Damon Lister.'

She doesn't reply.

I'm about to straighten back up when I spot an out-of-place brick, slightly redder in colour than those surrounding it. I run my hand over it and discover it's plastic. It springs open when I push it to reveal a key. It unlocks the front door and I make my way along the reasonably bright hallway, and trace my finger through the dust on the surface of a console table. The house smells as if it hasn't been aired out for some time.

'Helena?' I call again. 'It's Damon.'

I poke my head around the first open door and find her sitting in an armchair, a book in her hands. It's called *Dead in the Water* by Ed James. I smile to myself. It could also be the title of my autobiography.

'Damon, how lovely to see you,' Helena says with surprise. She places the book on an adjoining table and uses the arms of the chair to push herself up and shuffle unsteadily towards me.

This is the first time I have seen my foster mother since Melissa and I invited her to our wedding six years ago. We've stayed in touch, but only intermittently. When I texted her once to ask if I could visit, she admitted she was in hospital awaiting an MRI scan following a handful of mini-strokes. Concerned, I told her I could be there by the afternoon, but she said her sister was with her and that she'd be staying with her for a while at Helena's house as she recovered. Each time I offered to come visit afterwards she had another excuse, and I took the hint that perhaps she wasn't ready for people. Also, I didn't want to encroach on her recovery.

I conceal how thrown I am to see how she's aged. She must've been in her early forties when she came into my life, and she was strong in both presence and opinion. The version before me now is approaching sixty and a sliver of her former self. Her Afro-style, raven-black hair is now almost completely white. Her irises are the colour of faded amber and there are lines below her nose that her lipstick bleeds into. The left-hand side of her face droops ever so slightly. The hands that once held me as I cried are curled like claws. I only realise how skeletal she is when I hug her.

I hand her the flowers I bought from Euston station and she thanks me. 'Who did you think it was when you said I knew where the key was?' I ask.

'Oh, no one really,' she replies vaguely. 'A friend who said they'd stop by.'

'I tried calling before I came but it keeps going to voicemail.'

'I don't turn my phone on very often, which is quite cathartic,' she says. 'If people want me, they know where to find me. Anyway, how are you?' She gives me another hug before I can answer. 'It's so nice to see you.'

She uses a hand to steady herself against the fireplace. There are a pair of framed photographs on it. Seeming to catch me looking at them, she shifts to obscure them with her reed-thin body.

'Can I get you a tea or coffee?' she asks.

I'm thirsty but I don't want to put her to any trouble. I point to the daffodils. 'Why don't I find a vase for these, then put the kettle on?'

She says yes and I leave the room, recalling where the kitchen is. I lived here briefly, soon after my mum's death. Helena was a stopgap while social services located somewhere suitable for me to remain long-term. She is my life's true constant. My only link between my hazy past and lately lurid present. I return with two steaming mugs and note that the framed photographs have now been positioned face down. Neither of us mentions it, but it feels as if she is keeping something from me.

CHAPTER 13

DAMON

As I settle into the sofa, Helena asks me about my life and I tell her little has changed. Am I still in touch with anyone at the children's home, and do I still get the nosebleeds that plagued me as a boy? I answer no to both queries, but tell her that out of habit, I continue to carry a handkerchief. That rag, with two holes in it and my initials embroidered on the corner, is the only keepsake I've retained from my childhood.

'And how is Melissa?'

'She's good. We still see each other a lot.'

I decide not to mention we and Adrienne are trying for a baby. I don't want to risk her responding in the same negative manner as Tommy did when I told him.

'It's not only Mel you're doing this with, is it? It's Ade too,' he reminded me. 'You'll be tied to them for the rest of your life. Mel broke your fucking heart, mate. I was there. I saw how much it took out of you when she left. If I'm being honest, I don't think you've ever really recovered from it. I don't want you thinking this is a way of winning Mel back, because it's not going to happen.'

'I know that, and it's not,' I protested.

'If you have this baby, it's another excuse for you not to move on with your life and find someone else. Mel thinks she's doing you a favour by asking you to get involved. But she's using you.'

Tommy and I haven't spoken about it since.

Now, I gather myself. 'Can I ask you something?' I say to Helena.

'Of course.'

'Do you have any recollection of something in my records about the death of a child?'

'The death of a child?'

I take a deep breath and recount what I saw when I drowned five weeks ago. I don't tell her that I keep hallucinating his presence.

'Oh, how awful,' she says, then shakes her head as if trying to rid herself of the image I have planted there.

'He can't have been much older than twelve or thirteen,' I go on. 'Dark red hair, blue eyes, pale skin.'

'And you have no memory of him at all?'

'Nothing. I remember everything else I saw, but not him.'

'You never mentioned anything regarding a dead boy when you were living with me. Might it have been something you watched in a film or saw on television? Or something you read in a book?'

'I don't think so. It felt too real for that.' I hesitate before I ask my next question. 'You don't think . . . I could have had something to do with his death?'

'You?' she says in surprise. 'Why ever would you think that?'

'The way I saw myself crouching over him, how I wasn't trying to help him.' I still don't admit to my continuing hallucinations. 'And you know I have gaps in my memory after what happened with Mum,' I add.

'Which is understandable,' she says. 'You were only a child then. Look, I'm no expert, but it sounds to me as if your brain is playing tricks on you, which makes sense given the circumstances.

When I had my strokes, I was convinced I could drive, but I've never had so much as a lesson! And there are books and films my sister told me I used to love which I now have no recollection of ever reading or watching. Like me, your brain has gone through considerable trauma, Damon. You must give it time to recover.'

This makes perfect sense, and should put my mind at rest, given I trust her. So why doesn't it? Another happy product of my seashore trauma: I've misplaced the ability to take comfort offered by someone I know cares for me.

I change the subject and remain in her company for another half an hour or so before I explain I need to be back in Northampton by early evening to work a late shift. I promise her I won't leave it so long before I make a return visit, and we hug our goodbyes at the front door.

I'm halfway up the path when I turn to wave again and something catches my attention back inside the house. Helena is leaning against the wall with one hand. Her look of concern switches to a smile when we hold each other's stare.

But just beyond her is the red-haired boy.

He stands three stairs up, stretches out his arm and points to me. And from his black hole of a mouth, I hear him scream something I can't properly make out. Repeatedly he yells it, as cold waves, like the ones I drowned in, wash over me. I want to ask him what he means but the words snag in my throat. Instead, I turn quickly and stagger away, my heart racing.

CHAPTER 14

HELENA

Her house returns to the silence it held before Damon's unexpected visit. Knowing he has matured into a well-adjusted, compassionate and caring man should have filled her with warmth. Instead, he's left her restless. She drums her fingers against the arm of the chair, unable to shake the unease that descended upon her the moment he mentioned his drowning and the vision of a dying boy.

Helena recalls that when Damon left her charge all those years ago, she would call him on a phone she had purchased for him, to check in. He had left her care, but not her thoughts. They were more intrinsically linked than he would ever know.

She closes her eyes and Damon's image emerges like it has done many times in the past. He is never the teenager or the man he is now, only ever the frightened, vulnerable little boy she was persuaded – no, *begged* – to take in.

Then something ominous crawls over her, pinching her skin with its razor-sharp pincers. His vision of the dead boy. If this is all happening again, it is so unfair. Damon deserves better. And she resolves to do anything within her limited means to protect him.

But deep down, Helena fears it might already be too late. That what Damon thinks he saw might only be the beginning.

That he is going to learn the truth.

CHAPTER 15

DAMON

Night and day, the dead boy appears. He intrudes on my dreams, and when he awakens me, the whites of his eyes shine through the darkness of my bedroom. Sometimes he is a shadow hovering by the window. At other times, he's leaning over me, his face so close to mine I taste the cold, metallic tang of his blood, as though it has dripped from his mouth into mine. He leaves when he is ready, only ever on his terms.

So once again, I turn to the internet to search for help, for answers – and, failing that, to distract myself. Websites, YouTube, self-help e-books – all in search of a way to make myself remember if the boy is real. But nothing has worked.

I've passed sleepless, lightless hours imagining ways I might die, learn more about that boy, then bring myself back to life. At one point, I even found myself in the kitchen, filling the sink with water. The boy wasn't shrieking or slamming about the room now, but simply watching me in a curious silence as I pulled off my top, let all the air out of my lungs and dunked my head in the water. My skewed logic had suggested that if I could remain underwater long enough to black out, my life might start flashing before me. Then my legs would buckle and I'd fall to my knees on the floor, the jolt bringing me back to full consciousness.

However, my distressingly robust survival instinct meant that each time the panic and the pain became too intense, I'd simply withdraw my head, gasping for air, like a fish in a polluted pond. Three times I tried, and three times I failed. My brain wouldn't stop fighting against itself. Mentally and physically exhausted after my last attempt, I lay sprawled across the damp floor until I fell asleep.

When I eventually came to on the floor, cold and damp and ravaged by aches, another idea occurred to me. Something a little more logical and that didn't depend on me pulling off my own journey to death and back. Which is why I am here this morning, standing in a doorway in Northampton's market square. I'm a few minutes early for my appointment, so I take my third disposable vape from a packet and take a few long puffs. The clouds above are ominously black and the rumbling of thunder is followed by a white streak of lightning over a multistorey car park in the distance. My body twitches with its own answering electric charge of fear. I've always had an irrational terror of storms, particularly electrical ones. It's ludicrous, but I can't even be around toy plasma globes, the ones where you place your hand on the side of the glass and its electric tendrils follow your movements. They break me out in a cold sweat. Melissa searched online once for what I'm experiencing and apparently electricity-related anxiety is an actual thing. Electrophobia, it's called. Maybe that should be my Marvel superhero name.

I'm distracted by the ping of a text message from Melissa. It's a new appointment date for a counselling session at the IVF clinic – followed, if I pass, by blood and urine tests. They need to ensure my DNA isn't at odds with Adrienne's, which could lead to genetic abnormalities in our child if she conceives. She has accepted my apology for suddenly 'falling ill' during our last session. I blamed it on a bug doing the rounds of my supermarket colleagues. Melissa didn't seem as convinced by my explanation as Adrienne was, but then, she knows me better.

Thick raindrops appear and I look up to see an office above a betting shop. I press a video doorbell and it isn't long before I find myself inside a pleasantly decorated office. A woman in her forties greets me. She has a helmet of chestnut-brown hair and I smell mints on her breath.

'Damon.' She reaches out to shake my hand. Hers is firm and warm; mine is like ice in comparison. I wonder if she notices. 'I'm Jodi, it's lovely to meet you. Can I take your coat?'

She makes small talk as she hangs it up, and a shiver runs through me. The post-death freeze continues. And it's not only skin-deep, but deep in my bones. I take a seat and I cross my arms and legs.

My defensive body language isn't lost on her. 'A little bit unsure of what you're getting yourself into here?' she asks softly. I nod. 'Most of my clients arrive with a little trepidation or scepticism. When all else has failed, hypnotherapy is a lot of people's last resort.'

Penultimate resort, in my case, but I keep this to myself.

'Your online inquiry said you want to try and recollect something from your past, but you're not sure what?' she continues. She tilts her head a little. 'A repressed memory, I assume?'

My face heats up. Once I begin talking, I'm aware of how far-fetched this must sound. Especially when I reach the part about the boy. 'I'm frightened I might've had something to do with his death,' I admit.

She shifts in her chair. 'Okay,' she says, and taps her cheek with her index finger as if puzzled by a sudoku. Clearly not a typical inquiry. 'Well, let me explain a little about what I do. Firstly, I need to clarify that while we can use hypnosis to uncover memories, we can never be sure they're accurate. Our memories don't always remain the same and can alter over time. So even if we do locate what you want to find, there is no way of knowing the actual truth of what might have happened to that boy. I'd rather you were aware of this now than leave later, disappointed.'

'So if I do remember something while under hypnosis, it could bear little resemblance to true events?'

'Yes. Think of it like watching a TV series or a film that comes with a disclaimer telling you it's been inspired by real-life events, rather than re-enacting them.'

I feel myself deflating. 'I'd like to give it a shot anyway,' I reply, but with a note of dejection.

'Okay. Make yourself comfortable and let's try our best, shall we?'

CHAPTER 16

DAMON

Jodi presses a button on a remote control and a window blind unfurls. She points to a lamp in the now dimly lit room. Her voice, already smooth, takes on an even more honeyed tone. She could melt chocolate with it.

'So Damon, I'd like you to focus on the lamp ahead of you. If you try not to blink, the edges will appear fuzzy and blurred. And as you concentrate on the lamp, only listen to what I'm saying . . . think of nothing else but what you hear and see.'

I do as I'm asked.

She continues to talk about relaxing and, despite the self-consciousness I'm feeling, the rhythm of her voice soon accomplishes that. I don't know how long it takes – two minutes or thirty minutes – but I want to drift off to sleep. She suggests I imagine I'm floating on a cloud with the sun heating my face and body. And for the first time since I drowned, I feel something approaching warmth inside. She gradually counts down from ten to one . . .

'You're back in the water Damon,' she says, 'and this time you're safe and the sea is as warm as a bath. You know nothing bad will happen to you. If you look around, you'll see the water is a beautiful turquoise colour, and as it touches your body, it feels like the softest, warmest blanket. As you gently slip under the surface, I want you to tell me what you see when you begin replaying the stories of your life.'

And just like that, I find myself recalling with clarity some of the events I saw then – the toys I played with as a child, the people I loved, the places I visited. For the first time in I don't know how long, I feel something akin to peace. I have found my sanctuary, my place of security where I belong and where the harsh winds can't reach.

'And now I want you to think about the red-haired boy,' she says, her voice remaining unruffled and reassuring. 'Imagine you're streaming your life's events on a television screen. You're using a remote control to stop and start whenever and wherever you please. What do you see?'

'It's daylight and I'm on a path between trees and bushes,' I hear myself explaining. 'I see him ahead of me.'

'What is he doing?'

'He's lying on the ground. I'm getting closer and I can see blood coming from his mouth and ears. I think I'm saying his name.'

'Can you hear what it is?'

I shake my head. 'No.'

'What is he wearing?'

'Light-blue jeans and a T-shirt with a drawing of a surfboard on it.'

'What else can you see around you?'

'I hear cars in the distance. I think we're on a path, close to a road.'

A sense of unease is creeping towards me, cooling the soft summer breeze I've grown accustomed to.

'Look around you, Damon. Are there any signposts or landmarks?'

'I don't like this,' I tell her.

'It's okay Damon, remember this is a safe place. Nothing can hurt you.'

Time skips forward because now I'm crouching by the boy's side. He's trying to say something but I can't understand him. I'm trying to pull something from my pocket. A mobile phone maybe? He's holding his eyes wide open and I can see the fear in them. He lifts his arm and stretches his hand towards me.

I'm aware of my escalating heart rate and a weight on my chest making it increasingly difficult to take anything but short breaths. I try to focus only on what I'm saying and on Jodi's voice, but now something is muzzling that. Running water, a tap maybe? Though gradually, it grows louder and louder until it is deafening. Then I realise what it is. I'm no longer in warm, turquoise water; I'm deep inside the freezing temperatures of the Channel. I begin to cough, to choke on this memory. I'm drowning again! My lungs are filling up with water and I can't breathe.

My eyes snap open as I try to get my bearings, then I dash towards the window.

'Open it, please!' I beg her and Jodi reaches for the remote control and the blind lifts. I unclasp a catch and now the window is wide open. I lap up the fresh air like a dog poking its head out of a moving car window.

I'm only aware Jodi has approached me when she places her hand on the centre of my back. I flinch and turn quickly, staring daggers at her until she withdraws. I don't know what's come over me.

'Deep, calming breaths,' she says, trying to mask that she's a little ruffled by my hostile reaction. 'In through the nose and out through the mouth. Take as much time as you need.'

I become aware of a tickling sensation at the top of my nostrils, like something is running down the back of my throat. A nosebleed. I pull the handkerchief from my pocket and hold it under my nose while leaning forward to stop myself from swallowing the blood. Then I pinch under the bridge of my nose and wait. A few moments pass before I check the handkerchief. It's bone dry.

I turn to Jodi. 'I was almost there,' I say. 'I was so close.'

'Perhaps you aren't ready.'

If I approached him when he was dying, that would suggest I found him and didn't hurt him, wouldn't it? And if it was a phone I was trying to remove from my pocket, then I was trying to call for help? This should reassure me, but it doesn't. Because the look he has given me while I was under hypnosis and in each hallucination suggests he hates me. And the only reason I can think of for that is if I did something to him. If only I could remember what happened next.

'I want to try again.'

'I'm not sure,' she says hesitantly.

'Please?'

We return to our seats and she repeats her earlier script. But I'm too wound up to relax. The more I try to concentrate on the orange glow of the lamp and her voice, the less I succeed. Reluctantly, I'm forced to give up, and in frustration I slap my palms down on the arms of the chair. The noise is louder than I anticipate and I apologise.

'What's wrong with me?' I say. 'Why can't I remember?'

'It's not uncommon to hide from trauma,' Jodi explains. 'If this happened when you were quite young, you might not have had the cognitive capacity to understand everything that was happening. Brains prefer to avoid reliving trauma, so they build protective shields.'

'So you don't think I'm making it up? That what I saw is real?'

'As I explained when you arrived, we can never really know. If you want to delve deeper, I know a counsellor who might be able to help?'

I bristle, but I don't know why.

On the way back to the car park I become aware I'm being followed. I don't need to turn around because I recognise his deathly cold breath brushing against the back of my neck. Instead, I pick up the pace and gradually leave the boy behind. But I don't know for how long.

CHAPTER 17

MELISSA

It's a bright March morning and Melissa finds Damon sitting alone at a table at the rear of Caffè Nero when she arrives. There's already a caramel latte waiting for her in a large white mug and a wrapped biscotti on the saucer.

'Hey,' they say in unison and she takes a seat, removing her sunglasses to take him in.

Ten days have passed since she was last with him at the fertility clinic. Lately, her job at the ambulance service has had her working nightshifts. Yet several times, she has offered to sacrifice daytime sleep and swing by the home they once shared, for a catch-up. But he's been fobbing her off with excuses. A headache, a stomach bug, late shifts of his own.

Something isn't right.

She's spoken to their mutual friends, and they haven't seen hide nor hair of him either. So she was delighted when Damon texted her, suggesting a coffee.

The lighting at this end of the room is purposefully moody, but Melissa still notices dark rings developing under his weary eyes. He's also lost weight and hasn't shaved in days. He reminds her of the heroin addicts she and her crew sometimes find overdosed and blue-light to Accident and Emergency. Some people react to negativity and stress by comfort-eating. Damon is the opposite. He starves himself.

The last time she saw him like this was soon after admitting she wanted them to separate. It was the hardest thing she has ever done, and the guilt still gnaws at her. She corrects herself: second-hardest thing. Only Adrienne knows what trumps it.

'You don't look so great,' she begins. 'Do you still have that bug?'

'It's on its way out.'

'Did you go to the clinic appointment yesterday to finish the counselling?'

'Sorry,' he mutters. 'I wasn't feeling up to it. I'll remake it.'

Melissa bites her tongue as a niggle makes its presence felt. He keeps looking over her shoulder towards the doors.

'Are we expecting company?' she asks.

'Sorry, no,' he says, but offers no explanation.

He's hiding something from her, she is sure of it. But she knows the fastest way to send him running is confrontation. For a fraction of a second, she allows her brain to consider whether asking him to be their baby's father was a good idea. When she and Adrienne first discussed starting a family, it was Melissa who put his name forward.

'Damon, as in your ex-husband?' Adrienne had asked, clearly surprised. 'You want me to carry your ex-husband's baby?'

Melissa nodded. Though she was aware of how crazy it sounded once she heard it coming from someone else.

'I don't know, Mel,' Adrienne replied, shaking her head. 'I mean, you know I don't have a problem with you two being close, but this relationship belongs to you and me, not you, me and Damon.'

'He's kind, he's caring, he's loyal and he's empathetic,' she argued.

'So is a spaniel.'

Melissa ignored this. 'And you know he'd make a good dad.'

'He's also still in love with you.'

'He's not,' Melissa replied, though she knew that wasn't strictly true. He hadn't moved from the flat they'd shared and, on her insistence, had only recently replaced a framed honeymoon photograph that had been sitting on the mantelpiece. Sometimes she'd catch him staring at her before quickly looking away, a blush in his cheeks. He'd been on dates in the four years they'd been apart, but eventually deleted the dating apps when Tommy had pointed out that every girl he chose was a carbon copy of Melissa. Later, when Melissa asked Damon what was wrong with the girls he'd met, he'd told her simply: 'They're not you.'

She'd been equal parts frustrated and flattered. And she'd also made the mistake of sharing the exchange with Adrienne, which accounted for the raised eyebrow earned by Melissa's attempted dismissal of the notion that Damon still held a torch for her. Melissa could only look away.

Adrienne had pressed on with her examination of Damon's candidacy to father their child. 'There are other factors to consider too.'

'Like?'

'Like – and this is going to make me sound like such a bitch – he's a twenty-eight-year-old supermarket shelf-stacker. A little ambition wouldn't go amiss. I want our child to look up to its parents, to see how hard they've worked, to want to be like them.'

'Would you rather he was an absolute arsehole, but pulling in a six-figure salary?'

'What I'm *saying* is there might be better options for us. And isn't the notion of having two mums and a dad on the scene a little . . . outdated? A bit Generation X?'

'You'd prefer an anonymous sperm donor?'

'Perhaps it's something we should consider.'

'Just because Damon hasn't found his path yet doesn't mean he won't. Maybe having the responsibility of a child is what he needs to reassess where his life is going.'

'It shouldn't take a baby for him to want to do that,' said Adrienne. 'And are you sure the real reason you want him to be our baby's dad isn't because you want to give him the family he doesn't have?'

Tellingly, Melissa had hesitated before she said no. As, yes, it had been a factor in her decision. She shared a close bond with her parents, three brothers and sister, but Damon was alone. No siblings, no cousins, no granny or granddad. Only two dead parents. She hurt for him. She wanted him to have a biological link with another person in this world. Not that he ever admitted it, but she was convinced that never having had a regular father figure in his life was an open wound for Damon. Becoming a dad himself might help him to heal.

But there was more to it than that. A reason she didn't like to dwell upon, because she hated herself for it. A reason she intended to keep from Damon until her dying day.

She and Adrienne continued talking long into that night and over the following days, until they finally reached the same page and presented the idea to him.

But that was long before Damon drowned.

Because the version of him who sits before her today in this dim little café is different. He is on edge, struggling to maintain eye contact. He taps at the semicolon tattoo on his wrist, a sure sign he is anxious. She glances at three empty espresso cups on the table and she wonders how long he has been sitting here alone.

'What's going on?' she persists. 'What aren't you telling me?'

CHAPTER 18

MELISSA

'Damon?' Melissa asks when he doesn't reply. She is trying hard not to show how worried she is about him. *Treat him like a patient*, she thinks. *Listen, assess. Don't judge.*

He takes a deep breath. And for the first time today, he maintains eye contact. 'I'm not doing so well.'

'Is it something to do with Brighton?' She purposely avoids using the word 'drowned'. It's ghoulish, and neither of them needs reminding of it. The reality of his death still haunts her. 'If you need to see a doctor, I can drive us to A&E right now. We'll be there in ten minutes.'

'And spend all day in a waiting room only to be told what I already know?'

'Which is?'

'That there's nothing physically wrong with me.'

'Then what is it?'

He cocks his head and hunches his shoulders over the table so he is closer to her.

'Him,' he says. 'The boy.'

'What boy?' she asks, genuinely perplexed.

'*The* boy,' he repeats, placing emphasis on the definite article. 'The one who was dying.'

Now the penny drops. 'The kid you thought you saw when you were in the water?'

His lips purse. 'There's no *thought* about it, Mel. I know what I saw. What I keep seeing.'

She frowns. 'What do you mean, *keep seeing*?'

To her quiet disbelief, he reveals how, for the last six weeks, he's had repeated visions of the dead, bloodied child, a hole for a mouth, shouting something unintelligible at him. She nods along as Damon speaks – *don't judge, don't judge, don't judge* – fighting to maintain her composure and act as if what he's telling her is all perfectly normal. The rapid decline in his mental health profoundly disturbs her.

'What you keep seeing,' she says with a forced calmness when he's finished, 'is in your imagination.'

'I know that. I haven't totally lost grip on reality,' he replies, pushing himself back into his chair. 'But I'm convinced his presence in my memories is *based on something I witnessed*. And I need to know if I am responsible for what happened to him.'

'Of course you're not. I know you. You wouldn't hurt anyone, least of all a kid. It sounds to me as if you could be suffering from Post-Traumatic Stress Disorder. A by-product of PTSD can be psychotic symptoms like hallucinations. I mean, why *wouldn't* you be? And that's all perfectly treatable.'

'I'm not psychotic,' he snaps.

She bites her bottom lip, because she knows, to the untrained ear, what she has suggested probably sounds a lot worse than it is.

'Ade knows doctors at the hospital who work in the private sector,' she goes on in an even tone. 'I could ask if one of them could talk to you? Maybe they could help—'

'You're not listening!' Damon slaps the tabletop, hard. This is the first time she remembers him ever losing his temper with her. Even when their marriage was crumbling and he was powerless to prevent it, he never yelled at her. Instead, he withdrew into himself, which was probably worse – watching a beautiful soul disintegrate, and knowing she was responsible. But today, she has clearly misjudged the depth of his stress.

The room has quietened and heads have turned to stare at them.

'Are you okay?' a woman two tables away mouths at Melissa.

'I'm fine.' She nods, grateful that, even though Damon is no threat, a stranger wanted to check on her well-being.

'Stop treating me as the enemy,' she tells Damon. 'I'm on your side.'

'I'm sorry,' he says. Now it's his turn to rub hard at his face with his palms.

'I want to help you.'

He drops his hands into his lap and meets her eye. 'If you really want to help, there's something you can do.'

'Name it. Anything. I'm here.'

Damon nods, looking her dead in the eye before he speaks.

'You can kill me.'

CHAPTER 19

MELISSA

Melissa assumes Damon is kidding and lets out an artificial laugh.

'I tried that once already, remember?' she says and sips her latte.

She realises there's no humour attached to his expression.

'Are you being serious?' she asks, lowering her voice. And slowly, he nods. 'You want me to kill you?'

'Yes. And then resuscitate me.'

Now it's Melissa's turn to sit back in her chair. She glances around the café, hoping no one has overheard. 'I can't do that!' she half talks, half whispers. 'We are supposed to be trying to get pregnant . . . you know, *creating* life.'

Damon matches her pitch: 'The only way to know for sure that boy didn't die because of something I did is for me to go back to when it happened.'

Melissa shakes her head in disbelief. 'Do you realise what you're asking of me?' He nods again. 'Oh, well. Good. We're clear on that. But, the insanity of *that* aside, this isn't like that stupid *Flatliners* movie we watched, Damon. This isn't some silly ghost story where you can die – *die!* – and "confront your past", then spring back to life.'

'It's not about confronting it. It's about finding the truth.'

She takes a breath and releases it slowly before looking again into his bloodshot eyes. 'Do you know how lucky you are to even *be* alive after last time?'

Melissa looks to the ceiling and runs her hands through her short, cropped cut. She blinks long and hard, partly hoping that when she returns her attention to him, she might be the one who's hallucinating and that she's sitting here alone and arguing with herself.

'Damon, I love you with all my heart, but this is singularly the most stupid thing I have ever heard you say.'

'I'm running out of options,' he tells her, and lists every way he has tried to unlock what is hidden inside his head. 'Nothing works. The only way to discover what happened to that boy is if I die again. I'm sure of it.'

'No,' she replies. 'You can't be possibly sure of it.'

'He is *all I can think about*, Mel. The hallucinations are coming so thick and fast that I can't sleep properly. I haven't worked in a week because he's there in the supermarket aisles, the warehouse, even the damn toilets. I am *desperate*. Don't you think if there was any other way, I'd be all over it?'

'If our roles were reversed and I was begging you to kill me to help find a ghost, what would you say?'

'I'd say no, because I don't have the training you have. But you're a paramedic. You can bring me back.'

'I am trained to save people, I'm not the Grim fucking Reaper.'

'You've already resuscitated me once.'

'What medical evidence do you have that I'll be able to do it a second time? None. Who lives and who remains dead is a lottery, no matter how much medical expertise is involved. It is far too risky. And do you really think I want to have your death on my conscience?'

'You already do.'

That wounds. 'Go to hell,' she says. 'I already feel like the worst person on earth for what happened to you. I have nightmares where you're within my grasp before a wave drags you away.' She feels hot tears running down her cheeks and chin, and wipes them away with a paper napkin. 'And now you're asking me to relive one of the worst days of my life? That's colossally selfish.'

'No,' he counters. 'Refusing to help me when I'm clearly this desperate is.'

Melissa shakes her head. 'God knows what damage dying once has already done to you. And even if I managed to bring you back again, it could take so long that you're starved of oxygen and permanently damaged.' She tosses her napkin on to the table. 'So, if not wanting to put you in a vegetative state makes me selfish, then yes, that's exactly what I am. And for the sake of our friendship, we are never talking about this again.'

She rises to her feet, leaving her latte unfinished.

'Then I'll do it by myself,' Damon says.

'Empty threat. You can't die and bring yourself back to life,' she scoffs. 'It's not medically possible.'

'I'll find a way,' he replies with childish contempt. 'I'm doing this either with or without you. And if I can't, will you really be able to live with yourself?'

'Fuck you, Damon,' Melissa says, turning her back on him and walking away. She slips her sunglasses back on before reaching the door so the other customers can't see her crying.

This isn't the same man whose life she saved. She doesn't recognise him. But she has never witnessed him more passionate or determined about anything than he is about wanting to die for a second time.

And it terrifies her.

CHAPTER 20

DAMON

My phone vibrates but I don't answer it. Only when it stops do I check the screen. Melissa is calling again. I put the phone face down on the kitchen worktop. She is the last person I need to speak to tonight.

Sixteen days have passed since she refused to help me die, and it's the longest we've gone without talking in I don't know how long. I miss her company, but I'm not yet ready to talk. I'm still angry at how quick she was to dismiss me, and I'm also pissed off with how stupid she made me feel for asking for help in the first place. I didn't need her to tell me how crazy my request was, or inform me of the gravity of what I was asking her to do. I'd hoped she'd hear me out and at least agree to think about it.

It wasn't bluster when I told her that I was going to die and come back with or without her help. Because tonight, it's going to happen.

She was right when she told me I couldn't do it on my own. I've tried researching ways to pull it off, but Google is more interested in dissuading me from dying by prioritising helplines and websites that promote life. All of which would be useful if I was caught in that dark place, but I'm not. I want to *visit* death, not remain in its company indefinitely.

I've researched cocktails of medication powerful enough to end my life, how long it might take for me to drift towards unconsciousness and when I would need to call 999 and be resuscitated. But there is no guarantee I'll be reached in time. And if they can bring me round and pump my stomach, much of my brain might be irreparably damaged by the lack of oxygen. And then there's the list of long-term effects the pills themselves might cause, which is frighteningly extensive. Liver and kidney damage, seizures, cardiac issues . . . it goes on.

I thought I'd found my answer on a forum where a poster suggested attaching defibrillator paddles to my chest and placing the machine on a timer so I could be shocked back to life. Rash, I know, but in my excitement I sold my PlayStation 4 to Cash Converters so I could afford to buy a second-hand set from eBay. Then, when it arrived, I realised the button requires continuous pressing before the shock is administered. I can't do that alone. I suppose I was a little relieved given my fear of currents. The thought of charging them up and being that close to a device that could shoot volts of electricity through me is more than a little queasy-making.

So I've had little choice but to think outside the box and search for help elsewhere. That's when I stumbled across him, hiding within the depths of an obscure internet message board catering for people like me, fixated on what lies between life and death. Within an ongoing topic discussing our 'life reviews', as they're known, I shared my own experience under the username Jude St Francis from the novel *A Little Life* by Hanya Yanagihara. Those users aware of that story and its many references to suicide would appreciate how fixated by death I was. Albeit temporarily.

As far as I can see, the only way to find out more about my missing past is for me to die again, I typed, but without mentioning the murdered boy. *And I don't know how to do that alone.*

Soon after, a message appeared in my account's inbox.

I read your thread with interest, he wrote. *To clarify, your dilemma is not the means by which you end your life, but how you return to it?*

Yes, I replied. *I've searched and searched but I can't find a way of doing it alone.*

Minutes passed before he responded.

I might be able to help you. If you're serious.

I stared at the words on the screen, my stomach beginning the first in a series of somersaults.

How?

I can assist you with ending your life. And then I can bring you back. If that's what you want.

I pushed my laptop to one side, took a few deep drags on my vape as my mind raced. I was desperate, but I wasn't naive. What kind of person volunteers to end another person's life? How could I be sure he wouldn't leave me after I died? I should have dismissed his offer, deactivated my account and shut down my device. But I didn't. I couldn't. I knew he might be my last hope. So I responded.

He went on to explain how he understood why I was compelled to do this. How, like me, he wasn't afraid of death. He claimed to have medical training, and that he'd do his utmost to resuscitate me in time. Nothing he said suggested he was anything aside from genuine. However, I remain conscious of the risk of inviting this stranger into my life, and giving him the power to take it away from me. And I can't rule out the possibility he might not even turn up. He could still be a fantasist.

Regardless, I have accepted his offer. Only today have I dropped a pin in a Google map and sent him my address. He should be on his way to my flat now.

I inspect the bedroom again, because this is where I plan to die. It contains a built-in wardrobe with a metal railing that can support my full weight. I've tested it in the past with chin-ups during my periodic fitness programmes. And I have a rope all ready.

The overly aggressive door buzzer sounds and my stomach cinches as I stare at the black-and-white image of him from the camera installed one floor down, above the front door. He's wearing a baseball cap and is holding his head down, doing his best not to be filmed, I assume. I don't blame him. I only realise my hand is trembling when I push the button to allow him entry.

I hear his feet echoing lightly up the flight of metal stairs, and when I open my door, we are finally face to face. I hesitate because I'm a little taken aback. Throughout all our chats, I assumed him to be male. But this is a woman.

'Hi,' I say.

'Hello.'

'You must be The Good Samaritan,' I continue, referring to their message board username.

She nods. 'Call me Laura.'

CHAPTER 21

LAURA

She is immediately reassured by how ordinary he appears. He's skinny, and at about five foot seven or eight, he is only slightly taller than her. She hides her enthusiasm and tries to mimic his nervousness to help put him at ease. His apprehension quietly pleases her. He poses about as much threat to her as plankton might to a shark. However, she's aware looks can be deceiving. She is evidence of that. Butter wouldn't melt in her mouth, she's been told. Which is precisely what allows her to behave as freely as she does.

She glances around the room. No sign of a third party: no shadows behind cracked-open doors, no shoes visible in the gaps between doors and floors. No stray noises. Damon appears to be alone, but she will remain hypervigilant regardless. That's how she operates. With care. She doesn't take unnecessary risks. Well, not anymore. She has learned from her mistakes.

Having been sent his address, she knew what to expect from the flat itself before reaching it. She found images cached on property website MoveMe's pages from the last time it was up for let seven years ago. A phone call to the local council tax department in which she masqueraded as a debt collection agency revealed its sole occupier.

Lister. Why was Damon's surname familiar to her? She didn't recognise his face when a Google search offered images of him in a five-aside football team, then a charity fun run. A DBS search on the dark web revealed no criminal record. She must have been mixing him up with someone else. For all intents and purposes, he was who he said he was and posed no threat. So she thought no more about it.

The flat is open-plan but compact, to say the least. If Ikea made coffins, she'd be standing in one. There's about enough room for a double sofa and a single chair in the lounge, a circular dining table and four chairs by the window overlooking the town, and a light-grey galley kitchen with a metallic splashback. No art on the walls, the only ornaments on surfaces a Lego *Friends* Central Perk set and something *Star Wars* related. This manchild's bachelor pad has all the personality of an Airbnb.

She removes her baseball cap to reveal blonde hair scraped back into a tight ponytail. She wears frameless glasses, a little make-up, and is casually dressed in jeans and trainers. Nothing that might make her stand out if she was ever caught on CCTV. She may have reached her mid-forties, but she's confident she can pass for a decade younger because people tell her that. It pleases her when they're surprised by her age. She puts it down to her vegan diet, vitamin regimen, moisturisers, Pilates, jabs every four months to paralyse her facial muscles – and, most importantly, to what she takes from people. What she is about to take from Damon.

He introduces himself, asks for her coat, then leaves it hanging loosely over the back of the armchair. She'll have it dry-cleaned tomorrow. He's about to close the door behind him but she insists they leave it ajar. He doesn't protest, and props it open with a thick copy of *A Little Life*. 'My favourite book,' she finds herself saying aloud, and he smiles. It's true: no other written words have placed as much joy in her heart as that novel. Aside from *We Need to Talk About Kevin.* A bookmark protrudes from a page towards the back of the tome, suggesting he's almost finished reading it. The irony of the plot and Damon's situation isn't lost on her. She knows that his username and the book are indications he is serious. He wants to die. And she wants to help him.

'It's not that I don't trust you,' she adds as she continues to look around, 'but I was let down in the past by someone who wasn't who they claimed to be.'

'Were you helping them like you're helping me?'

'No, Rya—' She stops herself. He doesn't need to know the hell that man put her through, and it won't benefit her to rehash something that happened nine years ago. She has spent the time since replacing him with others so that she can forget about him. Yet still he lingers. And she can't put her finger on why. Perhaps it's the excitement he brought to her life, the challenge. Or maybe how their story played out.

'He was a very troubled person,' she suffices to say.

Damon offers her a drink, but she declines. She only consumes what she pours herself. Besides, she can't be sure how clean his crockery is. Value-brand dishwasher tablets are a false economy; they leave dirt the naked eye can't see.

He takes a couple of puffs from a vape, conjuring blanched white clouds above him like he's switched on a fog machine that's vomiting up the synthetic scent of watermelon.

'Have you travelled far?' he asks.

'London.' Humouring him, though she's here for a reason, which isn't to make small talk. 'But I know Northampton well.' No need to let on how familiar she is with the town.

'You said online you've witnessed people dying before,' he says. 'That watching me . . . die won't be something new to you. Can you elaborate?'

He thinks he's interviewing her for a job. Should have brought along a CV. References in the form of the file of death certificates she keeps hidden inside a picture frame housing an image of her and her three children.

'No,' she assures him, 'you won't be the first.' She must choose her words carefully. Can't sound like an amateur, but she doesn't want to frighten him off, either, by reeling off her bona fides. 'I have . . . assisted people when no one else was willing to step up. And for a number of years, I worked for a helpline for people in emotional distress. Several ended their lives while I was on calls with them.'

Of all the jobs she has worked over the years, she misses that one the most. Nothing has been able to replicate the challenge of identifying who needed her extra help, the thrill of the chase or the end result. There's a wistfulness in what she admits next. 'I'm accustomed to death. Sometimes I think it follows me around like a shadow.'

A fleeting image of her father and her twin sisters flashes into her mind. Where it all began, behind that closed bedroom door. The one she'd been excluded from entering. She will never really know why it happened, but it doesn't stop her from reflecting. For now, she blinks the memory away.

'Can I ask why you sent me that first message?' Damon continues.

She thinks for a moment. 'You sounded desperate. And I want to help people like you. I see it as my mission.' Laura isn't fast enough to curb the small smile creeping across her face, followed by a dash of frustration. There are so few people like her. She should be able to talk freely about what she has to offer. But until the world has become as emotionally evolved as she has, she will be forced to keep it to herself. Eventually, she hopes, they will understand.

'Where do you plan to do this?' she asks.

'In the bedroom,' he replies. 'I've set everything up, ready for us.'

'And does anyone else know I'm here? Have you mentioned me to friends or family, in person or by text or email?'

'Nobody. And I've done as you asked and deleted my message board profile, my WhatsApp messages and the search history on my laptop.'

Nodding, she glances around the room again, this time spotting a handful of off-white rectangular marks on the walls, suggesting pictures or photos once hung here. The only one left is of him and a woman – clearly taken years earlier, going by his haggard appearance now. They're holding hands, so it's not a sister. Laura concludes he's now single and hanging on to the past. She has been guilty of that on more than one occasion.

'No one else lives here?'

'I live here alone,' he says, a touch regretfully.

He leads the way from the lounge and into the bedroom, and she scans this room like a forensic scientist. It's so boring in here she's surprised spiders haven't started weaving the words 'Please help us' instead of webs. Laura asks him to close a slight gap in the curtains, not that anyone would be able to see anyway, as she doesn't think his flat is overlooked. But she can never be too sure. She turns up the dimmer switch to full so the room is bathed in light. She doesn't want to miss a thing. She also asks that he turn off his mobile phone and laptop. Laura is wary of any devices with the ability to record and that don't belong to her.

She picks up a coil of synthetic decking rope lying on the bed and yanks it to check its strength. The defibrillator he told her he bought is plugged into the wall. A green light flashes, indicating it's ready for use.

'Would you like me to record what happens?' She removes her phone and holds it in her hand.

'Why?'

'In case you say anything you might later forget when I bring you round. I have a way I can send it to you afterwards that can't be traced back to me.'

She masks her disappointment when he declines.

'I guess we should get on with it,' he says.

She nods, cricks her neck from side to side until it clicks, then slips into a mode so familiar to her, it's like donning a second skin.

CHAPTER 22

DAMON

I'm as anxious as hell as I sit on the floor, my hands trembling as I pick up the rope and start to form a noose. I memorised a YouTube tutorial, but despite practising it, I might as well be wearing boxing gloves for all the control I have over my fingers.

'Wait, no,' Laura says suddenly. 'It's all wrong.'

For a moment, I think she's backing out of this. And if that's the case, a small part of me might feel a tinge of relief. Would it really be such a bad thing if she walked out?

'You're tying a hangman's noose, and that only works when there's a drop,' she clarifies.

'Oh.'

She takes the rope from my hand and joins me on the carpet like an adult teaching a child how to tie his shoelace. 'There won't be a drop in your case,' she goes on with exaggerated patience as she works the rope, 'because you're doing this on the floor. So I'm going to use a clove hitch.'

If I needed any more evidence that Laura knows what she's doing, this is it. She exudes confidence. And unless I'm misreading the room, I sense an eagerness about her. Perhaps more than just a desire to be a Good Samaritan. Whatever. Her motivations are her own concern. I care only for results.

She sets to work and I feel the warmth radiating from her hands and face as she positions the circular hole a little below my jawline and above my Adam's apple. Her nose is so close to my mouth now it's like she is drawing in my breath. It feels strikingly intimate, almost sexual. It crosses my mind how she might respond if I moved a little closer and placed my lips on hers, but the thought leaves almost as soon as it arrives.

Next, she attaches the rope to the clothes rail and pulls at it to ensure it won't come loose. And finally, she binds my hands together behind my back with a cable tie she removes from her pocket. Does having it so at the ready demonstrate how serious she is taking this, or is it a red flag?

'Your survival instinct will be working against us,' she explains as she works. 'This'll stop your fists from lashing out.' She offers me a wan smile. 'I'd rather not leave here with a broken nose.'

'Sure,' I say. 'Okay.' *Absolutely. Truss me up like a pig. Carry on.*

'I'm going to add a little pressure to your body to try and spare you the pain of asphyxiation,' she continues. 'So you'll black out before you pass away. Hopefully, you'll find answers to your questions. And I'll be right here and ready to bring you back.'

Then, without warning or checking with me one last time if this is still what I want, Laura pulls the rope around my neck so tightly, my hands instinctively reach to try to create a gap between it and my skin. There isn't one.

Nothing if not efficient, within what feels like seconds Laura has me back in the cold, cold sea. Only, this time, I am bone-dry and it's not the elements killing me, it's Laura. The terror is the same. Knowing my life is about to end right now is no different to the time before. And even though Laura is here at my request to help me die, I still look to her in desperation, begging for help.

Instead of calming me or offering me reassuring words, a smile shines through the gaps in her face. A different smile from the one she showed me earlier. She remains on the floor with me, but now she is beginning to back away towards the defibrillator. Only, she's unplugging it and pushing it away with her foot, out of reach.

She wants me dead, but not in the same way I do.

CHAPTER 23

DAMON

Oh fuck. This isn't how it was supposed to go. Laura isn't here for me, she is here for herself. And I'm helpless to make it stop.

Now she is holding her phone out in front of her and she touches the screen. I think she's recording my death.

'Don't fight it, and it will be a lot easier and so much quicker,' she says, over the sounds of my coughs and gasps. 'Trust me.'

But I don't. Instead, I try to free myself, however, she has done far too good a job of securing my hands and the knot around the noose. It won't budge.

Now she has commenced slowly crawling towards me with the stealth of a cat approaching its prey, her phone trained upon me. I can smell her hunger as she draws closer. She takes deep breaths as if ingesting my panic. *Oh, no. No no no no.* I try begging her for help, to tell her I've changed my mind, but I can't get a word out. The rope is crushing my airway. And now the dead boy is standing next to her, reaching his hand out towards me, as if wanting to save me. *There's* a change. He opens his useless black mouth wide and his rasps mimic mine.

And then his expression alters. There's no mistaking it: he is silently laughing at me. He wants me dead. They both do.

Panic suddenly steps aside when my body floods itself with a naturally occurring chemical reminiscent of a sedative, numbing both my pain and my fear – my brain once again kicking in to protect me, pave the transition from this life to the next. An overwhelming sense of calmness washes over me. If there is a God, He has truly thought of everything.

And it's in that moment that another familiar sensation begins, one I have only felt once before, two months ago, beneath the waves. It's like the reverse of a Polaroid picture, as if a clear image of everything around me is slowly fading to black and is being replaced by a carousel of moving images that represent my life.

But then, in the remaining seconds before my exit from this world, the bedroom door bursts open.

CHAPTER 24

MELISSA

Melissa can't make sense of the scene before her. A woman she doesn't recognise is kneeling on the floor of Damon's bedroom, a phone in her hand, while he has a rope around his neck and his hands are bound. She briefly wonders if she has interrupted a kinky sex game before she notices they are both fully clothed. Then she registers Damon's eyes. They have all but rolled into the backs of their sockets, leaving milky white orbs. Only now does she realise what is happening.

This woman is killing him.

Melissa races towards Damon, ready to shove the stranger to one side. But the woman is lightning fast, back on her feet and weaving effortlessly past her. Melissa doesn't have time to stop her because she can tell from Damon's appearance that she is about to lose him for a second time. She attempts to loosen the ligature around his neck but it's too tight. She needs something to cut through it. She grabs a vegetable knife from the wooden knife block in the kitchen and hurries back, sawing through the rope, being careful not to go too deeply and accidentally slice his neck.

'Stay with me, Damon,' she begs him. 'Come on. I'm not losing you.'

Finally, the fibres of the rope splay as she severs it, the blade leaving a small cut on his neck. A sliver of blood trickles down it as she checks his vitals.

No pulse, no heartbeat. He is dead again.

Melissa begins the same procedure as last time, checking his airway is clear, then breathing into his mouth and launching a series of chest compressions.

They don't work. She repeats the actions, and still he fails to respond.

'For fuck's sake!' she screams at the top of her voice.

Only then does she register the defibrillator on the floor. She doesn't have time to consider how it got there. It's unplugged but she hopes it contains enough charge to work. She lifts Damon's T-shirt and attaches the pads around the left side of the chest under his armpit and below the shoulder on the right. Then she presses a button and stands clear as the first shock is administered, rocking Damon's inert body. Once prompted, she starts CPR again before preparing the machine for the next burst. But a second before she presses the button, Damon's eyes snap wide open and he gasps for air. He tries to sit upright, grabbing at his neck, trying to pull off the noose he thinks is still coiled around him.

'It's me, it's Mel,' she says over and over again. 'There's no rope, you're safe.'

He glares at her as if he doesn't believe it, and it takes several more reassurances before he accepts the truth. She takes the knife again and, this time, cuts through the plastic strip binding his hands before removing her phone from her pocket. 'I'm calling an ambulance,' she tells him as she dials.

'No,' he rasps.

'Damon, I need to get you to hospital,' she says, more firmly. 'You have to be checked over.'

'No!' This time, he swings his hand and bats the phone out of hers and across the floor.

'What the hell?'

'I saw the dead boy.'

She wants to shout at him, to tell him she doesn't care, to remind him that only minutes ago, he was dead. *Dead.*

'And he wasn't alone,' he continues. 'I saw her, too.'

'Who?'

Tears well. 'My mum. I saw my mum again.'

CHAPTER 25

MELISSA

It's too bright in here so Melissa turns the dimmer switch down. She slips her hands under Damon's armpits. They're damp with sweat and she helps prop him up against the edge of his bed. She can make out a small phoenix near his elbow in his sleeve of tattoos and she remembers when he had it done. But only now does she notice how it's rising from water, not flames. *How prophetic*, she thinks. She spots a handkerchief poking out from his pocket. She hates those bloody things. He didn't have a nosebleed in all the time they were together, but still he insisted on keeping one with him, just in case. They give her the ick.

Damon leans forward, resting his elbows on his thighs and supporting his forehead with his palms. She covers him with a blanket and takes a seat in the armchair opposite. She remembers buying it from a department store with gift vouchers they were given by friends when they married. He hides his face from her as his body trembles. She assumes it's out of shame. She is wrong. Minutes pass before he speaks again.

'Why are you here?' His voice is still hoarse but she hears anger in it. It takes her by surprise.

'Because you weren't answering your phone and you've stopped replying to my texts,' she says gently. 'Tommy, AJ, all your friends . . . you're ignoring everyone. We're worried about you.'

'You made it clear what I do is none of your business,' Damon says as he rubs his neck.

Again, she is taken aback by his animosity. Hasn't she just saved his life? *Again?* 'That's not fair. And it's not what I said. Killing yourself is very much my business.'

'You still don't get it, do you?' He sighs. 'I don't want to *stay* dead. It's a means to get to the truth. And I would have found it if you hadn't interrupted us.'

'What?'

'You ruined everything.'

'You're alive because of me!' she says in disbelief. 'Who was that woman?'

He hesitates. 'A friend.'

'Then why haven't I seen her before?'

'We only met recently.'

'Where?'

'Online.'

'What, Tinder? You discovered you had a shared an interest in strangulation, so you swiped right and invited her over to tie a noose around your neck? She was *killing* you, Damon.'

'Only because I asked her to. She was helping me because you wouldn't.'

'She was filming you as you were dying! She was getting a kick out of it. She wasn't going to bring you back.'

'You don't know that,' he replies, lying to himself because the reality of what her agenda might've been is too frightening to face. He rubs his neck again.

'If you saw the panic and then the absolute fury on her face when I interrupted her, you wouldn't be arguing with me. She was in it for herself.'

'She was about to resuscitate me.'

'Please, if you aren't going to be honest with me, at least be honest with yourself.'

Damon lifts his head and his gaze meets Melissa's. 'You refused to help me.'

'Don't try and make this about me.'

'You left me with no other choice. I had to find somebody else.'

'You did have a choice, and that was to forget about what you imagined. Put that little boy behind you and move on.'

'He won't let me! I see him *all the time*.' He taps his index finger against his temple. 'To get him to stop, I need to access what's locked in here. Why can't you understand? Jesus, Mel.'

Damon rises from the bed and makes his way into the bathroom, moving like a newborn foal, unsteady and awkward on his feet. Melissa trails behind him in case he falls. He retrieves a tube of Savlon antiseptic cream from the cabinet and massages it into the red imprints the rope has left on his neck. His hands are still trembling and he misses a patch at the back. She rubs it in for him. Together, they stare at one another through their reflections. A question lingers in her mind, one she both does and doesn't want an answer to. Eventually she relents.

'When do you see the dead boy?'

'Always. He's standing behind you right now.'

Melissa spins on her heels, raising her fists as if to protect them from an assailant. But of course it's only them in the bathroom. Well, her, him and his hallucination. She turns back to him and takes a deep breath.

'And he's not alone anymore,' Damon continues. 'Mum is with him.'

'Now?' She can't help it: again she whirls, and repeats her pointless search for the phantoms pursuing him. That his mother has now joined them throws her. He rarely speaks about her because he doesn't remember much, but her loss left a painful void. She's suggested many a time that he should consider therapy as a way of reconnecting with his past. And each time, he rebuffs her.

She faces him once more. 'Please,' she says, 'let me get you help. Outpatient, inpatient, you decide. I'll get you whatever you need, and I'll be with you every step of the way.'

He steps closer and slowly tilts his head forward until it rests on her hairline.

'There's only one way you can help me,' he says.

Melissa knows what he is asking of her. And she is conscious that if he is so desperate that he's willing to allow a stranger to take his life in her hands, then he has reached a frightening new level of desperation.

She doesn't answer him. Instead, she gives serious consideration to contacting the authorities to put the wheels in motion to have him sectioned under the Mental Health Act. However, it's not as simple as that – there are all sorts of hoops to jump through first, involving mental health professionals, assessments and searches for spare beds. And she knows how determined and stubborn Damon can be if he doesn't want to do something. If he refuses to go willingly, she can already foresee the complications that will bring. Once again, she will be the one who has betrayed him.

That's why she finds herself slowly nodding. Even as she's doing it, she knows it is stupid, irrational, a ginormous risk and completely wrong. She begins to cry. Not only for what is happening to someone she loves so much, but for selfish reasons. She fears motherhood is starting to slip through her fingers with every twist and turn in their relationship. She must find a way to turn the tide before it sweeps him away from her for good.

CHAPTER 26

DAMON

I pull at the collar of my T-shirt when it rubs against my neck. I can only wear T-shirts to work, not collared shirts, so I've borrowed some make-up from Melissa to cover the rope burn marks.

I'm on autopilot as I stack the shelves and fill my trolleys with other people's orders. All I've been able to think about is seeing my mum again. It's hard to put into words what it means because it was as overwhelming as it was intoxicating. She wasn't even attached to one specific life event; she was simply present, an amalgamation of thousands of repressed recollections, I suppose. I was able to hear the South London lilt in her accent, the faint lisp as she spoke, feel the softness of her fingers as they entwined with mine, I saw how the tip of her nose scrunched when she laughed and smelled the woody scent of her favourite perfume.

I wonder if her return was a one-off until I turn the corner of the aisle and there she is. I stop in my tracks, my mouth agape. It's the first time I'm seeing her in hallucinatory form and she's every bit as clear to me as the boy is when I see him. I can't stop a smile from spreading across my face, but it's momentary. Because there's something off about her – and I mean more off than the fact this is all happening in my head. The version of her I saw as I drowned is different to who I'm seeing now. She's a good few years older, with creases around her eyes and streaks of grey in her ash-blonde hair. Her sharp collarbones protrude from the off-white vest she wears.

Why, after all these years since she died, is she only now coming to me? Does she want to tell me something?

I approach her with caution. No one else can see her but me, yet the shoppers still walk around her, as if she is protected by an invisible forcefield. I'm no more than half a metre away when I stop. I see tiny clumps of mascara sticking together like little dead flies in her lashes. Her lipstick has bled into the skin around her mouth. But there's something else. Strange wisps of white smoke floating above her head.

I barely have time to address them when the dead boy appears from behind me and walks towards her. 'What are you . . .' I don't get to finish my question before he takes hold of her hand. For once, his mouth is closed, and he isn't scowling at me. His expression is impassive, mirroring hers.

'They're here together,' I whisper, as if saying it aloud will help it to all make sense. Of course, *nothing* about this makes sense. How do they know each other? This feels more than something my imagination has conjured up. Like two memories are merging to tell two separate stories with one common denominator. Me. If they are together in death, does that mean they were connected in life?

I return to the wisps of smoke above her head. It's not cigarette smoke, but another kind of burning. It appears to be coming from behind her. Curious, I follow the trail.

And I wish I hadn't.

CHAPTER 27

DAMON

I inhale sharply at the sight of Mum's exposed back. The surface level is a horrifying combination of red, raw, open wounds and blackened flesh. Smoke rises from her as if she is still smouldering.

I clap my hand over my mouth hard to stop myself from yelling, I taste blood. I've split my lip. I quickly return to face her, shaking my head in disbelief.

'What happened to you?' I gasp.

She says nothing.

I want to wrap my arms around her and hold her tightly, but of course I can't. I don't know yet how all of this works, but I do know that much. She isn't real. All I can do is glare at her.

I've never been told the complete story of Mum's death. I probably could have found out if I'd asked, but I've chosen not to. All I know is that she took her own life when I was twelve. And all these years later, it remains an ache I can't describe. So why would I make it worse by learning all the details?

At the time, it was only her and me sharing a flat, and I assume I must have found her body, which explains why there are so many blanks in my memory. Children often bury memories of abuse, neglect or distress. *It's not uncommon to hide from trauma*, the gentle-voiced hypnotherapist told me. But as I stare at Mum here before me in such a terrible state, perhaps it's time to confront the truth, no matter how hurtful that might be.

There are many moments before she died that I do remember, like being aware we were different to other families. Not because she and Dad weren't together. A lot of kids on our estate lived with only one parent. But they seemed happy. And Mum – well, she wasn't. She didn't smile as often as the other mums and dads did. Long periods could pass when she never smiled at all. And I'd wonder if it was my fault. Perhaps I wasn't enough to make her happy.

As a young boy I also remember Maud with clarity. She was a regular visitor for much of my childhood – Mum's special friend who came to stay, often for weeks at a time. A tall, much older, willowy woman with sapling arms, pinched features and eyes like black coals. She was unreadable.

'Maud's on her way,' Mum would warn shortly before she began spending more and more time in her room, or sprawled out on the sofa of an evening, in almost the same position as where I'd left her that morning.

'How long is she staying for?' I'd ask.

The answer was always a shrug because Mum never knew.

She'd arrive without luggage, only leaving the flat when Mum did, only ever returning to her own home when Mum was back on her feet. But despite these extended stays, Maud and I rarely spoke. I'd hear them talking behind closed doors, but if I entered the room, they'd fall silent until I left.

As the years passed, I began to sense those impending visits even before Mum announced them. She'd stop doing silly voices when she read me bedtime stories. Playdates weren't organised with other kids. There'd be zero interest in my days at school.

I remember wondering how many of Maud's visits were my fault. Maybe I made it too difficult for Mum to raise me alone. Perhaps I was the one who had pushed my parents apart. If they were still together, there would be no need for this stranger to intrude on our lives.

Now, in the supermarket aisle, my hallucinations of Mum and the boy are turning their heads as one, the attention of both fixed on me. They open their mouths. The boy's is still a black hole, and hers emits a puff of white smoke through the gaps in her teeth.

'Oodis,' he says. 'Oodis,' she repeats.

I'm about to ask them what this means when a customer distracts me with an inquiry about where to find cleaning products, and I point him to the correct shelves. Mum and the boy are gone by the time I return my attention to them.

Soon after my shift finishes, I'm driving towards the fertility clinic and hoping the next time I die I can carry more of her back to the present. Melissa is already there, waiting for me. There's a tension between us which is understandable after what I have twisted her arm to agree to do. Neither of us mentions it now. The counselling session that follows goes much better than last time – the boy is absent – and I'm told, there and then, that there are no concerns, so I undergo the first in a series of blood tests.

Ninety minutes later, I say goodbye to Melissa, and it's when I'm making my way back to the car park that I sense him following me again. The dead boy. I take an outdoor set of stairs to the sixth floor instead of the lift, as I don't want to be trapped in a confined space with him. It's only when I approach my car that I spot him ahead of me, yet I can still hear steps behind me. Is it Mum?

But before I can turn around, something pushes me head first into a wall and I drop to the floor in a daze.

CHAPTER 28

DAMON

I don't have the chance to gather my thoughts before a powerful pair of hands grabs me by the shoulders and yanks me up to my feet. A forearm slips under my neck and sets about choking me, while my own arm is twisted behind me so sharply I fear it might snap. I don't know who is hurting me but it's definitely not a hallucination. I open my mouth to yell in pain but before I can, I'm thrust forward until my chest slams into something metal and cylindrical. Only then do I realise where I've been frogmarched to.

The wall that separates the edge of the car park from the seventy-foot drop below.

Using all my strength, I wriggle and squirm and try to shake myself free, but I'm no match for the force of whoever has me in their grasp.

'Let go!' I yell.

Their response comes in the form of a thunderous blow to the kidneys. I've never felt such crippling pain, followed by an overwhelming urge to be sick.

I'm still dazed from colliding with the wall, but my vision returns to functionality as I'm lifted off the ground. Now my body is almost parallel to the top of the horizontal safety bar attached to the wall. My attacker's arms are around my chest and my thighs, like I'm a roll of carpet he's prepared to pitch into space.

Below me, all I can see are the tops of trees and shop roofs. The wind brushes against my face.

'What do you *want*?' I cry out in what sounds like a terrified child's voice.

The voice coming from my assailant is deep and unfamiliar. 'Finish what you started,' he snarls. 'You play until the *end*.'

I feel myself being held further and further over the railing. If he lets go, I'm a dead man.

'Do you understand?' he continues.

'Yes!' I say, but I really don't.

He holds me there for a moment longer until I shout 'Yes!' again, then he yanks me backwards and hurls me to the floor, face first.

'And if you tell anyone about this, my next visit will be to your ex. And Melissa won't be as lucky as you.'

I catch only the briefest glimpse of a black bomber jacket and heavy boots before he disappears behind a line of parked cars. I can hear him talking to someone on the phone, saying something like 'job done', before his boots begin to clomp down the staircase.

I'm dazed, my body is trembling and, a few metres away, the dead boy is silently laughing at me.

CHAPTER 29

DAMON

I turn on the tap, sit on the toilet seat and let my eyes glaze over as cold water thunders into the bath. I absent-mindedly rub an Elastoplast on my forearm through my long-sleeved top. I feel like a pin cushion after all the blood the fertility clinic took.

For much of the day, I've kept myself hidden behind a locked door, puffing vape after vape, curtains closed, only peering through a crack to see if I'm being watched from outside. I've yet to catch sight of anyone behaving suspiciously. It hasn't stopped my paranoia though. I've been through my phone, smartwatch and tablet many times, checking they haven't been compromised and that tracking devices haven't been embedded in them. To put my mind at ease, I even restored them to factory settings. But the reality is that if the man who attacked me knows who I am, then he is already aware of where I live.

I glance at the mirror on the bathroom cabinet, take a ball of cotton wool, and dab antiseptic on the red graze covering my cheek and eyebrow. What happened yesterday has left me a nervous wreck. It's also thrown up so many questions. Who was he? What's he after, and what game does he think I'm playing? And how does he know about Melissa?

The sensible thing would be to contact the police and report what happened. There are more CCTVs than people in this country, so some must have captured images of him following me into the car park, if not the assault itself. But I don't. Because nothing about what I'm going through right now could ever be described as sensible. Something tells me to stay quiet, for my own sake.

Mum is watching me from where she stands by the towel rail. Well, not watching. She stares ahead, not at me, but there's no doubt she's tracking me. There's a crackling sound which I realise is the embers and smoke coming from her body. Delicate wisps float from her skin up to the ceiling. While I'm fixated on her, she holds up her hands like a saint in a Renaissance painting, and I can see they're blistered and bleeding. Then she disappears.

I glance out of the open bathroom door at the spot by the wardrobe in my bedroom where, only four days ago, I sat with a rope tied around my neck. I don't know the truth behind Laura's motives for coming to the flat, but I am strangely grateful to her. Perhaps if she hadn't killed me, I might never have seen Mum again. Despite the state she is in.

There's about twenty centimetres of freezing water lying inside the bath now, along with the contents of half a dozen bags of ice I picked up from the corner shop in my only trip out today. I dip my hand under the surface and grimace. Good God, it's as cold as the sea I died in. My thinking is that the shock of the cold water filling my lungs might take me where I need to go more swiftly than warm water. The faster I die, the faster I can learn the truth about the boy and Mum's connection to him. Then Melissa can, fingers crossed, bring me back.

She has already refused to use the rope Laura insisted on, because she can't watch me die like that. She has witnessed the aftermath of deaths by hanging and strangulation. One continues to haunt her, a nine-year-old trans boy who ended his life in his parents' garage after online bullying.

Melissa slips into view in the bathroom doorway and I'm aware of her watching me. She's asked me countless times if I've changed my mind. And she called me last night when Adrienne was asleep, to tell me she's terrified that it won't work and she can't save my life. But I know that she will. It's a gut instinct that I doubt will offer her much reassurance.

I consider telling her about the man who attacked me, but I don't think she'd believe me. She already thinks I'm bordering on nuts with these hallucinations. Even with my facial injuries I don't think she'll accept someone was about to hurl me over the side of a car park. Besides, I don't want to give her another excuse to back out of tonight.

Melissa has been here for the best part of an hour. She came straight from work, so she's dressed in her paramedic uniform of green trousers, a polo shirt and steel-capped black boots. Laid out on the floor within easy reach is a defibrillator she brought with her, as she apparently doesn't trust mine. She ought to know. I know those sharp, intermittent bursts of electricity might save my life, but I hate them nonetheless.

'Did you smuggle that out of your ambulance?' I ask.

'And risk someone else's life so you can die?' she asks bitterly. 'No. I borrowed it from one of the rigs in the repair shop.'

No sense in clarifying I was kidding. She also has with her a small hand drill and two glass vials of clear liquid. I'm about to ask what they contain, but she reads my mind. 'Once you're dead, it's my problem and not yours.'

Her spikiness is no less than I deserve. I know I've become demanding and completely irrational. Her job is to save lives and I'm asking her to do the opposite with me. That's a hell of a thing to wrap your head around. First the trauma of finding me dead in the water, then doing it all over again when she caught Laura killing me. The third time figures to be no less agonising, I know.

'Have you said anything to Adrienne?' I ask.

'Oh, of course. I explained I was popping out to kill my ex-husband, and that she should keep the casserole simmering on a low heat because murder gives me an appetite.' Her eyes are slits. If she didn't still care about me, she'd have no trouble wishing me dead. 'What the hell do you think?'

'I think I should stop asking stupid questions.'

She examines her equipment for a second and then a third time. The defibrillators are charged. When she claps them together, the noise triggers something inside me and I recoil.

'For fuck's sake, Damon,' she snaps. 'Get over it and grow up.'

'Sorry.'

She takes my hands in hers. I have never seen someone who typically oozes such confidence appear so concerned.

'Are you sure?' she says. 'Are you absolutely sure this is what you want?'

'One hundred per cent.'

'Because it'd be so easy for me to accidentally fracture your ribs and cause internal bleeding or damage your internal organs. Then there's the danger of hypoxic brain damage if I can't bring you back quickly enough . . .'

She winds down. We've been over and over it.

Melissa takes a deep breath and pulls me in towards her. Her skin is warm and smells reassuringly familiar: the earthy tones of the argan oil she uses to moisturise her face, the grapefruit conditioner for her hair. Even now, if I walk into my bathroom and inhale, I think I can smell her, and for the briefest of moments, it's like she never left.

'Thank you,' I say. 'I love you.'

She doesn't say anything but is the first to leave our embrace.

I slip off my socks and roll them into a ball, then pull off my top. I turn my back to her, a little embarrassed by my ever-thinner frame. I kneel on the bathmat as if to pray, then rest my forehead on the edge of the bath as Melissa secures cable ties around my wrists and ankles to ensure I can't escape or accidentally hurt her.

Finally, I take three deep breaths and as I exhale the final one, I say, 'Now.'

Melissa takes my head, gently at first, then thrusts it powerfully down into the water. Its iciness takes my breath away and I immediately swallow a mouthful. It slides down my throat and deep into my chest. It's not salty like the seawater, but it's equally unpleasant. I cough and splutter. My body's reaction is primal, and I commence thrashing my head from side to side. But Melissa has a firm grip on me, she's pinning me down, her knees now on the back of mine, her chest pressing heavily against my back. Her restraint skills are why other paramedics want to work shifts with her, particularly on weekend nights, when the drunk and injured are more prone to aggression.

'Please don't fight,' she begs between sobs.

I cough again and water fills me up inside. And then, when I can take no more, the pain suddenly stops, the light dims, the dark of the water descends, allowing a film roll of my life to begin playing out once again.

CHAPTER 30

DAMON

I don't know how long I've been asleep but I wake up coughing, convinced I'm still under the surface of the water and Melissa's weight is pinning me down. It's only when I sit upright that I realise where I am – alive, and in the safety of my bedroom.

Even though there's no water left in my lungs or stomach, I continue to heave until my mouth fills with acrid bile – horrid yellow stuff that I spit into a pint glass by the side of the bed. I run my hands across my chest and face, but I don't know what I'm checking for.

Melissa is watching me from an armchair in the corner of the room. This 'aftercare' is another condition of her helping me, in case any complications arise. 'Secondary drowning,' she explained, and I stared at her blankly. 'Fluid can stay in your lungs and irritate them, which can affect your breathing. People die from it.'

Her legs and chest are covered by a grey, woollen blanket she's taken from the wardrobe. It's one of many things she left behind when she moved out. I know for a fact its threads still harbour her scent. They're getting a fresh helping of it, for which I'll one day be pitifully grateful.

'Do you need anything?' she asks.

'I think I'm alright.'

My voice is croaky, so I take a swig from the bottle of water she's left for me on my pillow. The sensation of it slipping down my throat is too familiar, though, and makes me gag. Looking to distract myself, I spy the defibrillator, the drill and unopened vials through the gap in the bathroom door.

'Did it work?' she asks.

I nod, then recall what I saw. I was watching Mum from a distance as she made her way towards a red front door in the middle of a row of what looked like terraced houses. She was holding the dead boy's hand and they appeared to be speaking animatedly but I was too far away to hear their conversation.

'He's called Callum Baird,' I tell Melissa. 'He was my friend. I saw him playing with me, the two of us chasing each other on scooters around a supermarket car park. He had a blue one and mine was black. Then I saw him again, this time back on the path where I think he died.' My voice tips past the vanishing point with that last word.

'What happened to him, Damon?'

'I don't know.'

Her expression sours. 'I thought the point of what you made me do was to find that out?'

'It's not like I can pick and choose what or who I'm going to see. But at least now I have his name.'

I'm also relieved that I've not brought anyone else back with me this third time. I don't know if my brain has the bandwidth to deal with what another hallucination might mean.

I switch on the bedside lamp, take my phone from the charger and input Callum Baird's name into a search engine, along with the word 'murdered'. Many pages appear. Most of the stories date back to the early 2010s. I read one of the more recent ones aloud.

The family of a twelve-year-old boy found dead close to his London home have renewed their appeal for witnesses on the tenth anniversary of his murder. The body of Callum Baird, who had been beaten and asphyxiated, was found on a quiet path, but a suspect has never been charged in connection with his death.

I recall once again what the hypnotherapist told me. How at a young age, I mightn't have had the cognitive capacity to understand each and every detail. And because my brain is reluctant to experience that trauma again, it has put up a shield to protect itself.

'So now you know he's real and what happened to him,' Melissa continues. 'This is over, right?'

'Not yet,' I say quietly.

She makes a disgusted, growling sound and drops her head back, hard, against the armchair. 'Why?'

'Because I need to know why I keep seeing him,' I counter. 'I think I should visit the place where he died to see if it triggers something else. And I need to know how my mum was involved.'

Melissa glares at me, as if I've caught her off guard with this, before her expression hardens.

'This is never going to end, is it?' she says sharply. 'The past is the *past*, Damon. It doesn't matter anymore. You are here and you are *bloody lucky* to be so. We are trying to start a family, a massively exciting and huge deal in all our lives. But instead of focusing on that, you're chasing ghosts.'

Before I can remind her they're not ghosts but hallucinations, she clambers to her feet, grabs the blanket, storms out of the bedroom and into the lounge, and throws herself on to the sofa.

CHAPTER 31

DAMON

It isn't long before I find the place I'm searching for. The pathway in South London where Callum Baird was murdered. I've used Google Street View and clips from old news reports uploaded to YouTube to find the exact location. In the footage, the path is bustling. Police officers come and go from behind blue tape before a body bag is removed from inside a white tent. All these years later, though, it's as if nothing ever happened.

I'm most of the way along the paved pathway when a coughing fit makes me so light-headed, I can barely continue. It's only when I stop to steady myself against a tree and try to control my breathing that I realise my heart is beating twenty to the dozen. Melissa keeps reminding me of the toll three resuscitations in nine weeks must be having on my body and how I should be at home resting. And that's where she thinks I am now. She'd go mad if I told her the truth. I wait until my heart rate levels before I continue.

A sixth sense tells me that a few metres ahead is the place where I found Callum dying. I half expect to find the hallucinatory version of him here now, awaiting my arrival. Contorting his face or screaming to scare the hell out of me. But he's conspicuous by his absence.

In my death three days ago, he was lying on his back on the ground, partially obscured by bushes and trees. His arms were at his sides, his legs slightly bent. I stared at his chest, waiting for it to rise and fall, but it was motionless. 'Callum?' I whispered, but there was no response. 'Callum?' I repeated, and then crouched over him, about to gently shake his shoulder. His sudden intake of breath scared the hell out of me, and I fell over as I scrambled to my feet.

'Help me, Damon,' he gasped. He looked so frightened.

I looked up and down the adjacent pathway for an adult. But we were alone. And that's when the memory comes to an abrupt halt. I can only assume I ran to raise the alarm at the actual event, but by the time I returned to him, it was too late. Now, I find myself wishing I could have done more. Ran faster, found someone to help more quickly, or at least held his hand so he wasn't alone when he died. Poor kid.

Back in the present and amongst the many other emotions I'm feeling, there's also relief. That I didn't hurt Callum. That he wasn't lying there injured because of something I did to him.

A metre-wide semicircle of ground catches my eye. Amongst the weeds and flowers with long-faded blooms lies a silver plaque with the name 'Callum Baird' embossed in capital letters, followed by the dates of his birth and death, and, in a handwritten font next to two cherubs: 'The angels will look after you now'. The neglect suggests no one has visited this spot for some time. I wonder why. A death or illness in the family, perhaps? Or maybe his relatives moved away, unable to bear living close to where they'd lost their son or brother.

Out of habit I reach for my phone to call Melissa and explain what I've found, but stop myself. I need to give her space. I see I've received a text from Adrienne though, reminding me I have another appointment at the clinic later this week. This time, they're testing my fertility. She's ended the message with an aubergine emoji and a splash of water, followed by a winking smiley. I try to extend the illusion that all is well with me by screengrabbing an image of a volcano erupting and sending it to her. She responds with a GIF of a solitary, tiny drip coming from a tap. Under ordinary circumstances this might have continued, but not today.

I hang around for a few more minutes, wondering if anything else might jog my memory. But for now, the well is dry. Perhaps Melissa is right and it's time to leave Callum here and move on with a life he doesn't have.

I continue along through the treelined pathway, keeping an eye out for a road with a bus stop that will return me to the Tube. A tower block of flats becomes visible, hidden until now by tree canopies. There's something familiar about it. I stop when I reach the car park below it and stare up at the eight floors above me. Each one has a landing framed by bright blue railings. That's when it hits me: it wasn't a terraced house I saw my mum and Callum walking towards in my last death. It was a series of flats. These flats.

And I think I used to live here.

CHAPTER 32

DAMON

There is something about this place that's both familiar and unfamiliar, if that makes any kind of sense. The colours of the rendering and front doors are different, but I know I've been here before. I direct my line of vision towards the fifth floor. That's where I need to be.

The lift stops outside number twenty-three. I saw my mum walking towards this flat with Callum Baird in my last recall. It has a red-painted door and chrome letterbox, and there's a cream-coloured net curtain draped across the windows. Several porcelain wolf figurines stand on the windowsill, glaring at me as if on guard. I press my face against the glass to peer inside, but the netting is too thick to see anything that might nudge free more memories.

This building must have played a large part in my childhood. So why can't I recall it? I review my memories of Mum and realise that most are set inside the flat, not outside it. I try to recall playing with other friends out here or in the park below, but draw a blank. There are more empty spaces from this period than I realised.

‘Can I help you?’ comes a voice to my side, all but ejecting me out of my skin. Only four days ago a man held me over the side of a car park railing and threatened to drop me to my death. You’d think I’d need no reminder to remain on guard at all times.

My paroxysm of terror triggers another coughing fit, so the elderly man who set this all off has to wait for my reply. He’s wearing a navy-blue flat cap and pushing along a silver walking frame. His stern expression is to be expected. He has no idea I’m searching for a trigger, not a flat to burgle.

‘I think I used to live here,’ I offer when at last I’m able. I take a step back and give him a disarming smile that most decidedly does not land.

‘Did you indeed?’ he says doubtfully. I detect a faint trace of stale alcohol on his breath. ‘And what, you can’t remember?’

‘It was a long time ago, when I was a kid.’

‘Well, you don’t live there now, so I suggest you move along.’

He clocks me spotting the cordless landline telephone in his cardigan pocket and raises it up to his shoulder to ensure I know he is ready to use it.

‘It’s okay, I’ll be off.’

When my second smile proves no more effective than the first, I start walking. Then I stop midway towards the lifts and look back at him.

‘I’m sorry, but could you tell me how long you’ve lived here?’

‘A good long time,’ he snaps. When that bit of ferocity doesn’t send me scurrying, he sighs. ‘Since the place was built,’ he offers up grudgingly. ‘In the mid-seventies.’

‘Then you must remember a boy called Callum Baird.’

His puffed-out chest deflates a little. ‘Course I do, we all do. Terrible business. Lovely kid. He lived in that flat you were paying so much attention to.’ His wrinkled brow knots further. ‘You a reporter or something?’

'No, no,' I say. 'I think he and I were friends when we were children. But my memory isn't so great, and I thought if I came back here, it might jog it.'

'What's your name, son?'

'Damon Lister.'

His puffs out his cheeks with the speed of a finger snap. He props himself against the railings with one hand and raises the phone a second time. But this time it's as if he's ready to hurl it at me.

'And you have the nerve to come *back* here, after . . . after *what happened*?' he shouts. Spit flies from his mouth and there's wildfire in his eyes. 'Go on, get out of here. Fuck off!'

I'm taken aback by his change in temperament. I'm no threat to him, but I raise my hands to my chest in a gesture of surrender to make it clear.

'I have no idea what you're talking about,' I say.

'Don't play dumb with me,' he hisses. 'Bad apples never fall far from trees.'

'Mate, calm down.'

'I'm not your mate!' he shouts, and he starts dialling three nines on the phone's keypad.

His raised, greatly agitated voice is drawing an audience. Two front doors along this row have opened.

'You alright, Jim?' asks a heavy-set man in a vest that barely covers his midriff.

'I'm leaving,' I reply, and hurry past that onlooker and the next, baffled by how badly that went and the questions it has thrown up. What did he mean by 'what happened'? Was he referring to Callum's murder? And who is the bad apple, and who the tree? Callum can't be either, as he's already referred to him as a lovely kid. It seems clear that one of them is me, or at least might be.

When I turn to take one last look back at the flats, my heart fills with warmth when I catch sight of Mum stepping through one of the doors and closing it behind her. Her halter top exposes portions of her back, and her skin is covered in horrendous burn marks. In that moment it all comes flooding back and hits with me with the force of a speeding train.

I remember how Mum died.

No overdose of prescription medicine, no hanging from a light cord or hacking at her wrists in the bath. Her death isn't the straightforward suicide I've spent so much of my life believing it to be.

CHAPTER 33

DAMON

I am watching a twelve-year-old me, standing at the rear of the flats, staring up at the fifth-floor window where Mum's bedroom is. The first drops of rain begin to fall from a charcoal-grey sky, landing on my forehead and trickling down my cheeks. I'm too transfixed by what's happening to wipe them away.

Mum appears from behind the window's net curtain, and even from this distance I can sense her panic. Her arms sway over her head as if trying to get my attention. Then she begins banging on the window with both fists, trying to break the glass. She is terrified of something.

She vanishes, only to return carrying a dining room chair that she hurls at the window. It rebounds off the reinforced safety glass and falls out of sight. It takes several more attempts before the window finally shatters, madly glittering glass showering to the ground in front of where I stand, as hard and fast as the sheets of rain now pouring down.

The sudden rush of oxygen from outside causes a plume of black smoke to swallow her in its rush to escape. Only then do I understand our home is on fire.

'Mum!' I scream and try running towards the stairwell that will take me upstairs to our flat. But someone grabs my arms, pulling me in towards them and holding me there.

'It's too dangerous,' a man's voice warns. I don't look at him because I'm transfixed by Mum.

A flash of lightning illuminates the sky, swiftly followed by a crack of thunder so loud it pulses through me.

'Help me!' she yells again and again before more smoke appears, choking her. She has something in her hand that she holds to her ear. I assume it's a phone and she must be talking to an emergency services operator.

Only then do I notice a crowd of neighbours gathering around us as others pour from the building while alarm bells ring, their end-of-the-world racket joining the thunderous rain to drown out the worried chatter of frightened tenants.

'Let go of me,' I yell to the man who has me in his grasp. 'I have to help her!'

But he holds me fast.

I hear others shouting back to her, urging her to hang on, promising that firefighters are on their way to rescue her. I doubt she can hear them above the roaring flames.

Mum turns to glance behind her, then down below, before her gaze locks on to mine. Another branch of lightning forks through the sky along with a second crack of thunder, and it's in this moment when she makes the decision either to remain where she is and succumb to the smoke and flames, or to jump.

The next image I see is of her hands on either side of the window frame, pulling her body up and perching there, like a fledgling gathering the courage to take its first flight from the nest. Now her phone is again pressed to her ear, and then in the next moment she reaches out her arms and, to a chorus of screams piercing the cacophony around us, she lets herself fall.

The sky ignites as Bobbi Lister's thirty-nine years on this earth are over in less than two seconds. Those around me shout and wail, but I'm unable to move, speak, or react in any way. Blood from a head wound has no time to pool before the rainwater carries it away in all directions. Then I'm dragged backwards and my face is covered by their hands. A kind gesture, but too late.

Today, as I stand here reliving that moment, I feel my body wanting to fold in on itself. I've spent many long years believing Mum left me because I'd let her down. That she chose death over me because I wasn't good enough. But now I know the truth. That in her final moments, and in a life blighted by depression, she was finally able to take charge. Perhaps it's selfish of me, but I'm awash with relief to know she didn't leave me through choice.

Suddenly I become aware of the old man on the landing yelling at me again. It returns me to the present.

'I know what I saw!' he yells. 'They didn't listen to me then, but I know!'

The sky is now clear, the people dispersed, and Mum's body vanishes from the ground. And I, too, leave with haste.

CHAPTER 34

DAMON

'What's troubling you, Damon?' Helena inquires with apparent concern.

'Why?' I ask and shift a little in my chair.

'How many years have we known one another?'

'Sixteen, or something like that.'

'So it's fair to say I might've learned a thing or two about you in that time.'

'I suppose so,' I concede.

'I haven't seen you in a while, and then you appear on my doorstep twice in a few weeks,' Helena continues. 'Don't misunderstand me, it's lovely to see you and you're always welcome. But I sense something is on your mind.'

I hadn't planned to return to her house so soon. But after reliving Mum's death yesterday, I needed the company of the living. Of someone I could trust.

Once again, it's her and me, sitting in her lounge. Every piece of decor in here draws from a palette of muted greys, browns and whites. It's as if the colour has been washed from both her and the room. The heads of the daffodils I brought with me last time hang limply over the rim of the vase on the fireplace. The framed photographs I couldn't see properly have vanished completely, leaving blank markers in the dust.

'There is something on my mind,' I admit. 'And it's them.'

I point to the space behind her, take a deep breath, and explain to her that it's occupied by Callum Baird, Mum and, now, a little boy perched on Mum's hip. I spoke too soon when I thought I hadn't brought anyone back from my last death four days ago. This latest addition to my family of hallucinations appeared for the first time early this morning, further chilling my already wintry bones. He either represents one step closer to the truth, or a further nudge towards being sectioned. The jury is out as to which. When he appeared, he was alone in the corner of my bedroom, sitting on the floor and staring at me. Now, he has one arm wrapped around Mum's back, the other clutching a blue chequered blanket. He's no more than six months old. He has a shock of blond hair and a dummy in his mouth. I check him out for similar burn marks to Mum's, but he's uninjured. I'm an only child, so we're not related. I don't know how he fits into all of this. Unlike her or Callum, there are no immediate signs this boy is dead until the world around us falls absolutely silent.

Then, all I can hear are the palpitations of his breaths. They're normal at first, then gradually turn short and sharp before the gasping begins. He reaches out his arms towards me in the same way Callum and Mum have done, as if I can help him. But I am powerless to know what to do. And then he stops breathing and the colour drains from his face. The more it pales, the more blue veins rise to the surface of his temples. His cheeks fold in on themselves before the whites of his eyes begin to spot like drops of pink dye in milk. Finally, his body flops to Mum's side like a ragdoll. Tears prick me for what this poor little mite must've gone through. I wish I could help him.

Helena turns slowly to see who I've become fixated by, but of course she sees nothing. I explain how I've died twice since I was last here a month ago, and she nods along with all this as if what she's hearing is perfectly rational. If she thinks I'm insane, she's hiding it well.

'I've given this a lot of thought,' I say, 'and it's time I applied to see my case records. I need to find out more about who I am.'

I'm expecting her to tell me that I need psychological help before delving into the past.

'And what's prompted this decision?' she asks instead.

I look away from her to the three figures she cannot see. I stare at Mum. I literally ache to have her hold me tightly in her arms one last time. I long to touch her, to fill my lungs with her scent. But all I can smell around me is charred flesh. I want her to convince me that everything's going to be alright, because she is going to make it so. But if she couldn't do that in life, I doubt she can manage it in death. It's time to stop burying my head in the sand and hiding from the other missing pieces of my past. And I trust Helena to help me. She has always been there for me. She had me removed from my first children's home when I was bullied by the other kids, and she visited me regularly in the next place until she was sure I was settled. She was the closest thing I've had to a guardian angel.

'I need to try and slot the pieces together to see if they fit,' I say. 'And it seems obvious the place to start is to read what was written about me.'

I go on to explain how I visited the location of Callum's murder and found the block of flats where I once lived. And how, in a flash, Mum's death came back to me.

Helena's gaze flits to a gold carriage clock on her mantelpiece, then back to me. Does she have plans? 'It seems the further you delve into what you don't remember, the more questions there are,' she says. 'And the more danger you're willing to put yourself in, searching for what you think might be the truth. Twice you have deliberately tried to end your life in the search for answers. That worries me a great deal.'

'I didn't want to remain dead,' I clarify. 'I wanted to come back.'

'But you are aware the odds are against you? Each time you try it, they become steeper and steeper. Many people who've been resuscitated even only once have suffered debilitating after-effects with their mental health. You have now died three times in all. You don't know what long-term damage that has already done to you.'

I think of the coughing fits I'm becoming prone to, along with the light-headedness and the racing heart. Let's not even get started on reanimating the dead.

'Is the truth worth dying over?' she presses. 'And what if you don't like what you discover? Where will that leave you?'

I don't know, is the answer.

'I'm typically an advocate for confronting your past in whatever way you find the most comfortable and that allows you to move forwards,' Helena adds. 'But in your case, Damon, I wonder if it might be best to let sleeping dogs lie. I'm concerned that what you might read in your records could have a negative impact on you. How has seeing your mum or those children benefited you so far?'

'Seeing her again and learning the truth . . . it's . . . it's hard to explain. It gives me a kind of comfort I didn't know I was missing. But yes, there's a longing that also comes with it which . . . hurts.'

'And the children? Do they draw the same emotions from you?'

'No. I feel bad for them. I want to help them.'

'Like I want to help you, Damon. You might only have been in my direct care for a few weeks, but the maternal instinct I feel for my foster children never leaves. I don't want you to be hurt when you have come so far.'

'I'm twenty-eight now,' I remind her. 'Perhaps it's time I made my own decisions.'

‘So if you’ve made up your mind, why are you here? You don’t need my permission.’

‘I suppose I want you to tell me I’m doing the right thing.’

She nods slowly and offers a half-smile. ‘You don’t need that. But you’re right, you are old enough to make your own decisions, and I apologise if it sounds like I’ve been trying to put you off. I have no idea what the report says, but I assume you’ll find an application form to access your records on Lambeth London Borough Council’s website.’

‘What do you remember me telling you about Mum?’

She hesitates for a beat. ‘So many memories from that time are clouded by my strokes. I wish I could help you.’

‘Try drowning. Works for me,’ I joke, but neither of us laughs.

She looks at the clock again and edges her way forward on her chair, as if preparing to rise. I sense she is drawing this conversation, or my visit, to a close because she’s waiting for someone.

‘Before you leave, Damon, I need you to promise that you aren’t going to risk your life again,’ she adds. ‘I’m positive that’s not what your mum, or any parent, would want from their child.’

‘Okay.’ I nod. ‘I won’t.’

It’s the first time I’ve ever lied to her.

CHAPTER 35

HELENA

Helena lets out a long breath she might have been holding for the last sixteen years. Her biggest fear is being realised: it's all starting to come back to him.

She knows a different Damon from the man who is preparing to leave her house. She remembers the troubled boy who couldn't be loved by his mother in the way he wanted to be. The one who felt abandoned by his father. The broken child who, despite herself, Helena briefly found herself caring for much more than she should have. The one she took a huge risk – not only professionally, but also with his well-being – to save. Everything could have fallen apart if she'd got it wrong.

Of all her charges, Damon made the greatest impression on her. Many followed, yet he remained rooted deep inside her, without him ever understanding why. The difference in him between that first day they met and the boy who left her home weeks later was immeasurable. They could have been two entirely different children.

No good can come of his digging, but she cannot convey to him why she's so sure of this without revealing her hand. He is not that twelve-year-old boy anymore, and she doesn't know how he will respond to the truth. She can't tell him what to do or how to live his life. She can't force him to leave the past where it is, buried with the shovel she provided. And she cannot go too far in her desire to dissuade him without him becoming suspicious of her motives. The last thing she wants is for him to believe that she has a hidden agenda, because he trusts so few and she's always had his best interests at heart. And she wasn't alone in that.

They both did.

Helena's chest tightens when she thinks of the opportunities that have been taken away from all involved. And, for a moment, she allows herself to imagine an alternative reality and how differently it could have been for her personally, had she written the script from the opening scene. She can't blame Damon for all of what happened, but there's no getting away from the significant but unwitting part he played. And that's why it's so important to her now that he doesn't learn everything. Because if he does, all the sacrifices they made will be for nothing.

Damon leaves soon after and she gathers herself for her next visitor, for they are due soon. She cannot appear flustered in front of them; they can read her like a book, and they'll know if something is troubling her. She doesn't want to lie to them, but they can never know the lengths she has gone to keep so many worlds from colliding.

CHAPTER 36

DAMON

I'm measuring my life in time stamps. Twenty-one days since I last spoke to Melissa, the morning after she drowned me and brought me back to life. Over five hundred hours of looking over my shoulder, waiting for my attacker to strike again. Almost three months since I first saw Callum Baird. And as I sit in a quiet corner of the stockroom at work, it's been more than two weeks of waiting for the white sealed envelope in my hand to arrive.

I take a hit of nicotine from the vape in my other hand before I tear it open, but that sparks a coughing fit. They're becoming more frequent, a hangover from filling my lungs with water too often. A lump of phlegm the size of a marble reaches my mouth and I spit it out into a nearby bin. It's a crimson and black colour; I turn my head, not caring to dwell on what that might mean. My heart palpitations are also becoming a more common occurrence but, like the coughing, I haven't had them checked out medically. I wonder how else I might have damaged myself.

Inside this envelope is a wedge of white A4 pages, and a covering letter with a logo at the top.

Dear Mr Lister,

Please find enclosed copies of historical records held by Lambeth London Borough Council Social Services as requested under your subject access request. Please be aware that redactions (blacked-out words) have been used. This may be due to third-party information being recorded where consent to share the information has not been sought or given. If you have any queries regarding your subject access request, please contact me using the address above.

I ready myself before I turn the page. When I do, the first thing I am struck by is how much has been redacted. Not the occasional word or sentence, but whole paragraphs and chunks of text.

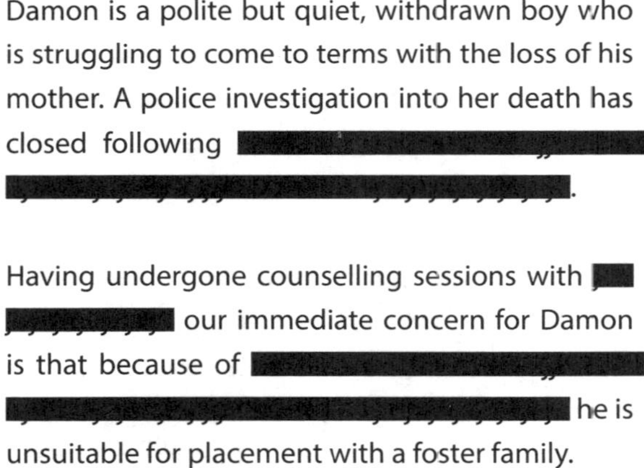

Damon is a polite but quiet, withdrawn boy who is struggling to come to terms with the loss of his mother. A police investigation into her death has closed following .

Having undergone counselling sessions with our immediate concern for Damon is that because of he is unsuitable for placement with a foster family.

I glare at the page. Why wasn't I suitable for fostering? I turn it over and the rest of the report follows the same pattern. Black line after black line.

has spent

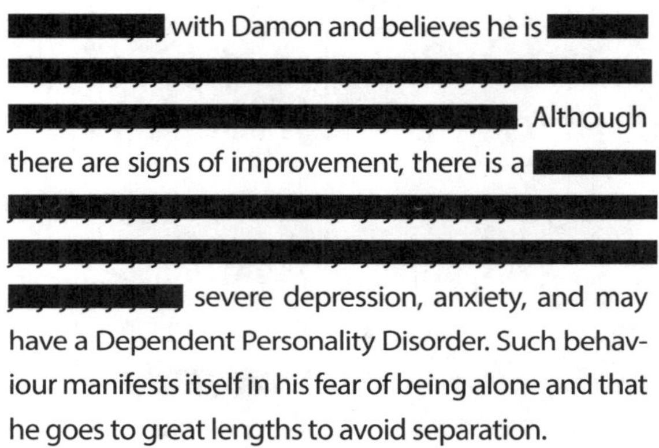

> with Damon and believes he is . Although there are signs of improvement, there is a severe depression, anxiety, and may have a Dependent Personality Disorder. Such behaviour manifests itself in his fear of being alone and that he goes to great lengths to avoid separation.

Some of that makes sense, I suppose. But a Dependent Personality Disorder? Surely all I exhibited was normal behaviour from a child who had recently lost his mum in such a gut-wrenching way. The rest contains minutes of case conferences about me, social workers' reports, their titles included but their names removed. It's as if they want to prevent me from identifying anyone involved in making decisions about me. So much is missing, so much unsaid. It continues like this for six more pages. I attempt to guess the missing words but it's like trying to complete a jigsaw puzzle when someone has stolen some of the pieces.

> For reasons stated earlier, his father, Ralf Lister, is unable to look after Damon.

Well, that goes without saying – he was dead by then. An accident at work, I was told. Again, something I have shied away from looking into. It's not that I don't think about him. Sometimes I used to imagine what my life might be like if he was in it. Even now I sometimes imagine picking up the phone and hearing him ask if I'd like to go out for a pint. But you can miss what you never had.

After a further page of text that has been almost completely redacted are two lines that confuse me:

> However, it has been requested Damon is not returned to care in the local Lambeth area for ████ ████ safety. ████ could be considered a danger.

Danger? Whose? Mine? Or other people's? Did they think I was dangerous? Why? The idea of this sends a shiver skittering down my back. I read on.

> We are in agreement ████████ it is in Damon's best interests to relocate him to a different area. For his long-term benefit, the move to Northamptonshire should be approved immediately.

And that's where it ends. This report was supposed to have explained so much to me: fill in the chunks of my life before Mum's death I can't remember, perhaps even my relationship to the two dead boys. Instead, I'm no clearer. In fact, I'm more confused than ever.

I consider leaving work right now and catching a train to London to talk to Helena about it. Perhaps something has come back to her since my last visit. Or maybe this could jog her memory? But I decide against it. This is my problem, not hers. If the authorities aren't willing to help me, then I'll need to find a way to discover the truth by myself. I stuff the report into my jacket pocket and make my way back through the warehouse.

Only now do I realise my fists are clenched as tightly as my jaw. Anger isn't an emotion I display very often, but I find myself picking up a broom and smacking the hell out of a pallet of shrink-wrapped toilet rolls.

I stop suddenly when I smell smoke. Looking up, I find my mum standing close to a forklift truck, watching me, holding Callum's hand, the little boy perched on her hip. Her face is redder than I remember it being last time. Black, patchy soot-like marks pepper her hands and forearms. Slowly her mouth opens and she sounds out that word, the one Callum keeps saying:

'Oodis.'

'What does that mean?' I ask. 'I don't understand.'

To my horror, Mum erupts into a ball of flames. Her piercing screams echo through the air as her body and face become engulfed in a swirling maelstrom of heat and fire. My face sears as the intensity of the blaze grows and spreads to the two boys. Now all three are flapping their arms wildly, their suffering unbearable.

I am jolted back to life and start yelling for help as I sprint towards an alarm attached to the warehouse wall. I slap the button and bells ring and a siren wails while a recorded voice instructs shoppers and staff to evacuate the building immediately. I spot an extinguisher and grab it. 'Fire!' I yell as I pull out the pin. 'Help me!'

I hear footsteps approaching when I turn to point the extinguisher towards Mum and the boys. But they are no longer there. There are, of course, no flames, no intense heat, no burning bodies. Only me, in an intense state of distress.

'What's happening?' shouts a colleague over the deafening siren. I turn to her, where she stands with two others.

'I . . . I . . . thought I saw . . .'

My voice trails off as a chasm continues to yawn between reality and the nightmare I've hallucinated.

She stares at me as if awaiting an explanation, but there's nothing I can say that won't have me sectioned within the hour. I drop the extinguisher and speed-walk past them, exiting the store, pushing my way through the crowds of ruffled customers gathered in the car park, only stopping when I'm inside my car. Then I scream as loudly as my lungs will allow before a coughing fit seizes me.

CHAPTER 37

MELISSA

'Hi Mel,' Damon begins. 'How are you?'

His unannounced appearance at her front door has taken her by surprise. It's been the best part of a month since she helped him bring about his death, then resuscitated him. She thought creating distance between them might be the wake-up call he needed. That limiting communication might help him rethink his choices. But there's an air about him that indicates this hasn't happened. The casual familiarity of his tone doesn't match his physical demeanour. His body language is awkward, he's tense and shifting from foot to foot, looking around her, not at her. He is forcing himself to give the impression he doesn't have a care in the world. As if holding his life in her hands didn't happen. No, she tells herself, he's not here to apologise. And a heavy weight settles in her chest.

'Good, thanks,' she lies back to him. 'What brings you here?'

'I thought I'd fill you in on how things are going at the fertility clinic. I gave them my second deposit today.' He looks beyond her and down the hallway. 'Is Adrienne around?'

'No, she's at the hospital.'

Her and Adrienne's shifts are often at odds, but they make it work. They've also planned out in detail what will happen if they conceive. While Adrienne will carry the baby, it will be Melissa who becomes the primary caregiver and takes the six months' maternity leave. But going by Damon's recent behaviour, she worries if they'll ever reach egg transfer day. She hasn't mentioned her concerns to Adrienne, as she doesn't want to hear a 'told you so' and be reminded it was Melissa's idea to ask Damon to be the biological father. Melissa clings to the hope she can still turn this around.

'Can I come in?' Damon asks.

She hesitates, then stands to one side and allows him to pass and closes the door behind him.

Melissa continues to struggle to reconcile the contradiction between ending Damon's life, then bringing him back, and her job as a paramedic, trained to prolong life. She is, however, a staunch supporter of assisted suicide, having watched her uncle lose his long, merciless battle with prostate cancer. She believes a person has the right to end their life when they want to, and on their terms. What if Damon had a terminal illness and begged her to help him die? Would she agree? Yes, she has decided, she probably would. So is it that much of a leap to help him die, then to resuscitate him? She wants to say no, it's not, but she'd be lying to herself.

When they reach the lounge, Melissa cuts to the chase: 'So why are you really here? You could have texted me with a clinic update.'

'I received my social services report,' he says before launching into a recap of all he has learned, and all that has been kept from him. He tells her it's not clear whether he was considered a danger to himself, or someone close to him.

'I'm sure it isn't you,' she says.

'I hope that's so. But neither of us can be a hundred per cent sure while I still have gaps in my memory.'

'I've known you since we were thirteen,' she says. 'Don't you think I'd have an inkling by now if you were a risk?'

'It's so frustrating,' he says. 'What's the point in sending me that report if they're not going to tell me anything?'

Melissa changes the direction of the conversation. 'I've been looking into EMDR, have you heard of it?' Damon stares at her blankly. 'Eye Movement Desensitisation and Reprocessing. It's a type of therapy that helps you process and recover from past experiences that affect your mental well-being,' she continues. 'I think it might be good for you. I have the address of a woman in Kettering who—'

'No thank you,' he says firmly.

'Why?'

'I haven't had much success with therapy, have I?'

Melissa knows what he is referring to. She had been the one to suggest they attend relationship counselling, despite knowing their marriage was over. She'd hoped it might provide a neutral territory for her to explain – and for Damon to understand – how she'd never be able to find herself if they remained together. In retrospect she realised that by suggesting couple's therapy, she'd given him false hope, only to hurt him even further when she finalised their separation. Adrienne thinks Melissa has been trying to make it up to him ever since.

'It won't be counselling,' she continues. 'It's more of a tool. A way of removing the emotion associated with traumatic memories.'

'But those memories only come back to me when I'm dying or dead.'

'How do you know you can't access them through EMDR?'

'I just know, okay? Now can we change the subject, please?'

'And talk about what?'

He hesitates and she knows what he is about to say before he says it.

'I need your help again.'

And the weight in her chest grows heavier still.

CHAPTER 38

MELISSA

Damon doesn't need to elaborate as to what he's asking of her. But she isn't going to make it easy for him. She wants him to spell it out. As if by hearing himself say it, he might suddenly understand that what he wants from her is cruel and unhinged.

'You need my help doing what?' she says.

'You know . . . *That.*'

'I don't know,' she replies. 'Tell me.'

He looks around the room, exasperated, and lowers his voice. 'I want you to . . . kill me again.'

'No,' she says, her expression a warning shot. This isn't up for debate. If they are to remain friends, he should not try to persuade her otherwise. And if he can't respect that, he should leave right now. But she fears Damon has lost perspective. He is too far down the rabbit hole.

'Please,' he says. 'Think about it.'

'What is there to think about?' she asks. 'No.'

Now it's his turn to become defensive. 'Why?'

Her laugh almost chokes her. 'Do you really need me to answer that? Because you have died *three times* in the last few months and

I'm the one who keeps bringing you back. Do you have any idea how fucking lucky you are?'

'Yes, but—'

'And how *unfair* you're being? You should join me in the rig for a few days and see first-hand the terrible condition we find people in, through no fault of their own. Maybe that'll be enough to slap some sense into you.'

'I know what I'm asking isn't easy . . .'

'Ha! That's the understatement of the decade. You cannot possibly imagine the pressure of holding somebody's life in your hands.'

'But you do it every day for work.'

'That's different. Most of my patients don't want to die.'

She shakes her head. Is this really the same boy she befriended at high school, when he was living in a children's home and she was a former army brat living off-base with her newly civilian parents? They were unfamiliar faces amongst the crowds. Others had already formed cliques and allegiances, but not them. They were like the loners in the John Hughes films of the 1980s they've been watching recently as part of their movie challenge. In fact, it was a movie they bonded over all those years ago, when she spotted the first *Harry Potter* novel poking out from his schoolbag. That was the catalyst for years of friendship. She has lost count of the number of firsts they shared. A kiss, a prom date, alcohol, a spliff, gig, love, marriage, divorce, and now death.

'I'm beginning to wonder if there's more to this than even you realise,' Melissa continues. 'If you enjoy watching your life flashing by because of the familiarity it brings. Like seeing your mum again.'

'No,' he protests. 'It's not like that at all.'

But Melissa hasn't finished. 'Or is this a convenient distraction because you're afraid of becoming a parent and the responsibility that'll bring? Is that what this is really about?'

He puffs out his cheeks. 'You are seriously doubting that I want to be a dad? That's all I ever hoped for when we were together.'

This pricks her conscience. 'You and I weren't in the right place to start a family.'

'It almost happened. But you didn't want to try again.'

'Okay, yes Damon, right you are. We all know it's my fault,' she shoots back. 'But I wanted more than marriage and motherhood. The miscarriage was probably a blessing in disguise.'

It's as if she's slapped him.

'I'm sorry,' she rushes in. 'I didn't mean it like that. What I'm trying to say is that things are different now. I'm in a better place.'

'Without me, you mean.'

She swallows the urge to tell him to stop being so childish. 'I'm trying to remind you I want you to be a part of this. But to do that, you must lose this obsession with death. You need help, Damon. Proper, expert care.'

'You think I'm mad, don't you?'

'Even you must know that something isn't right.'

He taps at the semicolon tattoo on his wrist with his forefinger. He is becoming more agitated. 'You want to lock me up. Out of sight, out of mind.'

'No,' she sighs. 'I love you, Damon, but you must admit, if you continue like this, it isn't going to end well. Let me find you help.'

His eyes narrow. 'No, you're the one who needs help,' he says, his tone taking on a sharper edge. 'Because without me, your dream of a family isn't going to happen. The clinic counsellor told me I can withdraw my consent at any time, with no explanation required. And no, before you say it, I would very much rather *not* do that. But if you do this one thing more for me, help me die again, then I'll do that one thing for you.'

Melissa's hands fall limply to her sides, and she's unable to draw a proper breath, much less respond. Damon swallows hard, suggesting he knows he has crossed a line, but that it's too late to retract his threat.

'There are four billion men in the world,' she says at last. The words sound tinny in her ears. 'You're not the only one with sperm.'

'But I'm the one who can get you over the finishing line quickly. Without me, you'll have to find someone else, which will take time and be an additional expense you can't afford. Do you really want to tell Ade I've changed my mind? And explain why, and what you and I have been doing? How do you think she'll react?'

Melissa shakes her head in disgust. She has never seen this side to him before, and God knows, she has tested him more than most.

'You've changed,' she says.

He takes his phone from his jacket pocket and offers it to her. 'You can call Ade right now if you like and find out?'

Melissa slaps it from his hand and sends it flying across the room. She doesn't know this man. She wants to yell at him to get the hell out of her house. But he's right, damn him: Adrienne would be devastated if they were forced to return to square one, and how much would it cost to find an anonymous donor and undergo more tests? It could set them back months, and it's money they don't have. But that isn't the worst of it. Melissa shudders to think of Adrienne's reaction to the truth about what they've been up to.

Damon appears to interpret her silence as acceptance of his demands. He picks up his device from the floor and turns to leave.

'Seven p.m., Thursday, at the flat,' he says without looking at her. 'See you then.'

He leaves without saying goodbye, and she sinks into the sofa before picking up a cushion and hurling it across the room.

CHAPTER 39

DAMON

I survey the bathroom one more time to ensure everything is in place. It's the same set-up as before, the same two people involved. We might be together in a confined space, but we are miles apart. Melissa and I are separated by tension and have barely spoken since she turned up at the flat earlier carrying the same two vials of liquid, tube and drill-shaped device as before. Last time, I didn't ask what they are for but this time, I do.

'Intraosseous drill,' she explains, her voice devoid of emotion. 'It's used to administer fluids and meds when intravenous methods don't work. It's faster than an IV. So if I can't resuscitate you, I'll drill in the head of your humerus or the tibia and inject you with adrenaline.'

She revs the device and I flinch. She's either testing my nerve or that it works. Probably both.

'Will it hurt?'

'You won't know. You'll be dead.'

Melissa refuses to look me in the eye. She hates me for the threat I made earlier this week. And I know it was unforgiveable. But I would never have followed through with it. I don't know why

I don't admit this to her now. Perhaps I'm afraid that, if I do, she'll walk out. Instead, my words hang over us like the darkest of clouds. I overcompensate by making small talk and reminding her of that scene in *Pulp Fiction* when Vincent Vega jabs Mia Wallace in the heart with a shot of adrenaline. Melissa isn't having any of my chat and tells me I watch too many films. I doubt we'll be rekindling our Friday movie nights anytime soon.

Compared to her, I feel a little underprepared, as all I have with me are a bath towel to stop the floor from getting too wet and some plastic ankle and wrist restraints to prevent me from thrashing around and hurting her.

'Your next appointment at the fertility clinic is tomorrow at five p.m.,' she says. 'Don't be late.'

I make a mental note to set an alarm on my phone and tablet. Then I suddenly launch into a coughing fit and spit what I hack up into a tissue. As before, there's blood in my phlegm. I don't mention it to Melissa.

Besides the animosity, there's another difference between now and the last time we did this. Melissa hasn't once asked if I've changed my mind. Neither by text nor in person. It reminds me of the last days of our marriage, before she told me it was over, when I wondered if she'd stopped caring. Or is she now in full paramedic mode, and I am simply another of her patients?

With everything prepared and no sign of further conversation, I take a deep breath and clear my throat.

'Right then, are we ready?' I ask.

'Not yet,' she says and pulls out her phone. She taps the screen and hands it to me. 'Record a statement of intent,' she says.

'A what?'

'Video yourself setting out, for the record, what you are about to do, what you hope to achieve and why you're doing it. That this is your idea and it's entirely voluntary. And that you don't hold me responsible in any way. Because if you stay dead, then I am royally fucked. I'll lose Adrienne, my freedom, my job and my house. My whole life as I know it will be gone because of you.'

If she wants to pile on the guilt, it's working. I feel terrible for putting her through this. But not terrible enough to call it off.

'At least this way,' she continues, 'if you die and I have a recorded confession, a court might go a little easier on me.'

I don't argue. I take her phone, press record and, with much stuttering and stumbling, I explain exactly what is about to happen. I end with a smile, and Melissa saves the video.

Then, without further discussion, she binds my wrists and ankles together and drowns me.

CHAPTER 40

DAMON

'Damon!'

The voice is shrill, and I feel hot breath against my cold ear. My body shakes with the same violence as the sea's waves.

'Damon!' she screams again, and I'm aware of hands upon my shoulders.

I open my eyes to find Melissa using all her force to rock me back and forth. I almost immediately spew water on to her face and chest and she pushes my head towards the floor as I vomit ice-cold water across it.

Now she knows I am alive, she begins to cry. I turn briefly and make out rivulets of tears pouring down her cheeks.

'What happened?' I whisper, my voice barely audible. It sparks a coughing fit so powerful, I worry I might pass out.

'I thought I'd lost you,' she sobs. 'I didn't think I could bring you back.'

Her face is wet with my vomit and is as white as a ghost. She holds me tight and we remain like that for a while, the heat of her body warming up the coldness of mine. I have missed her holding me like this, her skin pressed against mine. For so long she was my home. My world.

Finally, when her grip eases, I use my little remaining strength to push myself upright, my back now leaning against the side of the bath. I let out a gasp as a sharp burst of pain shoots through me and I clutch the left-hand side of my chest. It's agonising.

'It took longer than last time,' she says, sounding hollowed-out. 'I might have cracked some ribs when I gave you compressions, then you didn't respond to the defibrillator.'

She helps me to my feet. That's when I also become aware of a stabbing pain deep in my leg. I sit down on the bath's edge and look down to discover the leg of my cargo pants has been pushed up. A needle protrudes from it. She must have drilled into my bone marrow to get the required medication into my system fast.

Then she moves towards the sink to splash water on her face. She leans over the sink, resting on her elbows. I can sense her swelling resentment towards me from here.

'How long was I . . . ?'

'Sixteen minutes,' she says. 'You've been dead for *sixteen fucking minutes*.'

'Oh,' is all I can say, because the fact I am still here and with the cognitive ability to think and reply is a minor miracle.

She begins questioning me, asking my name, where I live, what day of the week it is, who she is, how we met. She relaxes only slightly when I answer correctly. Is it possible to build a tolerance for death?

I'm still shivering, but I don't know if it's because I'm cold, because I've just been brought back to life or because of what I saw when I died. Melissa takes a duvet from the bedroom and returns with it, wrapping it around my shoulders.

'Tell me it was worth it,' she says without looking at me. 'Tell me it was worth the living hell you have put me through.'

Slowly, I nod. 'Yes.'

However, Melissa doesn't give me the opportunity to reveal what I saw. Instead, she removes the cannula, bandages up my leg, packs up the equipment she arrived with and leaves my phone within reach on the lip of the bath.

'Call 111 if you have any difficulties breathing or heart palpitations.'

'Can you stay? What about secondary drowning?'

She shakes her head. 'I can't be around you.'

My heart sinks as Melissa closes the door behind her. She leaves me with my body in the present but my head in the past. I feel so overwhelmed by what I witnessed in death that now it's my turn to cry. I sink into my bed, my brain swimming with memories I've carried back from the dead like holiday souvenirs. There's so much I need to unpack, and I don't know how to do it alone.

This time it's a girl I saw.

A dead girl with half her face missing.

I turn my head to one side. And there she is, lying next to me.

CHAPTER 41

DAMON

I feel like a dozen knots have been wound around my stomach and they're all being pulled together. All night, I haven't been able to stop thinking about this third child and how badly disfigured she is. Half her head has been crushed, making her left eye, lower jaw and an ear nearly impossible to determine. A trail of blood drips from a gash in the side of her head, above her ear. It drops down her neck where it has been soaked up by her sodden T-shirt.

She appeared in only one of my life event recollections. She was lying lifeless on the ground, but not in the same place as Callum Baird. However, I can't identify where. Her blonde hair is spread out behind her head like a halo. It was hard to pinpoint her age as she was so mutilated, but I'd hazard a guess she was a preteen. There was a little, baby-pink gloss on the two half-lips that remained, and liner around her right eye. Emblazoned across her top was the graffiti-style graphic used to promote the 2012 London Olympics. Hanging from her arm was a green backpack with a flag poking out of a pocket reading 'Archbishop's Park Fun Day'.

I wrap my arms around myself as if to protect myself from the cruelty of the world and what it has done to the children I have seen. How many more are left for me to find? I can only hope she is the last. I keep going round in circles because I still don't know what they want from me. Did I hurt them? Is that why I keep seeing them? Or do they appear because they need something from me? It must be the latter because I've never wished ill on anyone. I haven't been in a fight in my life, neither at school nor as an adult. Violence isn't in me.

Soon after dawn breaks, I pick up my phone and google keywords that might identify the girl. It takes a few minutes, but I think I have found her in a story dating back sixteen years.

> *Police searching for a 13-year-old schoolgirl who vanished on her way home from a pre-Olympics family fun day have recovered a body in an industrial estate two miles from her home.*
>
> *A search party had been deployed around the Lambeth area where Daisy Barber was last seen. A police spokesman has confirmed a body was discovered at 11.30 a.m. yesterday.*
>
> *It has yet to be formally identified.*

'Daisy Barber,' I repeat to myself. The name is unfamiliar. Further stories include a report of her last-known sighting. She had spent the day with her stepsisters and their friends at the park, enjoying fairground rides. Then, at some point, they parted ways, and police believed she'd walked home alone. That was when she vanished.

I search again and follow her story in date order. I learn that, almost four weeks after her killing, someone was arrested in connection with her death and was being interviewed by police.

They weren't named for three days until they were charged with her death and made their first court appearance.

And that's when the coldest of chills surges through me. Colder than the sea I died in and the ice I pour into my baths.

Because I recognise the name of the person who pleaded guilty, admitting to what they'd done.

It's all too familiar.

Ralf Lister.

My father.

He is the man who killed Daisy Barber.

PART THREE

IMMERSED

CHAPTER 42

MELISSA

Melissa is sitting at a table in one of Northampton General Hospital's cafés when Adrienne arrives. It's mid-morning and the area is bustling with staff and visitors, but Melissa might as well be on a desert island for all the attention she is paying them.

'Hey,' Adrienne begins, startling Melissa with a peck on the cheek. 'Are they for me?' she asks hopefully, pointing to a banana and a cup of green tea with the string and label from the bag still wrapped around the handle.

'Yes,' Melissa says, failing to mention that, a few minutes earlier, she wolfed down a Snickers bar, an almond croissant and a can of cherry Coke before dumping the evidence in a recycling bin. Adrienne has put them both on a low-cholesterol, low-fat diet. But Melissa rarely sticks to it. More secrets, more lies. But by no means the worst.

'You're a lifesaver,' Adrienne says. 'Sorry, but I've only got fifteen minutes. I'm covering for Penny.'

'Where is she?'

'Morning sickness again. She's having a tough time with this second pregnancy, poor thing. But I've never been more envious of why someone has called in ill. Fingers crossed I'll soon be the one vomiting granola and moaning about my vanishing waistline.'

Adrienne snaps her banana in two and slides half to Melissa. She doesn't eat it. All she can think of is how she has found herself torn between the two people she cares about most in the world, striving to please them both in starkly different ways.

'Have you heard how Damon got on with his appointment?' Adrienne asks as she chews.

The mention of his name raises the hairs on the back of her neck. 'It's not until five p.m.'

'It should be a walk in the park, shouldn't it? He only needs to have a wank behind a closed door and hand a pot of sperm to a receptionist. It's a busman's holiday.'

Melissa picks off tell-tale flakes of almond from her sleeve.

'He hasn't been around much lately,' Adrienne continues. 'Is he okay?' When Melissa looks down at the table and hesitates a beat too long, Adrienne presses her. 'What are you not telling me? He hasn't changed his mind, has he? Oh God, has he found himself a girlfriend? That would be the worst possible timing. How many women would be happy to learn their new boyfriend is fathering a child with another woman? Let alone their ex-wife's girlfriend.'

'No, no,' Melissa says. 'It's not like that. I think he's been going through something recently. Ever since the accident, he's been struggling.'

'With what?'

'With where he is in life,' Melissa replies vaguely. 'With what he wants.'

Adrienne frowns. 'He's a bit young for a midlife crisis, isn't he? Does he still want a baby?'

'Yes.'

'And you?'

'Me what?'

‘Do you still want a baby? Because Damon isn’t the only one who hasn’t been himself lately.’

Her girlfriend’s perceptive nature shouldn’t surprise Melissa. She’d hoped she’d masked how she’s been coping – *not* coping – with the two, very separate demands of the people she loves. Apparently not.

‘You barely comment on the Instagram posts I forward to you,’ Adrienne continues. ‘I suggest baby names and you don’t seem to like any of them. I can’t even look at changing tables or car seats without you telling me I’m moving too fast.’ She reaches out her hand to take Melissa’s. ‘I know you’re more of a realist than I am, and I’m aware there are no guarantees IVF will work. But I need you to meet me halfway and be open to discussing the future more. I want to enjoy this experience, but I’m struggling because you won’t let me.’

‘Are you absolutely positive now is the right time to be trying for a baby?’ The question falls from Melissa’s mouth so suddenly, it even catches her off guard.

Adrienne withdraws her hand. ‘So you have changed your mind,’ she says flatly.

‘No, no, of course not,’ Melissa backtracks. ‘We’ve talked about starting a family ever since we got together.’

‘Is this like when you and Da—’

‘No.’ That was a conversation they had soon after they first met and it’s not one that Melissa wants to rehash. ‘I’m only asking because we’re both currently working such long hours to build our careers. Eventually you want to reach consultancy level and we’ve spoken about how one day I might like to explore positions in the military.’

‘And none of that has to stop because we have a family,’ Adrienne counters. ‘Anything is possible if we’re determined.’

Melissa wishes she'd kept her thoughts to herself. The last thing she wants is for her girlfriend to begin doubting her commitment.

An awkward silence emerges. Adrienne is the first to break it.

'I know what this is really about, Mel,' she says. 'I'm not an idiot. I've overheard you on the phone to Damon telling him you're terrified and asking him what happens "if you can't do it". It doesn't take a brain surgeon to work out what you're referring to.'

Melissa's stomach churns. Adrienne knows. Somehow, she has discovered Melissa and Damon's supercharged game of Russian roulette.

'Ade, I'm really sorry,' she begins. 'I shouldn't have—'

'It's okay, I understand,' Adrienne interrupts. 'Being responsible for a child for the rest of our lives is a massively scary thing. And you're right to be cautious, we might not even get that far. But then we might be lucky. And think what it'll mean if we are?'

Melissa waits for her pulse to stop racing before she replaces her hand in Adrienne's.

'You're right,' she says. 'I'm sorry. I promise I'll be better from now on.'

'It'll be amazing, babe.' Adrienne's beaming. 'Trust me.'

Melissa wishes she could do that. But if she can't trust herself or Damon, how can she trust anyone?

CHAPTER 43

DAMON

The truth hits me like a punch to the face. It's not me who killed a child, it's my dad. This should feel like a weight lifted from my chest, but it doesn't. Instead, it feels heavier.

All morning I have been leaving and returning to my phone as if hoping that if I go back to the story, the letters spelling out the name on the screen will magically rearrange themselves into something else. But each time I look, the words 'Ralf' and 'Lister' remain. I press against my damaged ribs with my fingertips to check I'm not seeing things, that my hallucinations haven't expanded from reanimating the dead to rewriting the internet. The pain alters nothing. But I still don't want to believe it. My father can't be the only man in the world with that name. Or even the only man in the London area. Nine million people live in the capital; there must be more than one Ralf Lister.

And then I spot a photograph, one snapped by a determined photographer running alongside a prisoner transportation van as it left court. The flash has overexposed his face and he looks ghostly and startled. I haven't seen Dad for almost two decades, but there's no doubt it's him. I read the accompanying story.

A man who pleaded guilty to the manslaughter of 13-year-old Daisy Barber has been sentenced to sixteen years in prison.

Ralf Lister, 39, from Lambeth, South London, admitted to killing the child then dumping her body on a disused industrial estate.

Pre-sentencing, Lister was described as a prolific career criminal with previous convictions for theft, aggravated assault, battery and robbery.

Justice Mrs Stacy Denton at the Old Bailey told electrician Lister that what he had done to the girl was 'unforgivable'.

After sentencing, senior crown prosecutor Malcolm Davies of London CPS said: 'While Lister pleaded guilty to manslaughter and saved Daisy's family the further pain of a trial, he has never given a full and frank explanation of where, how or why she died. But the fact remains, he took their daughter. This sentence reflects the brutality of his crime.'

The victim's mother, Sandra Barber, told reporters on the steps of the Old Bailey, 'Nothing will bring back our darling girl. The cruelty of her loss is unbearable. We hope that he rots in prison, where he belongs.'

That man is my father. No matter how many times I tell myself this, it refuses to completely sink in. I need time to process this. I call in sick to work again so I can spend all day familiarising myself with the case. I've barely been there recently, one day won't make any difference. Dad was apparently adamant he hadn't deliberately killed Daisy, and the police couldn't prove murder. CCTV cameras caught him moving Daisy's body from his car into the industrial estate, where he stripped her of her clothes and left her hidden behind an old outbuilding.

I want to believe Dad is innocent and that there's been a huge miscarriage of justice, but I know there wasn't. And if that's not enough to poleaxe me, I discover something else in another online newspaper report.

> A spokesman for the Metropolitan Police confirmed that the previous year, Lister was questioned, but not arrested, in relation to the murder of schoolboy Callum Baird. The case remains open.

I put my phone down on the bed and make my way to the bathroom to splash cold water on my face. Now I know this is why I keep seeing Callum. Dad likely killed him, and not me. But why have Callum and Daisy chosen me as their conduit?

I also have a terrible fear I know where Mum and that little boy she carries come into the story. That Dad somehow ended each of their lives, too.

Because my dad isn't only a murderer. He's a serial killer.

CHAPTER 44

DAMON

I disappear down another online rabbit hole and stare at the mugshot of my dad that the police released to the media. It's clearer than the one taken in the back of the prison van. We share the same oval-shaped eyes, clefts in our chins, slight bends in our noses and low hairlines. I close the page, worried that, from here on in, when I look in a mirror, all I'll see is his reflection.

Dad's past convictions tell me why his appearances in my childhood were so sporadic. Much of his time was spent behind bars. Mum must have thought she was doing the right thing by keeping this from me.

The noise of my ringing phone distracts me, but I don't answer when I see it's a withheld number. Instead, I think back to the elderly man hurling abuse at me on the landing of the flats where I once lived. Now I understand he was referring to my dad when he told me, 'Bad apples never fall far from trees.' Ralf Lister has made me guilty by association.

Everything is becoming a little out of focus. I put my phone back down on the bedside table and lie back. My hollow stomach rumbles, reminding me I haven't eaten at all today. But I'm too exhausted to even order myself a Deliveroo. I must have drifted off to sleep again because I wake up later with a start, aware I have company. All four of my hallucinations are here in front of me, together for the first time. But there has been a sharp decline in their appearances, which I wouldn't have thought possible.

Chunks of Mum's hair have been burned to the scalp and the red marks and soot on her arms are now bright blisters that extend to her hands and face. Callum's eyes are wide and panicked and he coughs as if he is choking on something. The boy Mum holds is so pale he is almost translucent. His fingertips have blackened as if dipped in ink. Daisy's appearance remains so damaged, so grotesque, I want to cry when I look at her.

'I'm so, so sorry for what he did,' I say. 'Please tell me how I can help you?'

Callum is the first to reply, but a combination of static and unintelligible words come from his black hole of a mouth. 'Oodis' is the only word I can make out, but still, it makes no sense. 'Oodis,' he says once again.

'I don't understand,' I reply. But I desperately want to.

Callum moves towards me and I unconsciously shift a little further back. Daisy is the next to edge closer to me. My phone vibrates again, and when I glance at the screen, I realise I've missed five more calls from the same withheld number. There's also a text message from Melissa.

You're a lying, selfish fucking arsehole, she's written.

I look up and I'm alone again.

I'm about to respond with *why?* to Melissa when I remember what I've done to provoke her wrath. I had an appointment at the fertility clinic this afternoon to make another donation. That's who the withheld calls were from. I know I should rearrange the appointment for tomorrow instead, but the way my ribs hurt and where my head is at, I doubt I'll even manage to become aroused, let alone climax. So instead, I shower, get dressed and make my way downstairs to the designated parking area under the flats, and prepare to drive to Melissa's house and beg her for forgiveness.

I climb into the car, slip the seat belt on with one hand while closing the door with the other. But I don't get the chance to shut it fully as someone grabs it and yanks it open.

Before I even turn my head, I know it's him. The man who threatened to kill me a month ago. And before I can defend myself, his hands clamp around my head as he tries to drag me out of my car.

CHAPTER 45

DAMON

My neck ligaments stretch like he is trying to rip my head off. But unlike the last time he attacked me, my awkward positioning weakens his grip, so he isn't strong enough to completely overpower me. I dig my fingers into the tendons of his arms and he loosens his hold ever so slightly. Enough for me to reach out and press the car's ignition button.

'I told you last time, this isn't a game, but you didn't fucking listen,' he snarls, throwing his body towards me inside the car to try to undo my seat belt.

I still have no idea what he means, but I don't have time to figure it out. I know I'm no match for his brawn, so instead of trying to push him off me, I push the gearstick paddle on the steering wheel into reverse, then slam my foot on the accelerator. The car shoots backwards, as does my confused attacker as he is pushed along by the driver's door, until there's a crack of bones and crunch of metal when his body and the door collide with a concrete post. He crumples to the ground like a bag of bricks. I scramble to close the door, but for an excruciating moment my savaged ribs won't allow me to do anything but shriek in pain. And when I do finally get hold of it, I learn the door's hinges must have overstretched because the damn thing won't shut.

'Shit!' I scream and shift gears instead, this time lurching forward. But I know I won't be able to get the vehicle out of the narrow car park with a wide-open door, so I hit the brakes again. I desperately try to close the door again, but it won't budge. A movement in the rear-view mirror catches my eye. My dazed attacker is slowly climbing to his feet.

It's him or me.

A new sensation comes over me. One that I'm unfamiliar with. Panic and fear have made way for anger. I want, *I need*, to hurt this man.

I slip the car into reverse and floor the accelerator. He can't move quickly enough. The rear bumper hits him with such force that he vanishes from view – under my wheels, I can tell by the way the car heaves beneath me. My knuckles are white as I grip the steering wheel and shoot forward again, my tyres bumping over him before I manage to stop the car.

My stare is fixed on the rear-view mirror and the reflection of the motionless heap lying on the ground. I can't leave here without knowing if he is alive or dead.

Slowly, I exit the car. I've watched enough films to know this is the part where the bad guy springs back to life, but I can see from here the unnatural twist in his neck and part of his cracked-open skull. Not even the toughest Hollywood bad guy could survive the damage he's suffered.

My rage slips away and I return to myself. But I'm conscious I don't have time to dwell on what I've done. It's far too late for me to call an ambulance, and I know the police will say I've gone beyond what constitutes self-defence. Also, if any of my neighbours in the flats above suddenly appear to pick up their cars, then I'm done for. I need to save myself and dispose of his body right now. I look around me and clock the bin storage section in the corner of the car park. I grab him by the ankles, but one of them is broken and moves like jelly.

My stomach churns when I realise we are not alone. Someone is watching me. I turn, and see my mum. It's a relief, as if she's here to assure me I've done the right thing. That I had no choice. However, she makes no attempt at communicating this. Instead, she watches as I set to work covering my tracks.

CHAPTER 46

DAMON

It takes all my strength to drag the man twenty metres to the bin storage. Each step delivers a dagger to my ribs and I'm in tears by the time we're inside. I close the bin storage's doors but I can't rest. Inside are a handful of galvanised wheelie bins, and I choose one labelled 'non-recyclables' knowing that after it's tipped into the back of the collection lorry, its next destination is a landfill site.

The stench is overpowering as I open the lid. And going by the list of dates attached to the wall by the private refuse firm, tomorrow is collection day. It's almost full, which will make it easier to hide him, if I can only succeed in getting him inside. I slowly climb in to empty it, tossing dozens and dozens of bags over the side until it's only two bags deep. I'm covered in other people's uneaten food, sanitary products, nappies and general household trash, as fetid bin juice leaks and seeps through my jeans and jumper.

He is far too heavy for me to lift and drop inside the bin, so I tip it on to its side on the concrete floor, climb in again, and drag him in after me. Adrenaline is keeping my pain to a bearable limit, but I know I'll pay for this later. Tucked in tight with stinking refuse and the corpse of the man I've just killed, I search his pockets to try to find out who he is . . . who he *was*. But he has no wallet and no mobile phone. Might've been good information to have, but not a top priority.

After I clamber over the nameless man out of the bin, it takes me what feels like forever to push the bin back upright, then cover him up with the bags I chucked out to make room for him. By the time I've finished, I'm drenched in sweat and I reek. But finally, I shut the lid. All I can do now is hope that when he ends up in landfill and buried under tons of rubbish, he will never be found.

I hurry back to my car and park it in its space, kicking and kicking my sprung driver's door until at last it shuts. There's a tap near the bin storage so I fill an empty water bottle lying on my back seat and turn to wash his blood off the ground. It's at this point that it dawns on me there might be CCTV cameras in here and that everything that's happened has been recorded and stored on a server somewhere. But when I've scanned the roof and walls, it still seems possible that luck might finally be on my side. I can't locate a single lens.

Finally, ensuring there is no one else around but Mum, I hurry back upstairs and take a long hot shower I never want to leave.

CHAPTER 47

DAMON

A young woman takes me by surprise when I turn to walk along Helena's drive. She is making her way from the house to the street. She looks wary of me and I don't blame her. I'm hardly a picture of health.

I quietly make my way unannounced into the house using Helena's hidden key. It's so silent in here I assume I am alone, until I find Helena in the lounge. She is in her armchair, head bowed, chin resting on the top of her chest. It is deathly silent in here. A chill blows through me as, for a moment, I worry she might have slipped away. I don't know if I can deal with a second dead body in a matter of days. But to my relief, I hear the faint sound of her ragged breathing. No one in my life seems to remain dead forever.

Well, except for the car park man. At least, I *hope* never to see him again.

I take a moment to really see Helena as she is today. It saddens me to admit how much she has deteriorated. I recall the woman she was and try to imagine who she might have become had the strokes not taken away the life she knew. I find myself thinking about all the children out there today, desperate and alone as I once was, who have been denied the care she could have offered them.

A part of me wants to admit to her about the man whose life I took three days ago. To offload that, like my dad, I am a killer. That stranger has been almost all I've been able to think about as I replay each moment again and again. I still don't know who he was or why he targeted me. And everywhere I go I'm constantly looking over my shoulder to check if I'm being followed by someone else. In case he wasn't working alone. Each time I question my response to his actions, though, I return to the same conclusion: I did what I had to. It doesn't prevent me from feeling guilty for purposely taking a life, but I one hundred per cent believe he was going to kill me. I look at a sleeping Helena again and decide against offloading on her. She doesn't deserve that burden.

The day after killing him, I watched from inside my car while refuse collectors attached the bin holding his body on to the back of their truck, hoisted it aloft with its lift, and tipped its contents out of sight. The rubbish from the next three bins helped to bury him deeper. I've been regularly checking news feeds but, as yet, there have been no reports of bodies found in the Cambridge plant where Northampton's refuse is transported and sorted. But even if he is discovered, I don't think there's any way he can be linked to me. I hope to God this is over.

As Helena sleeps, curiosity takes hold and carries me up her staircase – slowly, as my ribs are still tender – and into the room where I stayed during my brief time here all those years ago. The curtains are closed and all that remains is an empty chest of drawers and two single, unmade beds. As hard as I try, I can't recall how it felt to be here. It's all so muddled. I can only assume that, with Mum's passing, I was as traumatised as I was confused. But the overriding feeling this house offers is of safety. Perhaps it's why I keep returning to it of late.

I know it's intrusive, but I push open the door to Helena's bedroom. Inside is an open wardrobe full of identical blouses, jumpers, trousers, and a rack of flat-soled shoes. The third bedroom contains a cabin-style bed, with a desk below it. Dots from oily putty residue mark the walls where photos and pictures were once stuck. I get the impression this was also someone else's home, and perhaps not that long ago.

'You're back,' Helena says when I return to the lounge. I jolt as her voice catches me off guard. She shifts in her seat and her bones crack when she stretches her arms before her.

'My social services report,' I say as I take a seat opposite her.

'Have you received it?'

'Yes. And it hasn't shed any light on the gaps in my memory.'

She sighs. 'I suspected that might be the case.'

'Then why didn't you warn me?' I find myself snapping at her. 'Why did you let me get my hopes up?'

'Would it have stopped you from applying if I'd told you some of it might be redacted?'

'No, but it might've managed my expectations.'

'I told you it wouldn't necessarily give you the answers you want, Damon.'

I lean towards her. 'My report isn't the only reason I'm here.'

Helena opens her mouth, hesitates, then closes it again. If I didn't know better, I'd think she might have an inkling as to what I'm about to say next.

'My dad.'

We stare at each other in silence as she considers her response.

'And?' she asks.

'He killed Daisy Barber,' I say. 'Then attacked her dead body so viciously, her parents weren't allowed to identify her. And he was also questioned about the death of Callum Baird. But you know this already, don't you?'

She gives a slow, deliberate nod. 'Rightly or wrongly, I made a judgement back then not to tell you. You had already suffered so much with your mum's passing, I thought it was in your best interests not to compound that pain.'

A grudging nod. 'I understand why you didn't when I was a kid,' I reply. 'But you could have brought it up since. You must've known I'd find out eventually.'

'Damon,' Helena says calmly, 'let me ask you the same question I asked you last time. Has the experience of dying three times—'

'Four,' I correct.

'Four?'

'There was another,' I reply, as if I had no control over it. 'Last week.'

She works to disguise, then recover from, her fluster at this news. 'Has it helped you retrieve any positive memories from your forgotten childhood?'

I wish I could say yes, that seeing Mum again has given me something I thought I'd lost all those years ago. But how she died and the state she is in upsets me. So I shake my head.

'Just because I don't like what I remember doesn't mean you should have kept it from me. Is there anything else you're not telling me? Like who that little boy is who Mum holds?'

'I can't help with that one, I'm afraid.'

'What about why Dad killed Daisy Barber? Or if he murdered Callum Baird? Is that why I keep seeing him?'

She shakes her head and breaks eye contact with me. It's only for a second, but long enough for me to register it. Is she hiding something?

'What do these kids *want* from me?' I ask in desperation. 'Are they punishing me because of what Dad did? Are they trying to tell me something about why he killed them?'

‘They’re not trying to tell you anything, because none of this is real.’

Not her too. I sit back on the sofa and let out a long breath. Silence fills the room as she patiently waits for me to gather my thoughts. I change direction.

‘So when did Dad die? Because I’m confused by the timelines. I assumed it was way before Mum. I remember him not being around for ages, and then something about him being killed in an accident at work.’

I recall someone telling me this very matter-of-factly. Mum, perhaps? He had been such an irregular presence in my life that it had the same impact as being told a neighbour had passed away.

I continue. ‘So I assume he died after he was sentenced?’

Helena grips the arms of the chair and pushes herself up. She carefully shuffles across the floor to join me on the sofa.

‘Damon,’ she says as she clasps my hands in hers. ‘Your dad isn’t dead. He is still very much alive. And he’s a free man.’

CHAPTER 48

HELENA

'What have I done?' Helena says aloud, a small part of her hoping the empty room might offer her reassurance.

She reminds herself she had no choice but to tell Damon about his father. That he wouldn't have needed to dig much deeper to discover the truth by himself. And where might that have left the two of them? Damon would likely never trust her again. At least she can manage him, now he's heard it from her. Well, as best she can. Sometimes she forgets he's a grown man and no longer that quiet, confused little lad who came into her life a decade and a half ago, with only the clothes on his back. Then, she was in control and he did what she asked of him.

Helena recalls how she rejected him outright when he first turned up on her doorstep.

'Absolutely not,' she said firmly, and crossed her arms. 'He can't stay here. It wouldn't be right.'

She had always maintained a distance between her personal life and her job. Taking Damon in wouldn't so much blur the lines as erase them. However, she allowed herself to be talked into it. To take him in, to take him on. But she agreed only on the provision it was her way or not at all. And she meant it. She gave them no choice but to accept.

And her way proved to be in the boy's best interests. By the time Damon left her care a couple of months later, he was a different child. The transformation surprised all involved. In the years that followed, he checked in with her less and less often, but she didn't take that personally. It only meant she had done her job. And while the strokes then did their best to ensure the demise of her fostering career, she could take comfort knowing Damon turned out to be the best version of himself any of them could have hoped for.

But today, the ill wind she's harnessed for so many years is threatening to develop into a storm. And there are going to be casualties, now he knows Ralf Lister is still alive. Before Damon left, she tried talking him out of tracking down his father. She hopes she made a persuasive argument, warning him of the irrevocable harm he might do to himself to meet a man like that. A man who had admitted to such brutality.

'I know how introspective you can be, how much you question yourself,' she'd told him. 'How you can dwell too much on the negative side of your character and how that can impede your progress through life. I worry that confronting your dad might make you question yourself and who you are. Remember: he hasn't shaped your personality. *You* have. DNA is all you have in common. And you are so much more than that.'

As Damon bade her farewell soon after, Helena was still trying to convince herself she might have succeeded in persuading him to let the past lie. But if Damon is willing to literally *die*, again and again, in his search for his truth, then why would her words make him stop now? Not when he is closer than ever.

Perhaps she shouldn't have got involved. Not asked an old colleague of hers to redact the report to hide the facts.

The stress of the unknown, of what is to come next, aggravates her. Her head pulses and she pushes her forefingers into her crown. It's become a more common occurrence since Damon came back into her life – and she can't keep blaming it on a migraine. It's more than that. When black spots interrupt her vision, she can do nothing but shut her eyes tightly in the hope they will go away. But she knows they won't. *Because this is what happened before.*

CHAPTER 49

DAMON

I recognise my dad immediately, despite not having seen him in God knows how long. He's in the aisle of a DIY store, loading a pallet of paint on to a shelf. His hair has receded, leaving a fluffy tuft at the front and short-cropped patches across the top. He is attempting to make up for it with a beard that hangs at least six centimetres from his chin. His shirt sleeves are rolled up, and as he lifts four cans at a time, the purplish veins in and around his broad biceps snake down his tattooed arms. His shoulders are wide and his waist is narrow. I guess that's what a third of your life in prison does to your body if all there is to do is exercise.

Tracking him down has taken a lot of digging, and some dumb luck. The police refused to tell me where he was, as did his former lawyer. And there was no trace of him anywhere on social media. So I lied when I contacted victim support services and pretended to be a relative of Daisy Barber, concerned that my niece's killer had been released and was living within the local vicinity. My dumb luck came in the form of the kind soul I drew for that call, whose empathy for my loss and outrage over my current situation inspired her to not only confirm that he was indeed living within fifty miles of the scene of Daisy's death, in Basingstoke, but let slip he'd secured work at a DIY store three streets from a school. Ten minutes of Google Maps triangulation and a confirming telephone call later, and I'd located him.

Now, I'm pretending to consider paint samples from a spectrum of colour cards, flicking through fifty shades of grey and black. The colours mirror my mood. I keep stealing glances at Dad. The tattoos scattered about his arms and hands seem faded and blurred. I struggle to make them out from this distance. I wonder what the designs are and if he's the reason I've been inked too. Many of mine were conscious choices, like the chorus to Bruce Springsteen's song 'Bobby Jean' because it reminds me of a song Mum would play. The semicolon on my wrist symbolises the number of times I could have ended my story with a full stop but carried on regardless. The ensō symbolises how life is in a constant flux and that everything must eventually end.

There are others I found through surfing the internet or flicking through the tattooist's portfolio, such as the girl hiding her face behind a white flower, a night sky with lightning bolts (despite my irrational fear of electrical storms), and the Grim Reaper hovering over a clock, whose hands are at ten minutes to six. I've also included some of my own drawings that I don't really understand the origins of. Random stuff like a candle flame and a grid of random numbers.

I begin studying Dad's mannerisms for shared traits. Do we walk the same? Are we both left-handed? Does he tug at his right earlobe when he's deep in thought? Does he feel the same guilt I do for taking another life? I doubt it. Because I think he took three more.

Helena explained Dad had been released from prison on licence. Jails were overcrowded and he'd been a model inmate. So while he was technically still serving his sentence, it was now in the community instead of at His Majesty's pleasure. I was surprised to learn that no one had protested it until I learned Daisy Barber's parents had died in the intervening years. I assume no one tipped off the tabloids, otherwise I'd have found online long-lens shots of him passing a school or a playpark and a story reminding the public what a danger he was to every child in his radius.

A customer approaches him, and Dad's smile catches me off guard. It makes the dimples in his cheeks more visible. Mine are the same, although my smiles are few and far between these days. I'm conflicted as to how this should make me feel. A few days ago, I was alone in the world. Now, there is someone here I can relate physically to. Only, it's a child killer.

Dad leads the woman into the next aisle along. I wonder how she might react if she knew what he's done.

Anger begins to boil inside me. The same way I felt when that man in the car park was trying to kill me.

When Dad reappears I'm dwelling on what else we might share aside from our career prospects, which are unlikely to extend further than stacking shelves for a little above minimum wage.

I hate that I am a reflection of this man in so many ways. I also hate what he did and the aftershocks his behaviour has delivered, and still delivers.

He needs to know this.

He is a physically intimidating presence, and the relentless drumbeat of my heart echoes in my ears as I start towards him. And then, from deep within, a confidence I didn't know I possessed surges to the surface. I stride over and he steps aside as I pick up one of the five-litre cans of emulsion he has stacked on a shelf. He watches as I lift it above my head, turn and hurl it down the aisle away from us. My throbbing ribs serve as a sharp reminder of what I've put myself through to get here today.

The lid bursts open upon impact and paint leaps out, covering the floor and splattering products on shelves in a sunburst of brilliant, silky white.

I turn to glare at him, and he stares back at me, bewildered by what's happening. I know he has caught the rage in my eyes. *Our* eyes.

'Oops,' I say. 'Sorry, Dad.'

CHAPTER 50

LAURA

Laura stares from the passenger window of her car at the building on the opposite side of the road. She absent-mindedly taps her fingernails against the door handle. It's midday and the upstairs curtains remain closed, which suggests he is either too lazy to open them or he worked long into the night and is catching up on sleep. She dials his number, but like it has over the last six days, it goes straight to voicemail. She has yet to leave a message. It's frustrating, not knowing why he's not answering. Is he simply ghosting her? That's what people are calling it nowadays, or so Laura's youngest daughter told her when her eldest, Effie, stopped answering her calls.

Her patience worn thin, she exits her car, slamming the door shut. 'Bloody fuckwit,' she says aloud as she crosses the road and makes her way up a short driveway to his front door. The front garden is unkempt, with an old leather armchair dumped in the centre of it. She suspects *Country Living* magazine won't be begging for a photo shoot here anytime soon.

No sound comes from the doorbell so she knocks three times. No answer. She looks over her shoulder to check she's not being watched by a nosy neighbour, then slips around the side of the house towards the rear.

It's as messy back here. It could be a scrapyard, with all these spare car parts littered about. Again, there is no answer at the back door, so she takes a tissue from her pocket and uses it to turn the handle. It opens. Careless, but unsurprising. He's not struck her as a detail person. Just as well in this case. She quietly lets herself in, leaving it slightly ajar should the need arise for a swift exit. It's happened twice now elsewhere, and luck won't always be on her side.

She's always had a heightened sense of smell, and her nose crinkles at the odours in here, a fetid combination of weed, barbecue-flavour pot noodles and, yes, the unmistakable tang of the regular masturbator. Laura spies a mobile phone lying on the kitchen table, which suggests he's here.

'Garry?' she calls in something more than a speaking voice but less than a shout. Not a word in reply. She scans each room of the ground floor, hesitating at the bottom of the stairs. She's reluctant to go up there in case an even worse stench is readying an assault on her nostrils.

'Garry? Are you awake?' she calls. Nothing. She sighs and climbs the stairs. A cautious sweep of two empty bedrooms and a filthy bathroom follows before she returns to the kitchen. 'Where the hell are you?'

Nobody leaves the house anymore without their mobile, she thinks, but then she recalls she warned him not to take it on the job she assigned him. 'If the shit hits the fan, it can be used to trace your movements,' she warned.

But that was days ago. His continued silence suggests all hasn't gone according to plan.

She switches his phone on but the battery is dead. The charger lies next to it so she plugs it into the socket and, after a wait of several minutes, it bursts into life. His code is, predictably, set to six zeros – probably as high as he can count. But she isn't using him for his brain.

Curiosity takes hold and she scrolls through his phone. He's part of a few WhatsApp groups where like-minded Neanderthals share home-made pornographic video clips with each other. The main thing is, she supposes, that he's found his tribe. *Oh, no.* Garry is featured in one video, and she can't help but watch as he high-fives a fellow tattooed gorilla over the back of an unconscious woman they are top-and-tailing. Laura might have some sympathy for the woman if she hadn't been wearing such hideous knee-length, white PVC boots.

Scanning the rest of his messages, she's pleased to see he has followed her advice and erased all correspondence between them. Then she deletes the logs of all her calls.

An app on his home screen catches her eye. It's called Find My Car Key. She glances out of the window and realises there's no sign of his vehicle, a garish purple Vauxhall Astra she remembers he souped up with styling kits and a chrome exhaust. He really is the man that taste sidestepped. She opens the app and doesn't have to wait long before it pinpoints to the nearest ten metres where the keys, and he, most likely are.

She's puzzled when she recognises the address.

The car is parked beneath Damon's block of flats.

CHAPTER 51

DAMON

In the blink of an eye, the past my dad thought he could hide from has returned to haunt him.

'Damon,' he says, unnerved.

'So you remember me,' I reply rhetorically.

He looks me up and down before regaining his composure, clearing his throat and glancing around quickly to check no one is close enough to overhear us. 'What are you doing here?'

'You should never have been released from prison. A hundred years behind bars can't make up for what you did.'

'I'm getting on with my life.'

'I'd like to do the same, but I keep seeing your victims.' I tap my temple with my index finger. 'They're stuck in here.'

He doesn't understand. And why should he? I must sound insane. But he doesn't ask me to expand either. Instead, Dad turns on his heel and begins to walk away towards the mess I've made further down the aisle, which only serves to rile me further. I grab another tin of paint from the shelf, my cracked and bruised ribs screaming as I do so, and launch a second five-litre can of emulsion after him. It lands to one side of him and, as with my first salvo, the lid flies off when it strikes the floor. This one doesn't spray us much, though. Instead, its contents shoot free and flow down the aisle beside him like white-water rapids.

I watch his fists clench at his sides, and I half expect him to come racing towards me like the thug he is. Instead, he walks on, stops when he reaches his trolley, and removes a large brown bag.

'What do you want from me, Damon?' he asks gruffly. Then he walks back my way a few steps, opens the bag and scatters sawdust over the paint. He's close enough to me that I spot my name tattooed across the knuckles of his left hand, and for a second, this catches me off guard. The letters are dark blue, blurred, barely legible. It suggests he must have cared about me enough to put my name on his skin. On the knuckles of his other hand, I can make out a 'b' and an 'o'. Bobbi, I assume. My mum's name.

He's now on his knees, gloves on hands, mixing the sawdust with the paint like he's kneading dough.

'I died recently,' I continue, and he turns sharply to stare up at me. 'I drowned in an accident.'

I don't know him well enough to recognise concern or confusion.

'Chunks of my life that I didn't know I was missing flashed before me,' I continue. 'And now I hallucinate. I see Daisy, two other kids, and Mum. They follow me, they watch me, sometimes they scream at me. And I can't get rid of them.'

He stares at me, lost for words. He doesn't know what to process first: death, hallucinations or the children. He finally chooses the latter.

'Who were the other kids?' he asks in a hushed voice.

'Daisy Barber is one, but you already know that, then there's Callum Baird, another familiar name, and the other is a kid no more than a few months old, who's always carrying a blue chequered blanket.'

He drops his gaze and his lips part ever so slightly, then close again as if he's had second thoughts about what he was planning to say.

Instead, he takes two pieces of cardboard and begins to scoop up the paint and sawdust and drops it into a second, empty bag. I remain standing, arms folded, casting a shadow over him as I await his explanation. I want him to attempt to justify what he did, to give me something to hit back against. But he says nothing.

'What?' I say eventually. 'Is that it? Aren't you even going to try and defend yourself?'

Again, his fists briefly clench and I know he is forcing himself not to react. But I want him to. I want to meet the real him. 'I don't know what you've come here expecting from me,' he says. 'But whatever it is, I can't give it to you.'

I am not a violent man – at least, that's what I thought before I ran over and killed someone – but at this moment I'm so consumed with rage, it scares me. It takes all my strength to stop myself from stepping back for another of those paint tins and staving in his face like he did Daisy's. But I possess enough self-control to know that would make me no better than him. I may have taken a life, but it doesn't mean I will do it again. I am not my father, I remind myself. *I am not my father*. Tears begin to form and I curse myself for showing weakness.

'If there's only a shred of decency left inside you,' I say, 'if you ever cared for me at all, you'll help me to fill in the blanks. Tell me why you hurt those kids.'

Still on his knees, he holds his head down, and I wonder if, like me, he is pushing his tongue against the back of his front teeth as he formulates a response. He looks up at me again.

'You need to leave,' he says firmly.

It's not the answer I wanted. My anger surges and I return for another can and hurl it into the space between us. The tin bursts open, spinning as it does so, splashing us both, this time with red paint.

This gets me what I'm after. He rises to his feet like a grizzly bear, under threat and unfolding. His eyes are blazing and his jaw is tight as he tosses his bag of sawdust to one side, raises both fists and marches towards me. Instinctively, I take several steps back.

'Ralf?'

The man's voice comes from behind him. Dad stops in his tracks and turns to look. A badge on his white shirt reads 'Deputy Manager'. 'What's going on?' the man asks, surveying the mess.

Dad can't say anything more to his boss than that he's sorry and it was an accident.

'So,' I shout, 'you can apologise for some spilled fucking paint, but not for what you've done?'

His manager steps in between us. 'I don't know what this is about, mate,' he says, 'but we have a zero-tolerance policy for customers who abuse our staff.' He speaks into a walkie-talkie and asks for urgent assistance in aisle 23b.

'Do you know who he is?' I ask, pointing to Dad. 'Do you know what he did? He's a child killer, and you've given him a job.'

The man attempts to hide that this is news to him. 'Our parent company is part of the government's Right to Work programme,' he manages, 'and our head office decides who is suitable—'

'I don't care!' I bark at him. But before I can continue, a burly woman wearing a black-and-orange security jacket approaches us, assessing the situation with admirable cool. The deputy manager orders her to eject me from the store.

'*He's* the one you should be kicking out,' I say, glaring at Dad.

The manager gives me one last chance to exit of my own accord. Realising I'm not going to accomplish anything else here, I make my way along the aisle and towards the sliding entrance doors.

I turn to take one more look at my dad, now back on his hands and knees, scrubbing the crimson-and-white concrete. I can see myself in how pathetic he looks and it's deeply unsettling. I rub my damp fingers together and see splashes of red paint on them.

We both have blood on our hands.

CHAPTER 52

DAMON

Confronting Dad today has drained every ounce of strength left in me. Maybe even more so than after a drowning, or killing that man in the car park. Which reminds me: before I try to get some sleep, I type into my phone words like 'landfill', 'refuse collection' and 'body', but no news stories appear. If he isn't found by the end of the week, I don't think he will be. But I don't know if I'll ever be able to rest with something like that on my conscience. It is beyond my understanding how my dad has lived with what he did to Daisy Barber. Or any of the others if, as I suspect, he was responsible for their deaths, too.

For much of the train journey from Basingstoke to London's Waterloo, I'm drifting in and out of a hypnagogic state, traversing consciousness and sleep. Luckily a commuter's briefcase brushes against my knees and stirs me as we pull into the platform. I make my way towards the Northern line where I'll catch a train home from Euston. At least, that's the plan. But at the last minute, I drag myself into a carriage heading south.

I'm too exhausted to make the almost two-hour journey to Northampton from here, so I make a snap decision to visit Helena instead and ask if I can crash in her spare room for the night.

When she tried to talk me out of seeing Dad, I let her believe that perhaps I'd listened. It was easier than pleading my case to deaf ears. But I'll admit to where I've been when I see her. I'll also apologise for taking my frustrations out on her last time. Now I've met him, I can sort of understand why she didn't warn me earlier that Dad wasn't dead. She didn't want me to get hurt, either physically or emotionally. And clearly he is every bit as volatile now as he was when he killed Daisy Barber. Helena has my best interests at heart.

As the Tube train enters the tunnel and I catch my reflection in the darkened window opposite, I'm relieved that my fears of seeing Dad in my own appearance aren't realised. *I am not him.* Unfortunately, I'm distracted from this gratifying epiphany by finding Mum and all three children sitting on either side of me. I turn to the left to look at Callum first, but the seat is empty. My hallucinations must only available today in reflected form. We five stare dumbly at each other uninterrupted until my train pulls into Lambeth North station, which triggers their vaporous exit.

My phone signal reappears, and I spot a voicemail from Adrienne's number. It briefly crosses my mind that Melissa can no longer cope with the guilt and has told her girlfriend everything. And now she is gunning for me. I nervously press play.

'Hey, it's Ade,' she says cheerfully, putting my mind at immediate ease. 'Just a quickie. I wondered if you'd spoken to Mel lately? I sense there's something on her mind, but each time I ask her, she says she's fine. Do you think you could check in with her? I'm not asking you to breach any confidences or anything like that. I'm hoping she might tell you if there's something troubling her. Thanks, hun. See you soon.'

Guilt takes a jab at me. What I've put Melissa through is beginning to come between them. Once upon a time, I might have been quietly glad of that. Seeing them together has become easier over the years, but it won't ever feel painless. I'm reminded of how I was introduced to Adrienne. It was at AJ and Nisha's engagement party. AJ asked in advance if I was comfortable if they invited my ex and Adrienne. I wanted to tell him of *course* it was going to make me feel awkward, that seeing the woman I loved being around the woman *she* loved was going to destroy me. But I didn't. Instead, I kept up a facade all night to prove to our friends I was capable of behaving like an adult, while the child inside me sobbed in a corner.

I think Adrienne was more nervous than I was when Melissa introduced us. She was smart, funny, self-deprecating and beautiful, and it wasn't hard to see why Melissa had fallen for her. I tried to find fault and hate everything about her. It was impossible. By the end of the night, the three of us were doing Sambuca shots together at the bar. In the meetings that followed, I'd find myself absent-mindedly staring at Adrienne, wondering what she had that I didn't, and what had led Melissa to fall so deeply for her. It never took long to arrive at half a dozen good reasons.

Even now, a small part of me resents Adrienne for giving Melissa what I can't. But if I don't manage it, if I allow it fester, I'll lose out. Having only a part of Melissa in my life is better than having no Melissa at all. Which is what I risk now with my demands on her. She was right to have branded me a selfish arsehole for missing that clinic appointment, because that's exactly what I am.

I let out a long sigh as the reality of my situation kicks in. I don't know if I can do this anymore. This constant need to try to find out more about myself is taking away more of me than it's adding. Helena was right to ask me if the truth is worth dying over. If seeing visions of the dead has benefitted me in any way. The answer to both questions is a resounding no. All I'm doing is punishing myself and those closest to me. Meeting my dad was the final straw. If I continue in the way I am, I fear this will ultimately destroy me. I must find a way to focus on the future, on making things right with Melissa and preparing for parenthood. If it's not too late.

Shortly after I exit the Tube, I arrive at Helena's house. After being attacked, I've developed the habit of checking over my shoulder to see if anyone is following me. Night is falling and when there's no answer at her door, I let myself in again with the hidden key. My voice echoes through the gloomy hall and I enter the lounge. She's not there. I flick on the switch to see more clearly, but no light appears. I try another switch and it's the same. I find the fuse box in a cupboard under the staircase and it's still switched to 'on'. Outside, the neighbours' windows aren't illuminated, either. There must've been a power cut.

'Helena?' I shout again, and gingerly remove my phone from my pocket and switch it to torch mode. Still no reply. I check upstairs, but I'm alone.

On a table next to her armchair in the lounge, a Dictaphone and a brown, sealed, padded envelope catch my eye. My name is written across the front of the latter. Curious, I open it. Inside are seven small cassettes, each containing my name on the inlay card as well as the label stuck to the tape. There's a note, too.

> Helena,
> As discussed, here are the recordings of our sessions. And to reiterate, this is not a clinical diagnosis as we are not navigating official channels here. I am doing this as a favour to you because of your relationship with the boy and your vested interest in his family situation. More thoughts to follow. In the meantime, I have – albeit with

apprehension – set up an appointment with Dr Fernandez-Jones as you asked and have briefed him on the situation. Should you decide to proceed, please keep in mind all I have warned you about. Tread carefully.

Dr Hugo Dahl, BPsych Hons.

CHAPTER 53

DAMON

I assume I am 'the boy' in question. But who is Dr Hugo Dahl, and what are these 'sessions' he mentions? I'm unfamiliar with the name. But as I've become aware of my past, I've realised there are more gaps in my memory than a moth-eaten jumper, so it's not inconceivable that we've met.

I take a seat in Helena's armchair and remove the cassette marked '#1' from its box and insert it into the device. I hesitate, unsure of where this sliding door moment might take me, or if it's a journey I want to be on. Ten minutes ago, I was done with all of this. But Helena must have left the tapes out for me to find for a reason. I rub my thumb over the empty bare spot on my ring finger and press play.

A man's voice is audible. It's deep and has a soft, Scottish lilt. Something about it is vaguely familiar.

'Hello, Damon, my name is Dr Dahl, but you can call me Hugo if you prefer.'

I don't move an inch as I wait to hear myself speak. But my present self and the recorded doctor are greeted with silence.

He continues. 'A mutual friend of ours, Helena, thought it would be a good idea for us to meet because we might get on well. My job is to spend time with young people, like you, who have lived through some challenging experiences. And I'd like to try and encourage you to talk about what you've gone through to help it make sense.'

So Helena sent me to a shrink. Is he the reason why I bristled when the hypnotherapist and Melissa suggested I might benefit from seeing a counsellor? Did something bad happen between Dahl and me?

'Helena told me you've had trouble finding your voice since you lost your mum,' he continues. 'It's a perfectly normal reaction to something stressful. Sometimes you want to curl up into a ball in the corner of the room and not say anything to anyone.'

The silence is broken by a faint shuffling, as if someone is moving.

'The Lego in the corner of the room has caught your attention. Shall I bring it over?'

I imagine myself nodding and hear a large clunk and rattling as a box, I assume, is placed on a table. Now the only noise is the shuffling of plastic bricks, then a clicking as I begin to build.

A few more minutes pass as Dahl explains a little more about what he does. He asks if I've heard of the word 'psychoanalyst', then explains it's a fancy term for a listening doctor. Every so often, there's the sound of Lego pieces falling against a wooden surface. Dahl talks about himself a little longer and I wonder if, back then, I was listening to anything he said or if I was too absorbed by my own grief-stricken building-block world.

He continues to try to engage me like this for another forty minutes until he draws the session to a close, telling me he'll see me tomorrow, before the recording ends. He doesn't sound disappointed, though. Perhaps he relishes a challenge. Some people thrive on that. I press eject and turn the cassette over.

We are twenty minutes into our second session before I finally find my voice. Hearing it catches me off guard. It's familiar, yet alien. I was twelve and it hadn't broken, yet it still surprises me how childlike I sound. Dahl has been asking me about Mum and our relationship.

'When can I go home?' I ask optimistically.

Dahl pauses, considering his answer. 'I'm afraid that's not possible,' comes his gentle reply. 'Sadly, your mum passed away the day of the fire. Do you remember?'

'No, she didn't,' I say adamantly. 'She's in hospital. She's getting better. She will be home soon. I always help her get better when she's sick.'

My heart breaks for this version of me, convincing himself there is hope. That things will return to our version of normal.

There's a rustling of papers before I speak again.

'It's like last time,' I insist, 'when she was too sad to look after me and the doctors sent her to hospital. After a week she was better, and she came home.'

Adult me doesn't recall that.

'Where did you stay when that happened?' Dahl asks.

'With my dad and my gran.'

My gran? I have absolutely no memory of her, or of this happening at all.

The conversation between Dahl and me travels back and forth, like two tennis players competing in a rally. Dahl keeps attempting, in the gentlest possible way, to convince me that Mum is dead, while I try to make him believe she's in hospital. Listening to myself now, I understand why I couldn't accept it. God only knows what it must have been like for a twelve-year-old to process watching his mum fall six storeys to her death on to the concrete before him. But eventually, I waver.

Both versions of myself, old and new, begin to weep.

CHAPTER 54

DAMON

'Were you and your mum close?' Dahl asks.

It's the first question on a tape recorded five days after my second session.

I assume I must've nodded, because he asks another question.

'Was that because for such a long time it was only the two of you?'

'I told you before, I look after her when she's poorly,' I say. 'I help her.'

It's only now that I realise I'm still talking about her in the present tense, even though by the end of the second recording, I seemed to have accepted she'd died.

'Does your dad help, too?'

'Mum doesn't like him coming around.'

'Why?'

'I don't know.'

'How do you feel towards him?' I hear the rustle of clothing. 'You're shrugging. Why?'

'I don't like him.'

'Why?'

'Because he doesn't like me.'

'What makes you believe that?'

'Because if he liked me, he'd have stayed.'

That feeling remains with me today. Even though now I know Mum had no choice and Dad was frequently behind bars, I still hear an echo of not being good enough for either of them to want to be around me.

'What was it like for you when your mum was depressed?' Dahl continues.

'She doesn't want to do anything. She just lies around the flat or stays in her bed for days. The television is on all the time, but she never really watches it.'

'Can you tell me how that made you feel, Damon?'

'Like she doesn't care about me.'

'You missed her attention.'

'I make her food, I read her books and I try to make her laugh. She likes my silly voices.'

'And did that work to bring your mum back to you?'

'Sometimes it does.'

'But not every time.'

'No.'

'And how did that make you feel?'

'I get sad.' I mutter the next part: 'Then I get angry.'

'I think I'd feel like that too,' says Dahl. 'How did you show your anger?'

'Sometimes I cry and I shout at her and when that doesn't work . . .' My voice trails off.

'It's okay, you can tell me. This room is a safe space, remember?'

I can barely hear myself. 'I hit her.'

'You hit her?'

'Yes,' I whisper.

'Where?'

'On the arm or her chest. Sometimes her face. But I don't mean it and I say sorry as soon as I do it.'

The adult me recoils. Another memory I have blocked out. The only explanation is that I didn't know how to express my frustration in any other way.

'What was it like having to share her with her boyfriend?'

Boyfriend? What boyfriend? I don't recall my mum ever dating anyone. But before I can give it any more thought, my younger self answers.

'I didn't like him.'

'Why?'

'Because he took Mum away.'

Dahl pauses before he speaks again. 'And was jealousy the reason why you stabbed him?'

CHAPTER 55

DAMON

Stabbed? What the hell? I barely have time to process Dahl's question before the conversation continues.

'I didn't mean to,' I say on the tape. 'He made me angry.'

'What did he do?'

'I don't know . . .'

My voice trails off, allowing silence to reign.

'Most of the time,' Dahl says, 'we only lash out against other people when we think we have a reason to.' His tone is never judgemental. *When we think we have a reason to*. That echoes in my mind, conjures up the face of the man I killed. 'Were you scared he was taking your mum away from you?'

I don't answer him.

'When grown-ups start new relationships, it can be an intense time,' he continues. 'They want to know more about each other, so they spend a lot of time together. And sometimes that means the people they love the most are often left out.'

'It wasn't fair,' twelve-year-old Damon blurts out, his frustration now evident. '*I'm* the one who looks after her. When she was sick for weeks, *I* made her better. But when Maud left, instead of spending time with me, she was with him. He was always in the house, eating with us, watching TV and drinking beer. I wanted it to go back to her and me.'

'And that's why you tried to hurt him with the scissors.'

'It was an accident,' I say. 'I was using them when he said he wanted them, and I told him to wait a minute. Mum told him she'd find him another pair but he yelled at her. Said I needed to do as I was told. She tried to say something else but he slapped her in the face and she fell on to the floor. Then he tried to grab the scissors from me and he lost his balance, slipped, and they went into his arm.'

Relief floods through me, knowing it wasn't deliberate. That I am not like my father.

'What do you remember next?'

'He punched me. Three times.'

It comes back to me in a flash. A repressed memory buried for almost two decades. A blow to the stomach and two to the side of the head. I didn't burst my eardrum falling against a coffee table like I was told. Mum's boyfriend did it. And now I remember her pulling him off me before he began kicking her in the face and stomach.

'There was lots of screaming and the police came,' I tell Dahl. 'We never saw him again after that.'

'You're smiling,' says Dahl. 'Can I ask why?'

'Because then it was me and her again. For a while. But then she got sad again, she started sleeping more and Maud came back. I don't think Mum liked it being only me and her.'

'Can I ask you more about her friend?'

I listen to myself as I describe Maud – her willowy body, angular features, pale face and unreadable eyes. She was like a dark cloud that descended upon us and remained for weeks.

'Damon, I wonder if Maud was a real person.'

'What? Of course she is.'

'Did your mum ever use the word "depression"?'

'No, she'd tell me Maud was on her way.'

'How did they come to meet?'

'She said she'd known her ever since she was a child, but that sometimes having her around felt like going for a walk with a huge bag of bricks strapped to her back. And more bricks keep being added the further she travels. Until finally, her knees buckle under the weight.'

'Do you know the word "maudlin"?' Dahl continues. 'It's a word that's fallen somewhat out of favour nowadays that was once used for people displaying the symptoms of depression. I wonder if your mum humanised her condition by naming it rather than admitting to what she was suffering? And that, to understand it, you created a physical manifestation – a woman – out of something you couldn't see?'

'No,' I protest. 'Maud visited us lots of times.'

'It's understandable if you did make her up,' says Dahl. 'There's nothing wrong with that.'

I press pause on the Dictaphone. And as I think about her now, I'm beginning to wonder if he is right. Perhaps Maud was an invented caricature and not flesh and blood. Forever dressed in dark clothing, lacking in warmth, having little interest in me, coming into our lives uninvited, always outstaying her welcome. Like a Disney villain. Perhaps my hallucinations have been a part of my life for much longer than I realise.

What I hear in the recordings that follow sets my mind spinning with further insights into my childhood that perhaps – more than perhaps – explain my adult behaviours. Like constantly living with a fear of rejection. I'm supposed to be embarking on the greatest journey of my life with parenthood, but instead I've been doing my utmost to push Melissa into cutting all ties with me. I'm forcing her to reject me for a reason I can control instead of one I can't, like when we split up.

I've been acting similarly with friends. I haven't responded to their messages in weeks. Even before all this, I'd go through phases of keeping them at arm's length because I fear if they really get to know me, they'll recognise how much of a sad mess I am. Reject them before they reject me. I'm literally dizzied by the continuing cascade of revelations. Rejection: my terror of it is why I haven't shown any career ambition, in case I'm told I'm not capable. And I'm always the one to check out of a relationship early. None of the girls I've dated since Melissa have worked out because I immediately fall to developing exit strategies. There's always this lingering thought in the back of my head that if I wasn't enough for my parents or my wife, I won't be enough for anyone else. Why should I be?

I press play again, but Dahl gets little else from me in these sessions. Until day twelve, when he drops his biggest bomb so far.

'Damon,' he begins. 'Can we talk for a moment about what happened to your brother?'

CHAPTER 56

DAMON

Brother? I don't have a brother. I'm an only child, I always have been. And for a split second, I wonder if I have got this all wrong, and this isn't me on these recordings but another troubled kid, and the tapes have been mislabelled. I squeeze one of the cassettes in the palm of my hand to make sure they're real and this isn't another hallucination.

Then it hits me like a punch: it's the young boy I see with Mum, perched on her hip, clutching a blue chequered blanket. I blink hard and I see them together now, in the corner of Helena's lounge. I crane my neck towards them as they edge closer. In this dusky room, I can just about make out a name embroidered on the blanket. It reads 'Bobby'. And I realise the faded tattoo on Dad's knuckles wasn't referring to my mum, Bobbi, but to a brother I didn't know existed. Both his sons emblazoned on his hands for all to see. For a moment I forget that if I can see the boy now, he must be dead.

'Do you remember much about him?' Dahl continues.

'He died when I was little,' twelve-year-old me replies.

'Did your mum talk about him?'

'Not really.'

'But when she did, what would she say about him?'

'That everything she loves is taken away from her. So what's the point in expecting more?'

I didn't realise quite how alike she and I are. It's sadly reassuring.

'Do you know what happened to Bobby?' Dahl asks.

'I think he got poorly when he was sleeping because in the morning, he wouldn't wake up.'

'It's commonly referred to as Sudden Infant Death Syndrome, or cot death,' he says, then goes on. 'What do you remember about that day?'

'Mum screaming, Dad already being there, an ambulance arriving, me watching lots of Disney films at a neighbour's house.'

So Dad was there when he died.

'Do you think losing Bobby and your father leaving might be why your mum would have these depressive episodes?'

'She still had me,' I mutter.

Dahl continues to gently press me, encouraging me to open up about Bobby. But I must have had enough of his questions by then, as he receives short shrift from me for the rest of that session.

Back in the present, a yawn catches me. I am so drained, I want to turn off the Dictaphone and return to the moment before I joined Melissa in the sea at Brighton Beach. I wish I'd told her no, I wasn't going into that water. How different things would have been. How different *I* would have been to who I am now.

One cassette remains, dated two weeks after these sessions began. I stare at it, preparing myself to tackle the final hurdle in this gruelling steeplechase.

'Can you tell me about your friendship with Daisy?' Dahl asks soon into the recording.

The girl Dad killed was my friend? I cock my head to the side, waiting for a reply. But my younger self says nothing.

'I believe you and her were close?'

'I don't want to talk about her,' I say, my tone flat.

'For a while, she even—'

'I don't want to talk about her,' I reply, a little louder.

Dahl often changes the subject when I sound uncomfortable, but eventually circles back to it. But not this time. He isn't letting me off the hook.

'I think it's important that we find a way for you to talk about her, Damon, because of what happened,' he continues. 'You and I know what your father did . . .'

A low humming is coming from the recording.

'Damon,' says Dahl.

The humming gradually becomes a little louder, so Dahl says my name again. Then I realise it is me making the noise. I'm shutting down. I turn the volume up to maximum before the recording suddenly falls silent. Is the session over so soon? I flash the torch light on to the cassette itself and see the spool is still half-full. I pick up the device and hold it closer to my ear.

A piercing scream erupts so loudly that I think it's coming from here in the lounge. I drop the Dictaphone on to the floor in shock, and scramble to my feet as fast as my broken rib will allow. I shine the torch around the room, but I'm alone, it's only me, no hallucinations. Now the recorded scream is joined by a loud clattering and smashing, as if objects are being thrown around. Dahl has raised his voice but I can't make out what he's saying before the recording suddenly goes silent.

What the hell happened back then?

I rewind the tape and play it again in case I've missed something. I'm desperate to hear more, but the rest of it is blank. 'Fuck!' I shout in sheer frustration.

The tingling sensation in my nose appears again, a warning of the nosebleed to come. I position myself and hold my ragged handkerchief under my nostrils, but they remain dry. It leaves me with the makings of a headache though.

I glance at the time on my phone. It's past midnight. I conserve my phone's battery by moving it to low power mode before searching Google for Dahl's name. But all I can find is a mention of his name in industry magazine *The Psychologist*. It's an obituary. Dahl died after a brief illness in 2017. He's literally a dead end.

I need to rest. The heart palpitations that have come and gone in the last few months are back with a vengeance. Bruised ribs, torn neck ligaments and constant exhaustion are making me feel a hundred years old. I try not to think about my dead baby brother, my father the murderer, stabbing Mum's boyfriend, killing that man in the car park, and why Helena isn't here. It's all too much for me to unpack.

By some miracle, sleep takes hold of me. And I don't move from this spot for the rest of the night.

CHAPTER 57

LAURA

It's approaching 7 a.m. when Laura's car pulls up outside the block of flats where Damon lives and the trail of breadcrumbs has led her. A little over five weeks have passed since she last visited him here. Then, it was at his invitation, after he begged her to help him to die. And like the Good Samaritan she is, she agreed. They almost accomplished their shared goal before they were interrupted by an unexpected gatecrasher.

She switches off the ignition and recalls how she didn't stay to find out who the intruder was or why she was there. Instead, she raced from Damon's flat, jumping down the staircase two steps at a time, out of the lobby to the road. Then she continued running for at least a mile, before, exhausted and panting, she came to a halt. She took a seat inside a bus shelter and cried.

Laura wept for her unfulfilled expectations, for being unable to complete what she'd set out to accomplish and for again putting herself in a vulnerable position. She should have learned from the mistakes of nine years ago. Of Ryan. She flinched as she recalled his name. The pain he'd put her through. But conversely, how he had been the catalyst for the most exciting period of her life. It had proved impossible to replicate. And God knows, she had tried.

Once she pulled herself together, she retraced her steps to where she had parked her car, close to Damon's flat, and drove back home to London, stopping off at a motorway service station to find out all she could about him. She had done a little due diligence before they met, but clearly not enough. She had allowed her overwhelming desire to be there with him as he exhaled his last breath to cloud her judgement. And that made her angry with herself.

It didn't take much scrolling through Facebook before she found Damon's profile. It was set to private, but his banner photograph was a wedding picture. She screwed her face up at his pale green suit: something a laundry basket would spit out.

She recognised the image of his bride immediately. It was the interloper who had stopped her from killing him. Tagged as Melissa Lister. The combination of first name and surname amused Laura. Quite the tongue twister. If it was her, she'd have kept her maiden name. But going by how much Damon's flat screamed 'single man', it was clear to Laura they were no longer together. *Lister*, she repeated to herself, not for the first time. Why did that sound so familiar?

Melissa's Facebook page was also set to private, but she wasn't as guarded with her Instagram page. And Laura's hunch was right: there were no images at all of her and Damon. But there were plenty of Melissa cosying up to another woman. It was obvious they were a couple.

The plot thickens.

Throughout the remainder of the car journey home, Laura ran through every possible explanation as to why Damon's need for help in ending his life might've been a scam. But try as she might, she couldn't think of a plausible motive. She kept replaying Melissa's reaction to what she'd interrupted: it appeared to be disbelief. But her arrival being merely unfortunate timing didn't mean Laura was going to let Damon off the hook. He owed her his last breath.

Over the following days, she gave herself time to formulate a plan. For years she'd been a regular fixture at *End of the Line*, a Samaritans-style charity helpline established to listen to the worries of lonely, desperate and suicidal callers. Some she had actively encouraged to end their lives, but these scenarios weren't frequent enough to satisfy her appetite, so after a number of years, she had left. The palliative care offered by the nursing home where she now volunteers offers close to what she needs, and on a much more regular basis. When patients have no family or friends to be with in their final hours, she works extra shifts and quietly inhales their final moment. But these are easy pickings. They are fruit offered to her on a plate. She longs to fill her lungs with more than the stale death rattle of the terminally ill. She has longed for someone like Damon.

Laura was at the breakfast table eating from a bowl of yoghurt, blueberries and chia seeds when it struck her from nowhere why she might recognise Damon's surname. Fifteen minutes later, and following a rummage through her house and a dive into the dark web, she found her answer. She had to push her laptop to one side and draw in a long breath. What she had learned was a game changer. Killing the same person twice was always going to be a first for her. But this was an even better opportunity, almost too much for her to comprehend.

It was more important than ever that she not let Damon get away.

Today, she hovers on foot by the key-coded entrance to the car park under the apartment block. She doesn't know the entry number, but she doesn't have to wait long before a tenant appears and picks up their vehicle, and she slips inside the car park before the gates close.

Laura almost immediately finds what she is looking for: a souped-up Astra parked close to the entrance. She recognises it as the one belonging to Garry, the man who was supposed to have made it clear to Damon that Laura is not done with him yet. The man she sent to taunt him simply because she can. What use is a mouse to a cat, after all, unless it can be toyed with?

But why has Garry since vanished, and left behind his prized possession – not to mention his smartphone, back in his awful flat?

The car's doors are still locked, but as she peers inside, she can see a set of keys lying in the central console. *Odd and odder.* She considers smashing a window to gain entry, then checks his phone again. Amongst the other pointless customisations that scream 'pizza delivery boy', he's also had a keyless entry system fitted. She opens the app and the door immediately unlocks.

She's not sure what she is looking for when she slips inside and closes the door. There's certainly nothing immediately surprising. The passenger footwell contains empty cans of Red Bull and polystyrene boxes with the remnants of takeaway meals inside. He is what he eats: cheap and disposable. There is nothing of interest in or on the back seats or inside door pockets, but she does find a small unlabelled bottle – complete with pipette – containing a transparent liquid in his glovebox. GHB, the date rape drug, she assumes. She has found it useful in the past, although she doubts it's for the same reasons Garry has.

She's about to leave when she spots a small, dashboard-mounted camera. Its green light suggests it's either recording or live-streaming. She scrolls through his phone again and finds the accompanying CamMe app inside a folder. In another minute she's scrolled back a week, to the date she asked Garry to drive here and up the ante on Damon, and presses play. The video begins with him following another car into the car park and positioning his vehicle in a spot opposite a bin storage area. She fast-forwards three hours until she spots a figure she recognises. Damon entering his car.

It's rare she is left speechless, but that's what happens when she watches the events of that confrontation play out. It's only then that she realises how much she has underestimated Damon. And how he has the potential to be one of the most thrilling chapters of her life so far.

CHAPTER 58

MELISSA

Melissa checks the equipment in the back of the ambulance ahead of the day's shift. She is tired and tetchy and lets out a yawn so wide, her jaw clicks. It's the result of another fitful sleep in which she dreamed about Adrienne drowning a newborn baby in the sea while Damon stood watching from the beach. Each time she ran towards Adrienne, her feet sank deep into the pebbles. It isn't the first time the dream has haunted her. And every night she has it, she awakens to find herself sitting upright, face and chest drenched in sweat, and Adrienne rubbing her back, assuring her it's not real and that she's safe. Her girlfriend is understandably concerned where this is coming from. Melissa has tried to reassure her that all is well.

When she left Damon, she vowed that in her next relationship, she would be honest about everything right from the start. Only, deceit has crept in again. Because she isn't excited by this baby. Not anymore. Damon's demands have put paid to that. The joy she felt in the beginning of their journey has been replaced by guilt over what she's allowed Damon to persuade her to do. She knows the longer they continue, the more they are living on borrowed time. And the less chance there is of them completing their IVF journey.

As Melissa wipes clean the green plastic stretcher cushions, she wonders how life might've been had she stayed in her lane. Had she and Damon begun the family he'd longed for. She thinks back to a year before she and Damon married, when she admitted she had grown tired of her job as an assistant manager at a hotel on the outskirts of town.

'It doesn't fulfil me,' she told Damon. She knows now she could also have been referring to their relationship. 'I want more out of life.'

'Such as?' he asked.

'I've talked about being a paramedic for as long as we've known each other. Perhaps now's the time to start looking into it properly?'

'But we get married this time next year and then we agreed to start trying for a family,' Damon argued. 'So where will training to be a paramedic fit in? You'll only have to give it up when you get pregnant.'

In those three short sentences, there was so much she wanted to take him to task over. But she held back. 'Well let's delay our family plans,' she said instead.

'How long for?'

'Only until I'm qualified, and then we can reassess.'

Damon didn't try to disguise his disappointment, and he barely spoke to her for the best part of a week. She understood why. She was removing from the table something hugely important to him.

Now, when she reflects on her marriage, she realises this moment was where its decline began in earnest, and her awakening commenced.

Later, and shortly after she'd made their separation permanent, she spotted an attractive young nurse filling in forms in A&E. They chatted for a while, and it was Adrienne who asked Melissa if she had time for a coffee. The spark between them was instant. Afterwards, Melissa couldn't stop thinking about her. And, despite long shifts and unsociable hours, not a day passed when they weren't with one another.

A year later, when Adrienne asked her what she thought about the two of them starting a family, Melissa didn't shrink into herself like she had with Damon. Because it felt right. *This is how love is supposed to feel*, she told herself.

A noise approaching her from behind returns her to the present. The familiar shuffle of his feet gives him away.

CHAPTER 59

MELISSA

Melissa turns to find Damon, paler and skinnier than when last she saw him, his features more pinched and strained. His jeans hang off his hips and bunch at his ankles. His T-shirt looks two sizes too big. Instinctively, she wants to pull him to her and ask if he is alright. But she holds back, reminding herself his immediate welfare is no longer her concern. She must put herself and her needs first, not his.

Damon clears his throat. 'I know I'm probably the last person you want to see right now.'

'No shit,' she mutters.

'And you have every right to hate me. But I want to let you know I went to the fertility clinic today to make my last donation.'

Melissa doesn't express any gratitude. Instead, she feels a pang of shame over her first thought at hearing this, which is to wonder what the staff must have thought of his appearance. She is grateful the three of them passed the ethics board panel before his recent decline.

She throws one wipe away and removes two more from a container and methodically cleans the metal frame. She senses his awkwardness and a small part of her enjoys it.

'Mel, please,' he says. 'Don't be like this. It's unfair.'

'You don't get to tell me what is and what isn't unfair,' she snaps. 'I'll be the judge of that.'

'Last time we . . . you know . . .' She does know. All too well. A hollow pit opens in her stomach every time she thinks about killing him, which is far too many times every damn day. 'Anyway, I saw someone else,' he continues. 'A girl, this time. She had half a face. And I know what happened to her. My dad killed her.'

This momentarily punches the anger out of her. 'Your dad?' she repeats in a whisper, and he nods.

'I found her story online,' he says, 'and learned my dad admitted to it.'

Melissa shakes her head as she takes a seat on the stretcher.

'That's not all,' he continues, capitalising on her attention. 'I went to see him.'

'You found his grave?'

'No. He's still alive. He served fifteen years of a sixteen-year prison sentence for manslaughter before getting parole last year. I tracked him down.'

Her head slowly spins as Damon recounts their heated confrontation and how his father offered no reason for his actions. Then he explains how Helena left recordings of his childhood counselling sessions for him to hear. Listening to them blew him away, not least because he's learned he once had a brother. Melissa is stunned by how much has happened in such a short time frame. Each new revelation chips away at the anger she holds towards him.

'What else am I hiding in here?' asks Damon, pointing his finger towards his forehead. 'Because I know there's more.'

'Can you visit your dad again?' she suggests. 'Ask him, once and for all, to be honest with you about everything?'

'I don't think he'd be very receptive to me asking more questions. If his manager hadn't arrived when he did, I think he'd have wiped the floor with more than just the sawdust.'

'Then perhaps you have no choice but to come to terms with never knowing the whole truth.'

'There is another way,' he says.

She is about to ask what that would be before she reads his expression.

CHAPTER 60

MELISSA

Her fury returns and erupts. She pushes herself off the trolley, grabs Damon by the arm and pulls him up a step and inside the vehicle, slamming the door behind them. He winces at the sudden movement and clutches at his ribs. She must really have cracked them when she brought him back to life last time. *Good*, she thinks.

'What are you going to threaten me with this time if I don't do it?' she barks. 'Are you going to tell my family and Adrienne what we've been doing? Or the NHS Trust and have me fired?'

'No, no no,' he says, and appears genuinely horrified by her suggestion. 'What I said last time, I promise, I'd never have gone ahead with any of it. I was angry and tired and confused and I lashed out at you when I shouldn't have.'

While she is partially satisfied by his apology, it matters less whether he'd have carried out his threats and more that he thought to use them against her in the first place.

'You seriously expect me to do that to you again?'

'I've found a hospital that will help me,' he says. 'A psychiatric unit in Leicestershire.'

He removes his phone from his pocket, locates a bookmarked website and passes it to her. Melissa is aware of it. A former colleague now works there.

'They will admit me if I tell them I'm a danger to myself,' he continues. 'If you help me this one final time, I'll say anything it takes for me to be accepted there as an inpatient. And before that, I'll make a statement to the police about everything I remember about finding Callum Baird's body. At least I can put it on record in case Dad hurts anyone again. But I need your help to fill in the last few gaps.'

Melissa clenches her fists, willing herself not to become emotional in front of him.

'When is this going to end?' she asks.

'When I have my answers and when I can help these kids and Mum,' he replies. 'Please believe me, this isn't a threat. And I'm not trying to guilt-trip you into doing it. But you must know, I've come too far to stop. I'm going to do this with or without you. And then I'll get help and we can go back to how things were. I swear.'

Melissa knows that pregnancy or no pregnancy, their friendship cannot return to how it once was. Far too much has happened. She looks him up and down. Mentally and physically, Damon is disintegrating before her. And she is his only hope of survival.

An image of Adrienne appears in her mind. She loves that girl with all her heart and desperately wants to make her happy. But she knows she can't do that until Damon's questions are resolved.

'Go and see your dad one last time,' she says.

'You weren't there,' he argues. 'You didn't see how quick he was to lose his temper when I told him what I remembered. It's pointless.'

'Your *death* is pointless,' she counters. 'So talk to him again. And if he isn't willing to help you, then I will.'

CHAPTER 61

DAMON

I've been sitting in a KFC restaurant for the best part of the afternoon but have yet to order anything from the menu. It's close to the DIY store where Dad works, and I'm waiting for him to finish his shift. When he finally passes the window, I scramble to get my coat and bag and leave without losing sight of him.

My plan was to confront him in the street, where he can't hide behind a security guard as before. Where there are witnesses. Instead, curiosity gets the better of me and I follow him. I maintain a safe distance for close to half an hour until we reach a row of terraced houses. I'm unfamiliar with Basingstoke, but I get the impression he doesn't live in the best part of town. His front door and window face directly on to an area of litter-strewn greenery. Still, I'm sure it's better than his view was from a prison cell window. He lets himself in and switches on a light as the door closes.

I remain where I am, by a tatty playpark, ignoring the curious gaze of a pack of young people roaming the area on BMXs. I try to rehearse the conversation I need to have with him, but I don't really know why I'm bothering. I'm not expecting much from him. I'm only here because of a promise I made to Melissa to press him for the facts of our family's past. I was tempted not to bother: to keep myself safe and lie to her. But after all she's put on the line for me, she deserves more than that.

My heart thrums as I approach his front door with its flaking yellow paint. I don't know what to expect, but maybe this time if I don't provoke him, we can at least have a conversation. There's no bell, so I pluck up the courage to knock once, twice, then a third time. Eventually he answers, every bit as surprised to see me at his home as he was at his work. He recoils ever so slightly before regaining his composure and puffing out his chest. Without saying anything, he begins to close the door on me.

'We can do this out here if you like,' I say, raising my voice. 'Do your neighbours know who they're living next door to?'

He hesitates, then reluctantly allows me inside. I follow him along a gloomy hallway where I'm half expecting him to suddenly turn around and pin me up against a wall. Instead, he leads the way into a lounge. It stinks of stale tobacco in here. There's an old black leather sofa, and next to it an armchair with three stacked cushions to offer extra height. In the corner of the room is a small circular dining table and two chairs. A half-full ashtray lies in the centre with the remnants of charred roll-ups. There's a television that predates flatscreens with the six o'clock news on mute. I wonder if this is where he lived before he was jailed, because it doesn't appear to have been updated in years.

'Why are you here?' he asks, keeping his tone measured and the volume to a minimum.

'There's more to your story than you're telling me,' I reply. 'I don't think Daisy Barber was the only person you killed. I think Callum Baird keeps coming to me because you killed him too.' I know the answer to my next question, but I ask it anyway. 'The third kid was my brother Bobby. Is he dead, too, because of you?'

'No! Of course he's not.'

‘He comes to me like the others.’

‘What are you talking about?’

‘I told you before, I hallucinate them. All day, every day. In fact, he’s behind you right now being held by Mum.’

My dad turns quickly, but of course he sees nothing. This time neither do I. I just wanted to catch him off guard. He turns back to me and puffs his chest out again, but his eyes give him away. He’s either scared of what he thinks I’m seeing, or of his own son’s madness.

‘You need help,’ he says.

‘You don’t know the first thing about what I need. Because if you did, you’d tell me the truth. What did you do to Callum and Bobby?’

‘I’d never have hurt Bobby. You boys were the only good things in my life and I loved you both. And your mum,’ he adds in a sudden moment of emotional vulnerability.

‘But you killed Callum, didn’t you.’ I don’t pose it as a question but as a statement of fact. It’s almost imperceptible, but I think he nods his head. Or am I imagining it? Was it only a casual movement? ‘How many others are buried inside me waiting for me to find them?’

‘None.’

‘I don’t believe you.’

‘And I don’t care.’ He takes a step forward, the sliver of sensitivity he allowed me to witness now swallowed by his shadow self. ‘Now are you going to leave by yourself, or am I going to drag you out of here?’

But I’m not yet ready to back down, no matter the consequences.

CHAPTER 62

DAMON

'You don't randomly hit your thirties then suddenly start killing kids,' I press. 'There must have been more. And, FYI, if you can't be honest with me, I'll get myself killed again tomorrow and come back with the truth anyway.' I can tell by his expression that my statement of intent has once again wrongfooted him.

'I'm going to drown myself again,' I clarify. 'Each time I've done it before, I learn more.'

His jaw drops. 'You . . . you can't. It's insane.'

'You almost sound like you care.'

'This is not worth dying over. Nothing is. Please, don't.' He runs his fingers through his beard then tugs at it.

'Then spare me the trouble.'

He moves swiftly from bravado to exasperation. 'There were no others,' he insists, his voice rising.

'Did Mum know what you'd done?'

He says 'No' too quietly for me to believe him.

'You're lying. She found out, didn't she?'

And then a sudden, unsettling thought appears from nowhere.

'How did that fire start in our flat?' I ask. Dad doesn't reply. 'Was it deliberate? Did you do it? Did you kill Mum too?'

'I absolutely did not hurt her.'

'Then what does she want from me? Because I know she's trying to tell me *something*.'

I might not know this man, but I recognise his mannerisms. His rubs his thumb against a tattoo on his wrist when he's anxious, as do I. He is holding back.

'You didn't answer when I asked if the fire was deliberate,' I say.

'They investigated it. Said it was likely a cushion set alight by a fallen candle.'

'I don't care what an investigation said. I'm asking *you*. And please, no more bullshit.' I hesitate before I ask my next question. 'Did Mum kill herself because she knew what you'd done to those kids?'

Dad's gaze leaves mine, which gives me my answer. My emotions jump back and forth like a needle on the Richter scale. After years of believing Mum's death was suicide, I moved to grappling with the truth that she'd died because her only choices were to leap from a burning building or burn in the flames. Now I know he gave her no choice. He took her away from me. He might as well have pushed her himself.

Dad looks up and catches the storm escalating in my expression. I lose who I am and return to the person I became when I killed the man in the car park. It doesn't matter how much larger and stronger Dad is than me. Adrenaline numbs the pain in my ribs and I rush towards him, tackling him by the waist and sending us both tumbling to the ground. The back of his head slams into the wooden television unit and I clamber on top of him.

I have never hit another person in my life, but here I am, fighting with my father. I punch him in the face. When I raise my fist again, he turns his head and this time I catch his brow. Now there's a sharp, shooting pain burning its way through my knuckles, but I don't give in to it. Instead, I hit him again and again, colliding with his nose, his eye, and then his mouth.

'I fucking hate you!' I scream. '*You* should be dead, not those kids or my mum.'

Now I raise both my hands and bring my fists down upon his face once more. He isn't trying to defend himself. He is letting me hurt him. He wants to feel my pain for what he did, because somewhere inside him, he knows he deserves it. And I am all too willing to oblige.

The first time I killed was because I had to. This time it's because I want to. I am a carbon copy of him. *Bad apples never fall far from trees.*

Then the expression on his battered face alters. It's momentary: his eyes flit to something behind me. I don't have time to process it or turn before something heavy crashes against the back of my head.

CHAPTER 63

MELISSA

It's been a long, fourteen-hour shift by the time Melissa returns home from work. It's past six and she picked up a microwavable jacket potato and a tin of baked beans from a garage en route. She made sure to leave the empty full-fat Coke bottle and two Twix wrappers out of Adrienne's sight in the car's glovebox, because Adrienne wants them both to be as physically healthy as possible before they become parents. She has no idea the chances of motherhood are becoming more and more remote. And the further away they recede, the more Melissa craves the comfort of junk food.

Her stomach is still rumbling as she walks up the short drive to their detached home on a modern estate. She edges her way around the rocks and bricks that her dad excavated as he prepares to replace the stones with block paving. She curses him as she almost trips over a mallet and spirit level he's left close to the porch. The house itself is a characterless copy of every other property in the neighbourhood, but it will do until they can afford something that suits their tastes better. After willingly leaving Damon with almost all their shared belongings, everything inside this house embodies the last, and best, years of her life.

Melissa locks the front door behind her, then makes her way to the kitchen and spots Adrienne's handbag lying on the floor. She is supposed to be working a late shift tonight. Melissa finds her sitting at the breakfast bar, an iPad lying face down on the marble-effect worktop.

Adrienne's head doesn't turn to meet her lips when Melissa kisses her. There's clearly a problem.

'What's happened?' she asks.

Melissa lowers herself on to a barstool, and from that angle, the lighting reflects Adrienne's eyes. They're pink and puffy, as if she's been crying. Which is unusual, because it's Melissa who's typically the more emotional of the two.

'Babe?' Melissa asks. 'Are you okay? Has someone died?'

Adrienne nods.

'Oh my God, why didn't you call me?' Melissa asks, now panicked. 'Who?'

Adrienne turns to look her girlfriend in the eye.

'Damon, apparently,' she says. 'And more than once.'

CHAPTER 64

DAMON

'Stop it!' shrieks someone from behind me. 'Get off him!'

I'm slow to react and I turn, just as I'm about to be struck again. I can't move fast enough to avoid it and it slams into my head for a second time. The impact of what sounds like metal against my skull is so forceful, my vision blurs. I lose my balance and tumble off my dad. Then I'm hit once more, this time on the shoulder with a thwack so hard, I fear it might've fractured my collarbone. I try to roll away but come up against a wall.

My vision flickers on and off like a light switch, leaving me with barely enough clarity to register an arm being raised and the weapon about to fall on me again. I can't make out what it is.

'No, Mum!' comes Dad's voice.

I brace myself for a fresh blow, but it doesn't come.

Only now, as I refocus, do I realise my attacker is an elderly woman. She supports herself with a walking frame in one hand, and in the other, she brandishes a metal coal shovel.

Then I realise what Dad's called her: *Mum*. My grandmother is the one who has ambushed me. The woman I share a past with, but have no memory of.

She glares at me, her face ablaze with wrath. 'Stay away from him,' she hisses at me, 'or I'll kill you.'

Now Dad and I look at each other. His face is bloodied and raw with open wounds. I return to myself, the person I was before tonight, appalled that I lost control and did this to him.

'He's served his time,' my grandmother continues. 'Now leave him alone. Fucking vigilantes.'

Dad clambers to his feet and I refuse the hand he offers. I push myself up off the floor, then balance against the wall as the pain makes the room swim. An almost unbearable flash of heat causes my knuckles to pulse.

'Go,' says Dad. 'Now, Damon.'

This time, I don't protest.

'What did you call him?' my grandmother says.

'Go!' Dad says to me again, with more urgency.

'Is that . . . him?' the old woman asks, turning to me.

Neither of us answers as she regards me, searching for signs of familiarity. She doesn't have to look too hard: facially, I am a carbon copy of my father. Her fearlessness is replaced by disbelief, and I think she's about to open her heart and her arms to the grandson she hasn't seen in so many years. Instead, she pivots effortlessly to who she was a moment ago. Her face is a picture of rage. As I move past her towards the door, she manages to turn and smack me one last time across the middle of my back with the shovel. It pushes me into another wall and comes close to knocking me back to my knees. I recover from my stumble just in time.

'Get out, you little cunt!' she yells.

'Mum, *stop*,' Dad shouts and steps between us, snatching the weapon from her hand and throwing it across the room. Then he takes me firmly by my injured shoulder, and frog-marches me back along the corridor and towards the front door. He opens it and I spin around to face him. He spits a mouthful of blood over the doorstep and on to the pavement. A string of red saliva drips into his beard, then he locks his eyes on mine. They are cold and hard and full of fury. I am seeing the real him. And it floods me with fear to see myself reflected in his glare.

'That was your only shot,' he warns. 'If you ever come back again, what I did to all those kids will be nothing compared to what I'll do to you.' He slams the door closed between us, but bellows through it: 'Now stay the fuck away!'

CHAPTER 65

MELISSA

Melissa's stomach folds in on itself as Adrienne turns her iPad face up, accesses a shared Cloud app and a video appears. How could she have been so stupid? It's the clip Melissa demanded Damon record before she helped him die the last time, in the hope of exonerating her if she were unable to successfully resuscitate him.

'This is nothing,' Melissa assures her, hoping Adrienne won't spot the goosebumps or fine, raised hairs on her arms. 'We were being silly. You know what we're like when we've had a few drinks.'

She tries to take the iPad from Adrienne's hand before the clip finishes playing, but her girlfriend moves swiftly to snatch it away. 'Don't lie to me,' she says. 'I've watched it a dozen times and nothing about this video suggests you'd been drinking or were "being silly".'

'We were drunk,' Melissa insists, trying to keep her intonation light. 'Damon was talking about going swimming in the sea again and I told him not until he makes a video clearing me of any responsibility if something happens. It was a bit of fun.'

Adrienne bangs her fists on the worktop. 'I'm not an idiot, Mel!' she shouts. 'Every day I'm around patients who lie to me. Lying because they want more meds; lying because they're in more pain than they care to admit: lying that they've injured themselves falling when they've been beaten by an abusive partner. My bullshit radar is pretty damn good.'

The game is up. Melissa rests her head in her hands, too ashamed to look at her.

'Why?' asks Adrienne.

'Because if I didn't help him, he was going to do it alone, and he can't bring himself back to life.'

She goes on to explain how, each time Damon dies, he discovers chunks of his childhood he's forgotten and returns with hallucinations of dead people.

'So instead of getting him psychiatric help,' says Adrienne, 'you're facilitating and actively encouraging him.'

'You have to believe me, I begged him to change his mind. But when I first told him I was having no part of it, he found some psychopath online who was trying to kill him and had no intention of resuscitating him. If I hadn't walked in on them, he'd be dead now. At least if I'm with him, he has a chance of coming back.'

Adrienne shakes her head. 'And how many times have you done this with him?'

Melissa hesitates, so Adrienne repeats the question.

'Twice, since Brighton,' Melissa eventually answers.

'Twice,' Adrienne repeats, as if trying to make sense of it. 'How do you do it?'

'I . . . I hold him under the water in the bath until he drowns.'

She wants to say it sounds a lot worse than it is. But of course it isn't. Adrienne gasps, pushes back her barstool and begins pacing the kitchen. Without looking at Melissa, she asks, 'How do you bring him back?'

'Chest compressions at first, but then I had to use the defib and an intraosseous drill.'

This forces a disbelieving, despairing sound from Adrienne. 'It'd be bad enough if you were there to witness him dying of his own accord and not stepping in to help,' she says. 'But to deliberately end his life with your own hands? That's *murder*, Melissa. Do you understand that? Murder.'

'He gave me no choice.'

'You killed your ex-husband!' Adrienne all but shouts at her. 'And you *keep* killing him! That is *your* choice, because you don't have to do it.' She stops pacing and stares at her, wide-eyed. 'What if he stays dead? That video won't prevent you from being prosecuted.'

'I could make a jury understand he wanted me to do it. It's no different to assisted suicide.'

'Are you stupid or just naive?' She grabs her phone and types something into it as she continues to talk. 'The law won't care if Damon wanted this. You're still the one who's killing him.' She turns the screen around to face Melissa. 'It says here eighteen years is the average prison sentence for murder. You'd be approaching your mid-forties before you're released.'

Melissa tries and fails to hold back her tears. 'I thought that if I agreed to it, he might've got his answers by now and we could return to normal.'

'Normal?' Adrienne scoffs. 'That is never going to happen.'

'I was doing it for you too, for us, so that we could have our family.'

Adrienne's laugh dies in her throat. 'The baby's father dead and his mum jailed for murder? How did you think that might've helped us? How could I explain that to our child?'

'Damon threatened to withdraw from the IVF donations if I didn't help him. And I know how desperate you are for us to have a baby. I tried to tell you at the hospital café this might not be the best time.'

Adrienne glares at Melissa and her voice deepens. 'Don't you dare try and put this on me.'

'No, no, that's not what I'm saying,' Melissa backtracks. 'I didn't want to disappoint you, that's all.'

Adrienne draws an invisible line around her face with her finger. 'Look at me. How do you think I feel right now?'

'Now you know, perhaps you can help me talk him round? Make him see sense. Help him to realise that he doesn't need answers. That he can have everything he ever wanted when he becomes a dad.'

Adrienne shuts her eyes tight and Melissa's heart sinks. 'Do you think I really want to co-parent a child with someone as unstable as Damon? That is most definitely not happening.'

'But you know how much it means to him.'

'Him, him, him. I'm sick of it. What about us? Was Damon thinking about how much this means to him when he missed his clinic appointments? When he was threatening to withdraw his consent? No, he doesn't think of anyone but himself.'

Melissa wants to fight back, but her arsenal is empty. In her heart, she knows everything Adrienne is saying is valid.

'Are you sure you don't want to be with him?' Adrienne asks suddenly.

Melissa tilts her head slightly, unsure if she has misheard. 'Yes,' she says emphatically. 'Of course I don't want to be with him. Where is this coming from?'

'I'm a patient woman. I don't complain when I'm not invited to your Friday film nights. When the dinner I've cooked is getting cold because you're in the other room FaceTiming him. Or even when you go over to his flat because you're worried he's lonely. I accept you two are close. But what you've been doing is so completely beyond what you might expect from a friend. Can you blame me for questioning if there's more to your relationship than exes?'

'Ade, I swear to you, there's not.'

But Adrienne doesn't appear to be registering Melissa's answers. 'You loved him once, perhaps you're not ready to admit those feelings have returned. Maybe I was an experiment.'

'As a *friend*,' Melissa says earnestly. 'I love him as a *friend*. You are the person I am *in* love with.'

She watches as Adrienne paces the kitchen once again, trying to push together pieces of a puzzle that don't fit.

'You keep telling me you wish Damon would move on,' Adrienne continues, 'but you're not allowing him to. He isn't the only one clinging to the past.'

'I'm not clinging to anything.'

'You have allowed and encouraged this co-dependent relationship to develop. I think subconsciously, you want him to keep needing you.'

'No, it's not like that.'

'If we are to stay together, you cannot allow this to continue.'

'Listen to me, I won't do it again,' Melissa pleads. 'I promise you.' And she means it. No matter how desperate Damon is and how much he begs or threatens her, she is unwilling to risk losing what she has with Adrienne.

Adrienne shakes her head. 'No. That's not enough. You and him . . . it must stop. Right now. Tonight. You do not see him or speak to him again. You block his number, you delete his texts and that video.'

Melissa's heart sinks. 'I can't do that,' she says. 'What if he tries to die again without me?'

'That will be his decision, not yours. I'm warning you now, if you are willing to throw your freedom away for his crazy obsession, then you are throwing away our relationship too. And that's already on very shaky ground, because I don't know if I can be with someone who is willing to kill another human being. And I don't care how good your intentions are.'

Tears stream down Melissa's cheeks as she watches Adrienne storm up the stairs and hears the slamming of their bedroom door behind her.

CHAPTER 66

DAMON

So he did it. He killed all of them. Daisy, Callum, Bobby and, most likely, my mum. Four deaths and no explanation. Dad's words ring in my ears like tinnitus. *If you ever come back again, what I did to all those kids will be nothing compared to what I'll do to you.* I hope if I see him again, he's in the back of a hearse, en route to his funeral.

It's unlikely he'll ever tell me why he did what he did. Do I even need his reasoning? No, probably not, because it'll never make sense to me. There's no justification for taking another life. Then the man I ran over in the car park comes to mind. Well, perhaps there is, sometimes. *Case-by-case basis, then.*

Point is, I know for certain I am the son of a serial killer, and I don't know if I have the mental space right now for what that means. But this isn't over now I have the truth. Because I still don't know what those kids want from me or why they haunt me and not him. And if they won't tell me, how am I supposed to find out? Or will they live rent-free in my head for the rest of my life? I really hope not because I don't think I have the strength for much more of this.

I stop by a chemist on the way back to the station to buy painkillers, and a kind pharmacist takes pity on me and tapes up my sprained or broken fingers. I can still move my shoulder, so I don't think my collarbone is fractured, but it feels like I'm being stabbed by something red-hot and jagged.

Then I call Melissa as I board the train but it goes to voicemail, so I leave her a message asking her to ring me back. I pick a seat in the corner of the carriage, curling up against the window, my arms wrapped around my chest and stomach, as if protecting myself from an imminent attack. I spot the reflection of a man about to take a seat next to me. He changes his mind when he clocks the state of me and I start coughing and spitting blood into a paper tissue. He moves to another section instead. I don't blame him. I'm a mess.

I begin to replay the events at my father's house. I don't know who that person was who attacked him. It certainly wasn't me. At least not the me I have known for twenty-eight years. It was as if someone else took over. Dad unleashed a primal rage in me. I wanted him to grasp the gravity of what he has put me and others through. And I truly believe that had my grandmother not interrupted us when she did, I'd now have two deaths on my conscience. She's fiercely protective. The maternal bond must be a powerful one for her to allow Dad back under her roof. I'm almost jealous of it.

I wish I knew where Helena is. She might be able to help me glue together the fragments of sanity I have left. I'm desperate to hear a familiar voice, to be reminded of who I am and not who I was in the presence of my dad, so I call Melissa twice more but I don't leave messages.

An hour and a half later, I'm back in the lobby of my flat, collecting post from a box I haven't opened in two weeks. I wait until I'm in my kitchen before I begin sifting through the letters.

Some are bills – reminders or final warnings – but two are from the Human Resources department at work. The first informs me they have been trying to get hold of me to discuss my continued absenteeism. I've been deleting the voicemails they've left without listening to them. The second warns they have no choice but to begin disciplinary procedures and lists the reasons why. They can fuck off. I don't open anything else and sweep them all into the recycling bin.

In the process, the postmark on one of them catches my eye. 9 May. I look at the date on my watch. It's 11 May. It was my birthday two days ago, and I missed it. I wasn't alone in that. So did Melissa and every one of my friends. In my twenty-ninth year on this earth, I've been forgotten by everyone I have ever cared about.

I curl up on the sofa, knees bent, arms across my chest again, lonelier than I have ever felt. I have no one. Absolutely no one. People have stopped calling because I don't reply. I've deactivated my social media accounts so I don't have to watch them living their lives while I'm trying to end mine, over and over again. I'm not dead, but I'm not living, either. I'm a year away from turning thirty and have less to show for it than when I was twenty. I'm stuck fast in purgatory, and I don't know how to escape. Or even if I can. Perhaps this is it for me. Somehow, sleep catches me and carries me away.

A throbbing in my knuckles and shoulder awakens me sometime in the early hours. I push two painkillers out from a blister pack and swallow them with water, followed by another two for good measure. I'm always fully stocked with medicines. Melissa used to tease me for having so many in this flat that I could open my own pharmacy. Even in less complicated days, every now and again I'd experience phases of debilitating headaches. It feels like a pressure expanding inside my skull that leaves me dizzy. She nagged me to see a doctor, but they'd only refer me to the hospital for CAT or MRI scans, and there is no way in hell I'm going inside one of those machines, my head in such close proximity to the electrical currents used to generate magnetic fields and radio waves. So I self-medicate instead.

I'm about to return the pack of pills to the medicine cabinet when a little voice in the back of my head stops me. Swallow them all and you'll get all your answers, it urges. It won't solve the problem of how I bring myself back to life, but does that even matter anymore?

I survey what I have. There are boxes of paracetamol, aspirin, co-codamol for an old work-related back injury, ibuprofen, and even some antidepressants I was prescribed after Melissa and I separated.

The little voice is not so little anymore. It's big and booming and ever so persuasive. It guides my hand and I remove everything from the cabinet and carry its contents into the kitchen. Then I empty each bottle or packet, one by one, into a cereal bowl. Finally, I remove a bottle of San Miguel from the fridge, twist open the cap and return to the bowl.

I am powerless to stop myself picking three different-coloured tablets and swallowing them. Then another three. *This is it*, the voice tells me above the sound of waves crashing. *This is where you'll find your truth.* I'm about to continue when a message flashes up on my phone. I don't recognise the number so I'm ready to ignore it until I see there's an attachment. Curiosity gets the better of me. It's a video, so I press play. And the moment I do, I wish I hadn't.

It's footage of me in the car park below, driving over and deliberately killing a man.

CHAPTER 67

DAMON

I shove three fingers down my throat until I spew six partially dissolved tablets into the toilet bowl. My heart races as I hurry back into the lounge and watch the video footage for a second time.

Like I do when I'm viewing my life events playing out, I'm a spectator as I reverse the car until the door and my attacker collide with a concrete post. Then I drive forwards before pausing, slipping the car back into reverse and knocking him down again. Next, I see myself dragging him into the bin storage area and shutting the doors behind me. The stench of rotting food and death is as strong in my memory as it was in that moment, as I recall the effort it took to hide him inside one of the dumpsters.

I put the phone face down on the coffee table for a moment, hoping this is a hallucination. It's wishful thinking, though. When I pick it up again, the message is very much real. The static positioning of the camera and the slight reflection from a windscreen suggests this was taken from inside a car. I'm so angry at myself. In my haste to get rid of the body, I didn't give myself a moment to think of how my attacker got there. If he'd travelled by foot or by vehicle, and where he might have parked it. Now I know. It was almost directly opposite mine.

Someone has sent this to me for a reason. To tell me they know what I have done. But who? I check the number against those in my phone's address book, but none match. I brace myself for the response as I call the number, but it doesn't connect. The call simply ends. There's no voicemail either.

Think, Damon. Think. Is the car this was filmed from still downstairs? I doubt it, if the footage has been taken from it. But it's worth checking out.

I hurry down two sets of stairs, through the double doors and into the basement car park. I stand in front of my vehicle, parked in its allocated space, and survey the area, comparing it to the angle of the film. Opposite me are two cars that I cautiously approach. Only the Astra is unlocked. I open the door and take a seat inside, noting a plastic mount on the dashboard in which a camera might fit. This has to be it.

My mum suddenly appears in the passenger seat, but there's no sign of the young boy who so often returns with her. She now has a hole in her cheek and in her mouth sit red embers, which she begins to spit into the footwell.

'You died because you found out what Dad did. He as good as admitted it,' I tell her. 'I don't know what you want from me. Please help me to understand you.'

She looks at me with hollow eyes before her neck bends with a series of cracking sounds until her ear touches her shoulder. She diverts attention from me towards something in the door pocket. It's a book.

I swear I can feel the heat coming from her as I lean over and reach for the book. I recognise the cover instantly. *A Little Life*. And I know who left it here for me to find.

CHAPTER 68

DAMON

I ring the doorbell of a house in the Shropshire countryside and a housekeeper with a stern expression answers. She invites me inside, leading me into a room that overlooks immaculate gardens. It appears to be a working office. There's a desk with a dark brown leather chair behind it and I'm surrounded by grey filing cabinets. A trolley next to a mobile gurney contains electrical equipment. Knobs and dials are labelled 'Pulse', 'Duration', 'Frequency' and 'Current'. There's a device with the words 'Sigma EMR' written across the side. On top of two cabinets are computer monitors and a keyboard. Even to my uneducated eye, much of this equipment looks dated. Now I must wait for the man I'm here to see.

I've encountered the name Dr Owen Fernandez-Jones only once before, when Dr Dahl included it in the note he sent to Helena, along with the cassette recordings of our sessions. But it came with a warning, advising her to 'tread carefully'. What with everything I learned from those tapes, his name must have been pushed to the back of my mind until I had the mental capacity to take it in. And that moment came a few nights ago, during a fitful sleep. It was a welcome distraction. Because each time my phone's screen illuminates, I'm convinced it's going to be another video from Laura. She sent that clip of me in the car park and left the book in the car for a reason. She'd commented on it being a favourite of hers when she spotted a copy in my flat. But in the seven days since, she's yet to respond to my messages.

What the fuck do you want from me? read the last one I sent.

Nothing. It's as frustrating as it is frightening. I can only assume this is all part of the game. That she revels in the torment of making me wait. Perhaps I should have swallowed those pills after all and brought an end to this chaos. But I didn't. Because my story isn't over yet. Not until I help those children and Mum. I owe it to them for what Dad did.

I've been trying to take my mind off her by tracking down Fernandez-Jones, which hasn't been easy. There's barely a mention of him online, suggesting he paid for his digital footprint to be erased or suppressed by search engines. A red flag appeared in my head. Then after making a post on Threads appealing for help, a user sent me an email address and a link to a biography buried so deeply on the web, I wouldn't have been able to find it myself. It described Fernandez-Jones as a pioneer in the field of something I'd never heard of.

> Electroconvulsive therapy (ECT) is a physical treatment that uses an electrical current to pass through the brain and cause a brief seizure. The procedure is performed under general anaesthesia and affects areas of the brain that control mood, thinking, appetite, and sleep. ECT is often used to treat severe depression, catatonia, or mania. Up to forty per cent of patients can have temporary memory problems while they are having ECT. Rigorous scientific research has not found

> any evidence of physical brain damage in patients. The most serious potential long-term side effect is that a patient might forget events from their past. A small number report gaps in their memory about events in their life that happened before they had ECT. Sometimes these memories return fully or partially, but these gaps can also be permanent. Recent research suggests that seven per cent of people report some persistent memory loss a year after ECT.

My heart throbbed as it slowly sank in that I must have undergone the procedure. Was my response to Mum's death more intense than I remember? Did Helena arrange for me to meet Fernandez-Jones because I met one or more of those criteria? It would explain the gaps and missing events I didn't even notice had vanished until recently, along with distorted my memories. If Dad and Helena weren't going to tell me the truth, I thought, perhaps Fernandez-Jones might.

Now, as I await him, vultures have swept in and eaten the butterflies circling in my stomach. I lied to get myself an invitation here, calling myself David Smith and explaining I was a mature student studying psychology at Northampton University. I told him I was fascinated by his pioneering work in the field of ECT used to treat depression. He initially declined my invitation and recommended former colleagues I might speak to. He only agreed when I assured him that anything he said would be for research purposes only and strictly off the record.

Suddenly the door opens, and whatever I was expecting, he is not it. A short, squat man barrels into the room and shakes my hand firmly before throwing himself down on to the chair behind the desk. He must be in his sixties, but the skin of his face is unnaturally tight. He has a deep, even, ochre tan, sparkling white veneers, and a thick head of hair that could only be the result of a transplant. He looks more like a gameshow host than a doctor. He asks if I found his place okay, then wants to hear a little about my course, and I recall and recount what I've read about it on the university's website.

'Right,' he says as he entwines his fingers and stretches them out in front of him until the bones crack. Then he offers me a smile that leaves creases around his eyes. 'Let's cut the pretence. Do you want to tell me why you're really here, Damon?'

CHAPTER 69

DAMON

His recognition has me on the backfoot. I glare at him, unsure of how to respond.

'I may no longer be practising or teaching, but I still have contacts in academia,' he boasts. 'There is no one with the name David Smith enrolled on the university course you claim to be studying.' I have a feeling he enjoys having the upper hand. 'I prefer to fly below the radar these days, so David Smith must've had a reason to track me down here. I assumed at first you might be a journalist or one of those irritating podcasters or TikTokers, trying to put their own spin on events of the past. Attempting to portray me as a modern-day Frankenstein because I dare to challenge the norm. So I planned to correct their misconceptions. And then I saw you approaching the house and I recognised you immediately. And you are a far more interesting guest.'

'So you remember me?' I ask.

He looks me up and down. 'I rarely forget faces. And you haven't changed that much.'

'It's been sixteen years.'

'You were here three times a week for over a month, which leaves a lasting impression. You've grown out of your nosebleeds, I hope? You were like an old man, always carrying a handkerchief, because you suffered from them so frequently. But the most important question should be is: do *you* remember *me*?'

'No.'

'Then what led you here?'

'Your name was mentioned in notes left by a psychotherapist I saw as a boy.'

That creates a frown line in his unnaturally smooth brow. He removes the lid from a chunky fountain pen and makes some notes in a lined notebook.

'Do you know what one of the most persistent adverse effects of ECT treatment is, Damon?'

'Memory loss. So I assume you used ECT on me? Even though I was only a kid.'

'Let's bypass the accusatory section of this tête-à-tête and accept that as a given, shall we? And "retrograde amnesia" is the correct terminology. Some patients may have gaps for events that occurred around their time of treatment. But in some cases, that amnesia can stretch back years. Such as yours.'

'But now my memories are returning.'

His brow arches and he leans forward. 'Explain.'

'I witness events that have happened in the past, but only when I die,' I begin, before recounting everything that's happened to me since the first time I drowned. He hangs on my every word without interruption and makes furious notes. He only asks questions when he's sure I've finished. It's the hallucinations that fascinate him the most. He presses me about who I see, what they look like, how obvious their injuries are, how frequently they appear and what they tell me they want from me.

'"Bleeds",' he says when I've answered. 'That's the name I have ascribed to them. It's not uncommon. Memories bleeding from your subconscious into your conscious. But what, or whom, you see isn't tangible.'

'I'm aware they're not real,' I say. 'I'm still the right side of crazy.'

Only just. And I'm not sure he believes me. I'm also unsure if I care. 'Are you the reason why I've forgotten so much?' I continue. 'You used that machine to pick and choose which memories to erase?'

'No. The fields of neurophysiology and neuropsychopharmacology have yet to advance with such great strides,' he admits. 'The hippocampus, located in the brain's temporal lobe, is where episodic memories are formed and indexed by you to access later. That's the area I targeted.'

'"Episodic memories"?'

'They're tied to everyday specific events and experiences. Like what you watched on television last night, how you travelled to my house this morning, what snacks you ate in the car. By targeting them with electricity, some of those memories can be erased. But we can't choose what you retain and what you lose. If we could, there'd be a queue a mile long outside my front door begging me to consign bad behaviours to the past. However, the more cases we treat, the more we learn.'

'And you're still treating people?'

He tenses. 'Not presently.'

The way he says it, almost with indignation, suggests he's keeping something from me. I hold his gaze and we remain in a stalemate until I suggest, 'You were struck off.'

He sighs as if responding is tiresome. 'A common misconception, accepted and disseminated at the time by an uneducated, disingenuous, mainstream media,' he says. 'I resigned.'

'You jumped before you were pushed.'

He ignores me. 'British medical science once led the world with its comprehensive mental health services. But a lack of continuing government investment, an unwillingness to risk pioneering treatments and a generation of woke, spineless bureaucrats mean we now lag behind many other countries. And when experts such as myself formulate revolutionary ideas that challenge and expand upon current procedures, we are pilloried. When, in fact, we should be celebrated.'

'For doing what?'

He answers as if the reason is obvious. 'For helping young people like you!'

'And how exactly did you help me? Because, from what I can tell, all you've done is take things away. Like the truth.'

Something about his expression brightens when I ask him this, as if a spotlight only he can see is now shining upon him. He reclines in his chair.

'Are you sure you really want to know?' he asks.

He is toying with me. And I have no choice but to play along. 'Yes.'

'I should be celebrated for ensuring you have never killed again.'

CHAPTER 70

DAMON

I stare at him blankly. Either I've misheard or he knows I've deliberately killed a man. Maybe Laura has given him recorded footage, and together they plan to use it against me. No, that doesn't make sense. They can't know one another. My mouth opens, ready to tell him it was self-defence, that I had no choice. But I struggle to find the right words.

'Well?' he says. 'In all the years since I treated you, have you taken another life?'

It's the way he phrases the question that confuses me further. *Another?* 'I haven't killed anyone, ever,' I lie.

He offers a condescending smile. 'And how can you be sure of that?'

'Because I know who I am.'

'You know who you are now, but not who you were then. With your hand on your heart, can you claim to be one hundred per cent certain that you have never cut another person's life short?'

I think we are talking at cross purposes here, but how can I explain that without admitting to what I did in that car park? 'Because . . . because I'd know if I hurt anyone,' I say. 'The memory might be gone, but that feeling of remorse would remain.' And as I've learned recently, it certainly does.

'Then why do you think Helena and your father brought you here?'

'My dad?'

Fernandez-Jones nods. This revelation about my father's participation surprises me because, from what I have seen of the man, I doubt my mental health would've been high on his list of priorities.

'They must have brought me here to treat me after Mum died,' I reply. 'I assume I was in shock or a deep depression. After seeing what happened to Mum, anyone would be, regardless of their age. I needed help.'

'You came here six weeks after she died, if I recall correctly. I wouldn't have performed ECT on a child grieving their mother's passing.'

'Then why did you?'

He forms a steeple with his fingers in front of his mouth. He leaves me in no doubt he is enjoying this.

'First, permit me to recount a case study in the early 2000s by an American institute I was involved with that focused its efforts on rehabilitating career criminals,' he begins. 'Not, petty, occasional criminals, but those who posed a real, physical risk to other inmates and to the general public. When we electrically stimulated the prefrontal cortex of their brains, it reduced the urge to carry out violent antisocial acts by half. *By half*, Damon. Do you understand what a difference that can make?' His question is rhetorical. 'The more case studies we performed ECT upon, the more markedly their behaviour improved. So our belief was – *is* – that we should introduce ECT on purposefully selected offenders before they are released from prison to commit another crime. Think about it. What if the most antisocial and feared offenders – the murderers, the paedophiles, et cetera – were subject to mandatory ECT before being freed? How many people might we protect if we eliminated or drastically reduced their criminal urges? Why should offenders have freedom of choice when their victims don't? Some of my more vocal critics claimed my proposal was inhuman. But I say no, what's inhuman is allowing people back on our streets to bring pain to the lives of others.'

I'm reminded of the film *Minority Report* Melissa and I watched last year as part of our movie challenge. Tom Cruise plays a detective attempting to arrest murderers before they commit their crimes. That is science fiction. What Fernandez-Jones is claiming, is fact.

He admits his proposal ran into difficulties after being granted access to a South American supermax prison – the most secure level of custody – which allowed him to experiment on a dozen prisoners. Two suffered irreversible brain damage, one later took his own life, and four others reoffended. He casually brushes this off.

'Not the results we were hoping for, granted. But the most important thing to remember, and what continues to be ignored by the naysayers, is that my treatment didn't have a negative impact on all of them,' he adds. 'The remaining *five* offenders never committed another crime. But the vocal minority used the ammunition of the less successful subjects to have my funding withdrawn, to ensure I was blackballed by my peers and deemed a danger to my profession.'

I look around at the equipment and electrical devices surrounding me. Some remain plugged into sockets.

I can't listen to any more of this and rise to my feet. 'I came here looking for answers, not bullshit,' I say. 'It was my dad who killed people, not me. At least three children and probably my mum. And I suspect he's guilty of others too.'

Fernandez-Jones has also got to his feet, and now he moves around his desk and perches on the edge in front of me, blocking my path.

'But Damon, your dad didn't kill anyone.' That damned smile. 'It was you.'

CHAPTER 71

DAMON

'Move out of my way,' I snap. 'You're crazier than I am.'

Fernandez-Jones is unfazed.

'When your father brought you to me, he told me he knew for certain that you had killed.' He speaks in a softer, more even tone now. 'You freely admitted it to him and your mother. There was something inside you that you couldn't control. He also knew that, for all intents and purposes, you were also a caring, loving young man and he was desperate to keep that side of you as the dominant one. He wanted to prevent you from hurting anyone again.'

I shake my head so vigorously that the tendons in my neck seize up from when the only person I know I've killed attacked me. I don't believe Fernandez-Jones. I don't *want* to believe him. 'If that was true, why didn't you go to the police?'

He offers a humourless laugh. 'Damon, why would I do that when you offered me the perfect case study? You were an otherwise normal, even endearing boy, who happened to possess antisocial aspects to his personality and who acted aggressively with poor impulse control and elements of Reactive Attachment Disorder. That you traversed many typical diagnoses made you difficult to pigeonhole. Some of your behaviour was undeniably psychopathic, but that was fleeting. You were able to form genuine emotional bonds, you had empathy and felt immense remorse for the pain you had inflicted. The dual aspects within the same persona fascinated me. You had your whole life ahead of you. A life that I could shape through my treatment. We were all in agreement that you needed help to make you forget what you had done, and to steer you on to a different, better path.'

'Rubbish,' I say. 'You're trying to justify using your illegal methods on a child. And now you're trying to cover your own back. You already told me that ECT can't erase specific memories. Now you're saying that's what you did.'

He doesn't offer a direct answer to this. 'With repeated procedures, I was able to accomplish what I set out to do: take away your murderous impulses and help you to forget. And you cannot deny that it worked, until your recent brushes with death. Think of your brain as you would a computer you are disposing of. You can't erase everything by deleting the hard drive. It reassigns that space so that more recent files – or in your case, new memories – can be added. Only, these new files are now competing for space with the old. Perhaps it's time to jig them around again.'

An intrusive thought appears from nowhere and sets my skin prickling like it's charged with static. I imagine, in spectacularly vivid detail, punching Fernandez-Jones to the ground, shoving a fistful of electrodes down his throat and turning one of his machines up to full power. Then I watch as his body fits and spasms with shock after shock, until he bleeds violently from each and every orifice. I wave the scene away. Where the hell did that come from? Being here is clearly no good for my already fragile mental health.

'This is over,' I say. 'You're wasting my time.'

I turn my back on him and approach the door.

'Callum Baird,' he says. I'm stopped in my tracks. But I don't turn around. 'You know the name, don't you?'

'What about him?'

'He was one of the children you killed. You told me yourself.'

Without warning, the ground beneath me begins to crumble. I haven't mentioned the boy to him by name, so how could he know him? *Dad*, I tell myself. *Dad killed him and told Fernandez-Jones I did it.* But why? What would he gain from doing this? I steady myself against the wall as the dead boy appears to me again, standing in the corner of the office. I glare at him as he places his fingers inside his mouth and begins to pull something out. It's a piece of material. Not once in my previous hallucinations did I realise his dark hole of a mouth was actually a cloth stuffed inside it. Slowly, it unfolds and I eventually recognise what it is: one of the handkerchiefs I used for my nosebleeds. The initials DL are embroidered in the corner.

Fernandez-Jones is clearly oblivious to the boy's presence.

Of course he is. The boy is mine alone.

I suddenly become aware of my racing heart and how light my head is. I need air. I need to get out of here. I hurry out of the room and retrace my steps through the house as Fernandez-Jones follows. I get lost and panicky but eventually I locate the front door. By now, my stomach is churning and I bend over and begin to dry-heave over the lawn.

'You might not remember what you've done, but you know I'm right, don't you?' Fernandez-Jones asks my back. 'You know that you're capable of killing. And I wonder if you've done it since?'

I turn to face him. 'Yes,' I whisper. 'Once.' My answer lights up his face.

He suggests we could begin another course of ECT therapy, but I shake my head.

'Allow me to help you again,' he persists as I walk up the gravel path. 'This time I can help you remember or help you forget. You decide. I can make it happen if you let me.'

I slow my pace until I stop, then turn to him. I no longer possess the ability to read a person. I cannot tell if he is looking at me with the eyes of a devil or an angel. His crooked smile doesn't help.

'Come back inside, Damon. What do you have to lose?'

I want to tell him to go to hell and that I don't need him, that I've never needed him. But I don't.

'I want to remember,' I say.

And I follow him back inside.

CHAPTER 72

DAMON

It's 2009. I am eleven years old, and neither Callum nor I know it yet, but within weeks, I will kill him.

For now, I watch us in his lounge, logged into his dad's Xbox account, building animated fantasy football teams and competing against one another in FIFA tournaments. A few months earlier, Callum moved into the flat next door with his father, following the death of his wife from cancer. As kids often do, we built up an instant rapport, spending most evenings and weekends playing together. I'm drawn to his dad, Lloyd, as much as I am Callum. Mum says my own dad has begun working on a building site nearby, but he hasn't bothered to drop by. He has a knack for making me feel worthless even when I haven't seen him in months. So why as an adult did I think he'd died a couple of years earlier? More unanswered questions.

However, my relationship with Callum at school isn't mirroring our time away from it. From morning until mid-afternoon, I don't exist in his life. He is a year above me and has his own friends. He gives me the cold shoulder each time I try to become a part of their group. Being pals in public with someone younger than you isn't cool, he reminds me. And I reluctantly accept it.

Mum has taken a shine to Callum and the feeling is mutual. Especially when his dad begins travelling cross-country as a delivery driver. Lloyd slips Mum money each week to keep an eye on his son and ensure he's fed and dressed in clean clothing. So Callum is a regular face around our breakfast and dinner table and Mum makes us both packed lunches for school. The extra responsibility seems to bring out something different in her. Maud visits less frequently, and Mum smiles more. I enjoy having a brother figure, even if it's only on his terms. But it's all odd. Until it isn't.

Now it's a hot Sunday afternoon and I watch as Callum and I return to my flat. I'm pouring us drinks when I hear him giggling by the lounge door. It's slightly ajar, and when I peek through it, I see Mum and Callum's dad together on the sofa, kissing. His hand is down the front of her joggers. Up until this point, I thought I liked Lloyd. But watching him and Mum together makes me uncomfortable. Going by the smile enveloping his face, Callum thinks differently.

Our parents are red-faced and flustered when they realise they've been caught. My gaze fixes on Mum, but she struggles to maintain eye contact with me when they sit us down and explain how they enjoy spending time together. I suddenly feel stupid for believing Mum has begun wearing make-up and started doing her hair because I've made her better. It's all for him. And it makes me wonder why he's enough to keep Maud away, and I'm not.

Soon after, Lloyd and Callum are spending all their time here with us, even though their own perfectly adequate home is next door. Dad must still have some friends around here who have told him Mum now has a boyfriend, because I've spotted him inside his van in the car park opposite. For twenty minutes I watched him from behind the net curtain, waiting for him to come up. He'd driven away by the time I gave in and made the first move. I spotted him again yesterday driving slowly past the flat.

Being around Callum is becoming a strain and I resent him for taking Mum's attention. I'm also angry at Lloyd because I'm sure him being around is stopping Dad from coming by to see me. The stress of it is making my childhood nosebleeds heavier and more frequent. A handkerchief becomes a permanent fixture in my pocket, much to the amusement of Callum and his friends. He says my initials on the edge, DL, stand for 'dick licker'. One day they jump on me in a quiet corner of the school playground, pushing me down and shoving two tampons up my nose. Then they wrap brown tape around my head to keep them firmly in place, and laugh as they run away. I rip out so much hair taking it off. Mum's response is that it's only a bit of fun.

'Your mum is dead,' I cruelly remind Callum the same week, to hurt him like he's hurting me. 'And you'll never have another one.'

'We'll see,' he replies cryptically and wanders off.

My situation further declines when Lloyd's job expands into Europe. He'll be gone for days at a time. I cry and shout when Mum announces Callum is moving in with us permanently. I beg for it to be her and me, even telling her I don't mind if Maud comes to stay again. The argument ends when I storm out of the kitchen to find a smug Callum in the hallway.

Our flat only has two bedrooms, so Lloyd gives Mum money to buy a bunk bed. Callum sleeps on the bottom. Sometimes I imagine waking up to find he has died in his sleep. Or I fantasise about holding a duvet over his face until he stops breathing. I feel it with such clarity, it's less like a fantasy and more of a re-enactment.

I grow to hate everything about him. The clicking noise his jaw makes as he chews; his constant sniffing and tuneless singing along to songs on the radio. And how he instinctively knows how to goad me, frequently finding ways to make me jealous of his relationship with Mum. He'll wait until I'm in the room before telling Mum how much he loves her. She soaks up every word before wrapping him in tight hugs. All the time, he's looking my way to view every second of my reaction. Callum and I get into our first fist fight the day he starts calling her 'Mum'. He wins, and I'm left bruised in body and ego.

Our relationship at school further deteriorates. He lies to everyone, telling them I'm a bedwetter; that I'm a pervert who likes to listen through the wall as our parents have sex, and that my real dad is a child molester and that's why he doesn't live with us. My life there becomes equally as miserable as it is at home. I report him to my teacher, who gives him a week of detentions, but Callum is still too pig-headed to stop. He just keeps on and on. I start doing stupid things to pay him back, like setting fire to his favourite West Ham football shirt and two of his schoolbooks with a box of matches I find in the kitchen. I do it in the bathroom, failing to understand it will warp and melt the bath itself. Mum catches me and puts it out with the shower before it can spread, then screams at me and grounds me for a fortnight. She also takes all my birthday money and spends it on a new shirt for Callum. I wish I'd set fire to him instead.

'You know you're not going to be living here much longer, don't you?' Callum begins one afternoon, out of Mum's earshot.

'We're not moving,' I reply.

'*We* aren't, but *you* are. When Dad gets back from Estonia, he's going to ask Mum to marry him.'

My heart sinks. 'Liar.'

'He showed me the ring he bought her. And once they're married, you're going to live with your paedo dad. She said there's not enough room in here for two kids, so you'll be staying with him. But don't worry, you can visit us. I might even let you stay in my room, once Dad's redecorated it.'

His words tap into my worst fear – being separated from Mum. A fear generated years earlier by Dad's departure. Maud hasn't succeeded in pushing us apart, but this cuckoo is.

And I won't allow it to happen.

Something takes charge of me, a raw, unrelenting rage that's unlike anything I've ever experienced before. I hate this boy so much that it burns each part of my body. It radiates from the blood surging through my veins and boiling my skin, to my skull that wants to explode under the seething pressure. And I instinctively know the only way to release this suffocating tension is to hurt the source of it.

I grab a pair of scissors from Mum's knitting basket. Then I turn to face Callum.

CHAPTER 73

DAMON

Now I watch myself chasing Callum Baird along the corridors of our block of flats. He is showboating, screaming with devilish laughter as he runs. He isn't taking me seriously. But he should.

'Help,' he yells, pretending to be in fear as he runs down the staircases, before sprinting across the estate and towards a tree-lined pathway. 'The paedo's son is trying to grab my arse!'

He is faster than me, but I'm no longer the Damon he thinks I am. I should not be underestimated. I have more determination and more staying power. He turns as he runs, to see how far behind I am, and I see from his expression that I'm much closer than he was expecting. We pass a man leaning against a building, a can of lager in his hand who swears when I almost knock into him. I recognise him now as the man who yelled at me when I revisited the flat all those years later.

Callum leaves the path and runs through some patchy undergrowth. But as he turns again to see where I am, he stumbles and falls into an adjacent street. Almost before I can process what's happening, a van clips him and his body is thrown over the vehicle and he lands on the road. The vehicle screeches to a halt and the horrified driver hurries out.

It's my dad.

I'm returned to who I was before I saw red. Still furious but trying to make sense of what's happened.

I stare at Dad. He looks nothing like he does now. He's slimmer, his tattoos fresh and his build more athletic. He is as white as a ghost and it takes a couple of seconds for him to register me, before he turns his attention to Callum's motionless body.

'I – I didn't see him,' Dad stutters. 'It was an accident.'

I say nothing. He looks behind him and then to the other side of the road, but there are no other cars or pedestrians in sight. Meanwhile, I'm fixed on Callum. Dad has taken his life and it feels like an anti-climax. It should have been me.

'Help me,' Dad says suddenly. 'Take his legs.'

I hesitate, unsure of his plan.

'Damon!' he yells and I snap out of my trance. He doesn't see me slip the scissors into my pocket. I do as he orders, and Dad lifts the boy under his arms before we place him on the path.

'I need you to call for help,' he says.

'Why can't you?'

He is in tears and his hands are trembling. 'I'm still on parole and the van isn't insured. I'll be straight back inside. Please, go and find someone. Tell them you found him like this. Don't say we moved him, or anything at all about me. You promise?'

I nod and Dad looks nervously around him. 'I need to go,' he says and he starts back towards his van, then turns to look at me. 'I'm sorry. I'm supposed to protect you, not the other way around.' Then he hurries the rest of the way to the van, pulls away and vanishes as quickly as he appeared. It's only when he leaves that I spot a silver cigarette lighter that has fallen from his pocket. I pick it up and keep it for myself – my solitary possession of my dad's.

Now it's only Callum and me. I stand over his body, regarding him. My fury has died down and I see him for what he is. Skin and bones and a heart that no longer beats. He is not a threat to me. There are no obvious injuries to his body, with the exception of an angular elbow. It looks as if he is asleep. But then his eyes suddenly open and I jump.

'I need help,' he groans between laboured breaths. 'I can't move my legs.'

'I'll go get help,' I say. I'm about to start running when he speaks again.

'You called him Dad.'

My stomach clenches. 'It was an accident,' I say. 'He didn't mean to hurt you.'

'You did this together. I'm going to tell the police.'

'No, please don't,' I say, panicked. 'I'll find help. I can make it right.'

'You'll never see Mum again,' he manages to taunt while still struggling for breath. He cannot help himself. Even like this, when his life is in my hands, he is taunting me.

'She loves me,' I argue.

'No she doesn't. Nobody does.'

No, no, no, I think. I cannot let this happen again. Because if I raise the alarm and he is right, I'll be alone. I'll lose everything to him. I will not let him ruin my life any more than he has.

So I lower myself on to him, pressing into his stomach and further constricting his ability to breathe. And for the first time since I've known him, he is scared of me.

'Get off,' he wheezes.

Then I take the handkerchief he's humiliated me for using and thrust it into his mouth and deep down the back of his throat.

Now too weak to fight me off, he begins choking on the cloth. His expression switches from panic, to imploring me to stop and spare him. But I can't – I won't – risk losing everything because of him.

Finally, the boy's eyes glaze over and the fight leaves his body.

I have murdered Callum Baird.

CHAPTER 74

DAMON

By the time I get home to the flat, the anger that consumed me has vanished, leaving behind it a frightened schoolboy. Callum is late returning home, but Mum isn't worried. He is rarely punctual. Then later, when swarms of police descend below the flats, and white tents are erected and sniffer dogs are deployed, Mum joins the other neighbours downstairs to find out what's happening. Word-of-mouth spreads, and Callum's name is mentioned.

The fallout begins.

His dad is driving his truck back from Estonia when the police contact him. My distraught mum breaks the news to me as we await Lloyd's return, then she holds me tightly as we cry in each other's arms – her tears for the loss of a boy she cared about, mine in gratitude for having Mum to myself again. I play the part of the grieving friend well, asking all the right questions, becoming upset when necessary, accepting sympathy from schoolteachers and whoever else offers it.

I know what I have done to Callum is wrong. But he was terrible and bent on my destruction, and it has given me the outcome I wanted. So was it really so awful?

In the days that follow, I devote all my attention to my devastated mum, ensuring she eats regularly and rests. I field visits from worried friends and make the police family liaison officer cups of tea when he comes round. He tells me a witness claims to have seen a boy matching my description chasing another child at the time of Callum's death. But he says the man is alcohol-dependent, so can't be relied upon. Weeks on from the discovery of Callum's body, I will hear that man shouting over the balcony at me, 'I know what I saw! They didn't listen, but I know!'

For the most part, it's only Mum and me for the first time in ages. It's like old times. Even Maud is nowhere to be seen.

Dad appears one morning shortly after breakfast. Mum allows him in and he tells her how sorry he is. His stubble looks prickly and his hair greasy, like he hasn't washed it or shaved in days. He and I make eye contact several times but it's never only us together. We say nothing about what happened. About what I am allowing him to believe he did. I keep my hand in my pocket, balling the handkerchief in my palm. In the other I clutch Dad's cigarette lighter.

Lloyd returns and blames his son's death on Mum for not keeping a close enough eye on him. His words devastate her, and the last time we see Lloyd is days later, when he packs up his clothes and terminates their relationship. I can't stop smiling. Callum's exit is the gift that keeps on giving.

I attend Callum's funeral alone as Mum can't even leave her bed. Even as I watch his white coffin being carried into the church on the shoulders of pallbearers, I can't pretend to feel remorse. Because every time Mum holds me tightly like she's afraid to let go, I know what I did was right.

CHAPTER 75

DAMON

My heart sinks the moment I recognise a familiar face in my next life event being spooled out for me by Fernandez-Jones's tatty but still quite functional equipment. Because I remember who he is and what happened to him. The little boy my Mum carries so often is my baby brother. And he is the first person I ever killed.

I'm almost three years old when Mum and Dad bring him home from hospital. Their faces are exhausted, but delighted. I can smell the scent of fresh cotton as Bobby is carried into the living room. Dad asks me to be a little quieter in case I wake him up. He shows me how to use gentle hands when I stroke the velvety skin of my brother's face.

Mum and Dad are still together when Bobby arrives. I don't know if he creates ripples in their relationship or if he is here to paper over existing cracks. But if it's the latter, it isn't working. In the weeks that follow they are arguing more than ever. If it's not in front of me, then it's behind closed doors, but the flat is small so I can hear every fraught word.

I don't think Bobby is the easiest of babies. Dad now sleeps on the sofa and my brother screams long into the night. There are many appointments with health visitors, and I tag along for regular trips to the doctor's surgery. But no one can diagnose what the problem is or how to solve it. He's only, apparently, being a baby.

The more attention Bobby requires, the less I get. Something has to give.

It turns out to be Dad. He starts spending more and more time away from the flat, leaving Mum to cope alone.

I watch myself clinging on to his leg, understanding he is leaving, but not why. He tries to explain he'll be staying with my grandmother but it's only for a few days. He says he is putting me in charge of looking after Mum and my brother. Minutes later, his role in my life switches from regular fixture to bit-part player. He never spends another night under our roof. It's me, Mum and a screaming baby who doesn't know he's responsible for tearing our family apart.

Later, Mum moves a then six-month-old Bobby from her bedroom into mine, and just like that, dosed up on the special tablets she gets from Florence who lives downstairs, she's rendered herself deaf to his cries for attention. It's left to me to try to soothe him back to sleep. I talk to him, show him my picture books, leave my soft toys in his cot and sing him songs I learn at nursery.

Dad has been stopping by, but Mum punishes him for abandoning us by not allowing him inside. I stand watching from behind a crack in the lounge door as they have furious rows on the doorstep in front of the neighbours.

My three-and-a-half-year-old's logic suggests that if Bobby can sleep through the night, Mum will go back to her old self, she'll be nicer to Dad, and he'll move back in with us. None of this would be happening if Bobby behaved as well as I did.

So later that night, as Bobby shrieks in his cot, I take a blue chequered blanket he sleeps under and hold it over his face. I stroke his fine, blond hair and gently shush him as his little arms and legs flap, then I sing him 'Rock-a-bye Baby' until he finally falls silent. My plan has worked. I've got him off to sleep. I grin as I place the blanket back over his little body, ready to go and tell Mum. I change my mind; she needs her rest. So I slip back into my own bed and wait until morning to inform her that she can call Dad and tell him to come home because I can make my brother sleep.

Only, before I have the opportunity, I awake to screams ringing throughout my bedroom. The next moments I witness happen fast and furious. Paramedics arrive; my distraught dad appears and a hysterical Mum blames herself for why Bobby won't wake up. And while I understand that I am now the reason for this, something deep inside urges me to remain silent.

Sometimes I crawl into bed with Mum and she holds me for hours like I'm a teddy bear. I don't complain. I need it as much as she does. When new visitors arrive, I see myself asking if they can show me their wrists. Then I put my fingers on them trying to find a pulse, mimicking what I saw the paramedics do with Bobby. Only when I'm happy I can feel one do I walk away and leave them.

But my closeness isn't to last. Because this marks the first appearance of her friend Maud.

I know as an adult that my childhood actions came from a good place, even if their consequences were devastating. And I wonder if they're the foundations that created the boy I became? Perhaps I learned from my brother's death that to get what I want, I have to take control. Because it worked with Bobby and then Callum Baird. Though not so much later in life, with Melissa. It didn't matter how much I loved her or wanted her to stay, she still left me. And it certainly didn't work with Daisy Barber. I couldn't control her.

That's why I had to kill her instead.

CHAPTER 76

DAMON

I first meet Daisy a few months after Callum's death. She has joined the school midway through the September term. She tells me she recently moved to the area after her mum separated from her father. I am completely besotted, and she seems to like me too. I love everything about her, from her poker-straight, dark blonde hair, pushed back and held in place with an Alice band, to the way she smiles or glances at me with her piercing amber eyes, which makes a tingling sensation spread from my stomach to more intimate areas. And she smiles and glances at me a lot, much more than at the other boys in our year.

We might both be twelve but she has a maturity I lack. It doesn't stop her from choosing to sit next to me in shared lessons and at lunchtimes. She doesn't ask me before buying double portions from the school canteen when Mum is too distracted by Maud to remember to give me money for food. She invites me back to her house for tea and we play for hours. There are times when I try to pluck up the courage to kiss her, but I'm always too nervous to risk rejection. So I keep my feelings – and my lips – to myself.

I want our relationship to remain like this forever. Her and me, the best of friends. But life moves on and I watch as, to my dismay, so does Daisy. Her mum begins dating a work colleague, an older man who drives a brand-new Mercedes and has two mid-teen daughters of his own. Soon, Daisy starts spending more of her weeknights with them than me.

Her appearance is altering too. She starts wearing baby-pink lip gloss and a little eye make-up. Her T-shirts now expose her belly button and her skirts are creeping up above her knee. When we are together, she is barely off the brand-new iPhone her mum's boyfriend bought her. She's messaging and replying to names that flash across her screen, people I've never heard of. She is leaving me behind. That's when my inherent possessiveness rises to the surface.

I do my best to try to prevent it. I even try to shoplift a pay-as-you-go phone from Tesco so I can join in with her text chats. But to my shame, I'm caught by a security woman and my furious mum has to come to the store to pick me up and apologise. I feel sick when I discover Daisy had a thirteenth birthday party she didn't invite me to.

But I don't want to give up on her. I ask her to join me at a family fun day at Archbishop's Park, close to where she lives, to celebrate the forthcoming London 2012 Olympics. She apologises, saying she can't because she's poorly with 'girl's problems', and I pretend to know what she means. Despite my disappointment, I go alone.

The familiar tingling sensation appears when I spot her amongst the crowd of thousands later that day. I assume she must have changed her mind and come to find me. I raise my hand above my head to wave, stopping short when I see she's with a group of older girls and boys I don't recognise, along with the daughters from her recently blended family.

Witnessing them all in this tight-knit group suddenly makes me self-conscious. They're dressed in cool T-shirts and trainers, their hair is styled, and they carry portable speakers playing music. I am not like them. I'm angular and awkward, skinny and clad in clothes bought from Brixton Market. I know nothing of their world. So for much of the afternoon, I watch from afar as Daisy dances, laughs or yells in faux-terror as fairground rides spin her in different directions.

I continue to follow her until dusk begins to fall and the event prepares to draw to a close. As her new friends make their way towards the Tube station, Daisy is left alone. She sets off by foot through a much quieter section of the park until she crosses a road then reaches a second area of greenery. There is no one else about so I take my opportunity to talk to her alone.

'Oh hi,' I say, appearing from the darkness behind her.

'Damon!' she shouts, her face flushed. 'Oh my God, you scared me to death. Why are you creeping up on me?'

'I wasn't, I was on my way home from the park when I spotted you. Are you feeling better?' I ask, even though we both know she has lied. But it doesn't matter. I'll forgive her for anything. That's what you do when you're in love.

'Yes,' she continues. 'My stepsisters asked me if I wanted to join them.'

So they're already family to her. 'You should have called me.' I smile. 'I'd have tagged along.'

'It was a last-minute thing and you don't have a mobile phone.'

My face reddens. 'Well, do you want to do something tomorrow instead? I'm free all day. We could get McFlurries from Maccy D's? Or take our bikes round Victoria Park?'

Her flinch is slight, but it's there.

'What about a film?' I persist. Movies were our thing. During the Easter school holidays, she'd rent at least one DVD a day from

Blockbusters and I'd borrow them from the library. 'We could watch the new *Toy Story* movie at the Odeon?'

'That's a kids' film,' Daisy scoffs.

'But you liked the other ones.'

'When I was twelve, but I'm thirteen now.'

We walk in silence while my brain races through other suggestions. The thought of losing her makes me anxious.

'Do you want to be my girlfriend?' I suddenly blurt out.

Daisy stops in her tracks. 'No thanks,' she says firmly.

'Why?'

'Because you have to love someone to be their girlfriend.'

'But we're together all the time.'

She eye-rolls. 'Things change.'

'Why?'

'They just do. Anyway, I said I'd go to the cinema with Luke tomorrow.'

A chill skitters across my shoulders. 'Who?'

'I met him at the park. He told me he thinks I'm pretty, and he asked me out.'

I know the boy she's referring to. A tall lad with snow-white Air Jordan trainers and Beats by Dre headphones hanging loosely around his neck. He was stuck to her side like a leech for much of the afternoon.

'I think you're pretty too,' I offer. 'And he's old. He must be like, fourteen.'

Her forehead furrows. 'How do you know Luke?'

I can't lie quickly enough. 'I saw you with him.'

She scrunches up her face. 'If you were spying on me, that's creepy.'

Daisy picks up her pace. This is going badly. So in a last-ditch attempt to prove to her how much I care, I grab her arm, spin her around and plant my lips on hers. I desperately try to find an opening in her mouth with my tongue like I've seen men do in the porn films Callum used to show me on his dad's computer. *Hard and fast*, that's how they like it. But her response is to shove me backwards. I lose my footing and fall to the ground, landing on my side.

'What do you think you're doing, you weirdo?' she yells. 'You don't *force* yourself on a girl!'

'I didn't!' I reply. 'I'm showing you how much I love you.'

'Damon, get this through your head. I don't love you and I'll never love you. You're just a boy.'

'No, I'm not. I'm more of an adult than you.' She laughs and I desperately try to find something, *anything*, to make her stay. Make her realise I'm more mature than she knows. 'I killed someone once!' I blurt out in desperation.

Her face pales. 'What?'

Shit! What have I said? I know I should stop, tell her I'm joking and walk away, but I can't help myself. 'His name was Callum. He was bullying me and tried to poison my mum against me, so I killed him. I couldn't have done that if I was just a kid.'

'I don't believe you,' she says. But when my expression doesn't falter under her scrutiny, I see she knows I am telling the truth. And instead of it demonstrating I'm more mature than she believes, she's scared. She turns her back on me and hurries further down the path and deeper into the encroaching night until she is little more than a wavering shadow amongst the trees and a flickering streetlight above. Nobody but she and I know we are here.

The girl I adored wants nothing to do with me. The rage that first made its presence felt the day I killed Callum returns within the blink of an eye. My head pounds like thunder rolling through the sky above us and I know the only way to relieve it is to hurt her like she is hurting me. So I clamber to my feet, pick up the first object I can find – a rock – and now I'm running after her. She must hear the crunching of gravel under my feet because she also begins to run, but she is no match for my grit and urgency.

I hit the back of her head so hard with the rock, she staggers forward, which makes it easy for me to shove her to the path. I turn her over and mount her, forcing her to see what she is making me do. But she is impossible to pin down properly and keeps squirming and turning her head to one side, in a vain attempt to protect herself as she yells for help.

Instead of trying to silence her cries by stuffing a handkerchief down her throat like I did with Callum, I hit her once more with the weapon, and then over and over again, until no one can ever call her pretty again.

CHAPTER 77

DAMON

Back in the present, I stare at Fernandez-Jones as I lie on the bed in his office. There's a bitter aftertaste in my mouth from the two anti-sickness tablets I've swallowed. I don't, I can't, speak. Nothing has ever overpowered me like the ECT I've just undergone. Not even my childhood urges to kill. He warned me that both nausea and migraines might follow treatment, and how they'd be more severe if I insisted on refusing his offer of a general anaesthetic or even a muscle relaxant. He doesn't understand that I've spent too much of my life as a spectator. That I now need to *feel* the things I fear the most, including the electrical current going into my brain.

The details of what happened when he got to work on me are scant, but I do remember my whole body jerking then stiffening. Fernandez-Jones tells me now the seizure was brief, half a minute at most, but it felt much, much longer to me. Now, he has his notebook out and his fountain pen in his hand and he's asking me questions, but I don't have the cognitive capacity to listen or respond. Instead, I'm thinking about what I've learned. In a few short moments he has given me the clarity I've spent months searching for. And as a result, I know almost everything. Memories that were taken away from me have returned. Not all, but enough to paint a more detailed picture of my past.

I think I must fall asleep, because I don't remember catching him moving to the chair behind his desk. He's writing again in his notebook, too busy to spot me regaining consciousness. He hasn't seen me watching the man who's returned so much of what he once took away. I'm aware that guilt at what I've done in the past should be clawing at me like an animal trying to scratch its way out of a locked room. I should be spiralling and racked with self-loathing. But I don't feel those things. Instead, a calmness has descended.

I'm no longer the person I was a few days ago, or even earlier today, when I first approached his front door. I have returned to the one they tried to erase. The one Fernandez-Jones met with when I was twelve.

The one he is about to become the first person to witness the return of.

I'm aware of Callum in the room with us, and before I turn to face him, he opens his mouth, once again pulling at the handkerchief I wedged into it. He is muttering that familiar phrase that always sounds something like 'oodis' as he tugs at it.

'Oodis,' he continues as he slowly pulls more of it out.

'Youdis,' he is saying.

No: 'You dis.'

Now he holds the handkerchief in his hand. And finally, I understand what he has been trying to tell me, ever since he first appeared.

'You did this.'

A sudden rush of energy passes through me and I hear what sounds like the crackling of static electricity. I know I'm imagining it, but I still look to Callum to see if he heard it too. He knows what I'm thinking because the corners of his mouth lift as his eyes narrow. My head feels thick and heavy, like a crushing weight on my shoulders. There is only one way to alleviate it. My expression mirrors Callum's and we nod to one another.

Together, we look at Fernandez-Jones, who is completely oblivious to our candid exchange.

CHAPTER 78

LAURA

Laura reacts to the video of Garry twice being run over by Damon as casually as she might respond to a TikTok short of pets doing silly things. This clip is something she returns to regularly. Sometimes she'll replay it to see if it prompts an emotional response, as she has yet to muster up a shred of guilt for sending Garry to his death. Today is no different. She feels nothing. She can justify her lack of concern by reminding herself they weren't really friends, so the murder of a drug-dealing rapist is no great personal loss to her. A minor inconvenience. The only emotion she concedes to is a small pang of jealousy for the moment she views Damon leaning over Garry's body, and how he might have caught his last breath without even realising it. Without *appreciating* it. It's like eating caviar on a digestive biscuit.

'How far do you want me to go with him this time?' Garry asked, when they last met face to face at a café close to the hospital where they once both worked. She'd been a volunteer visitor and he was a porter, wheeling patients in chairs and beds from ward to theatre. One day she had watched from a doorway as he'd pocketed medication from the sleeping and unconscious. He later admitted, when pressed, that he'd sell those meds on the nights he moonlighted as a nightclub doorman. She'd promised not to report him, but told him in return she might one day need a favour. A year later and she had called on him for help with Damon.

'What we did last time wasn't enough for him to take me seriously,' she said. 'That's my fault. I need you to up the ante.'

'Kill him? Because that ain't my—'

'No. I want him to come away terrified of what I'm capable of doing to get what I want. I want to make his life hell.' So hellish, in fact, that death would become a more attractive option than life.

He nodded. 'And what did he do to twist your tampon?'

'He took something away that he promised to me,' she replied vaguely. It was better Garry didn't know the ins and outs. He wouldn't understand.

Three weeks have passed since Garry was run over. When Laura discovered his car, she also checked each refuse container to see if one contained him. There was no trace of his body, so she assumes he's in a landfill somewhere with the rest of the rubbish. *Such a waste, quite literally*, she thinks, then chuckles.

She switches from that video clip to another, the footage she recorded in Damon's apartment. Specifically, the moment before he was supposed to die. His taut limbs, the fear in his face, the guttural gasps travelling up his throat as he tried to fight her. While this video encourages her brain to release enough dopamine to cause her skin to tingle, it stops short of giving her that feeling of euphoria she craves. There's only one way for that to return. And it is all dependent on Damon dying again.

It's been a fortnight since she sent him the clip of Garry's last moments. He has been left to stew for long enough. Laura scrolls through her WhatsApp messages and rereads his twenty-seven replies she has yet to respond to. There's a lightness in her chest when she thinks of his increasing anxiety, signalled by the arrival of each successive message. They're a delight to review, becoming angrier and angrier and eventually more threatening. She rereads his last few.

What the fuck do you want from me? he wrote. And now she is ready to reply.

We had an agreement, she texts.

His response comes almost immediately. *You had a rope tied around my neck. You were trying to kill me. Not bringing me back wasn't part of our agreement.*

Do you believe everything your ex-wife tells you?

A minute passes before he responds.

What do you want from me? he asks.

What I'm owed.

And what do you think that is?

For her own amusement, she responds with three emojis. The first, a rope with a knot in it. The second is a face exhaling a puff of air. And the third is a coffin.

She hits send, then switches her phone off and enjoys a second dopamine influx.

CHAPTER 79

DAMON

I place my phone face down on the coffee table without replying. So Melissa was right: Laura planned to kill me that night. I think I doubted Melissa's interpretation of events because I didn't want to admit to myself I made a huge mistake in trusting a stranger to be honest about their reasons for helping me to die. And now Laura has made it clear she wants to finish what she started. Only she doesn't know who she's up against. I'm not the same man she tried to kill last time, or even the person she sent that video to. Now I know the truth about myself, I fear nothing and no one. But for now, I'll allow her to believe she has me over a barrel. It's easier to fool the enemy when they're blinded by arrogance.

I open the fridge door in search of a bottle of beer. It's devoid of both food and alcohol, so I slip on a jacket, pull my hood up and leave the flat.

My neighbours who argue so often are at it again. They are walking up the staircase towards me as I descend, the first time I have actually seen them in person. They can't be any older than their late teens. How can two people be so dysfunctional at such a young age? He is yelling at her again, telling her she is a waste of space and he can do better. I feel an unexpected and frankly exhilarating hostility swelling up inside me and clench my fists as we prepare to cross paths. I purposely catch him with my shoulder and he loses his balance, falling backwards down three steps and landing flat on his back.

'The *fuck*?' he manages, while clearly winded.

'Sorry, mate,' I say, and stop to grab his arm to lift him back to his feet. And as I do so, I whisper in his ear. 'I have a spare key to your flat,' I inform him, 'and if you talk to your girl like shit again, I will stab you to death in your fucking bed.' He's standing on his own again now, but I hold on to his arm. 'Understand?'

He's not sure he's heard me correctly until he looks into my eyes and sees who he's talking to. Who I really am. He doesn't know I'm lying to him, of course. About the spare key part, anyway.

He nods quickly, then I leave him, and as I make my way to a minimart a few streets away, there's a rush of something pumping through my veins that leaves me excited. What I did, what I said, to that kid wasn't me. I don't behave like that. Yet I did, only a few minutes ago. And it's left me buzzed.

'You okay, mate?' asks the man behind the counter as I pay for my six-pack of San Miguel, a vape and a pack of refills. I'm a regular customer, so he recognises me. I catch a glimpse of myself in the convex mirror behind him. I'm a ghost of my former self. I look worse than those I hallucinate. Yet inside, I've never felt stronger.

'Long Covid,' I say, covering my mouth. I pay him and leave.

In need of a change of scenery, I make my way to a local park. I twist the cap off my first beer bottle as I lower myself on to a wooden bench. A bearded man of indeterminate age shuffles past me, pushing his worldly belongings in a shopping trolley and humming to himself. I wonder what's led him to where he is now. Perhaps he is thinking the same about me, because we are not that dissimilar. For a fraction of a second, a pulse of energy bubbles under the surface of my skin, a spark in search of something to ignite. I imagine smashing my bottle on the pavement and tearing it across his throat until his flesh is shredded. The moment passes almost as soon as it arrives. He glances at my stash, then at me, and without either of us saying a word, I offer him one. He nods his gratitude and wheels himself away.

I'm halfway through my own bottle when Daisy Barber takes a seat next to me. Her undamaged side stares ahead at a tree-lined island in the centre of a pond.

'Hi,' I say, but she doesn't respond.

I now understand how insecure and weak I have always been. So frightened of being left behind, left alone, of being unloved, I'd rather take a poor girl's life than allow her to hurt me any further.

I wait for the first of many tears to fall. Only, they don't arrive. I think I should cry for the lives I have taken away and the families I have destroyed. But my cheeks remain dry. Because I am awake and because monsters don't cry.

They simply behave . . . monstrously.

CHAPTER 80

DAMON

I look up at the building ahead of me – the DIY store where Dad works. I need to tell him what I now know about myself and hear in his own words why he took the fall for Daisy Barber's death. Why he sacrificed fifteen years of his life in prison for my behaviour. But no matter how he answers, I know we won't see each other again after today. He deserves a life more than I do. One far away from me and that I cannot taint. I will leave him to get on with what remains of it.

I stretch out my fingers and wince. I've removed the splint from my broken knuckles, but still they nag at me. And my ribs still ache from when Melissa resuscitated me a month ago. We haven't spoken since, but I intend to make things right on that front as well. One reparation at a time. And if she doesn't forgive me? I will find a way to make her.

I continue my inventory: I'm still walking with a stoop ever since my grandmother hit me across the back with a shovel. And the man who attacked me in the car park surely caused some degree of ligament damage to my neck when he tried to wrench me out of my vehicle. How I'm even still able to physically function amazes me.

The sliding doors to the store sweep aside for me as I make my way inside, hoping I'm not seen by either the security guard or the deputy manager who escorted me out last time I was here.

I've decided to approach Dad at his place of work instead of at home again so I don't cause my grandmother more unnecessary stress. Not that I care about her; she's a stranger to me. And besides, she strikes me as being a hardy old bird who can take care of herself. Like I can now.

'I've come to see Ralf Lister,' I say to the young staff member behind the customer service desk. 'Is he working today?'

'Can I ask what it's about?' she asks hesitantly.

'He's . . . my dad.'

She moves towards a microphone and her amplified voice asks a person whose name I don't recognise to come to the desk. She must have misheard me. I clench my right fist ever so slightly.

'I'm sorry,' I say. 'It's Ralf Lister I wanted.'

She looks me up and down and offers an apologetic smile but says nothing. Another sudden rush of energy passes through me along with the crackling of static electricity. With some effort, I overcome the urge to grab her by the collar and slam her face down on to the cash register. These urges are becoming more frequent and insistent, yet I'm still able to resist them. Does she thank me for this? No. Instead, we stand in silence until the deputy manager arrives. There must be a photo of me behind the desk and an order to contact him, not Dad, if I reappear. He's gathering himself to speak, but I pre-empt what he might have to say.

'I don't want any trouble,' I begin, and hold my hands up to my chest in mock surrender. 'I want to talk to him.'

He looks to the assistant, then back at me, and asks me to follow him into the lighting aisle. And what an accommodating fellow the deputy manager proves himself to be, for there Dad is, waiting for me a few metres away. His face is bruised and I spot a trickle of dried blood running from his ear to his neck. *Shit.* He looks rougher than me. He glares at me, but says nothing. It's the deputy manager who clears his throat and speaks.

'I'm very sorry to have to be the one to tell you this,' he says to me, 'but I'm afraid your dad died a couple of weeks ago.'

'What are you talking about?' I say. 'He's standing behind you.'

But as I point to the space Dad occupied an instant before, I see that he's vanished.

CHAPTER 81

LAURA

Damon's flat is even more depressing on her second visit than it was on her first. She remains by the front door, surveying the open-plan lounge, diner and kitchen. There are unwashed clothes blurring the lines between furniture and laundry, and uneaten food left inside open cartons cluttering the kitchen worktops. The air is suffused with a musty odour, somewhere between a gym changing room and a place where ambition crawls away to quietly die. She makes her way inside, pushing aside detritus with her boots.

She already knows Damon isn't here, as she watched him drive out of the car park twenty minutes ago. That's how long it took for her to find the supervisor's office and convince the young man working there that her boyfriend had taken both sets of house keys with him when he left and that his phone was now switched off. The touching effect of the rolled-up jumper tucked under her coat and the protective hand placed lovingly upon her pregnancy bump probably didn't require the distressed tears she summoned to convince him to allow her in, but she takes pride in her work.

It's by no means the first home Laura has gained entry to under false pretences, and she doubts it will be the last. However, these are typically homes of elderly people who have been admitted to where she works. It doesn't matter if she plunders the belongings of the terminally ill. She's a firm believer in the old saying 'You can't take it with you.'

Laura checks her watch. She doesn't know how long Damon will be away, so she gets to work. She would rather not be here, putting herself at risk, but he's given her little choice but to up the ante. It's a week since she sent him that text message, clearly spelling out what she expects from him. What he owes her. And how has he responded? Well, he hasn't. Not a single word. Either he is burying his head in the sand and pretending this isn't happening, or he doesn't appreciate the lengths she will go to – and has done in the past – to get what is rightfully hers. Each time she thinks about it, it's like a balled fist slowly expanding in her stomach. It stretches her insides so tight that sometimes the pain of not having what she wants makes her almost scream. She is so close to getting it that she can taste death in the back of her throat. And it is beautiful.

She glances around his home. She would like to believe that she will be doing him a favour by taking him away from all this, but she can't fool herself. His death will be infinitely more for her benefit than his. What he has to offer her is markedly different from all the others she has helped. Damon is someone completely unique.

Her plan for today was to merely add or alter something in his flat. Nothing threatening, on the order of what she once served up to a man who crossed her, which involved a pig foetus and his dead pregnant wife's wardrobe. And even now, when she thinks about it, she smiles at her innovativeness. Such extremes won't be necessary with Damon, however. She will only need to do enough to immediately make him realise his safe space has been compromised. Turn a sofa ever so slightly; move the cutlery in a drawer around; rearrange his bookshelf so the spines are colour-coded; rebuild his *Friends* Lego into something a little different.

But now that she is here, she realises this place is in far too sorry a state of disarray to carry out this scheme. So she wanders from room to room until she spots on a shelf an Audite – a second-rate Alexa-style virtual assistant – and a smile spreads across her face. That will do perfectly.

CHAPTER 82

DAMON

Sleep isn't always a given these days, but when it occurs, I can fall so deeply into it, it's like I'm dead in the water again. Because my dreams have become so crystal-clear, it's as if I am reliving moments I only ever witness when I'm drowning. Or when I had ECT again.

I don't know for how long I've been asleep, but a raucous, thundering noise brings me back to consciousness. Music plays at a high volume in the disorienting, near pitch-black of my bedroom. I try to grab the lamp on my bedside table but misjudge the space, and as I switch it on, I accidentally send it crashing to the floor. 'Hey Audite,' I yell over the noise. 'Stop music.'

However, it's playing at full volume so it cannot hear me.

In my groggy state I scramble to my feet and move towards the device to turn it off manually, when the chorus plays. I assume it's a software glitch because I haven't asked the Audite to play this. But when I realise the title of the song, I know who is responsible. It's 'Every Breath You Take' by The Police and includes lyrics about the protagonist's obsession with watching someone and how they have left them with a trail of broken promises and vows.

Laura has been inside my flat. And she wants me to know it. She wants to scare me, but it doesn't. Instead, I let out a laugh before I turn down the volume and ask it to play the song again. I actually admire Laura's tenacity. She's a psychopath who hates to be ignored. Don't they all, I guess. But she will have to wait a little longer before I give her what she wants and reply.

CHAPTER 83

DAMON

This place doesn't resemble any crematorium I've visited before. I exit my taxi and my sunglasses slip down my nose as I scour the immaculately landscaped gardens. It's more like the grounds of a plush country hotel than a place to bid farewell to a loved one. I count the number of other vehicles parked here. There are so few that I check my phone to see if I've made a mistake with the date. No, I have it right.

I make my way towards a set of wooden double doors under a tall arch, aware I probably shouldn't be here. I look around and half expect to see Laura, waiting to remind me of the debt she thinks she's owed. I finally replied to her a few days ago, confirming she will get what she wants but that I need to tie up some loose ends first. I first spelled loose with an 'n' by mistake and almost didn't bother to correct myself. Gallows humour, quite literally.

When? she replied.

Soon.

WHEN, came her response.

SOON, I replied, amused by her lack of patience. I have plans to capitalise on her frustration.

Two black vehicles appear. The first is a hearse with my father's coffin inside. The only flowers propped against the dark wooden box are a white floral letter tribute, spelling out the word 'son'. I take a few steps back and conceal myself behind a tree trunk as the doors to the second vehicle open and my grandmother steps out. A woman of a similar age supports her as my grandmother uses a walking frame to make her way inside.

Four pallbearers in identical dark suits and crisp white shirts carefully lift an inexpensive pine coffin on to their shoulders and carry it in. I wait for a moment before I follow, catching my reflection in one of the vehicle's windows. The black suit I wear that once fitted me now hangs off my shoulders. I hold my head down, hoping my grandmother doesn't see me, then make my way along the carpeted aisle until I reach the last row of wooden seats.

Organ music plays a hymn I don't recognise. I'm one of only nine people here. That's all my dad has to show for his fifty-plus years on this earth. Nine people who cared enough about him to want to say goodbye.

And that's my fault. Because who wants to remain friends with a child killer? If only they knew the killer isn't lying inside the coffin; he is sitting in the back of the room.

Finding where Dad's funeral service was to be held was a struggle. As no death notice was placed either online or in the local paper, I had to call almost every funeral director in the area until I found the one handling him. They were hesitant to give out details until I told them I was his son. The 8.30 a.m. start makes me wonder if they operate a special fast-track under-the-radar system for child murderers and other such monsters.

I pick up an order of service from the little stack on the chair between me and the aisle. It's one photocopied sheet and there's a mention of the only person Dad has left behind: 'his loving mother

Maisy'. There's a photograph of them together: him as a child, her in a café wearing a waitress's uniform.

A middle-aged man in a brown shirt, jumper and chinos takes to the podium and introduces himself as our celebrant. He explains this is a non-religious funeral that will honour my dad's life. I can't help thinking there isn't much to honour or celebrate. He talks about Dad's childhood, how his father died when he was young leaving his mum to raise him alone. I'm struck by our similarities and learn more about him in ten minutes than I have in twenty-nine years. There's a brief mention of Mum and the baby son they lost, but not of me. I don't exist in this version of events. There's also no mention of how Dad died. I wonder if our last confrontation was too much for him to handle emotionally and he took his own life?

Soon after, his coffin disappears behind a sweeping burgundy curtain, to the sound of the Oasis song 'Don't Look Back in Anger'. I've played this track a lot over the years, and several of the lyrics have been incorporated into my sleeve of tattoos. I assumed I gravitated towards it of my own accord, but perhaps I used to hear Dad playing it on the occasions we were together.

When I spot my grandmother rising to her feet, I bow my head so she can't see me. I give her five minutes after she leaves before I also go.

Only, she is standing outside, waiting for me.

CHAPTER 84

DAMON

I'm caught in the headlights of an oncoming juggernaut. I'm half expecting her to raise her walking frame and start clubbing me with it. And I don't think I'd try to stop her. I probably deserve all the pain she wants to inflict. Instead, she settles for glaring at me, venom present in her milky eyes. I'm intruding on her grief and I have never felt so despised by anyone in my life. Does it bother me? In all honesty and in my present state of mind – no.

'What the fuck are you doing here?' she snaps in her deep, fiery London accent.

'I wanted to say goodbye,' I say quietly.

'You think you deserve that privilege after what you put my son through?'

'I know you won't believe me, but I didn't remember anything about what happened back then, until recently.'

'I believe you, but I don't care,' she says. 'Do you know what you did to him?'

'I know he was innocent when he went to prison, and I can't imagine what he must have gone through—'

'No, you fucking idiot,' she interrupts, 'I don't mean then. I mean after you forced your way into my house. Do you know what happened?'

'I don't.'

My grandmother edges closer, and as one hand remains on her walking frame, she uses the other to jab me in the chest. Her nails are sharp like claws. 'Then ask me,' she says.

'Ask you?' I repeat.

'Ask me,' she hisses.

'What happened to him?'

'You killed him.'

She straightens her back and waits for me to absorb her words.

'I think you're confused, because he was alive when I left—'

'Fuck off,' she snaps. 'I might be old but I ain't away with the fairies just yet. When you pushed him and he lost his balance, he hit the back of his head on the TV cabinet. Later that night, he started complaining of a headache. I didn't think much of it as he's suffered from migraines for years.' *Like me*, I think. 'But then he collapsed. I called 999 but he was dead before the ambulance arrived.'

I'm unsure of how to respond, stifled by her revelation.

'The pathologist said it was likely a bleed to the brain. So you killed him, that's what happened. Like all the others, he's dead because of you.'

I ought to have known, because I hallucinated him in the aisle of his store. With the exception of Mum, I only see the people I kill. I should be overcome by emotion, or begging her for forgiveness, but I remain detached.

'What did he tell you about me before he died?' I ask.

'You mean before you *killed him*?'

I sense she is going to use every opportunity to remind me of this. I nod.

'When you left, Ralf told me the treatment they gave you all those years ago was wearing off. That you were beginning to remember. Like I always said you would. 'Cos evil don't stay buried for long. Good, I told him. Why should we be the only ones to suffer?'

'You knew what they did to me?'

'Yes, but I didn't agree with it. You were old enough to know right from wrong, *you* should've been punished for it, not my boy. He made me promise that if I ever saw you again, I wouldn't tell you anything.' Her brows knit. 'But I'm not like my son. I don't want to spare your feelings.' She points to the awaiting black funeral car. 'Get in,' she says.

And I do as I'm told.

CHAPTER 85

DAMON

As the vehicle pulls away from the crematorium, my grandmother orders the driver to roll up the partition. Now it's her and me alone together for the first time since I was a child. She stares from the window as the vehicle makes its way through the open gates and along the road outside. She pulls a small tin of tobacco from her purse and, without watching what she is doing, drops a pinch inside a rolling paper and creates the most perfectly symmetrical cigarette. I'm tempted to ask her for one. She lights it with a disposable orange lighter which has a black-and-white image of the Pope on the side. She doesn't unwind the window.

The sun's bright rays do nothing to defrost her. I don't really know where to begin, but I must find a starting point because I don't think she will. She might've told me to get inside but she isn't going to surrender what she knows that easily. And I doubt that after today there will be any other opportunities to have this conversation.

'What do I call you?' I ask.

She takes a long, deep drag on the cigarette. 'Nothing,' she replies. 'Because that's what you mean to me.'

Her point is valid. We are nothing more than strangers, bound together by blood. The blood of others I've shed, like my dad's.

'Why did Dad admit to killing Daisy Barber?' I ask.

'Why do you reckon?'

'He didn't want me to be blamed for it.' That's the only reason I can think of.

'If you know, then why are you asking?'

'How did he find out I was responsible?'

'I thought you said you can now remember everything?'

'Not all of it, no.'

She eyes me cautiously. 'If I tell you what you want to know, what's in it for me?'

I think for a moment. 'I don't know. I don't have much money . . .'

She offers a humourless laugh. 'I'm eighty-two years old. What would I want with blood money?'

'Then what?'

She leans closer to me. 'I want the truth to come out. I want you to admit to the police what you did to that girl. Tell them what you are and clear my boy's name.'

'What good will that do?'

'You took fifteen years of his life away from him. Then, when they set him free, you stole the rest of it. You owe him. An eye for an eye.'

'But he's dead.'

'I don't care!' she shouts, and she hits the armrest with her fist.

I look her squarely in the eye. She won't be backing down.

'Okay,' I say. 'I'll tell them.'

'Tell them what?'

'That I killed Daisy.'

She scans my face, searching for an almost hidden tell: a micro-expression that suggests I'm saying what she wants to hear.

'Detective Sergeant Barney Flynn.'

'Who?'

'Type his name into your telephone.'

'Why? Who is he?'

'Do as I tell you.'

I find a news story about him in which he discusses a manslaughter trial in which the defendant was found guilty.

'Where is he based now?' she asks.

'A station in Bromley-by-Bow. London.'

'I know where fucking Bromley is,' she snaps. 'Look it up. Is there a telephone number?'

'Yes.'

'Call it. You're going to admit right now, in front of me, to what you did.'

'I already told you I would.'

'I don't trust you as far as I can throw you, son. So if you want to know anything else, you'll call him now.'

I highlight the phone number on the website and call it. The twelve long rings it takes for them to answer are made more excruciating by the awkward silence in the car. 'Can I speak to DS Barney Flynn please?' I eventually ask.

The switchboard operator transfers me to another number. 'It's an answerphone,' I tell my grandmother, and I'm about to hang up.

'Leave a message,' she says.

'Saying what?'

'Work it out.'

I'm put on the spot. 'Hello, DS Flynn, my name is Damon Lister . . . my dad was Ralf Lister, who was imprisoned for the killing of Daisy Barber. I wonder if you could call me back.'

'Tell him why,' my grandmother interjects.

'Because I know my dad isn't guilty,' I add hastily. 'I'm responsible for her death and he was trying to protect me.'

I leave my number, hang up and look at her with daggers as equally sharp as hers. 'Happy?'

'As I'll ever be,' she replies, feigning nonchalance. 'So go on then. Ask away.'

CHAPTER 86

DAMON

'So what happened the day Daisy died?' I ask.

'Your mum came home early from work to find you burying a bloody T-shirt and jeans at the bottom of the wash bin,' my grandmother recalls. 'You tried to talk your way out of it like the born liar you are, claiming it was another one of your nosebleeds. But she didn't believe you. Too much blood. Finally you broke down and admitted to what you did. Bobbi called Ralf, bawling, and we got to hers to find her pinning you up against the fridge. She was hysterical. It was only after Ralf dragged her off you that you told them you didn't mean to hurt Daisy but that she didn't like you in the way you liked her.'

I should want to fold in on myself in shame, but I don't. I remain strangely collected.

'It was your mum who wanted to call the police,' she continues, 'but your dad talked her out of it. Said he'd sort it out. That what goes around comes around, whatever that meant.'

I'm about to ask why he did that, when I answer my own question. I assume he never forgave himself for making me complicit in covering up the death of Callum Baird. He told me before he drove away, leaving me to get help, that he was supposed to protect me, not the other way around. I don't mention this to my grandmother because I don't know if she's aware of what he did. Besides, she is satisfied with her own interpretation.

'Told me it was his fault you turned out a wrong'un because you didn't have no father figure around to set you straight,' she continues. 'Regretted he didn't fight harder for you.'

'What do you mean?'

She hesitates, as if she doesn't want to continue this story. As if whatever she has to tell me might be something I want to hear.

'What do you mean?' I repeat.

'He never wanted to give up on you even though he fucked it up for himself by getting into trouble with the law. He wasn't a bad boy – not like you – but he served three years for kicking the shit out of that bloke your mum was seeing, the one who knocked you both about. Crushed a bunch of discs in his spine. Never walked properly again. Then later Ralf got done for robbing a corner shop when your mum went all looby loo and locked herself in the flat and couldn't work or afford to keep a roof over your heads. The gun didn't even have a bloody trigger, but they threw the book at him. He gave all he stole to Bobbi, and what'd he get for it? Her stopping him from seeing you when he was released. He begged her for access, threatened to go to court, wanted shared custody, but she wasn't having any of it. She knew a court would never side with a criminal over a mum.'

For all these years, I've thought he gave up on me. Like so many other assumptions I've made, I was wrong.

'What did Dad do after I admitted I'd hurt Daisy?'

'Let's call a spade a spade, shall we? You didn't only *hurt* her. You fucking *ruined* her.'

Another attempt by her to get a reaction. I don't respond.

'Once you told them what you'd done with her body, he drove there and put her in his car to hide her somewhere else. Took her clothes off in case your DNA was on them. He didn't spot the security cameras recording him from a building nearby. That's why he was arrested a few weeks later and her hair and blood was found in his car.'

I return to something my grandmother said earlier. 'You said it was Mum who wanted to call the police?'

She glares at me through a grey plume of smoke. 'Bobbi had a total fucking meltdown. Started believing what some old alcoholic neighbour told her about seeing you chasing that Callum kid shortly before his body was found. Refused to believe it at the time, but couldn't hide from the truth any longer. Convinced herself you battered him because you were jealous. She couldn't handle having a kid capable of not just one murder but two. Your dad said he'd get you help. But she didn't want you anywhere near her. He wanted to bring you to mine, but I wasn't having any of it either. I said you should be locked up, that it wasn't safe for you to be out on the streets. Turns out you weren't safe to be indoors either.'

'I don't understand?'

My grandmother takes a last drag on her cigarette before stubbing the remainder of it out in the footwell. She gives me a hard stare.

'You really don't remember, do you?' she asks.

I shake my head. It feels heavy. She makes me wait for what she has to say next. The mean old cow is loving this.

''Cos indoors was where you killed your mum,' she adds.

CHAPTER 87

DAMON

My grandmother's unwavering gaze tells me she believes she's telling the truth. I don't doubt there's a lot she remembers accurately, but this isn't one of those moments.

'Mum killed herself,' I say. 'I was there. I . . .' The words catch in my throat. A hint of emotion for the first time in our face-off. 'I saw her jump from the window. I remember it.'

'Have you asked yourself why you were watching her from outside?' she asks. 'Why you weren't in the flat with her?'

I recall again what I saw when I drowned. My mum jumping to save herself from the flames. But I remember nothing of the moments leading up to the fire and how I ended up standing outside. 'I was probably out playing on my bike or something.'

'You were the first person on the scene,' she says. 'Some of your neighbours saw you staring up at the window as the heavens opened, even before the fire alarms rang. But you didn't call for help.'

'I was only a kid. I must've been trying to make sense of what was happening.'

'You were *twelve*. Old enough to know what a fucking fire looks like and what you should've done. So no, son, don't kid yourself. You were watching and waiting. You knew what was happening.'

I shake my head. 'She was my mum. I loved her.'

'You tried to lie your way out of it at first, telling your dad it was probably some old woman who was staying with your mum who started it. But none of us had ever heard or seen hide nor hair of this Maud bird. Then your dad found in your pocket the Zippo lighter you used. Recognised it straight away because it belonged to him before he lost it.'

'That doesn't mean anything.'

'It was half-full of lighter fuel when he last saw it. When it came out of your pocket, it was empty.'

'Then I'd probably been playing with it. It still doesn't mean I set fire to my home.'

'You had form. Tried torching something else in the flat once and almost burned the place down.'

She means Callum's football shirt and homework in the bath. It still doesn't prove anything.

'What you haven't told me is why I'd want to hurt her,' I continue. 'I had no reason to. She was all I had. It's not like your beloved son was banging on our door wanting to play dad, was it?'

It's a deliberate provocation that has the desired effect.

'Because she was giving you *up*,' my grandmother growls. Spittle flies from her mouth like small white rockets, landing on the lapels of my jacket until the tiny bubbles burst. 'She'd met with social workers to talk about putting you into care.'

I hesitate, processing what she's just said. She gauges my stunned expression before she further twists the knife. She couldn't be getting more pleasure from this if she tried.

'She stopped short of telling them what you'd done to Daisy or Callum because no one wants to admit their kid is a fucking psycho,' she adds. 'You begged her to let you stay, but she'd washed her hands of you. She wanted rid of you completely, and who can blame her? So while she was asleep in her bedroom, you set fire to the sofa. Then you watched from outside with everyone else as that place burned.'

I hear my own breath being released in sharp bursts as the wind leaves my sails. Since visiting Dr Fernandez-Jones, I have felt like a cold, distant version of my old self. Unfeeling, untethered, but in absolute control. And constantly wrestling with the urge to harm those who don't deserve it. But something about the way my grandmother tells me this with such certainty knocks me off that path. Suddenly, everything around me begins to blur and sway: the trees, the flowers, the cars – even her. It's as if I am able to feel again, but now I feel everything at once. Sadness and remorse . . . it's overwhelming, and I'm forced to steady myself with a hand against the car window. Her stare strips me into pieces until she's satisfied she has been able to deflect some of her suffering on to someone else.

'You're making it up,' I mutter. 'You can't know any of this.'

'I'm old and I'm mean and I'm fucking well vindictive, but I ain't no liar,' she says. I believe her.

She doesn't need to say anything else. She has won. I slump in my seat before, once again, the crackling of electricity and a suffocating pressure inside my skull announce the return of the cold version of myself. It pushes to one side the remorse for what I did to Mum, and instead I want to hurt my grandmother. Take my pain out on her. And to keep hurting her until there's no strength left in my body and every inch of saggy skin hanging off her wretched old body is black or bleeding. I even find myself drawing my arm back as if readying myself to act on my urges. It does not go unnoticed, but she doesn't so much as flinch.

'Be my guest,' she goads. 'You've already taken away everything I have to live for.'

She starts rolling another cigarette and continues to regard me, revelling in the wounds she's inflicted.

Then I suddenly feel something warm trickling down my nose. I put my hand to my nostrils and examine my fingers. Blood. In a panic, I search my pocket for the handkerchief I always keep on me. I tilt my head forwards to stop it trickling down my throat and making me want to vomit, then pinch my nose. Now it's as if I'm suffocating, but for once, it's blood and not water filling my mouth. I wind down the window and spit it out. A long few minutes pass before it stops and I can pull myself together. I catch my reflection in the partition glass. I look as if I've been in a fight.

'Finished?' my grandmother asks without concern.

'I didn't know about Mum,' I reply, aware of how weak I sound.

'You weren't supposed to know, were you? The only people who did were me, your dad and his girlfriend.'

'His girlfriend?'

'You didn't know?' she asks, surprised. 'I wonder why she didn't tell you. She was probably scared you'd kill her too.'

'Who?'

There's another dramatic pause as she prepares to deliver another big reveal.

'Helena,' she says.

CHAPTER 88

HELENA

Helena drifts to a place where Ralf's image emerges with such clarity, he could be in the room with her. She's glad he's not, though. She wouldn't want him to see her like this. They haven't been in touch for sixteen years, but it doesn't mean she can't remember his smile, his touch, his scent, his strength, his kindness, and above all, their connection. All these years later and a day doesn't pass when she does not think of him.

Back then, and following a string of failed relationships, a happily single Helena had recently celebrated her forty-third year when she was introduced to Ralf at a conference about integrating rehabilitated prisoners back into their estranged families. She learned there had been many spells in his adult life that he had spent behind bars. But with almost a year of freedom under his belt, he was determined to remain on the straight and narrow. His honesty with regards to his flaws was as refreshing as his willingness to expose his vulnerabilities.

However, fearing someone with his criminal history might pose a risk to her foster carer status, they kept their relationship a secret from her employers. And out of respect for her vocation, he accepted his needs would always come second to those of the children placed in her care. There were weeks when they barely saw one another, either when he was working away or she was looking after a child who feared the company of men. Yet they made it work by keeping the channels of communication open, via text messages, handwritten postcards and notes.

A sadness washed over Ralf each time he spoke of the sons he had loved and lost. Of how his ex-partner Bobbi had irreparably changed after the death of their baby boy. How it had led to their permanent split and how she had refused to allow him regular access to their other son, Damon, for fear of permanently losing him. Ralf was aware of the part he had played in the estrangement of father and son. How long stretches behind bars for attacking the man who'd assaulted Bobbi, and stealing to help her financially, had fractured their relationship to the point where it was beyond repair.

Then, one early evening, Ralf turned up at Helena's house unannounced and in a state of distress. She managed to maintain an impassive expression as he explained how, that afternoon, his ex-wife had died trying to escape a blaze in her flat, and as he'd comforted his son, he had felt something pressing against his leg. The boy's only possession was a silver Zippo cigarette lighter he recognised as one he'd misplaced a year earlier. An emotional Damon couldn't explain why he'd kept it or what had happened in the lead-up to the fire, only that there'd been another argument in which she'd ordered him to get out of the flat and never come back. He'd pulled the boy's hand towards his nose. Did it smell of lighter fuel? He couldn't be sure that it didn't. But he did know the Zippo was now empty.

It wasn't proof of his guilt, but it didn't paint the picture of an innocent boy either.

Helena stepped out of the room and into the garden, taking in long gasps of fresh air as she tried to unpack all Ralf had admitted.

It wasn't only the revelation of what Ralf's son was capable of that shocked her. It was that the man she could tell anything to without fear of judgement had been keeping Daisy's murder a secret from her for a fortnight. It hurt, even if she understood why.

'I know a solicitor who specialises in family law,' she informed him on her return. 'She can advise us on the best way to approach the police.'

'No, please, I can't,' Ralf pleaded with her. 'It's not Damon's fault, it's mine. I fucked up. I wasn't present when he needed a dad. He lost his moral compass.'

'A quarter of all households in this country are made up of single parents,' she argued. 'Your absence isn't the reason your son has done these awful things.'

'It's a huge part of it. If he's arrested, he will be swallowed up by the system and that will be it for him. I know because I've lived it. Damon wouldn't be able to cope.'

'But if he's done everything you think he has, he needs to face the consequences. They can help him.'

'But so can we. Please, meet him and you'll see he isn't a bad kid. There's just a dark side of him that he needs help to control. He's . . . he's here. Outside. In the car.'

Her face fell.

'I'm sorry, but there's nowhere else for him to go,' Ralf continued. 'My mum won't have him under our roof. And until I find enough money to put a deposit on a place of my own, you're my only hope. It won't be for long.'

Helena's love for Ralf influenced her to agree to meet his son. The moment the shy, withdrawn boy nervously stepped into her home holding his dad's hand, she was struck by how he was every bit as broken as many of the other children who were brought to her. Damon was small and slight for his age, his eyes a rich, soulful brown. He was barely able to function. She saw elements of Ralf in his appearance and body language, and despite Damon's horrendous behaviours, she found herself torn between her love for his father and her sympathy for his victims and their families. Eventually she followed her heart and agreed to let him stay.

Strings were pulled by friends of hers at social services to allow her to care for him temporarily – the son of a family friend, she claimed – until his father was able to look after him permanently.

Helena didn't know it then, but she can see it now. Accepting the boy into her life marked the beginning of the end for her and Ralf.

CHAPTER 89

DAMON

It takes a moment for my grandmother's most recent revelation to sink in.

'Helena, my foster mother? She was Dad's girlfriend?'

The old woman gives another condescending nod. 'Your dad talked her into letting you stay with her until they got you help.'

'Why hasn't she told me this?' My grandmother shrugs as if she doesn't care. 'And why would she take me in if she knew what I was capable of?'

'She was one of those women who can't resist a bird with a broken wing. Can't accept that not everyone can be saved. Not like me. If you can't fly, stay out of the fucking sky. Anyway, I only met her a few times, but I sensed she could handle herself. They tried to get you counselling to begin with, but that didn't work when you tried to smash a paperweight in the shrink's face. So as a last resort, he told her about a doctor he knew, one who used machines and electricity to fry parts of the brains of people like you. Put you on the straight and narrow. Reckoned he could help you start over.'

'I went to see him. He told me that.'

'Good for you,' she says wryly. If this surprises her, she doesn't let it show. I wait for her to continue but she doesn't.

'What did Dad tell you about the treatment?'

'I'm getting bored of this,' she yawns.

'It's my life we're talking about here!' I snap. 'I have a right to know.'

'And my Ralf and those kids and your mum had rights to their lives too,' she lashes out. And I can't argue with that. 'Your dad reckoned the treatment worked,' she says after a time, her gaze returning to the buildings we pass as the car continues to make its way through unfamiliar streets. 'But you lost more than only the memories of what you did. He tried to convince me to see you, 'cos you were a completely different kid. But I wasn't having any of it. A leopard doesn't change its spots, no matter how many volts you blast it with. Ralf was naive and had this stupid idea that, one day, you two could build a relationship and you'd live with him. I kept telling him life ain't no Disney film but he wouldn't listen. And soon after they started treating you, he was arrested for the girl you killed. He knew the only way you might ever live a normal life was if he took the blame for what you did.'

My racing mind is filled with images of what I recall and what I'm imagining as my grandmother speaks.

'So much of this I didn't know,' I say.

'Do you wish you'd kept it that way?'

'I think so, yes.'

'Yeah, well, this is what it's been like for me, carrying your shit like a fucking packhorse for all these years.'

I ask her about his aggressive behaviour towards me and his threat as he threw me out of the flat, the last time I saw him alive. She looks to my phone instead.

'That detective called you back yet?' she asks.

'It would've rung if he had,' I say.

'You could've turned the sound off. Call him again.'

'Come on,' I say. 'I'm giving you what you want.'

'Do it again.'

I repeat the exact same process as before, speaking again when I reach an answerphone. She appears satisfied.

'Ralf was worried that you seeing him would rake up more of your lost memories and you'd return to who you used to be. That's why he threatened you. So, once and for all, you'd believe he was guilty and leave us alone. Only it didn't work, did it? 'Cos here we are.'

Without warning, she raps her knuckles on the driver's partition, and it opens. The cigarette smoke that surrounds us finds a new area in which to drift.

'He's getting out,' she informs the driver, and the car comes to halt. I have no idea where I am. 'Don't ever let me see your face again unless it's staring at me from the front page of a newspaper after you've been sentenced,' she says, and returns to stare out of the passenger window.

I'm left by the side of a dual carriageway as the car pulls away.

CHAPTER 90

MELISSA

'You can't be here,' a panicked Melissa tells Damon when she opens her front door to find him there. She steps outside and closes it quietly behind her, hoping Adrienne hasn't heard the bell chime.

'You weren't answering my calls or texts,' he says. 'I was worried about you.'

Each time his name has appeared, she's automatically diverted it to voicemail. She has also deleted his voice notes and WhatsApp messages without listening to or reading them. Melissa hates having cut off all contact, but the choice was made starkly clear to her: life with Adrienne, or death with Damon.

Melissa grabs his arm and pulls him further away from the door, careful not to trip over the tools her dad's left here as he holidays before finishing their block paving driveway.

'Did you not think there might be a reason I haven't replied?' she asks in a half-whisper.

'I honestly didn't know what to think,' he says, 'but I assumed we were okay.'

'Well, I'm sorry, but we're not.'

Only now does she register his appearance. There are scabs on the knuckles of his right hand. His left shoulder is hunched more markedly and each move is accompanied by a small, sharp wince. He's so clearly damaged, in so many ways. She fights her instinct to ask him what happened or to invite him inside for treatment. But there's something else. Something different about him. Some slight shift in character that she can't put her finger on. But it's undeniable.

'I've got so much I need to tell you,' Damon persists. 'I went to my dad's funeral yesterday. Just to pay my—'

'No.' Melissa shakes her head. 'Please, stop. Don't tell me anything else. I can't do this anymore.'

It breaks her heart, but she takes a step back, readying herself to slip back into the house and close the door on him.

'I know who I am now,' Damon implores her. 'I know everything, and there's no one else I can talk to about it but you.'

'Damon, what we did, it was wrong. I should have been strong enough for the both of us to stop it from happening. I wasn't then, but I am now.'

'But—'

Melissa holds her hands up in front of her chest. 'But nothing. Please, if you care about me at all, you'll leave.'

A flicker of something passes through him – his expression momentarily hardens, his body tightens – but it's too fleeting for her to get hold of.

He continues: 'I need you to—'

To both their surprise, the door is suddenly flung open. Melissa spins to find Adrienne behind her. She's scowling, her jaw is tight. Melissa has never seen her so angry, even during their own confrontation about Damon.

'You need her to do *what*?' Adrienne directs at Damon. 'Kill you again?'

His gaze flits back and forth between Adrienne and Melissa as though measuring them.

'I found the video you recorded,' she continues. 'I know you've been manipulating Mel into helping you to die, and that she's been stupid enough to play along with it. But it's over, do you understand?'

Melissa wills Damon to say 'okay' and walk away. But she knows he won't give up that easily.

'Ade,' he says, 'please let me come in and talk to you both.'

Adrienne takes a step over the threshold and squares up to him. Inches separate them.

'Do you have any idea of what you have done already?' she snarls. 'We've had to put our baby plans back a year. That's how long it'll take us to save up for IVF and a new sperm donor. And that's if Mel and I last the course, because believe me, we're hanging on by a very thin thread here.' Her look sharpens. 'But then, that's what you've wanted all along, isn't it? To come between us? To win her back?'

'No, no,' Damon protests.

'I don't believe you. I tried my hardest to be your friend and to make you a part of our lives, because I know how much it means to Mel. But now I see you for what you are. A manipulative, selfish, jealous little prick. If you want to kill yourself, then go ahead. But don't drag my girlfriend into your fucked-up headspace.'

'We can sort this out,' he insists.

Adrienne folds her arms across her chest. 'How?'

'I'll get help. I can get better. Then we can continue trying to start a family. I'll go to all my clinic appointments. I'll do whatever I need to, and if you don't want me around for a while until I can prove to you I'm worthy, then I'll give you that space.'

'God, you will say *anything.* I don't give a shit if you get help or not. You might not value your life, but I value mine and I value Mel's.'

‘If you give me a chance, I’ll show you I can be a good dad.’

‘Damon,’ she says, leaning towards him. ‘You will never make a good father, because you’re too self-involved and too utterly obsessed with your admittedly horrendous past to be anything *but* that. I’m sorry about all that. I am.’ Here, she takes another small step closer. The tips of their noses are nearly touching. ‘But we live in a world of pain, Damon. People everywhere go through hell all the time, and they don’t make it worse for themselves and everyone around them, like you have a positively insane genius for doing. I don’t *blame* Mel for having that abortion.’

Melissa’s head turns so sharply to Adrienne it’s as if she’s been slapped. Adrienne’s steely veneer cracks as she realises what she has said.

Damon’s wide-eyed gaze fixes upon his ex-wife’s.

‘*What* did she say?’ he asks.

CHAPTER 91

DAMON

The sun is beginning its descent over the area of green space behind my flat. It's about a third of an acre comprising trees, grasses and a wild meadow the other tenants have planted. The windowsill at the foot of my picture window is large enough for me to sit on comfortably, so I draw my knees to my chest and lose myself in the world outside. This is me. Forever the spectator.

For a moment, I allow myself to imagine Melissa playing out there with the child she terminated. Our child. A boy, I've decided. My son. I've called him Samuel, which is Hebrew for *God has heard*, suggesting he is a long-awaited answer to my prayers. They are chasing each other around the lawn, shrieking with laughter, darting in and out of a sprinkler, trying to avoid the thin jets of water, but gradually dampening. He'd be almost four by now. But he is to forever remain a daydream, because Melissa robbed him of the opportunity to become an actual person. I shift my body, aware of the tension creeping across my shoulders and tightening my chest as I dwell on this. I curl my toes and bunch my fingers into a fist until the feeling disappears. I can't allow myself to think about a boy that only exists in my imagination. And I can't dream about Melissa.

Days ago, I was cold and unfeeling, but this has pushed me into a different realm. I have been a tightly wound ball of anxiety ever since I learned what she did. I'm the touchpaper on a firework waiting to be lit and explode in a thousand different directions. I'm unable to rest or eat and my sleep is peppered with vivid images of what could have been. Melissa took away everything I ever wanted, and I hate her for it.

The walls of the flat are closing in on me. I need to get out of here. I grab my keys and make my way downstairs to the car park. The entry doors are locked while maintenance work is being carried out on the building, so I must walk the long way around.

My grandmother's presence infiltrates my thoughts. Perhaps I shouldn't have lied to her. Maybe I should've left a message on that detective sergeant's answerphone and not pressed the mute button on my device before I spoke. All he'll have heard on both recordings is silence. But she didn't need to know that.

My thoughts are interrupted by Melissa approaching me. As she gets closer, tension fills the cracks that anger hasn't already seeped into.

'Leave me alone,' I snap before she has the chance to say anything, and I quicken my pace.

Her footsteps are following me and I feel rage building inside. I turn.

'You are the last person in the world I want to see right now,' I yell. She looks frightened and I don't care who else might be listening. 'All you do is hurt me and I can't take it anymore. So give me some space, alright?'

She opens her mouth to respond, but I turn my back on her. She's got the message and remains where she is. I have never spoken to her like that before, so she must recognise I am serious. I have forgiven her for ending our marriage and breaking my heart. But this? I don't know if I'll ever move past it. Because she hasn't only robbed me of one child, but of two: the one she was pregnant with, and the one I now cannot have with Adrienne. I have only ever wanted to leave something behind that is better than me. But that opportunity has been removed from the table. Now, it's impossible.

I reach my car. I've been unable to open the driver's door since hitting a concrete post to stop Laura's hired goon from attacking me. So I climb inside through the passenger side. It smells in here so I wind the windows down and begin puffing on my vape.

But before I put the key in the ignition, I take my phone from my pocket and send a text message.

I am ready.

CHAPTER 92

DAMON

I think I recognise the young woman opening the front door to leave Helena's house. I'm sure I saw her on a previous visit here. She can't be much older than her mid-teens. I cannot place why there's something familiar about her when the light makes her irises glint.

'You're Damon, aren't you?' she asks as she reaches me on the driveway. 'You've been here before, recently.'

I nod cautiously, unsure if this is an accusation. She senses this, because she adds, 'It's okay,' and smiles. 'I left an envelope out for you that I found amongst some paperwork in Mum's wardrobe. I'm Sally.'

It takes a moment for what she's said to register. 'Helena is your mum?'

'Yes.'

I had no idea Helena had a daughter and I'm briefly lost for words. But now it's obvious. She has Helena's huge smile and high cheekbones, but she's of dual heritage and her tawny skin glimmers in the late afternoon sun. We weren't supposed to meet. That's why her mum kept something so important from me. An image of Melissa comes to mind and I realise it's a common theme with people I love. Because Helena knows what I'm capable of, I bet she was concerned I might hurt her daughter. Was Sally in the photographs on the fireplace that Helena lay face down?

'I found the envelope,' I continue, 'but there was no sign of your mum. Is she okay?'

Sally's smile thins. 'She's not, no. She had another stroke – well, several, her doctors think.' My heart sinks. 'The first was probably soon after you last saw her and it knocked her for six. She was beginning to pull round when she had the second, which took a lot more out of her.'

Is this my fault? Did I put pressure on her? 'Oh, I'm sorry,' I reply. 'How is she now?'

Sally shakes her head. 'She's been moved from hospital and into a private nursing home. She's conscious but barely responsive. I can give you the address if you'd like to visit? I know you mean a lot to her.'

I briefly wonder how much Helena has told her about me. Whether Sally has heard the edited, redacted headlines or been told the whole sorry story. Maybe she has listened to those cassette recordings and it's given her a flavour of who I really was. No, if it was the latter, she'd have run a mile from me by now. I know I would've.

Without warning, it happens again. A pulse of energy bubbles under the surface of my skin and sends my thoughts scattering. Now all I want is to knock this innocent girl to the ground and strangle her until the blood vessels in her eyes burst. I can see myself walking through the doors of Helena's nursing home and clamping a pillow tightly over her face. I imagine being caught by a staff member and finding an object to attack them with, to stave in their skulls.

'Are you okay?' Sally asks.

I return to reality with a jolt. She stares intently at me, trying to read me.

'Um, I'm not sure I am,' I reply with honesty. Because now the thoughts are so easily and rapidly escalating to urges. And I fear I might not be able to control myself if I am around her for very much longer.

'Look, I'm leaving,' she says, to my relief. 'Why don't you go inside until you're feeling better? If Mum trusts you, so do I.'

'Thank you,' I say.

But first she takes my mobile number and promises to text me Helena's nursing home address. I have no intention of visiting her. I cannot guarantee her mum's safety if I do.

I make my way to the front door with no idea of who I am anymore. No, that's a lie. I do know who I am. I am him. The version Helena and my dad thought they had erased all those years ago. My grandmother's words remain steadfast.

It wasn't safe for you to be out on the streets.

The first thing I spot in Helena's house is the envelope addressed to me, now on the fireplace. As far as I can tell, each cassette is still present inside. However, knowing they exist is enough to send a wave of anger rippling through me. I don't want them here. I don't want them to exist anywhere in this world. So I take them into the garden, prise out a large stone from a crumbling rockery, and start smashing them with the same force I used on poor Daisy's face. I only stop when the contents of the envelope rattle. At the end of the garden is a gate and I hear movement behind it. Outside, refuse collectors are wheeling away a black bin. I slip the envelope into an as-yet-unemptied container and wait until it's pulled away.

I return to the house, lock the door behind me and scan the news feeds. The headlines on the BBC, Sky News, *Mail Online* and the *Guardian* all remain as they were an hour ago. There is no mention of anything related to me. I've been lucky so far. But time is my enemy. If I don't move quickly, what I have planned won't work.

However, I'm distracted by a scrunched-up ball of paper in the otherwise empty fireplace grate. I pick it out and unfurl it.

When I thought I had everything figured out, I'm caught off guard once again.

CHAPTER 93

HELENA

She has stopped counting how long she has been here. The days are interminably long and the nights drag on even more so. Everything has blended into one infinite nightmare. Lying in a care home bed, unable to move anything but her eyelids when she blinks. Even that is an involuntary reflex action. However, sometimes, when she focuses hard enough, she can hold them closed for a handful of seconds at a time. It's about the only part of her body and her life she has any control over.

Helena wishes her heart would listen to her brain and begin its descent towards death. Some days she prays for an infection to sweep through her useless frame, undetected by doctors until it's too late to treat. Or maybe a brand-new superbug that's immune to antibiotics. Even Covid, pneumonia or a heart attack would suffice . . . Anything, as long as it's fatal. Because she knows there is no coming back from where she now finds herself. Not this time. And that isn't only based on what she overheard the doctors telling Sally. Helena knows her mind and body are no longer symbiotic. They have formed two separate identities working independently and against one another. And she has had enough of both.

Helena doesn't like the specialists. They talk to her with loud voices and use oversimplified language, as if they're trying to explain something to a hearing-impaired child. She wants to remind them she is a grown woman in her late fifties and is perfectly capable of understanding long words and neurological terms despite her circumstances. They discuss her condition with one another, about how the stroke in her brain stem is on the higher end of the spectrum. She wishes Sally hadn't been the one to find her, lying in a heap on the dining room floor, her knickers soiled and her face drooping half an inch lower than it should be.

She passes the day listening to daytime television, when the staff remember to turn it on. Sometimes they forget and she'll be drowning in silence for hours. She'll sing songs to herself, Barbadian folk tunes her father sang when she was a little girl, to help her drift off to sleep. Or she'll focus all her efforts on trying to move a finger or a toe. No luck, as yet. She will also challenge herself to raise and lower her heartbeat only by concentrating on it. Sometimes it works, but if she goes too far an alarm sounds. A nurse will appear, check on her, then reset the machine and leave.

Sally visits most days. She tells her about what she's been doing at school, or Helena hears the pages of revision textbooks turning, keys on a phone being tapped as she messages someone. But Helena would rather Sally weren't here as often. She has her GCSE exams on the horizon – she's such a bright kid that she's taking them a year early – and she wants her daughter to concentrate on revision. She detests being a distraction.

Sally has always been adamant that, once her exams are complete, she will be returning to the family home. For a year she's lived with her aunt, uncle and cousins on the other side of London, closer to a school Helena wanted her to attend. Helena eventually agreed to her daughter coming home when her exams are over, but insisted the return only last until she gets her results and stays on at school for her A levels. With the way she is now, Helena fears Sally might follow her heart, and not her head, and find a school that's more local. More guilt to add to the ever-expanding pile. The pile that began the day Sally was born to a single, working parent and which has yet to shrink all these years later.

Helena regrets how much time was stolen from them by other people's problems. How foster parenting – never a nine-to-five job, requiring taking in children with little notice – forced her to not only work unpredictable hours but to rely on family and after-school clubs to care for her own offspring. How her headspace was often occupied by the needs of others. What saddens her the most is the certainty their lives would have been different had Ralf not moved Daisy Barber's dead body the day Damon killed her.

For a time, it looked as if there might have been a light at the end of their particularly bleak tunnel. When the counselling she had organised for Damon with Dr Dahl failed, Helena turned to an experimental treatment by an ECT specialist who believed electroconvulsive therapy could limit future aggression in criminals. The chances of it working on children, whose prefrontal cortexes have yet to mature, was undetermined. So Ralf was hesitant, but she talked him around. And her gamble paid off.

Helena witnessed the changes in Damon after three sessions in that first week. Sometimes he would return to her home in an almost zombie-like state. He suffered crippling headaches and gaps appeared in his memory: episodes of time and people that, when pressed to recall, he either barely remembered or had no recollection of at all.

She'd use Damon's vulnerable, confused state to provide him with an alternate history: to convince him he hadn't been responsible for his mum's death; that there had been no fire at the flat; that his vague memories of Bobby, Daisy and Callum were merely figments of his imagination. Damon was barely allowed to sleep even when he cried out for it. She wanted to take advantage of his bewildered state to expand upon Fernandez-Jones's work. One of them hid the past, the other shaped his future.

At times, it made Ralf uncomfortable and he begged her to stop. She knew it was unethical, illegal, and not far removed from brainwashing. But together, she and Fernandez-Jones convinced Ralf they must break Damon down to rebuild him.

It worked, until it didn't. Damon's pre-treatment behaviour caught up with them. Ralf was arrested in connection with the murder of Daisy Barber shortly before Damon's final week of appointments. Ralf asked Helena for her help one last time. He wanted to be erased from his son's memories. For her to convince him his dad had died years earlier.

'Why?' asked Helena in the police cell shortly before his first court appearance. 'Once you tell the police Damon killed that girl, they'll release you. I mean, you'll probably be charged with aiding and abetting or perverting the course of justice, but . . .'

Her voice faded upon reading his expression.

Ralf leaned across the table. 'You can't tell the police it was Damon who killed Daisy. They must believe it's me. Every day, Damon is getting better. He needs a second chance.' Now it was Ralf who'd become the true believer in his son's treatment.

'But Ralf,' she argued, 'if you plead guilty you will spend the next twenty years in prison.'

'I don't care. This is the only thing I can do to protect my son.'

'If we can show that his ECT is working,' she said, 'perhaps we can convince a jury that he no longer has these urges. That he can control himself. He might get a reduced sentence.'

'Fernandez-Jones will never admit to a court what he's done to a child.' He was right, of course. 'And I told you,' he went on, 'Damon could never survive a young offenders' institute then prison. It would kill him.'

Helena tossed her hands into the air in exasperation. She knew so much of this was of her own making. If she had not pushed him into getting Damon treatment, she might still have the man she loved.

'And where does that leave us?' she asked.

Ralf pinched the bridge of his nose and looked down to the tabletop. 'I'm sorry.'

'I'm pregnant,' she blurted out without preface. There had been no good time to tell him. 'I was late, so I did a test.'

It had been entirely unplanned. Helen had chalked up changes to her body and her period as perimenopausal. Until morning sickness began.

His face momentarily lit up and the corners of his mouth lifted. For a moment, she thought her news might make him reconsider. But his expression soon soured.

'I'm sorry,' he whispered.

Then he pushed back his chair, rose, and left the visitors' room without saying goodbye.

Ralf was charged with manslaughter later the same week – there was not enough evidence for a murder charge – and he refused to see Helena again. A few weeks later, Helena found Damon a space in a boys' home in Northampton. But he had formed an attachment to her and didn't want to leave. He'd come so far and she was tempted to keep him with her, partially to entice Ralf into repairing the bond with her he'd broken. But it was out of the question. She couldn't trust Damon around her baby after its arrival in a few months.

Damon's first accommodation didn't work out when other boys bullied him. Despite the apparent success of the treatment, Helen was frightened a rage might build up in him and he might eventually retaliate. So she found him somewhere else, a calmer place, and she received regular updates from its managers, a kind couple who kept an eye out for her former charge. They reassured Helena that Damon was a quiet and introverted lad who showed no signs of the violence Helena knew he was capable of. His memory loss was a small price to pay for that.

Ralf continued to refuse all her visitation requests, and even after sentencing, failed to respond to her letters. Not even the one she sent containing photographs of their newborn daughter. She called her Sally after the woman referred to in the Oasis song they liked, 'Don't Look Back in Anger'.

It was at that point Helena chose to close the book on Ralf, focusing all her attention on her daughter instead. Being a single mum wasn't easy, but with the support of sister Carolina and her husband Addo, she raised a daughter to be proud of. Sally was a relatively easy child, but there were still bumps in the road. At eight, she was diagnosed with a brain tumour, which although benign, created an intercranial pressure inside her skull. Its positioning made it tricky to operate on so it was left but regularly monitored, and steroids were prescribed to reduce inflammation when necessary. It did, however, lead to headaches, nausea and nosebleeds. The latter of which caused her to regularly carry a handkerchief or tissues.

Later, Sally's mental health took a downward turn after she witnessed a school friend suffer fatal injuries in a car accident. The trauma caused sharp spikes in her blood pressure, which increased the pressure inside Sally's skull, leading to frequent tension-induced migraines. Combined with the vivid memories of the collision, they altered her focus. She developed a fixation with death, poring over YouTube videos about it; searching online for images of bodies in war-torn regions across the world; submerging herself in gothic literature and accounts of international funeral customs and practices. Helena sought counselling for her. And Sally eventually channelled her childhood preoccupation in a more positive direction, by choosing subjects that would enable her to study forensic pathology if she earned the right grades.

Over the years, Sally had asked a few questions as to who her father was, and Helena had lied, claiming she was the result of a drunken one-night stand. She appeared to accept her mum's explanation at face value. Even though Sally was intelligent and mature, it was too much to expect her to understand her father was in jail for covering up a murder her half-brother had committed.

A voice from the doorway pulls her away from the past. 'Hello Helena,' it begins chirpily. 'What have you been up to today?'

She recognises it as belonging to one of the volunteer staff.

'Let me think,' Helena imagines herself replying. 'I lay here for a few hours, then I peed into a catheter, had breakfast pumped directly into a tube in my stomach, and tried and failed to hold my breath in a vain attempt to die. What about you?'

She's being unfair. There is something about this volunteer that is different to the others. She'll sit with her at night sensing when Helena can't sleep, holding her hand or reading to her from books and magazines. She seems to understand her, and tells her that if she wants to quietly slip away, it's okay. She'll hold her hand while it happens. That her family and friends won't resent her for it. She says she wishes she could help her, and that if maybe Helena could show her a sign that's what she wants, then she can find a way. That's why Helena has been practising trying to close her eyes, so that if this woman asks her if she wants to live or die, she might be able to communicate that she is desperate for the latter.

And then, God willing, this woman, this Laura, might take matters into her own hands.

CHAPTER 94

DAMON

She'll be arriving soon, so I take one more look around the bathroom to ensure everything is in place. The plastic restraints for binding my hands and ankles together are on the floor, along with scissors to cut them off when we have finished. The bathtub is three-quarters full of ice-cold water. The defibrillators I brought with me are lying on the floor, a green light indicating they're charged. I am as ready for her as I'll ever be.

We finally spoke yesterday, when I texted to tell her that I was ready to talk. She was angry, then hesitant when I gave her an address to meet me at. But finally, she agreed. It makes sense to do it here.

I slip my last cartridge into the vape and puff on it as I glance at a mirror above the sink. I wipe the dust clean with the sleeve of my jumper and take in my recently shaven face. My features remain pinched, but at least I look a little less like a character from a Tim Burton movie.

For the first time today, I'm not alone in here. Mum has joined me, and my baby brother is balanced on her hip. He's no longer carrying the blue chequered blanket I suffocated him with and she is not scarred by fire or spitting embers. Daisy is also here, her face intact, reminding me of the beautiful young girl I fell in love with. Standing next to her is Callum, now without the handkerchief stuffed in his mouth. I can see his lips and his teeth. And there's also the man who attacked me and whose dead body I dumped in a bin. I still have no clue as to his identity and I don't care to learn it. But he appears far less menacing than he was when he was alive.

Dad is next to them. His appearance is also different to when I last hallucinated him, bloodied and battered and standing in the aisle of the DIY store moments before I was told of his death. Today, he is uninjured and fresh-faced. He's no longer balding, bearded or grey-skinned from spending a third of his life behind bars. He is the spit of me before the first time I died: in his twenties, with the rest of his life ahead of him.

At one point or another, I have believed all these hallucinated figures to be reaching their arms out towards me, begging for my help. Now I realise it is the opposite: they were trying to push me away before I could hurt them again.

'They're here, aren't they?'

'Jesus!' I shout and turn sharply to face Melissa. Her head is cocked to one side, a shoulder casually leaning against the doorway. 'I didn't hear you come in,' I tell her.

My reaction amuses her. 'I'm right though, aren't I?' she says. 'They're in the room with us?'

'Yes.'

She casts a quick look around. 'I wish I could see them.'

'Trust me, you don't want to. It's like every terrible thing you have ever done in your life returning to haunt you.' She makes her way into the bathroom and takes a seat on the toilet lid. 'Thanks for being here,' I add.

She shrugs. 'Not that you gave me much choice,' she says, 'but we've come this far together, I might as well see it through to the end. Wherever that might take us.'

Melissa is the only person who truly knows everything about me. Even more so than Helena, I realise. She knows who I was, who I became and who I've returned to. She has witnessed my best and worst parts. Yet she hasn't turned her back on me. Still, she remains.

I absent-mindedly pick at the dried blood embedded in the dial of my watch. I've scrubbed it and picked at its crevices and crown with an unfolded paperclip, but it won't budge.

'Is Fernandez-Jones here?' she asks.

When the fog of my post-ECT daze lifted during our meeting and he turned his back on me, I raised the machine above my head and brought it down upon him. I remember the crunching sound, then the dull thud as he dropped to his knees before the second blow came.

'No, he's not,' I tell Melissa. 'So I assume he's still alive. But he must be only just.' Amazing how hard some lives can be to end.

'And you're sure there's no link between you and him?'

'I used a secure network for my initial contact, gave myself a fake name, and only his housekeeper can identify me on sight. Before I left, I took the book Fernandez-Jones was making notes in about me and grabbed my records from his filing cabinet.'

'What about your fingerprints or DNA?'

'They're not on any criminal database. If they track me down, well . . .'

My voice trails off, but I know she's aware of what that means. We both are.

'Why did you do it?' Melissa asks. 'I perhaps understand why you did what you did to the others. But aside from Bobby, it was always out of rejection or jealousy. What Fernandez-Jones did to you was morally abysmal, but he gave you a second chance, didn't he? You had sixteen years of normality. So didn't the end justify the means?'

'I didn't deserve one day of normality in those sixteen years,' I reply. 'I'm a danger to be around. He delayed the inevitable. Put everyone around me at risk.'

'Had I not dared you to do that swim, you wouldn't have died and seen Callum. And that's what started all this. I feel responsible.'

'No, I'm to blame, not you. If he hadn't appeared then, he'd have emerged another way. It was only a matter of time.' A moment passes before I speak again. 'Can you forgive me, Mel?'

She hesitates before answering. 'Yes,' she replies, as though surprised. 'I think so. And you? Do you forgive me for the ways in which I hurt you?'

'Of course. I always will.'

'But you hated me a few days ago.'

I will never stop loving this woman. 'No matter what you do to me, you will go to your grave with my heart in your hands.'

She looks behind her across the hallway at the closed bedroom door. 'Did you bring them here?'

'Yes. They're in the spare bedroom.'

'Can I see them?' she asks hesitantly.

'I can't stop you if you think you really want to.'

'I think I should.'

I nod then lead the way, stretching out my arm to push open the door. Here, Melissa regards her own and Adrienne's lifeless bodies lying on a bed, wrapped from head to toe in plastic sheeting and secured with tape.

I turn to gauge her reaction, but my hallucination of her has vanished as suddenly as it appeared.

CHAPTER 95

THREE DAYS EARLIER

MELISSA

'I don't *blame* Mel for having that abortion.'

'*What* did she say?' Damon asks Melissa.

The temperature between the three of them plummets. Damon's gaze narrows, his glare switching from Adrienne to Melissa. A flicker of something passes through him again and lingers before he can conceal it. Adrienne also seems to sense it and takes a step back, allowing space between them. She turns to Melissa, who is shrinking inside herself.

'What is she talking about?' Damon asks her.

She opens her mouth, but she cannot find the words.

'Mel?' he continues.

She watches his face pale as the truth begins to settle.

'You had an abortion?' he says. 'When?'

She says nothing, her focus falling to the half-finished driveway below her. She waits for the penny to drop.

'There was no training course in Harrogate, was there?' he asks. 'You told me we lost the baby there. But you had a termination instead, didn't you?'

'Yes.'

'Why?'

'Because I wasn't ready. Not then.'

She meets his gaze as his features harden. 'You killed my baby,' he says.

Adrienne jumps to Melissa's defence. 'No,' she says firmly. 'She didn't kill anything. At that point, "your baby" was barely more than a cluster of cells.'

Damon raises his voice. 'It was still *my* child.'

'And *her* body,' Adrienne argues. 'So she gets the final say. Don't try and make her feel any worse about it than she already does.'

Melissa finds herself at a loss for words. Instead, she is whisked back to one of the worst days of her life, when she made the decision not to move forward with the unplanned pregnancy. Up until then, her periods had been as regular as clockwork. And she'd chalked the missed one up to the stress of realising her marriage was crumbling. But when her breasts began to feel tender and the fatigue set in, she knew in her gut what it meant. A home-testing kit confirmed her suspicions. She said nothing to Damon, afraid that she might cave under the weight of guilt and remain chained to a life she no longer wanted.

She was an estimated ten or so weeks along when she underwent the procedure at a private clinic in Birmingham. In a cruel twist of fate, the pregnancy had been the result of the final time she and Damon had sex. She'd gone through the motions to please him, rather than admit to herself she was no longer attracted to him.

The abortion served as a turning point. Soon after, she plucked up the courage to leave him.

'I'm sorry,' Melissa whispers now.

'Damon, please go home,' Adrienne says, the edge gone from her voice, 'because if you don't, I'll have no choice but to call the police. You can't be here.'

It crosses Melissa's mind this might be the last time she ever sees him. A lump forms in her throat she can't swallow, no matter how many times she tries.

Damon finally appears to admit defeat. But the look he gives her before he slowly turns to walk back down the driveway is disconcerting. She has seen him hurt and she has witnessed his upset, but this is something altogether different. She can no longer read him.

'Are you coming?' asks Adrienne, but it's not inflected as a question. Melissa follows her inside.

But neither gets the chance to close the front door.

CHAPTER 96

TODAY

DAMON

A tear catches my eye as I realise this is the last time Melissa, Adrienne and I will all be in the same room together. Despite my resentment towards Adrienne for giving my wife everything I couldn't, we did enjoy some good times together. And we could have had so many more. I want to blame Adrienne for what happened to them, for telling me about the abortion and inviting the dark waters to come between us. I also want to blame Melissa too, for taking my child away from me. But I can't. I chose to kill them. Their deaths are my fault and mine alone.

My gaze remains fixed on their lifeless bodies, recalling the best I can what happened that night. As they returned to their house, I grabbed a mallet lying by the block paving and pushed my way through the front door they were readying to close on me. It was all such a frenzied blur, I can't be sure who I struck first. All I remember was that I caught them with such stealth, neither had time to protect herself or run. The sound of crackling electricity deafened me to everything else, so if they screamed, I didn't hear them. It was all over in less than a minute.

Then I recall standing over them, their bloodied hair tangled together, slumped over one another in a heap on the hallway floor. The murky waters cleared as I stared at Melissa, the realisation of what I'd done becoming clear.

I left soon after through an alley behind the house, careful to avoid the casual gaze of neighbours, and returned later that night with plastic sheeting and tape I'd bought at a DIY store. I cleaned them both up with wet cloths and towels, used their thumbprints to unlock their phones and change the settings to allow me access. I wrapped up their bodies, reversed my car into the garage and lifted them both into the boot before I left. Back at the flat, I scrolled through their phones to find email addresses of their work managers and messaged them, blaming their forthcoming absences on a bout of Covid. Then I texted their families to tell them the same thing. And I've been replying to well-wishers ever since, pretending to be them. It has bought me time.

Melissa and Adrienne remained in my car boot for two days until I made my decision on what to do next. Under the cover of night, I drove an hour and a half to Helena's house in London. I carried them through the garage and lay their bodies down carefully in one of her spare bedrooms. And now, as I whisper goodbye to Melissa, I wipe my tears and close the door on her.

I'm pushing up the sleeve of my jumper to check my watch when a tattoo catches my eye. It's the Greek Gemini symbol, one of my first inkings. I guess it makes sense now, with what I have learned about myself. Two halves of the same person. I roll my sleeve up further and scan my arm one last time. It's then that it strikes me like the lightning I so often fear: everything I have discovered about myself has always been here, in plain sight. I have been wearing my story all along.

The flower on my forearm that obscures half a girl's face is a daisy, like the girl I loved and killed. I have lyrics from the song 'Bobby Jean' – my baby brother's name – in which Bruce Springsteen sings about saying goodbye. Mum adored that song. The crackling lines of electricity between giant pylons are self-explanatory. A flame coming from a Zippo cigarette lighter was supposed to be in remembrance of Mum, but I think it's actually because it's how I set her flat ablaze using Dad's device. There's a grid of numbers on the outside of my bicep that I recognise a date in. It's of Daisy's death. Diagonally is the date Mum died, back to front is Bobby's death. Two rows of numbers I can't fathom out, but when I use my phone to google them, they are coordinates for the streets where Daisy and Callum were killed. Four beating hearts and a flatline speak for themselves. The words 'Offering Others Direction In Sorrow' running along my collarbone was a phrase I dreamed one night. It always felt as if it should mean something. Now I realise that when you take each first letter and put them together, it spells 'oodis'. *You did this.* And finally, I see a brightly coloured female skeletal figure clad in a long robe and holding a scythe. I take a photo and reverse-image search it. It's the Nuestra Señora de la Santa Muerte, a Mexican personification of death. She holds a watch in her hand with the time set to six o'clock. And when I check my watch, I find it's ten minutes to six. For all these years, my subconscious has been trying to tell me who I am and how my story will end.

A knock at the front door echoes up the staircase and I roll my sleeve back down. I make my way towards the door and offer my guest a narrow smile.

'You came,' I say.

She nods but doesn't move. She scans the space behind me. 'Whose house is this?' she asks.

'An old friend.'

She shifts from one foot to the other. 'Are they here?'

'No.'

I lead the way upstairs to the bathroom, where everything is ready for us.

Within a few minutes, I am bare-chested and restrained. She doesn't ask me if I am ready, because she knows I am.

'Thank you,' I say, but she doesn't respond.

Instead, Laura plunges my head under the water as the cold takes my breath away. And soon, she will claim my last.

CHAPTER 97

DAMON

The images flow as fast as the water that floods my lungs. I retread old ground, ashamed to watch the moments play out when I hurt people who didn't deserve it. I also relive my most recent killings: the man in the car park, my beautiful Melissa and Adrienne dying before me. Then something unexpected occurs, something that hasn't happened before. Instead of reliving the past, I begin to reshape it. I am rewriting my history to create alternative futures and new possibilities for me and the others I have impacted with my actions. I see what we could have been, not what was.

Imagined snippets run in a random order, beginning moments before I died for the first time. I'm swimming behind Melissa off the Brighton coast in the direction of the yellow swim buoys bobbing up and down in the swell of the sea. We take a moment when we reach them, before swimming side by side, fighting against the waves until we return to the shore. And once we're back on land, we tiptoe across the pebbles, then wrap ourselves tight in large towels, and start planning next month's challenge. It's my turn to decide.

Next, I see myself as a teenager walking along a brick pathway adjacent to a reservoir. Mum and Dad are with me, a few steps ahead. I can't see their faces but their joined hands suggest they're still a couple. My brother Bobby runs towards me with a net on a stick in one hand and a red plastic bucket in the other. His brown eyes are as wide with wonder as they are with kindness. 'Come on, Damo!' he shouts. 'Let's catch fish!' This is the first time I've given him a voice. I follow him to the water's edge, we slip off our socks and trainers, and wade in no deeper than our knees. He giggles as I demonstrate how to swoop the net back and forth under the surface. He beams with delight when he catches two mottled sticklebacks.

More illusory moments arrive. Me dressed in a smart pair of trousers and a shirt, with the words 'Deputy Manager' printed on a badge pinned to my jacket. I'm wandering up and down the aisles of the supermarket where I work, using a tablet to stock-check. Jason approaches me and asks if I have plans tonight. I apologise, I need to be home. Then I'm inside my car pulling on to the driveway of a modern townhouse. I let myself in with a key, and a small, enthusiastic Border Terrier bounds towards me. I kneel and allow him to lick my cheek, catching the name Oscar on a silver tag attached to his collar. Moments later, my wife comes down the stairs and kisses me and wishes me a happy anniversary as I hand her a bouquet of white daisies. What else could I have bought my childhood sweetheart?

Now, my grandmother is with me. She holds a walking stick with one hand, and her other arm is looped within mine. Her face is softer and alight with joy. My father accompanies us as we follow a line of people snaking through Buckingham Palace courtyard. We're all offered over-ear headphones and she appears fascinated by what we're learning from a recording about the history of the building. She squeezes my arm as if to thank me.

My mid-twenties follow and I'm sitting on a wooden bench in a pub garden with my friends when Callum returns from the bar with a tray crammed with pint glasses. He is now the man I robbed him of becoming. His red hair is scraped into a top knot and his beard is neatly trimmed. Symmetrical white teeth replace the black hole of a mouth that frightened me for so many months. For the first time, I realise I could've been a part of this group, not a spectator. I realise there is nothing wrong with feeling different from them. We are all different, and in being so, we are the same.

And now I'm two years in the future and kneeling on the carpeted floor of Melissa's lounge, supporting our toddler son as he takes his first few steps in the direction of his mums. To his delight, they clap and cheer as he reaches them. He turns to catch my eye, a huge grin enveloping his pink chubby face.

I skip forwards again, and Melissa, Adrienne, my mum, and Daisy and I are at our son Samuel's university graduation ceremony. It has certainly taken a village to raise him. Mum is an elderly woman beaming at me with pride as her grandson collects his diploma and waves to us from the stage. She wears a hospital identity bracelet, and it's only when I look at her properly that I realise how poorly she is. 'I wish your dad could've seen this,' she whispers in my ear as she places her hand upon mine.

All of these different paths they might have taken – if not for me.

Two twelve-year-old Callums appear in my final image. One lies dead on the path where I killed him, my handkerchief stuffed in his mouth. The second stands next to me, staring at the first. He turns his gaze to me.

'You did this,' he says in an even tone. There's no malice in it, nothing accusatory. He's simply stating a fact.

'I did,' I reply. 'I wish I hadn't.' And I really mean it.

He steps over the boy on the floor and begins to walk away, up along the path.

'Are you coming then?' he shouts over his shoulder.

I hesitate before I nod and follow him. The waters that once choked me are no longer dark, cold and murky. Now they're warm and clear as day, like the ones I swam in at the hypnotherapist's. And as they sweep me towards him, I know that in death, I am going to be the person I ought to have been in life.

Something jars this vision of what could have been. A voice. I can't be sure if I'm imagining it or if Laura is talking to me, because what she says doesn't make sense.

'First your mother and now you. I got you both in the end.'

Then I feel something soft planted on my lips, like a breath or a kiss, before the images fade into darkness.

PART FOUR

BEYOND

CHAPTER 98

THREE WEEKS LATER

LAURA

She likes to think of herself as an educated, articulate woman. But Laura struggles to put into words the emotions she feels watching somebody die and knowing she is responsible. It's a more intimate experience than sex, more profound than offering your body to someone who is craving the same pleasure as you. She feels more connected to a person she barely knows in their final throes of life than she does her own daughters. And the second she can inhale their last, desperate breaths is like no other sensation. It's more powerful than the most intense of orgasms, or the moment you realise you are hopelessly and completely in love. Or even the first time you feel your newborn child pressed against your chest. It's why when Laura holds their last, treasured breaths inside her, it's like she's protecting a precious jewel in a vault.

People in pain, like Damon, place themselves in her care because she understands them better than anyone else in the world. She knows what's best for them. She alleviates their suffering and brings all that is bad in their lives to an end. She will save them from themselves. She truly is a Good Samaritan.

Today, she sits in a café downstairs in the nursing home where she volunteers, her hands wrapped tightly around a mug, but not drinking from it. The patio doors are open, allowing the July sunshine to creep indoors, but she chooses to remain inside, distracted by the memory of finally killing Damon. She has no doubt that when he answered the door to her, he knew how this was going to end. Discussion was unnecessary. All that mattered were actions. In fact, she's sure that if he were being honest with himself, it's what he'd wanted all along, from the first time they corresponded on the online message boards.

After that initial encounter back in the spring, Laura kept herself to herself for a while. But she missed feeding from the despair of the desperate. She hungered for it. And she couldn't stop thinking about Damon. He was unfinished business. Then later, when she realised who Damon was and how, unbeknownst to him, she had been responsible for shaping much of his life, she saw an opportunity. To have blood from both mother and son on her hands.

CHAPTER 99

SIXTEEN YEARS EARLIER

LAURA

It was soon after Laura began volunteering for the telephone helpline *End of the Line* that she first crossed paths with Bobbi Lister. Bobbi was a caller prone to frequent bouts of depression that stemmed from the sudden death of her infant son some years earlier. These episodes would come and go, and the majority of the time, she either wanted someone to listen to the woes of a still-grieving mother or have someone impartial to vent her frustration at about the injustice of her loss.

She was fragile, conflicted, and carrying a heavy heart. Laura recognised something in Bobbi that B0bbi had yet to see in herself. Futility. Because nothing she, nor anyone else, could say was ever going to change how Bobbi felt about her life. Her only chance of releasing her burden was through death. And it was up to Laura to help her understand that. But it wasn't going to happen overnight. Laura would need to play the long game.

To keep Bobbi all to herself, she informed her what shifts she would be working over the next couple of months, so that if she called, she could be transferred straight to Laura. Slowly and over a series of many, many conversations, she began to work on wearing Bobbi down, planting seeds in her mind to make her believe her depression was having a negative effect on the parenting of the only child she had left. That the loss of her infant son was more through negligence than the cruelty of nature, and the death of Callum, her boyfriend's son, could have been prevented had she given him stricter curfews and paid him more attention.

With perfect timing, months of negative reinforcement were followed one day by a hysterical phone call in which Bobbi admitted to Laura that her son was responsible for the recent death of a child. Bobbi was overwrought to the point of incoherence as she sobbed. She kept repeating what a terrible mother and person she was, and how only a few minutes earlier, she had kicked her son out of the family home because she couldn't bear to be around him any longer. In the past, some of Laura's callers had threatened to end their lives, but more often than not, it was only talk. But there was something in Bobbi's tone that suggested she was at breaking point. And Laura was ready for her.

'I want to be erased from the world,' Bobbi told her. 'I don't want there to be any trace I was ever here. I'm cursed.'

'Are you sure about this?' Laura whispered, so neither of her two colleagues in the office she shared could hear. 'Because I don't blame you if that's how you feel. You must be so exhausted from letting down people who love you. I know you haven't meant to, but some people really can't help it.'

'I am,' she wept. 'I'm so, so tired. They'd be better off without me.'

An idea came to Laura. 'Do you know what some land managers and agriculturists do to clear areas? They start controlled fires to burn away underbrush and to stimulate new growth. If you want to truly erase yourself and everything you've tainted, a fire might do that. Everything gone in the flames, in one fell swoop. It would be as if you had never existed: you and your belongings now ashes.'

'I don't know if I could take the pain, Laura,' Bobbi replied.

'You won't have to,' Laura soothed. 'Almost all housefire deaths are a result of smoke inhalation. Perhaps a little coughing at first, but then you'll be unconscious long before the flames reach you. It will be swift and painless.'

'Do you promise?' Bobbi asked in desperation.

'I promise.'

There was a pause for a minute as an anxious Laura awaited her response.

'I know it's a lot to ask,' said Bobbi, 'but will you be there for me if I do it? Will you stay with me on the phone? I don't want to be alone.'

It was music to Laura's ears. 'I'd be honoured to.'

Minutes later, Laura was able to hear the crackling of flames as Bobbi's lit match turned her sofa into a roaring fire. Then she ran into the bedroom, barricading herself in. All the time Laura continued to reassure her it was the right thing to do for everyone. But not even Laura could prevent the panic from setting in as Bobbi began to choke on the acrid smoke.

'You said it wouldn't hurt,' Bobbi spluttered.

'It'll all be over soon,' said Laura. 'Hang in there.'

'I can't.'

'Bobbi? Bobbi?' Laura asked, but she didn't get her reply. Instead, she heard the sound of three loud thuds before the smashing of glass. 'What's happening?' Another interminably long pause.

'I've broken the window,' Bobbi eventually spluttered. 'But it's made the smoke worse. What have I done?'

Laura thought fast. There was only one option available to Bobbi. 'Jump,' she said firmly.

'I don't know if I can.'

'I'll be with you. Keep your phone held to your ear so you can hear me talking to you. You're doing the right thing, Bobbi. For yourself, for your son, for all who've known you. Don't give it another second's thought. Just do it.'

The last thing Laura heard was a final gasp of breath before two seconds of rushing wind, and then a clattering of the phone as it hit the ground along with its user. It couldn't have landed far because she heard what she had desperately hoped for – for all those months. Being there for Bobbi's last breath was like nothing else. Laura's body became awash with an overwhelming sensation of euphoria, and once she removed her headset, she retired to the office bathroom to recentre herself.

Bobbi was the first person Laura had indirectly killed. And it fuelled a spark inside her that she had no intention of ever extinguishing.

CHAPTER 100

TODAY

LAURA

Laura frowns when she takes a sip of her lukewarm coffee. She's spent too long reminiscing. She orders a replacement, along with a cinnamon swirl as a treat, before she settles back into her seat in the corner of the café and reflects on Damon's death.

When completing her due diligence before they first met, there had been something familiar about the surname Lister that she hadn't been able to place, not until weeks later. A search of souvenir death certificates belonging to those she'd helped to end the lives of contained one in Bobbi's name. Were they related? She wouldn't rest until she knew one way or another.

As a public record, it didn't take long for Laura to find Damon's birth certificate online, which contained the names of both parents. Bobbi was indeed his mother. Finally, when she had worn him down and he agreed to let her finish what she had started all those months ago, she decided to double down on her research into him to ensure this second invitation wasn't a trap. That he hadn't somehow found out about Laura's relationship with his mother and been out for revenge all along.

She paid to access a commercial satellite company that offered near real-time views of the new address in London he wanted to meet her at. Details were scant, aside from being an ordinary suburban home in London. However, when she researched the Land Registry for the property ownership, her head snapped back as she took a second look. Helena Obugachu was a patient she visited at the nursing home where she volunteered. How did she and Damon know each other? A chance meeting with the woman's daughter the next day in Helena's room revealed she had been a foster parent for many years. It was highly possible he had once been under Helena's care, and he felt a connection to the London address.

Laura sat back in her chair, scarcely daring to believe the opportunity the universe was offering her. Some might describe it as coincidence, but Laura knew better. It was the stars aligning. The wheel of fortune turning. Fate. Sixteen years after driving his mother to her death and hearing her last breath, she was about to do the same with Bobbi Lister's son.

When Damon answered the front door to her three weeks ago, she immediately knew by his puffy eyes that there was nowhere left to go for this man. She relaxed her grip on the taser in her pocket as he led her upstairs into the bathroom and a tub filled with cold water and ice. He explained this would work best for him. That by drowning, he was less likely to resist like he had with the noose. Laura was hesitant, disappointed even, because it's impossible to inhale the final breath of someone with their head underwater. Instead, she sought a compromise, eventually deciding to leave something of her inside him, by giving him mouth-to-mouth soon after he slipped unconscious. One puff, and certainly not enough to give him back his life. Just enough for her to live on in the dead.

Damon was easy to overpower as he thrashed around, his life slipping away, the two sides of his brain at odds with each another. It was in that moment she chose to whisper to him, 'First your mother and now you. I got you both in the end.' It didn't matter if he could hear her or not.

According to the recording she made of it on her phone, he was dead within one minute and thirty-two seconds, surprisingly fast. Laura assumed previous attempts and the frequent starting and restarting of his heart had weakened it. When he stopped moving, she dragged him from the bath, soaking herself in the process, and dropped him to the floor, rolling him on to his side. Once water had leaked from his mouth, she pressed her lips against his and offered him one long, solitary breath. It wasn't the same level of satisfaction she was used to, but it came pretty damn close. And then she left.

Today, she is overcome by an urge to do something she shouldn't. A smile creeps across her face as she glances around the room to ensure no one is watching her. Then she slips in her AirPods, scrolls through the photos folder on her phone and presses play on the video she has already watched dozens of times. When she first followed Damon into the bathroom, he pointed to a small metal stand on the side of the bath and told her she could attach her phone to it to record his drowning. She happily obliged.

Now, she pinches the screen to expand the size of the video. There's a thrill attached to watching this in a public place. Then she turns up the sound to hear his frantic splashing, and the moment when his head rose above the surface as he tried to gasp for breath before she forced it back under. A warm feeling spreads through her lower half when she remembers how desperate his body had felt, pressed tightly against hers as she pinned him in place. She fights the urge to slip her hand between her legs, and instead she checks her watch. She will give it another fifteen minutes before she returns upstairs to the hospice.

'Laura Murray?' A voice appears from nowhere and she slams the phone screen-down on the table so hard, her mug rattles against the saucer. She pulls out her headphones and looks up to see a smartly dressed man and a woman, both with grave expressions. The man's spiky hair and oval face has something of the pineapple about it. She considers denying it's her.

'Yes?' she says instead.

'My name is Detective Sergeant Mark Goodwin and this is my colleague DS Renee Price. We are here to arrest you in connection with an investigation into the death of Damon Lister, Melissa Lister and Adrienne Thomson.'

Who on earth are the second two? Laura's mouth dries and she tries hard not to swallow. She has had close calls before, but nothing like this. She thinks fast but this has blindsided her.

'I don't know who any of those people are,' she replies unconvincingly.

'You do not have to say anything, but it may harm your defence if you do not mention when questioned something that you can later rely on in court,' the detective continues. 'Anything you do say may be given in evidence against you.'

Laura remains seated. 'I think you're making a mistake,' she whispers, trying not to draw more attention to her than that already being given by curious staff and visitors.

'Could you stand up for us, please?' the woman asks politely, and as Laura rises she spots a recording device attached to the woman's jacket pocket. Her colleague takes Laura's handbag and turns her around, slipping handcuffs on her.

And when the detective picks up Laura's phone and puts it in a clear plastic evidence bag, Laura knows it's not only Damon's life that has come to an end.

EPILOGUE

CHAPTER 101

TWO YEARS LATER

SALLY

An atypical, billowing August wind slips through a small opening at the neck of her coat, where Sally hasn't zipped it up. Her aunt Carolina entwines her arm through her niece's as they make their way through the tree-lined cemetery and towards a section reserved for the burial of ashes belonging to those who have chosen cremation. Carolina carries a refillable water bottle while Sally holds close to her chest two posies she bought at a Waitrose store en route.

'You okay, sweetheart?' Carolina asks and Sally nods. 'Sure?'

'I'm sure.'

And she is okay. It's taken her time to reach this point, but she has made it. Keeping herself busy has helped. Despite the distractions, she learned last week that she passed all four A levels a year early with A* results. She has been offered a place at university and starts in October.

Two years have passed since *that* morning. Since she began the day catching up online with friends and scrolling through social media. Since she responded to the man she'd been chatting to on a dating app. Since she opened her email inbox. Since she read the first message that blew her world apart.

CHAPTER 102

SALLY

To: Sally.Obugachu_2010@gmail.com
Subject: Email 1: Helena
From: Damon.Lister@UKnet.com

Dear Sally,

Firstly, and most importantly, please accept my heartfelt apologies for everything I am about to tell you. And I mean *everything,* for I am aware this will be a lot for one person to shoulder. But I have no one else to explain it all to. So I am very sorry for the pain I will be putting you through and for what I will ask of you. I hope that one day, you can forgive me.

I'm your mum's friend, Damon, and I believe you and I have something in common. *Someone* in common. I think we share Ralf Lister as our father. I recently learned that long before I came into Helena's life, she and my dad were in a relationship. And they were very serious by all accounts. When I recently turned up at your mum's house and you and I met, I later found a discarded provisional driver's licence application in the fireplace with your name, date of birth and email address on it. I realised you were born shortly after Dad went to prison for fifteen years of our lives. I think you were conceived not long before he introduced me to your mum. Please know, Dad was an innocent man. He took the fall for something I did. He is no longer with us and that is my fault. But more of that later.

Sally's mouth was agape as she sat in the bedroom of her aunt's house, her hands gripping her phone tightly as she continued to pore over the message. Damon went on to explain what he'd done as a child which had led to him staying with Helena; his ECT treatment; how he'd gradually learned more about himself each time he died and the lives he'd taken since. He added that when she received this email – scheduled to arrive twelve hours after his death – he himself would be the last of his victims, thanks to the assistance of a woman he'd met online. He also expressed regret that all of this was to occur under her and Helena's roof.

By the time this email reaches you, I will be somewhere I can't return from. Somewhere better, I hope. I realised once I started scratching that itch, I couldn't stop the bleeding. Now I have all the answers I've been seeking. Your mum was right, finding the truth has done me no favours.

And I know that if I don't leave now, I will kill more people. It's the way I am.

This is the first of three emails you should have received by now. The second contains a live link to camera footage that was recording my death, the location of the hard drive it was saved on and the cloud it was automatically sent to for backup. There are also screen grabs of the conversations I had with the woman who ended my life, and all I know about her.

The third email goes into much more detail about what I now know about myself. There are names of my victims, dates, times and locations. You can forward this to the police too. It is your decision as to whether you read it first or not.

All there is left to do is apologise once again for this burden. I like to think that I'd have enjoyed having a half-sister (if it turns out my hunch is correct) but the reality is I probably would have hurt you like I hurt everyone else. I hope you go on to have the incredible life that our dad and Helena wanted for me.

With love and regret,
Damon Lister.

Sally remembers running downstairs to find her aunt and Uncle Addo in the kitchen and thrusting her phone at them.

'Is it true?' she asked Carolina. 'Do I have a brother called Damon?'

A bewildered Carolina read the email, her brow furrowing. She showed it to her husband before replying to her niece with a reluctant nod and a quiet 'Yes.'

'Why didn't Mum tell me?'

'It was such a complicated situation,' Carolina apologised. 'She didn't want you to be hurt by it.'

Sally pointed to the email on the phone. 'And do you think Damon has done all the things he says he has here?'

'Some I know to be true, because your mum told me, when she was pregnant and struggling with her separation from Ralf. But I really hope the rest are not. Perhaps the boy is having some sort of breakdown?'

'There's more,' Sally added. And after then reading Damon's full, unabridged third email containing a more detailed confession, they all watched in horror from the beginning, a link he'd provided to the video of his own death at the hands of a woman he identified in the accompanying notes. It ended when his phone's battery ran out of power.

Sally, Carolina and Addo drove through London's early morning rush-hour traffic to reach Helena's house. Sally spent much of it in silence, scrolling through her phone, reading newspaper stories about her father written around the time of his court case. The man she had spent her whole life wondering about had allowed the world to believe he was a child killer. She hated him for it yet reluctantly respected the lengths he'd gone to, to protect his own child.

Her aunt and uncle made her wait in the car as they entered Helena's house, returning quickly from upstairs, confirming Damon was dead inside and there were two other bodies laid out in a spare room. Addo removed his phone from the central console and prepared to dial 999. Carolina placed her hand over his keypad.

'I don't think we should,' she said. 'We need to think this through and the damage it could cause Sally.'

She turned to her niece in the back seat.

'If we hand the police Damon's email confession, it will put you in the spotlight,' Carolina began. 'There will be investigations and huge media interest, and social media will blow this up in a way we can't control. Your name and image will be everywhere . . . being the half-sister of a serial killer will be a terrible burden to carry. Much more than finding three bodies in your house. It will bring you the wrong attention at university, and will follow you for the rest of your life.'

'But I've done nothing wrong,' Sally argued.

'Of course you haven't, but that won't prevent people from believing you are guilty by association. The internet is a cruel, unforgiving place. And think of your mum. She fostered more than a hundred and fifty young people, but all her achievements will be forgotten because all people will remember is how she was complicit in trying to hide a boy who killed other children and even his own mother.'

'No one was charged in the case of Callum Baird,' said Addo. 'Mightn't it give his family some closure knowing who killed their son? What if we were in their shoes? Wouldn't we want to know?'

'Yes,' Carolina conceded. 'But if the police find that woman who helped to kill Damon, and she is charged, it could work in her favour if it becomes public that Damon made a deathbed confession that he was a multiple murderer. Will anyone believe his death is a loss to the world?'

Addo looked ahead at Helena's house, specifically the window of the second bedroom. 'And what about the families of those two women? Don't they deserve an explanation for what happened to their daughters? Even Damon wanted the truth to come out.'

Carolina shook her head. 'I don't care what he wanted. Sally matters, not the conscience of a dead man.' She paused before choosing her words carefully. 'I say we give the police the video link to his death he emailed to Sally, and that is all. Tell them she saw him here once and gave him her email address to keep him updated about Helena. Then we drove here and found him and two other bodies. Let them do the rest.'

'This doesn't sit easy with me,' Addo admitted.

'Me neither,' Carolina said, and returned her attention to Sally. 'But you are the one that matters. This must be your decision, not ours. Presently, the only link between you and Damon is that he once, briefly, was cared for in this house by your mum. There's no reason for anyone to ever think you and Damon are related.'

'Then how will I explain why he sent that email?'

'You met him once. You told him your mum was sick. So perhaps he confessed to you because he couldn't tell her.'

The car filled with an uneasy silence as Sally considered the pros and cons of her aunt's suggestion. Finally, she opened the email icon on her phone and deleted two of Damon's messages before removing them permanently from the trashcan.

'We need to find his phone and erase them from his email account too,' Carolina added.

'I'll do it,' Sally said.

'No, I don't want you going inside . . .'

But Sally was already opening the car door and climbing out before Carolina could finish. Both her aunt and uncle hurried to follow her, their protests ignored.

'I need to do this,' Sally explained with such determination, Carolina and Addo knew they'd be unable to change her mind. They anxiously waited downstairs in the hallway for her to return.

Upstairs in the bathroom, Sally came face to face with her brother. He was lying on his back, on the floor, eyes shut tight, his wrists and ankles tied with plastic restraints. She scanned his body from top to toe. His skin was so white it was almost translucent, except for a dry line of vomit beginning at his lips and ending on the tiled floor. That struck her as peculiar. All her research into death had taught her that after more than twelve hours, his skin should be more of a purplish colour by now, more waxy in appearance.

She looked around the room until she found his phone propped up against a bottle of shampoo in a soap dish and partially obscured by a shower curtain. It was pointed at an angle Sally suspected captured the whole room. The dead battery meant it wasn't recording her. She carried it with her back into the car, plugged it into a charger, waited a few minutes until there was enough power, then deleted two of the emails Damon had sent her. Then she deleted them from the cloud so they were gone for good. Finally, she turned the phone off and handed it to Carolina, who went back upstairs to replace it after both sets of fingerprints had been wiped off with Sally's handkerchief. All that was left to do was for Addo to call for help and wait.

The police arrived soon after the paramedics, swarming across the area, shutting off parts of the street with blue-and-white tape as forensic tents were erected. Statements were taken by scenes-of-crime officers, with details of how Sally, her aunt and uncle could be contacted again to arrange formal statements. Detectives were told of the friendship between Helena and Damon, but the family didn't admit to the biological link between the half-brother and sister. And, as Carolina had suggested, the police had no reason to search for one. Helena and Ralf had always kept their relationship under wraps.

Laura Murray – by a coincidence no one could explain – was a volunteer worker at Sally's mum's nursing home. She was tracked down through a combination of methods: screengrabbed images of their messages Damon had taken found on his phone; neighbours' Ring doorbell footage of her leaving Helena's house; an IP address given to them by the message board operators for the general area where Laura lived; cell tower triangulation recording her movements; and bank statements of the train and London Underground stations her Oyster card tapped in and out of on the day Damon died.

The deaths of Melissa and Adrienne were harder to pin on her. As Carolina had predicted, an internet frenzy began almost immediately, with amateur TikTok sleuths recording hundreds of videos broadcasting their theories as to how the ex-wife and girlfriend of a murder victim – and son of a convicted killer – had all ended up in the same house. Sally spent hours at a time scrolling from one clip to another, fascinated by the speculation.

Meanwhile, Laura had been charged with – and had of course denied – all three killings, despite the overwhelming video evidence against her for Damon's death. During her trial, the defence tried to paint Laura as a mere fantasist, claiming she thought she was involved in a role-playing game gone awry, and that she hadn't intended to kill him. When she realised he was dead, she'd given him mouth-to-mouth resuscitation. And when it failed, she panicked and fled without calling for help.

But Damon was far from innocent too, as it turned out. Police found footage on her phone of him killing a man who appeared to be attacking him in a car park, then dumping his body in a waste bin. Laura refused to explain where the clip came from or who the dead man was. He was later identified when investigators found his vehicle still in the car park. However, despite extensive searches of the Cambridge landfill site, Garry's body was never recovered.

Damon was identified by the housekeeper of a Dr Fernandez-Jones, who had been attacked in his home office and left for dead. He'd spent eleven months in a coma before sepsis killed him. No records of his involvement with Damon were discovered. More fuel to add to the fires of conspiracy theorists.

Then, midway through the trial, Laura unexpectedly confessed to Damon's manslaughter. However, she was adamant she had played no part in Melissa and Adrienne's killings. The only evidence linking her to their deaths were her fingerprints on the plastic sheeting wrapped around both women's heads, which had been partially opened to reveal their mouths. Additionally, faint traces of Laura's saliva were discovered on both Melissa and Adrienne's lips. She didn't offer an explanation as to how it had got there. After three days of deliberation, a jury found her guilty of the two murders by a majority of ten to two.

Months later now, here in the cemetery, Sally becomes aware of the cold and pulls at the zip of her coat to keep the wind from her neck.

'Here we are then,' Carolina says as they reach their destination.

Sally takes in the three small, brown wooden crosses, each with a brass plaque attached containing a different name: Helena Obugachu, Ralf Lister, and Maisy Lister, Ralf's mother.

They visit West Norwood Cemetery every so often. Helena and Ralf were never reunited in life, but they were in death when her ashes were buried next to his. It was Carolina who contacted Ralf's mother and asked for permission to do that. Sally considered visiting her grandmother to explain who she was, but her aunt talked her out of it. She feared Sally might be put in a position where she would be asked to help prove her father's innocence and outed as his daughter. Then, three months later, they read online her grandmother had succumbed to heart failure. With no known living relatives, Carolina and Sally organised the funeral and for her ashes to be interred next to her son's. Damon, however, was given a public-health funeral, one funded by the local council when no one else is willing or able to pay. Sally has no idea what, if anything, happened to his ashes.

Carolina uses her water bottle to fill three small vases, and Sally adds the flowers. She is arranging the second bunch when a figure catches her eye beyond the cemetery wall. A man with dark hair and an angular face is sitting midway back inside a bus. His head is turned towards her, his face expressionless. For a fraction of a second, she forgets Damon has died. He is there before her. Then the vehicle pulls away and he vanishes.

However, she knows for certain it's only her mind playing tricks on her. Damon is most certainly dead.

Because it was she who killed him, not Laura.

CHAPTER 103

SALLY

Carolina and Addo were all too eager to leave Helena's bathroom the day they discovered Damon's body inside it. However, Sally didn't beat quite such a hasty retreat when she went to retrieve his phone.

Death had always held a bleak fascination for her. She'd ruminated on life's fragility ever since witnessing a classmate being mown down and killed by a car outside their school. As others around them had screamed and cried, the then ten-year-old Sally had been captivated by the unnatural angles of little Poppy Harrison's contorted body and strawberry-blonde hair splayed across the road. But it was her serene expression that lingered in Sally's memory for the longest time. In her last throes of life, a faint smile had tugged at the corners of Poppy's mouth. It was as if, as she slipped away, she stopped feeling pain, and something else was holding her attention. Something far greater than this world could provide. Then, within the blink of an eye, she was gone.

In the years that followed, barely a day had passed when Sally didn't picture a dying Poppy. Or of standing behind her that day, both girls between parked cars, waiting for a gap in the road to cross. And of how light Poppy had felt when Sally pressed her hands into the small of the girl's back and shoved her into the path of oncoming traffic.

It was a spontaneous act, but one that had been brewing for a long time. All the way back to year one, with Poppy's refusal to invite Sally to her birthday party because she didn't want anyone there with 'dirty skin'. It hadn't seemed to bother Zara Chopra or Thandiwe Nkosi, but a humiliated Sally was more sensitive, more perceptive to injustice even at such an early age. Likewise, when Poppy had mocked her Afro hair or the brightly coloured clothes Helena wore to parents' evenings. Then there were the elbows to the ribs in the school changing rooms, her papier-mâché volcano that was mysteriously flattened in the classroom, and the mobile phone she left in her desk one lunchtime and returned to find doused in a sticky soda drink. Sally had been left with no choice but to retaliate.

Long after Poppy's death, Sally had wished she could witness it all over again, before the wish developed into an obsession. She'd admitted to her therapist Dr Dahl that she fantasised about hurting people who deserved it, but stopped short of confessing she'd once acted on those urges.

Five years later, a second opportunity to end a life presented itself. In the silence of the house she'd once called home, a dead Damon's skin colour fascinated her. Why had it remained white? Where were the purple patches where deoxygenated blood had pooled? It was when she moved closer to him that she got her answer: the faintest breath coming from Damon's mouth. It was so light, it was barely perceptible. She froze, unsure if she was imagining it. And then it happened again. So she crouched by his side, carefully placed her index and middle fingers to his neck, then his wrist, searching for a pulse. It was faint, but it was definitely present.

Her half-brother was still alive.

Sally turned her head sharply, ready to call her aunt and uncle who were waiting downstairs, but hesitated. Instead, she allowed herself to imagine what it might've been like to have had a father and an older brother in her life. A traditional family unit instead of only her mum. As loved as Helena made her feel, there had always been something missing in Sally's life. And the cause of that was lying on the bathroom floor before her. She felt a sudden rush of anger towards Damon, a resentment for what he took from her, and what he had stolen from countless other families and friends of those he'd killed. He'd got away with so much. As with Poppy Harrison, a sense of injustice reared its head. She was going to make it right.

So she took a handkerchief she kept in her pocket for unpredictable nosebleeds brought on by high blood pressure and stress, then she covered his mouth and nostrils with it and held it there. The fight had already left his body, so he didn't try to retaliate. He was dead in under a minute.

Sally felt only a grudging gratitude towards her brother for presenting her with the opportunity to watch a second person die. And in the final moments of his life, she saw something pass in Damon as she had seen in Poppy. A serene calm, far beyond Sally's understanding. She carefully wiped her prints from his skin and left.

It empowered her with the confidence to encourage the passing of her mother too. On Sally's sixteenth birthday, Carolina was downstairs in the nursing home's café when Sally was alone at Helena's bedside. There, she took the same, familiar handkerchief, and within a few short minutes, brought her mother's cruel suffering to a merciful end. By the time Carolina returned with coffees in both hands, the handkerchief was tucked back inside Sally's pocket. She and Carolina held each other and wept for their loss.

Sometimes Sally dreams about Damon. He reminds her they are the same. That because they share DNA, they share the same urges. She argues with him, but he refuses to listen and, in her frustration, she wakes up with a jolt and reminds herself she is nothing like him. She only does what she does for the greater good. The world is a better place without Damon and Poppy in it, and her mum didn't deserve one more second of pain. Three deaths, each for a very different, altruistic reason. Each justifiable in its own way.

Sally wishes she could talk to her mum more than she does. She hallucinates Helena every so often, but she can't control where or when. When she's here, she looks as she did when Sally was a child. A strong, beautiful and passionate woman, not the shell she became. She keeps Helena up to speed about events in her life. How it won't be long before she begins her BSc Forensic Science with Criminology course at the University of West London. How Carolina and Addo helped her find a buyer for the family home and that she hopes to purchase a flat not too far from the campus.

And how, next week, she will meet for the first time a guy she's been chatting to on a dating app whom she has a good feeling about. He's funny and handsome but a few years older than her. Twenty years older, to be truthful. She's never shown much interest in boys her age, but there was another older man she'd felt powerfully connected to. Helena had been so horrified to discover her fourteen-year-old daughter had been dating a twenty-four-year-old man that she had reported him to the police. Now, Sally can't help but wonder if growing up with only a mum has made her subconsciously seek father-like traits in relationships. Not that it really matters. As she once heard somewhere, the heart wants what it wants.

Sally hasn't told Carolina about this latest man because she is sure her aunt won't approve of the age gap, or that he has a child with his soon-to-be ex-wife. Or that he knows a thing or two about the complications families can bring. But Sally has a good feeling about Finn. She is sure they already have a lot in common.

Carolina's voice returns Sally to the present.

'I think we should go before the rain starts,' she suggests, her head pointed up at the sky. 'Are you ready, sweetheart?'

Sally agrees, but this time as they make their way back through the cemetery and to the car, it's not only Damon she hallucinates. Poppy is with him, her hair and face stained with blood. They are standing in the arched doorway of a church, alongside Helena.

Something tells her that once she starts university, it won't be long before they will need to make space for others.

ACKNOWLEDGEMENTS

This book was a long time in the making. The idea of someone's life flashing before their eyes first came to me three years ago. I dictated a couple of lines into my phone (as I do when I get a new idea) then put it to the back of my mind as I concentrated on writing the books I had planned – *The Stranger in Her House* and *You Killed Me First*. Then the time became right to explore the idea further. I hope you think it was worth the wait. And what a joy it was to bring back Laura from *The Good Samaritan* after so many years in the wilderness! I know from your feedback just how much you love to hate her . . . #PoorLaura.

All books are a collaborative process and this is no exception. First and foremost, thanks to my husband, Other John, for being my sounding board and the first person to read the books when they're in their early – and very badly written – stages. Thanks to Elliot for your patience as Daddy barricades himself in his office until these weird, made-up people transfer themselves from his head and on to the page.

Thanks to Kath Middleton for your proofing skills and to Tracy Fenton for your early feedback and eagle eye. I've been on this journey with both of you since the start and I'm so glad you've stuck with me for this long. To my mum, Pam, and to Rhian for being early readers and for giving me your opinions. Also to Louise

Beech, Emma Louise Bunting, and Facebook book clubs including THE Facebook Group and Psychological Thriller Readers. Myself, aka Freida, aka Colleen, all thank you. My gratitude also goes to Jules Swain (@thereadingpara) for your help with all things resus and paramedic like. Any errors are mine, not yours.

Thanks to my editors Vic 'Britney' Haslam and David Dowling and all the team at Thomas & Mercer and Amazon, including Rebecca Hills, Will Speed and Gemma Wain. I'm also grateful to the Audible team, plus my narrators, including Elizabeth Knowelden, who has contributed to all my psychological thriller audiobooks to date. I'm so lucky to have you bring my books to life. Gratitude also goes to my TV and film rights agent Jon Cassir at CAA.

And I'm also grateful to Lex Brookman and the team at Tandem Collective for spreading the word about my books and finding new readers. You've all been a blast to work with. Plus I'm hugely indebted to bloggers, Instagrammers and the TikTok community for talking about my books online.

And finally, thanks to you readers. Thank you for reading and listening to my stories, for interacting with me online and messaging me. You've had tattoos of my books inked on your arms, painted my covers on to bricks and iced them on to cakes, served them in suitcases at book clubs and dressed up as them for Hallowe'en. You're all chapter 39-ing insane. And I love you for it.

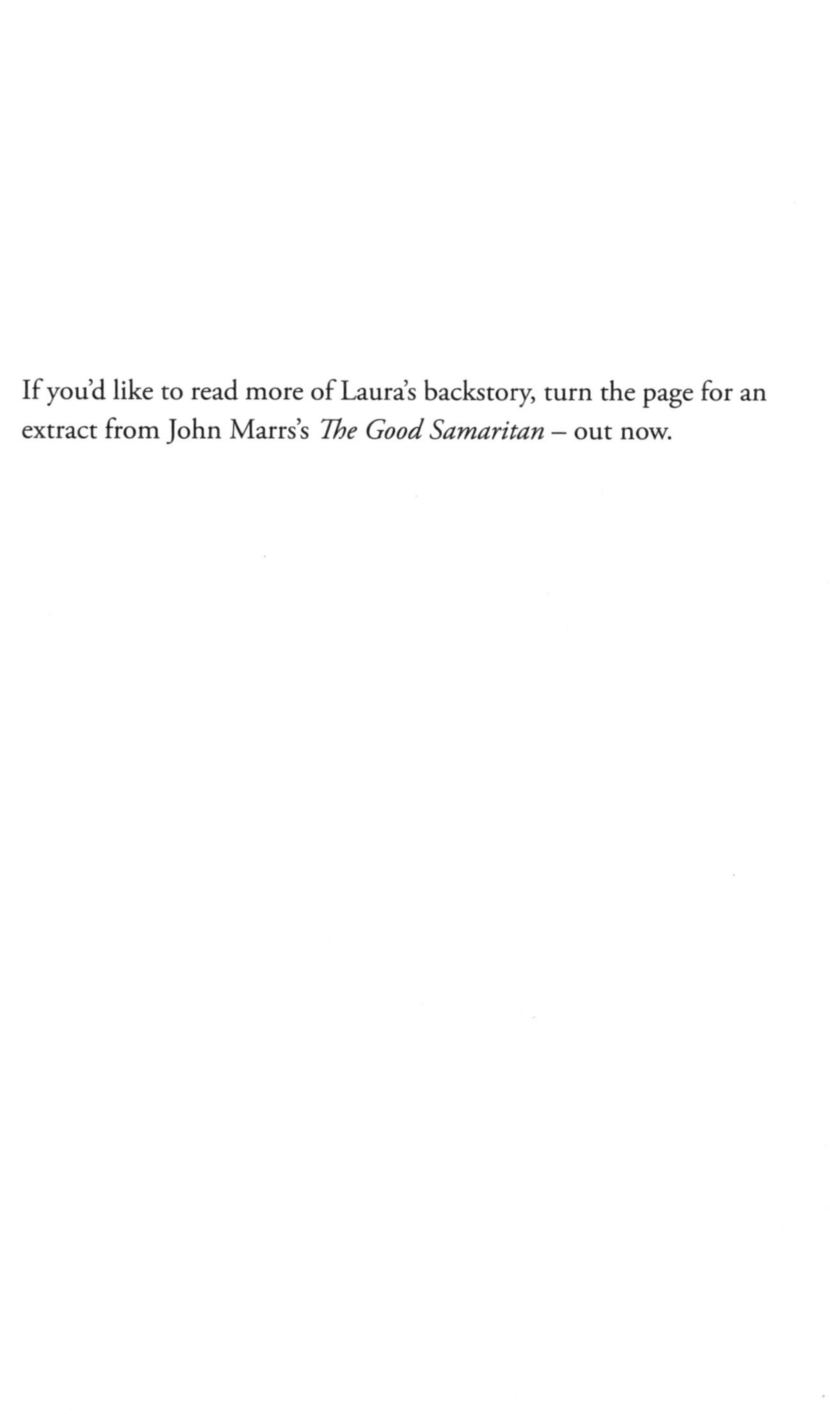

If you'd like to read more of Laura's backstory, turn the page for an extract from John Marrs's *The Good Samaritan* – out now.

PROLOGUE

'Where are you?' My voice was calm and my tone measured as I spoke softly into the receiver.

'My taxi has just pulled up in the car park and I'm trying to give away my loose change.'

'Why?' I asked.

'Because I don't have any need for it.'

'I understand.' I rolled my eyes. It felt like a waste of time and it concerned me that it might be a delaying tactic. But I couldn't pressure him. 'You do what you feel is for the best, and remember,' I continued, 'I'm with you every step of the way.'

I heard him mumble something to the driver, then he exited the taxi, closing the door behind him. I assumed it was raining lightly, because every few seconds I heard the rubber wiper blades squeak as they arched across the windscreen before the cab pulled away.

'How are we doing?' I asked, purposefully using 'we' instead of 'you' to emphasise that we were in this together, if not side by side then certainly in spirit. It was not my choice of location and I wondered if, once he saw its magnitude, it might give him second thoughts. If that were the case, I'd have to accept his decision. It had taken time for me to get in the right headspace, but now that I was, I wanted him to see it through to the end. And I'd make sure to remind him why he was there and how far we had come.

He read my mind. 'Don't worry,' he said, 'I've not had a change of heart.'

I let out a sigh of relief.

'Really,' he continued, 'I'm in a good place and I'm ready for this. Now that I'm here, now that I can see what's before me, I know one hundred and ten per cent that it's the right thing to do.'

I believed him. I don't think he'd ever lied to me, because he'd never had a reason to. He'd told me many times that he was more honest with me than with anyone he had ever known, and I was proud to hear it.

'Can you see her yet?' I asked. 'She's driving a red Vauxhall Astra. Registration number V987—'

'. . . THG. Yes, she's just flashed her lights at me. It feels like we're in a spy film and you've arranged for me to pass her secret documents.' He gave a nervous laugh and I pretended to laugh back.

'OK, let me give her a call,' I said. 'Stay where you are for now. We don't want to scare her.'

My number was automatically withheld when I dialled her. She answered after seven rings, too many for my liking.

'Hi there,' I began softly. 'How are we doing?'

'I'm not sure,' she replied. Her voice lacked the confidence of his. I'd accompanied enough people in her situation to recognise a heightened state of anxiety. I'd have to tread carefully.

'It's good to hear you,' I said soothingly. 'Did your journey go well? Did you find the place okay?'

'I got here an hour ago, so I had a cup of tea in a café up the road.'

This was another red flag. She'd had time on her own to think.

'Is there anything you want to talk about before we start?' I asked.

She hesitated. 'I'm really sorry, but now I'm here I'm starting to think I might not be doing the right thing anymore,' she replied.

I gritted my teeth. I was not going to let it end like this. I needed to reaffirm her sense of purpose.

'It's about the baby, isn't it?' I asked gently.

'Yes.'

'You're worried that you're making a selfish decision.'

'Yes,' she said again, this time in a barely audible voice.

I sank back into my chair. 'That's perfectly understandable, but you need to realise this isn't you talking, it's your hormones. They're giving you a false sense of what might be possible; making you think that everything could be all right in the end if you just give it time. Listen to someone who has learned from experience. When that child is born, things are only going to get so much worse for you. They'll up your medication so that your life is even more of a blur than it is now. You won't be fit for purpose as a mother, and the chemicals you've put into your body already are going to have a knock-on effect on your baby. It will grow up exactly like you, with exactly the same pain and problems you have; it'll be history repeating itself. Do you really want to be responsible for all that? Unlike you, I can see things clearly and I know that is exactly what is going to happen. Your baby doesn't stand a chance in this world. And deep down you know that too, don't you?'

'You're right,' she spluttered, no longer trying to fight back her sobs.

I'd been bad cop, now I needed to be good cop again.

'You know, I've been thinking about you all night and day,' I continued. 'I know how far you've come since you found me all those weeks ago. I'm so proud of you for your courage and strength. You know that, don't you?'

'Yes,' she replied. She didn't sound as convinced as I'd hoped. It was time to step it up a gear.

'I've been thinking about your family, too. They're very lucky to have someone in their lives like you, someone who is so selfless and so courageous. These are rare traits and I know that at first, it's going to be difficult for everyone to understand, but in time they're going to realise you loved them so much that you put their needs above your own. You've told me on so many occasions that you're never going to be the wife your husband needs. But that's not *your* fault, it's *his* for putting you on a pedestal. *He* has done this to you. Just keep reminding yourself of why you came looking for me in the first place. Together, we explored every avenue before *you* decided this was the only route that made sense. You are moving on and allowing everyone else you love to do the same. And I admire that so much.'

I'd spent so long repeating the same message, week after week, conversation after conversation, slowly reinforcing the belief that there was only one way forward. He, however, had required less work. There was no middle ground with him. Things were either black or white and never grey. He told me once I was like a rope that had pulled him from the quicksand and then set him on the right path.

'You're right,' she sniffed. 'Thank you.'

'Okay then. Well, blow your nose, take a deep breath and we'll do this together. Start by opening the door and walking towards him.' I tried to imagine I was there with them. 'Now, can you carefully describe what you're seeing in front of you?'

'I think that's him waiting for me,' she said. 'He's smiling. And behind him the sun is trying to make its way through the clouds. It's cold, but not freezing.'

I heard the crunch of the gravel under her feet, the pitter-patter of January rain bouncing off the shoulders of her overcoat, and the squawking seagulls above. I could almost smell the salty sea air around them. I switched telephone line to his.

'Hi,' I began. 'She's coming towards you now, but she's a little more anxious than you are. You will look after her, won't you?'

'Of course,' he replied, more assured than I'd ever heard him.

As they came face-to-face for the first time, I imagined them smiling at one another. I opened up both phone lines and heard a muffled, scratching sound of fabric against fabric, as if they were embracing. I'd told her to wear a coat big enough to hide her baby bump. The last thing I needed was for it to spook him now that we were so close.

I felt my skin burning under my shirt and adrenaline coursing through the sixty thousand miles of veins in my body, edging me towards a kind of euphoria.

Bide your time. Keep a firm grip on yourself, because too much can still go wrong.

I pictured them standing there, two perfect strangers who hadn't needed to speak to communicate. They were united in a common purpose and I had brought them together. Their lives would be forever connected because of me. I didn't know whether to laugh or cry.

'Can you both hear me?' I asked them.

'Yes,' they replied in unison.

'If you're still comfortable with it, I'd like to stay with you for as long as possible. So, when you're ready, each take a deep breath, then take hold of each other's hand and start to walk. No matter how tough it gets or how heavy your legs might feel, hold on to each other for support. Don't turn around and don't stop. We can do this together.'

'Thank you,' he said. 'Thank you for understanding me. You've been incredible.'

'It's been my pleasure,' I replied. In the past when I'd reached this point, I'd been so much stronger. But he'd been too big a part of my life for this not to hurt. I balled my fists as our journey came to an end. Now it was their turn to continue the story.

I closed my eyes tightly. I inhaled and exhaled in time with their breaths as they made their way further and further from the car park. The gravel faded into grass and the rain fell more heavily. She began to weep, but I was convinced they were happy tears. I was sure he was clasping her hand in his just that little bit tighter, offering her the strength I so admired in him.

And then—

Nothing.

Nothing but the sound of their last breaths and the coastal wind howling through their phones as they fell five hundred and thirty feet into the water below. And as their bodies sank and their souls soared, I bit my bottom lip hard until I tasted blood. It was over.

I gave myself a few moments before reluctantly replacing the receiver in the cradle. I took a tissue from my desk drawer, blew my nose, uncurled my toes and thought about my anchor until calmness once again took control of my body.

I lifted my head briefly and glanced around the room to reassure myself that no one beyond the confines of my booth had heard me.

'Are you all right?' Mary's honeyed voice came from the side, making me jump. She shuffled from the kitchen to my desk, sensing something was wrong. The years had not been kind to her face.

'I'm fine,' I replied.

'Was it one of *those* calls?'

'Yes.'

'They didn't do it while you were talking to them, did they?'

I nodded and she patted my arm with her hand. My skin prickled, as it did when anyone touched me uninvited. Such gestures had never comforted me.

'I'm so sorry,' Mary continued. 'You hope that when they call us, all it'll take is a friendly voice and someone to listen and it'll put them off ending their lives for that little bit longer, don't you?'

'Yes,' I lied.

'And I know we're not supposed to talk them out of it or even offer an opinion, but it's hard when you just want people to see that life is worth living.'

'It certainly is,' I nodded. 'I wish everyone could see the beauty of the world through our eyes.'

It was a busy afternoon and there weren't enough volunteers to man the helplines, so Mary made her way back to her corner of the office. When the red light on my phone began flashing to indicate another call, I cleared my throat and answered it, as required, within five rings.

'Good afternoon,' I began, 'you've reached the End of the Line, this is Laura speaking. May I ask your name?'

ABOUT THE AUTHOR

© 2025 Corrine West Photography and Media

John Marrs is an author and former journalist based in Northamptonshire, England. After spending his career interviewing celebrities from the worlds of television, film and music for numerous national newspapers and magazines, he is now a full-time author. This is his fourteenth book. Follow him at www.johnmarrsauthor.com, on Instagram @johnmarrs.author and on Facebook at www.facebook.com/johnmarrsauthor.

Follow the Author on Amazon

If you enjoyed this book, follow John Marrs on Amazon to be notified when the author releases a new book!
To do this, please follow these instructions:

Desktop:

1) Search for the author's name on Amazon or in the Amazon App.
2) Click on the author's name to arrive on their Amazon page.
3) Click the 'Follow' button.

Mobile and Tablet:

1) Search for the author's name on Amazon or in the Amazon App.
2) Click on one of the author's books.
3) Click on the author's name to arrive on their Amazon page.
4) Click the 'Follow' button.

Kindle eReader and Kindle App:

If you enjoyed this book on a Kindle eReader or in the Kindle App, you will find the author 'Follow' button after the last page.